P9-AFM-803

Also by André Brink

A CHAIN OF VOICES

WRITING IN A STATE OF SIEGE

THE WALL
OF THE PLAGUE

A NOVEL

ANDRÉ BRINK

SUMMIT BOOKS NEW YORK

Copyright © 1984 by André Brink
All rights reserved
including the right of reproduction
in whole or in part in any form
Published by SUMMIT BOOKS
A Division of Simon & Schuster, Inc.
Simon & Schuster Building
1230 Avenue of the Americas
New York, New York 10020
Originally published in Great Britain by Faber & Faber Limited
SUMMIT BOOKS and colophon are trademarks of Simon & Schuster, Inc.
Manufactured in the United States of America

10 9 8 7 6 5 4 3 2 1

First American Edition
Library of Congress Cataloging in Publication Data
Brink, André Philippus, 1935–
     The wall of the plague.
     I. Title.
PR9369.3.B7W3 1985   823   84-16325
ISBN: 0-671-54189-7

for
NANNA
because you are there

All I maintain is that on this earth there are pestilences and there are victims, and it's up to us, as far as possible, not to join forces with the pestilences.

ALBERT CAMUS, *La Peste*

The plague . . . is the revelation, the bringing forth, the exteriorization of a depth of latent cruelty by means of which all the perverse possibilities of the mind are localized, either in an individual, or in a people.

ANTONIN ARTAUD, *Le Théâtre et son double*

Because of these things . . . a variety of fears and delusions were born in the minds of those who remained alive, and almost all of them took a single cruel decision, namely to avoid and escape the sick and all their possessions, each thinking thereby to ensure his own health.

GIOVANNI BOCCACCIO, *Decameron*

Whither will you go, and what will you do? I would as willingly go away as you, if I knew whither. But . . . here we were born, and here we must die.

DANIEL DEFOE, A *Journal of the Plague Year*

But, in the last analysis, the most noticeable feature of the Black Death was not that some escaped but that everyone was to some extent involved and paid the price of involvement.

PHILIP ZIEGLER, *The Black Death*

PART ONE

. . . from this one died in five days. . . .
Guy de Chauliac, personal physician to Pope Clement
VI in Avignon at the time of the Black Death, 1348

First Day

Because I was there; had been there. (So many journeys travelled on a single trip.) Because I'd been exposed before to the quality of that light which once again struck me when, after so many days of aimless wandering, I crossed the Rhône in the small white Renault Paul had given me and faced the brown walls of Avignon. Not that earlier exposures had conditioned or even prepared me for it. After the first time one never fully comes to know a new place from the inside. Hence the restlessness, the resentment (even if dulled by habit), the feeling of never quite arriving or breaking free. In transit; in search; perhaps in flight. Boetie: "What's the blarry matter with you? Listen, man, if you got an itch in your arse, you damn well take it with you, no matter where you go." Surely Provence was just about the farthest I could hope to get away from District Six. But the itch had stayed with me. And what I still couldn't tell was this: was it because of my colour, this smooth brown skin so loved by Brian and later Paul? Or because I was a woman? Or because of something in myself, something that made me who and what I was, Andrea Malgas?

Back to the same landscapes, over and over. Like love, Paul had joked, that night among the old stone walls of the Auberge: "Some people believe that all the later loves of one's life are just repetitions and variations of the first. Not that you would have noticed, you're too young."

Come April, I'll be thirty.

"Who are you trying to repeat in me?"

"You're the exception that helped me to make a new start."
That was when, unexpectedly, mischief lighting up his green

13

eyes, he added: "You know, money is worth so little these days, one may just as well marry for love. So how about marrying me?"

That had been in Provence too, in July, at the blazing height of an improbable summer. The very landscapes to which I was now returning, this time in the more serene and basic patterns of late autumn.

I had no inkling yet, as I crossed the Rhône that afternoon, that I would have only five days at my disposal. In fact, I had been expecting to shed all concern for time, to see it expand into the space of those southern plains. (My God: that other, distant South!) And I'd been looking forward to being entirely on my own too. That had been the whole purpose of my brief escape: how was I to know that Mandla would follow in my wake so soon?

What determines such a journey? Coincidence, mere co-incidence? But what seems coincidence at the time may well look different later; link upon link. If they hadn't burst in upon Brian and me that night — If he hadn't brought me here to Provence to "find my feet" once it was all over (all over?) — If I hadn't turned to Frank for help in Paris — If Frank hadn't invited Paul that evening — If we hadn't spent the weekend at the Loire four years later — If we hadn't come down to Provence this summer to explore the setting of his film script about the Black Death — If I didn't have to contend with Mandla these five days —

All these wholly pointless ifs. Why should I feel any need to reply? Can one's whole life be conceived as an answer to a question (and put by whom)?

It was Paul who said: one lives forward; understanding goes backward. I thought it was just part of his male way of thinking. Now I'm not so sure. Whatever happens at any given moment may have been lying dormant in the blood for years. One may take one's health for granted. Until, one evening, quite by accident, stepping from a bath, one glances at a mirror, and stops to gaze, surprised and curious, naked, at oneself, to discover the boil in one's groin.

14

(Could these have been your thoughts? I have no choice but to presume. To guess, to imagine, to devise, to invent, offers at least a measure of comfort, it is something of an act of faith perhaps; not certainty. I can only try. Must. Forgive me in advance. "For God's sake, don't turn me into a story," you said.)

When I left my small attic flat in the rue Bonaparte — how long ago? it must have been a week or more before these five days in Provence; I really lost track of time — I had no intention at all of deviating from the route Paul had so carefully planned for me. He'd spent the night with me, of course; he'd woken me very early, when I was still limp with sleep, and I abandoned myself to his lovemaking; a man of experience and scars, who'd travelled far, through many women, and now could afford to take his time, not bound by the arrogant brevity of an erection, self-assured about his power and his potency, tender even in passion — and yet, in the sob of his coming, revealing the touching vulnerability of a boy who can still be surprised by bodies. He drew the blankets over me again and left me in bed while he made breakfast. Between my thighs the warm, sticky moisture leaking away, the sadness of loss: the pang I feel so often these days, the fierce wish that it shouldn't end like this but turn into a child. "Of course I want you to have a child, Andrea. But we must get married first. A child needs security." "Are you sure a child won't be a nuisance to you, Paul? Your own kids are married already." "I want your child, Andrea. That's why I asked you." I put a finger on his mouth: "Don't bring it up again. You must allow me this chance in Provence to make up my mind. I'll tell you when I come back."

Not even Paul, I think, could appreciate the urgency with which I had allowed the idea to take possession of me. Earlier, at the Cape, as a young girl, I'd always assumed that I would have children one day, lots of them. Now, suddenly, I was approaching thirty and it could no longer be taken for granted. I would have to make a start if I still wanted babies. A

15

conscious decision. Otherwise, just as consciously, I would have to resign myself to the prospect of a lasting emptiness, the very idea of which threatened and offended me.

From the bed I could see him moving about in the small kitchen. The vulnerability of his white narrow buttocks. His back still slightly tanned from summer, but already fading. A hint of grey in his tousled hair. But the body still youthful. I knew both its violence and its compassion. Struggling to contain the sadness at the thought of going away, I covered my face with an elbow to concentrate on the dull warmth ebbing from me. *(When shall I see you again? When will it be like this again?)*

"Is the bread fresh enough? Would you like me to go out and get some croissants?"

"No. Come back to me."

"Don't seduce me again. It's time you got up. There's a long trip ahead."

As I went about my preparations — showering, dressing, taking my time with my make-up — I could sense his growing impatience. Brian had had as much trouble containing his annoyance about my "fiddling". This male hurry to get prepared, to stride into the day: so many kilometres to one's destination, so many hours, time was of the essence. I couldn't care less. I know I tend to overdo it, but I need my leisurely start: wandering about in my dark red dressing-gown (Paul's favourite), contemplating possibilities, trying on clothes, picking up a garment or discarding it, hunting for something suddenly remembered, tidying a drawer, scrabbling in a handbag, sitting down with my make-up only to abandon it again to ponder or gaze or grope for dreams already half lost, trying to rearrange whatever has come unstuck in the night. Without it, I can get no grasp on myself and I know the day will not stop menacing me.

"Andrea, I don't want to rush you, but really — "

"It's not all that far to Avignon."

"Seven hundred kilometres. I don't want you to get there after dark."

16

I shrugged.

"Shall I close your suitcase for you?"

"Yes. No, wait, I still want to check my shoes."

It was our last morning together; he didn't want to spoil it by openly showing his irritation, but I could see he was finding it difficult and with perhaps a touch of provocation I dragged it out. It was past eleven when I left; in the rearview mirror he kept on waving. Would it all be cleared up and decided by the time I saw him again, two or three weeks from now?

Even when, rather impulsively, I took the road to Orléans rather than swerve into the denser traffic of the Autoroute du sud, I didn't think of it as discarding Paul's programme. I still meant to go to Provence. Not only because Paul and the director had wanted me to explore localities for the film (Avignon, naturally; and Apt; and the mountains of the Vaucluse), but because I myself felt the need to go, and to go there. Back to where we'd spent those summer weeks; and where I'd been with Brian, eight years before. Back: because what Paul had asked me had stirred to life again everything that had been dormant for so many years, peacefully, irrelevant.

At most, I thought, it would be a small detour. And for his sake as much as for my own. Driving through the Loire valley rather than following the autoroute: a return to the landscapes of river and vineyards and castles where he'd taken me the first weekend we had been together. A small gesture of devotion (for the way he'd awakened me that morning, for all his gentle, thorough care, to the point of personally booking me into the hotel at Avignon), in preparation of a decision which had perhaps already been taken and which required only this affirmation of the first discovery of an "us". What else, if I were sensible, if I were to obey both head and heart, could I offer him but my Yes? We'd shared so much already, in work and leisure; our bodies had become tuned to each other; there was infinite security in being together; and there was the prospect of a future, a child. Of course I would return to him to answer yes; of course. But first I needed this brief withdrawal.

17

As it turned out, I didn't reach the Loire after all; not even Orléans. Where the road forked just after Orly — Orléans left; Chartres right — I abandoned the more familiar route. This time it was a conscious decision: I would no longer reach Avignon that night. But did it really matter? — my time was my own now; Paul's programme had merely been a device to make things easier for me. "Go wherever you like once you get there," he'd said, hadn't he? "Keep an open mind. Anything you feel we can work into the film will be welcome. I leave it all to you."

Only, Chartres had nothing to do with the film. Which was why it attracted me. Just like three years before, when I'd got the news of Ma's death, the name made something take shape in my mind which I hadn't been able to grasp before. The Loire would have been an easy and obvious starting point. Chartres was more precarious, not a begining but a thorough-fare to more distant and dangerous beginnings which might have been better left undisturbed. Three years earlier, it had been Paul who'd insisted I go away for a few days; and at the travel agency I'd impulsively decided on Chartres. (A brochure on the cathedral, photographs of its windows.) I'd gone by bus, one of a motley group, but once there I'd stayed behind on my own, much to the dismay of the tour leader.

I think it was three days I spent there, in a cheap little hotel not far from the cathedral, in the lower part of the town. Bugs and cockroaches at night. Driven out into the dingy streets at all hours. Incessant rain. The misery of my hopeless, senseless longing to be back home: it was the first time since London that I'd yielded to that black despair. I spent most of the time sobbing in the protecting darkness of the great cathedral, only half conscious of the endless stream of tourists shuffling past. Dull light outside, no sun at all, but even that was enough to set the windows smouldering. It was that blue and red, that blue especially, I felt in need of now, a need as real as that of the body when it craves fresh fruit, or vitamins, or chastity, or sex. From the instant I turned right at the fork in the road to put Orléans out of reach the urge to be back in the cathedral grew inside me like hunger. At an incredible distance, across the ochre and brown of harvested fields, I was hypnotized by those two unmatched towers, disturbing in their lack of symmetry, obtrusive, unavoidable. Words suddenly tumbling into my mind from my earliest childhood: *Come all ye that labour and are heavy laden.* And I hadn't even realized that I was labouring or laden! I'd been feeling so content and fulfilled, well adapted, even happy, secure in a solid and challenging job, in the love of a man I could trust implicitly, and in my expectations of the future.

The exorbitant scale of the cathedral high on a hillside covered with haphazard buildings. Even after the unmistakable cleanups of modern times an impression remained of what it must have been like in the Middle Ages, an impossible hotchpotch of dwellings that had simply grown together like incrustations and agglomerations of shells on rocks. And high above it all, soaring and light in spite of its massiveness, the cathedral with its arms stretched out to the grey heavens. How difficult to believe that this greatness, this loftiness, had been designed by the same people who'd huddled together in the rabbit-warren of buildings down below. One could imagine them swarming into the cathedral for refuge in times of war or pestilence; how they would have scuttled through the squalor of their little hovels and tunnels to find sanctuary among those high walls against whatever threatened from outside. Their God had been no abstraction. His curse had been as real as His blessing. In that vast building they were safe from soldiers and arrows, blunderbusses, illness, plagues. *Come all ye.*

Now I was back. Through cool paved streets I found my way, having deliberately left my car a long way off so that I could absorb the feeling of the town before reaching the cathedral. Perhaps I was wary of a too sudden exposure to the grief I'd felt there before: even though something deep inside me actually wanted it. Small clusters of people in the gloomy streets through which I made my way. Nuns in black. Small girls in bright red stockings. An unexpected orange pumpkin cut in half in a market stall. Shopwindows filled with books, or food, or wines, or clothes. At a turn along a steep flight of steps I stopped to look back: a sudden view of misty distant hills. A cold grey drizzle had set in. Then I reached the cathedral. The architecture of my distant grief. Crumbling walls turning black in patches, streaked with moisture. Statues above the portals, half-ruined saints staring blankly into space above the demons and kings cowering below them.

I went inside. I'd skipped lunch and felt hungry; but that other hunger was more demanding. Only the burning colours of those tall windows, I knew in my guts, would lessen it. The pews stood motionless, a reassuring linear pattern in the dark. I chose a seat against a wall, away from the occasional groups of visitors, leaving a zone of emptiness between them and me. The transept stretched away from me like an avenue disappearing into the dusk. Far away, near the altar, a cluster of candles was burning undisturbed, unflickering. I made no effort to control my thoughts, and it would be impossible to try and retrieve them now. In fact, I was not really "thinking" at all, but simply abandoned myself to whatever was moving inside me. I know that at one stage it struck me how utterly out of place I was in that cathedral. A coloured girl from Cape Town hiding in Chartres. Outrageous and profound things must have happened to lead me there. Andrea Malgas, nearly thirty. For the first time since Ma's death I was — no, not "longing back", but simply exposed to an awareness of something lost, forsaken, given up, irretrievable. The church in Buitenkant Street, just opposite the Caledon Square police station. The long walk downhill on Sunday mornings; Gran never missed anything. The cast-iron railings of the gallery and the choir section. The heavy dark beams above. Arum lilies in front of the pulpit. The almost sobbing fervour of the singing, Gran's strident tremolo outdoing all the others. *The grace of the Lord Jesus Christ, and the love of God, and the communion of the Holy Ghost, be with you all. Amen.* The preacher's arms outstretched, tassels swinging from his gown, enough to convince the sternest unbeliever that he really had the authority to promise grace and love and communion.

20

Until we meet again.

I would be sitting there with my hair in corkscrew locks, Ma's pride and love and labour; swinging my legs, black shoes, white knitted socks, until in sheer abandon one foot would hit the pew in front and Ma would intervene with a reprimanding elbow in my ribs. All of us in a row. Gran and Grampa, he shrivelled and mousey, carefully measuring off his last small draughts of life; Gran large and impressive, like a great soft bundle of washing, watching with a seagull's fierce eye everything that moved around her. Her two spinster sisters, Aunt Joey and Aunt Myriam, always at hand, eagerly spying for signs of the end, whether in Gran or in each other. Ma, wearing a small hat that wouldn't cover too much of her head, for she was a hairdresser and felt the need to advertise her handiwork (with reason, too, for she really had beautiful hair, long and black with just a hint of waving, like my own). Brother Arie, provided he got the weekend off from the hotel in Hermanus where he worked as a waiter: his hair parted in the middle like an open Bible, and shiny with Brylcreem one could smell ten yards away. Sis Maggie, two years older than I and much more prim and proper, always buttoned up to the chin to ward off temptation; her clothes bought at cost from Garlick's, where she worked. Then me. And on my other side, unless he'd got away again, for he couldn't stand the inside of a church, was Boetie, a deep scowl on his forehead, his hands dangling from too-short sleeves. Sometimes Brother Sonny would be with us too, on leave from Oudtshoorn where he was a teacher, but that didn't happen very often and only when our father was away, for Sonny had been Ma's love-child years ago and had to keep his distance. My father? No, never. Not Dedda. Not in church. The times he was home from the sea, and those were few and far between and wholly unpredictable, he would keep Ma out of church to catch up.

All this was what I found in Chartres that afternoon. After the initial illusion of fulfilment brought by the windows glowing in the dark, came those brutal images of a smaller, lighter church, of people I'd already shut out of my mind, of

21

things I'd cut myself loose from years ago. And to my own dismay I began to feel so claustrophobic in the cathedral that I had to leave. I couldn't explain it at all. Surely I'd been freed from those painful memories long ago. Brian had taken me away for good; Ma's death had confirmed the break.

For good. Perhaps that was it. For it had never, really, inevitably, been "for good", even if I might have thought so. (Except that, for eight years, with one brief lapse when Ma had died, I'd never even wanted to think about it again.)

When I'd first left, I'd seen it as a way out. I'd made a new start, from scratch, first in London, later in France. I earned enough to keep me going. I had the men I needed or could stand (and sometimes others too; but one soon learned either to get rid of them or accommodate them). Then there was Paul. And I suppose it was inevitable that, sooner or later, he should ask what he'd asked me in the Auberge in Eygalières this summer. Nothing unexpected about it. A logical choice — yes; no — which might indeed determine one's future but need not tax one too profoundly. Except for the one thing which I must have been bearing blindly within me ever since he'd asked me, a heaviness like the weight of a child, the knowledge I finally faced in Chartres that afternoon: if we did get married, my life would be decided for ever. Then I would have to stay here; I could never go back.

I'd never *wanted* to go back, not for one hour in all the years I'd been here: not even when I'd suffered, not even when it had been hard or awful or miserable, not even when I'd cried my guts out. Never back to that place. South Africa had become the name of a bad conscience, an evil memory, a threat looming in my sleep; not reality any more. I'd put it behind me. It belonged for ever to the past. But now Paul's wish to get married had suddenly lent the weight of finality to what had come about by itself. If I said yes, we might well be happy together. But one thing would be excluded for good: the possiblity of choice. If we got married, we could no longer go back, whether we wanted to or not. Neither he nor I. He white; I coloured. And suddenly to discover that what you'd

22

never wanted to do anyway was now no longer possible, changed something momentous. It was different now, totally different. True, I'd never felt the slightest urge to go back; I'd made a habit of shunning people who came from there, because I didn't want to be reminded of anything I'd cut myself from. Yet, without ever having to think about it, return had always remained a possibility — *had I wished to*. Marry Paul, and I could no longer choose. I felt reasonably certain about myself. But what about him? Suppose, one day, he felt the need to return? He was becoming so curiously proud of his Huguenot roots: one day he might well wish to return to his other roots as well. He could go back on his own, of course; so could I. But not together. All right, it might even be possible for the two of us to go together — but then only with special permission, with a permit, with official sanction, a document branding us as exceptions to the rule, outcasts, deviants in their society, like paraplegics or monsters with five legs or two heads. And that would very effectively detain us. It would become the substance of our bond: the substance of what might, one day, begin to constrain us. The silent reproach building up in the eyes of the other, without ever daring to say openly: "Look what I've given up for your sake." It needn't ever come to that: it would be enough for either of us merely to suspect the other of it, to start looking for tell-tale signs. Not today or tomorrow, certainly not, but in a year's time, in five years, in twenty, as one grew older and began to feel, perhaps, more out of place, to yearn back for "one's own", whatever that might be. Would I be able to face that? This slow erosion, the undermining of a relationship that had become one's main defence against life, this nagging suspicion or reproach?

In Paris I'd been quite confident, as I was that afternoon in Chartres and the night I spent there (for I had to stay over; it was by then much too late to return to the autoroute), that I needed Paul and wanted him; wanted to spend the rest of my life with him. But would I still be so sure a year from now? Did I have enough faith for it?

That was what I had to settle in Provence. That was what

23

had inspired me to go there in the first place, although I'd never consciously considered it in that light. And now that I knew, I suddenly felt intimidated, reluctant to reach any definite destination, afraid of the finality of a choice that might demand too much of me.

So, from the next morning, I gave up all idea of a planned route. Do not ask me to retrace my wanderings on a map. I don't know where I was. I never opened the Michelin. That, together with the address of the hotel in Avignon, remained stowed away in the cubbyhole while I immersed myself in the vast French interior as if it were a sea. Mental skindiving: that is the only description I can think of for my experience during those uncounted, unmarked days of aimless travelling.

On a few rare occasions Brian takes her to Onrust to teach her how to skindive in the tidal pools. He is thorough and cautious; she plunges in regardless. She's always had this passion for the sea, her father's domain. ("I'm a Malgas. We're sea-birds." Her father's pride: that the family name means "gannet".) Brian is less reckless, daunted not only by the treacherous tide but by the constant fear of being seen together. Not that she is immune from it. How easily a single careless word dropped by a curious passer-by can end it all. The surge of fear intruding in one's dreams at night, sending one splashing through waves of sleep to jump upright with a gasp of terror: a fear that never slackens its grip, not even in the daytime. *(My God, Andrea, the man's white!)* So they check very carefully beforehand, to make sure that there's no angler or beachcomber in sight. Having parked the car among the milkwood bushes, they scurry across the small stretch of exposed beach to the shelter of the rocks. And then the pools, long deep gullies among the reefs. Goggles and snorkel. Spluttering and coughing at first, scared by the wheezing sound of one's own breath; until one gets used to it. Diving in, like immersing oneself in a dream. She often dreams of flying. Nights on end she spends flying, beyond the reach of all that threatens her by day. And diving repeats the sensation: gliding

24

smoothly over mountain ridges, limitless landscapes opening up below one, valleys and ranges and unexplored depths, as one moves through a world operating according to laws different from those in one's own. Shoals of fish flickering past, fabulous colours, the motion of anemones, entire faces of rock covered in strange growths. And over and through all this one continues, gliding along, accepted by crabs and fishes, mussels, crayfish, who hardly care to swerve or scuttle out of one's way. The silent ecstasies of a wholly new kind of existence.

Re-emerging, inevitably, at last, one stumbles clumsily over rocks and pebbles. All of a sudden one no longer feels at ease in what has always been one's "own" world. For a long time one will carry behind one's eyes the imprint of other realities, other dreams. One's feet will now feel ill-equipped to find their way, sounds will be different, harsher, more ominous. One feels driven by a dark urge always to stumble back to that submarine world so briefly glimpsed, so deeply lived. And yet, at the same time, one knows that permanent return is impossible: one can never *live* there. However magical it is, one can never be more than a visitor, an on-looker, an in-looker, an intruder in the other world. One remains conditioned by the requirements of lungs, the need for air. In there, one will always be a stranger, will never "belong". A brief, beautiful immersion — then the sad return, back to this side, to the place one has come from. Even if one knows one will, in future, never quite belong here either.

Travelling through the great French hinterland had even more of a submarine feeling about it because of the weather: occasionally, it is true, the sun came through; but mostly it remained cool and overcast, with a slight drizzle, a gentle opaqueness obliterating outlines and blurring individual objects. The liquid lines and masses of hills, large dark forests smouldering with autumn colours, undulations, the slopes of disappearing mountains. I stayed away from main roads. The moment I left the busy arteries, I abandoned the entire ordinary world of scheming and planning, of calculable time

25

and distance, order, schedules. Around me the limitless landscapes opened up, green and dense, humid, intimate, unde-
manding. Towns, villages, hamlets. The stern black slate roofs
of Auvergne, houses like nuns with their backs turned to the
light. Gradually more white and rusty red as one proceeded
south. Villages in the folds of hills; castles and ruins on the
ridges. Ancient walls now tumbled down and exposed to wind
and rain; small quick lizards in the crevices. From time to
time, when hunger reminded me of my body, I would look for
a roadside place to eat. Gloomy interiors, red-and-white
checkered tablecloths, smudges of rain on the windows; inside, a gentle cosiness, families with large lazy dogs, sharing
with me the food made from a recipe handed down for
centuries from mothers to daughters; stoneware carafes with
local wine; small cups brimful with strong hot coffee.
Occasionally a brief conversation with the plump *patron*
(white pinafore, dark veins on the nose, fish-eyes) or his wife
(hair dyed red, the black roots exposed, dark sensual eyes, the
smooth movements of a marine animal, slippered feet): "And
where would you be coming from, Mademoiselle?" (A quick
glance to my ring-finger for confirmation.) "South Africa" —
always with a touch of reluctance, not knowing what reaction
to expect. "My, my, all this way? But how come you speak the
language so fluently?" "Oh I've been living in France for eight
years now." "You must be missing your country in this
weather, no? — you always have sunshine, don't you?"

And then it was off again, through that green underwater
world with its ridges and dark growths and its comforting,
protective wetness.

For hours at a time I would cut myself off from the wide
misty country outside by immersing myself in a different kind
of water: music. All the cassettes Paul had sent with me.
Vivaldi. Chopin. Above all, Mozart. He doted on Mozart as
much as Brian had. They'd converted me too. But I couldn't
listen to Mozart *all* the time! I'd smuggled my own tapes with
me, the ones that drove Paul up the wall. So what? — this was
my music. Folk, country, rock, reggae. Bob Marley. Peter

26

Tosh. Police. Leonard Cohen. Jethro Tull. Linda Ronstadt. The most Paul had been prepared to concede in his lovable old-fashioned way, was Françoise Hardy, Joan Baez, possibly Jacques Brel. With him, I am separated from the music in my blood. On this journey I was free to abandon myself to my own — with sporadic concessions to his beloved Mozart — as I drove on through the hills and forests of the Dordogne and of Auvergne, of nameless regions far from the main road.

Small hotels overnight: not always easy to find, for most had already closed their shutters after the season. They weren't expecting visitors so deep into October. The weight of the wet nights. Dull bedside lamps casting light as heavy as dust over massive furniture and the dark patterns of the wallpaper. Propped up against a large square pillow (even after eight years I still hadn't got used to the long French sausages) I would sit making notes in the small green *cahier* I'd bought in Chartres — odd flashes, insights, memories, remarks — trying in this way to keep a hold on my fluid days. Otherwise I conscientiously sat reading through the material Paul had sent with me. The penultimate text of his film script. Books, pamphlets and photocopies about the Black Death and later pestilences that had scourged Provence. Macabre reading, indeed. Yet through the years it had become an intimate part of our relationship. He'd already been obsessed by the idea for his story at the time I'd first met him, when I was still living in Frank's flat in Paris.

"Why would this man want to meet me?"

"It wasn't he who asked, Andrea. I specially invited him, I keep telling you."

"Why?"

"He's a South African."

"Frank, you know damn well I don't care to meet South Africans."

"There's no need to avoid them like the plague either. What are you trying to prove? And to whom?"

"There's more than enough people at the party to keep me busy as it is."

27

"But I promised him I'd introduce you to him."

"Because I don't want to sleep with you, you think you can put me up for auction to your friends?"

"You're being very unreasonable, Andrea." Frank lifts his hands in desperation, but he seems to suspect that resistance will only make her more stubborn. "These past two years I've been introducing you to all sorts of people. Some of them have become very good friends, haven't they?" (A bitter swipe at the architect Stéphane, or Henri in the Department of the Interior?) "After all, Paul Joubert is something of a 'name'. I'm sure you've heard of him. Even if you've got a thing against South Africans: he's been living here for so many years he's no longer contagious."

They are interrupted by a stranger in the doorway of the cramped little kitchen.

"Talk of the devil," says Frank. "Well, here you are: Paul — Andrea." He seems ready to make his escape.

A sudden grin from Andrea. "On my right — on my left," she says. "So where's the boxing gloves?"

The stranger is studying her in silence. He must be aware of the defiance of her attitude, the straight back, the very dark eyes, wide apart, with the merest hint of an Oriental slant in the corners.

"You look like a gypsy," he says at last.

It's her turn to size him up: poloneck sweater, corduroys, well-worn Hush Puppies, a pipe in the corner of his mouth.

"You don't look very impressive," she remarks. "I thought you were a celebrity. Or is that just for show?"

"If you thought of sleeping with her, forget it," says Frank, seeing a chance for swift revenge. "She's already decided against it." He pulls a face at her: So you're safe, both of you." Adding, as he goes out: "Whatever you do, don't spend the whole night comparing notes about the long-lost land."

Which, in spite of themselves, is exactly what happens later that evening, after, clearly put out by Frank's remarks, Paul has mumbled something about offering her a drink. (Andrea: "Couldn't you think up a more original approach? But all

28

right, I'd love some red wine.") Glasses in hand, they stand in front of the window — curtains open; both frames swung out over the night sounds from the rue Mouffetard outside — she a little way behind him. Against one of the side walls, stacks of Frank's paintings, most of them with their backs to the room; the sharp odour of paint and linseed oil.

"This city has a smell all its own," says Paul, leaning out. "Have you noticed?"

"It's just the market," she says. "This morning's cabbages and carrots and onions and mussels and fish."

"That's not what I'm talking about. I can smell the stones. Can't you? No other city has this particular smell: stone worn smooth through contact with people, for centuries on end. Feet, breath, saliva, pee. Bodies. Stone as lived-in as old clothes. Come and have a smell."

"So you're one of those, are you?" she says. "You like anything that's old, just because it's old."

(Perhaps he'd like to retort: "I like you too"? Then it's just as well he changes his mind.)

"Our South Africa never smelled like this," he insists.

"Your South Africa," she reminds him, "has never been mine."

He ignores the deliberate challenge. "It's one of my most vivid memories," he says. "I don't often long back, but this is one thing I'll never forget. Writing in front of an open window at night. The large moths, the flying beetles. Crickets outside. And then this smell: there's grass in it, bruised green grass, but dry stalks too. If the wind comes up, it brings you a smell as tangible as dust stinging in your nose. Except it *isn't* dust. It's Africa. One gets so used to it one never even notices it any more — until you go away. Especially if you've been away for a long time."

"The Cape had a different smell," she counters. "The sea. The shithouse in the backyard. Fish."

"And the Mountain."

"One can't smell the Mountain."

"Oh yes, one can. Its weight. Its size. One can never get

29

away from it. It's that same smell I talked about." With something between a smile and a frown: "Perhaps you never noticed."

"Of course I smelled it!"

And then she has to laugh, he too, about what she's just conceded. But behind her laugh — it's only much later that she'll trust him enough to confess it — lies a memory so violently real that it causes her guts to contract. An intimation of birth. Something she's been able to suppress for a long time now, more than three years, but which can no longer be checked.

Her Cape: the small houses of District Six all huddled together. The tiny backyards. Washing. The closeness of people, always, everywhere. The foghorn at Mouille Point at night, if the wind is right. The wet winters, the quiet interminable rain, the green of soggy slopes, the crown pines on the shoulder of the Mountain. Curried fish. Braised *snoek*. Tomato stew. Sweet potatoes with cinnamon sticks. The children scattering into the Mountain to collect pinestones. Herbs and spices on the Parade. The outings to Kalk Bay on New Year's Day: swimming in the harbour, as the Whites have taken over the beaches. Cowboy flicks in the Gem in Woodstock, or the Globe down in Sir Lowry's Street. — Keep away from the Avalon and the British, that's where the Jesters and the Killers and the Dynamite Kids hang out. — The good strong wind in summer. Pentecostal prayer-meetings. Her Gran's knitting, from morning till night, strange elongated objects taking on unpredictable shapes in her gnarled hands. Gran, present at every birth and wedding and death in the District. Her father's boisterous homecomings. Her mother washing or "doing" hair. Maggie coming home with a new view of sin every weekend. Boetie slipping off into the streets with his mysterous, dangerous friends; jumping through the window at night as soon's the old people have gone to bed. — She's the only one to know, she is his eyes and ears, it's her duty to keep *cave*. — Brother Arie bragging about all the fancy people he meets on the job at Hermanus. Brother Sonny's

30

furtive visits; crumpled banknotes thrust in their mother's hand when Dedda is out to sea. Oh, Cape Town, Cape Town!

As the evening wears on, she and Paul slump down on the floor below the window, hidden behind a large easy chair (actually a splendid old train seat from the turn of the century, upholstered in stained and faded green velvet, which Frank has picked up at Kremlin-Bicêtre), like two precocious children playing immemorial games: *Show me yours, I'll show you mine*. The rue Mouffetard outside irrelevant now; the party guests excluded.

"Have you really been living in Paris for so long? That's what Frank said."

"It'll be fourteen years next October. Have you noticed how people always remember the exact month they first arrived in Paris?"

"I came the year before last, in February."

"You planning to stay on?"

"Of course. I can't go back. Didn't you know?" Stopping short; not wanting to say more; resentful for what he has already drawn from her.

"My family has never forgiven me," he says, as if he hasn't noticed anything. "Staunch Afrikaners, every one of them. Dad was a minister, I'd better warn you. If it hadn't been for my reckless aunt I might have been persuaded to follow in his footsteps. All the others thought she was raving mad."

She makes no effort to interrupt him. His talking makes it unnecessary for her to divulge what she would rather keep to herself; and somewhat to her surprise she discovers that she enjoys listening. (*So you're safe, both of you.*) Effortlessly, his talk washes over her, a broad and placid stream with occasional eddies of humour or gentle cynicism.

His father, dominie in a small village in the arid interior. Griqualand West. A vicarage with a high green roof and an attic; a canal of turgid water between house and stark white church. A brother and a sister, both much older, which means that the boy grows up very much on his own, rather frail and sometimes sickly, some chest ailment, shying away from the

31

boisterous company of his contemporaries. (There are secret and exciting games, though, with the sergeant's daughter, Elise, in the attic or the back garden, when they come home from tennis.) An omnivorous reader, picked on by some of the teachers because he always knows better, but braced by the confidence and sympathy of others. The maths teacher, whose flighty young city wife runs away with the chemist, leaving a baby behind with its father. ("Don't ever fall in love with a woman, Paul. There's not one of them has a heart. You want to know why not? Because you can't fashion a heart out of a rib.") The language teacher who inspires him to read and encourages his early writing efforts. Unlike Mum and Dad who can think of nothing but evil. *Humble yourself in front of the Lord, my son, and put these sinful things out of your mind.* Family holidays in the Cape: Dad's a Joubert, Mum a Roux, both descended from the Huguenots, and one should keep touch with the place of one's origins, not go to seed in the dusty interior. *Our ancestors fled for their faith, Paul. You must cling to that. It's all we've got.* As if the interior has remained untamed and only the Cape retained its Huguenot propriety.

Andrea: "Jeez, it's clear they never knew the Cape. Not the way I did."

And then the aunt comes to spend a holiday with them. His godmother, Aunt Katrien (later Cathérine), who left the country soon after his christening to settle in France where she married a Frenchman, not even a Catholic but an a-the-ist, the devil incarnate. Imagine an egg like that hatching in the nest of the Jouberts. Dear God, we offer Thee repentance on our knees. Paul has just turned fourteen when Aunt Katrien (sorry, Cathérine) announces her visit. Hardly able to speak Afrikaans any more. Recently widowed, if one can believe her. Everything possible is done to prevent her arrival: they'll rather drive the six hundred miles to Cape Town to spend a week with her there, if it pleases the Lord. But it pleases neither the Lord nor Aunt Cathérine and one sweltering summer's day she turns up on the doorstep, having taken a taxi

32

from the airport at Kimberley, a hundred miles away. Real leather suitcases, a New Look outfit (it's just after the war), a hairdo to make one gasp for breath, and, holy Jesus, that perfume! Paul wakes up from his first wet dream with the smell of her perfume in his nose. Hooked for life, both on wet dreams and perfume.

The family's futile efforts to keep Aunt Cathérine hidden from the Sisters of the congregation; and, for different reasons, from the Brethren. But she refuses to be hidden under a measure. (Causing Paul's father to accept the very first call that comes his way after her lamentable sojourn; as luck would have it, it takes them to the Cape; the Lord will provide.) Long walks in the dusty veld, the eager boy and his sprightly aunt, so exuberantly young and — ha! — already widowed. (No sign of mourning.) She talks to him about literature. About Louvre and Orangerie. At the very first opportunity, one Saturday morning, she takes him to Kimberley and loads him with armfuls of books. Rodin. Lautrec. Degas. Another wet dream is forestalled singlehandedly. Dad delivers a sermon on Oholibah and Mum has to be revived with sal volatile.

For weeks and months, for years, after Aunt Cathérine's departure her scent remains with him. And bulky parcels crammed with books keep on arriving in the mail (often intercepted by his father, until Paul arranges with a friend to use a different address). An entire alternative education begins to run parallel to his schooling. After matric, Aunt Cathérine invites him to spend a long holiday in France. "Over my dead body," threatens his mother. But the airticket is already in the mail; and after much grave and tearful praying the parents give way. That first exposure to Europe of a seventeen-year-old, virginally impressionable boy. Aunt Cathérine accompanies him· on his travels. Cathedrals. Museums. Music concerts. She even stuffs money and a French letter into his pocket, and sends him off in a taxi to the address of a specially selected brothel. A total fiasco; but the illuminating night-long conversation which follows amply compensates for the technical failure. The next morning they leave for the South: Aunt

33

Cathérine has a small villa at Villefranche-sur-Mer, and in the Mediterranean he can splash all guilt from his lusty young body. He also meets a little Aphrodite on the beach, washed up from the sea, with breasts as pert and perfect as anything ever painted by Botticelli: and this time, one night on the pebbly shore of Nice, his blind thrusts aided by her deft young hands, he doesn't fail. Her buttocks dented, his knees skinned and bruised. A week later he returns home to start a university career.

After an MA and a Teacher's Diploma his future as a teacher seems inevitable. But once again Aunt Cathérine intervenes. "No education is complete without a few years in France." "Now please try to understand, Katrien," writes his father, "we don't want to sound ungrateful, but it's time the boy started doing something useful with his life. We Jouberts —" "We Jouberts have never been scared to live life to the full," she writes back. "Paul is my godson, and it's my money, and it's time he saw something more of the country where his ancestors came from."

Comparative Literature at the Sorbonne. Vacations spent on all the highways and offbeat tracks of Europe, either on his own, or with the young-old Cathérine at his side, or with some new female companion. From the beginning Provence became his favourite haunt.

"One day," he promises impulsively — his legs stretched out on the floor behind the great train seat in the studio above the rue Mouffetard — "one day you must go there with me. I'll show you around."

"All right, I promise," she says. In a night like this nothing is too far-fetched to promise.

After two years he reluctantly has to go home, mainly because of his mother's emotional blackmail. "To be honest, there was another reason too," he admits. "But that's a different story."

"You may tell me if you wish."

"Later, perhaps. It depends."

"On what?"

34

He shrugs. (Would he like to say: "On you"?)

So it's back to South Africa. A lectureship at the University of Cape Town. But *repos ailleurs*. He tries to sublimate the urge (as he diagnoses it) by getting married. She's called Annemarie, carnival queen, mountaineer, intrepid adventurer. At the outset, that is. For there's a depressing change after the first baby (much too soon); and it gets worse after the second. Her new insistence on "propriety". There's a right way and a wrong for everything. Once one has sown one's wild oats, it's time to settle down. One has responsibilities. A family. Parents and relatives to consider. A society of one's "own people". This conviction takes root in her just as his first novel is published, to become something of a *succès de scandale*, exposing all the sacred cows of the *volk*. "It's obvious we simply don't have anything in common any more, Paul. So far and no further."

During the few years of domesticity the urge to be alone has already taken hold of him. Now, all of a sudden, he is free again: but what's the use? There's an insipid taste to life. At thirty-one is no longer twenty: as simple as that. Thirty—and what has he actually achieved, where has he got to? Even writing has lost its attraction. The first book had political overtones, as a result of which all kinds of people began to take an interest in him for reasons that had nothing to do with literature. Invitations to address meetings, to open congresses, to write prefaces, to sign petitions against apartheid, to promote causes. "To be a writer in a place like that," he explains to Andrea, disgruntled, "means that one is dragged into so many other things that in the end you have no time left for the one thing you set out to do, writing."

"Would you rather seal yourself up in a little fortress of beautiful words?" she challenges his resentment.

"Of course not. But one needs a certain kind of energy to go on like that and I didn't have it. Good God, why can't one sit down to write something just because you want to, because there's some private need you must come to grips with? I don't want to have a role forced on me, dammit. I'm not a social

35

reformer or a revolutionary, I just want to be a writer."

"Who're you trying to convince?" she asks quietly, pointedly. "I didn't reproach you for anything."

Impetuous, he rages on: "It really turned bad soon after the divorce, when I tried to get down to writing again. You know, trying to make sense of the mess I'd landed in. There was a sensation in the newspapers about a bunch of young people, students and suchlike, who'd got themselves arrested because of sabotage. Children from top families. There was a lot of talk of life imprisonment, even some speculation about a death sentence. In the end it turned out differently, but right then things were looking pretty bad for them. And the English press began to carry stories about how they'd been tortured by the Security Police to extract confessions. One girl, she was only eighteen or nineteen or something, came to court with her arm in a sling. Her companions — but that's beside the point now. What am I trying to tell you? That it very suddenly struck me that on the night they'd tried to express their hopeless resistance by committing sabotage, the night they'd got caught, I'd been sitting at my desk trying to find the right image to express a young man's state of mind after he's had sex for the first time. And on the day the cops had broken the girl's arm, on that very day, I tell you, I'd spent hours trying to decide whether the two parts of a particular sentence should run together or be divided by a parenthesis. See what I mean? That was what mattered to me — while other people were tortured and risked their lives. And what for? Not even for their own sakes — they were white, and rich, and privileged — but for others! Suddenly it just seemed obscene to go on writing sweet little stories. On the other hand, I was just too unpractical by nature, too hopeless a politician to get 'involved'. I tore up my manuscript, page by page, and threw away the lot."

"I suppose that was also a way of choosing," she remarks, her eyes obscured by shadow.

"Even that wasn't the worst. The worst, I think, was the resentment I felt afterwards. I thought: All right, this is the sort of thing one must expect. It happens. People destroy one

36

another, and oppress one another, or suffer, or die of hunger or of ignorance. I'm not denying it. But, for God's sake, does that mean I have no right to go on writing about what's important to *me*? What can *I* do to eradicate evil or change the world? Sweet blow-all. One thing I can do is write a book which some people may enjoy. But now I daren't, because my conscience is killing me. And all I get out of it is bloody frustration."

"You're a nut-case," says Andrea.

"You may be closer to the mark than you think. The point is, I got the impression that a country like South Africa has no place for people who simply want to carry on living, indulge in their little sins, have a good meal from time to time, enjoy a bit of music or a good painting or a good book. You're forced to walk right into the fire. Otherwise, the only choices you have are to go mad or to die."

"Sounds like the two choices a virgin imagines for herself," she says, unmoved. "Later she discovers she may just as well get fucked."

"I've never thought of myself as a virgin."

"One only realizes it afterwards."

"You obviously know all about it."

She doesn't answer; just sits there looking, unflinching, in his eyes.

"I'd like to know more about you," he suddenly says, with an urgency that surprises her, as if it is imperative for him to find out.

"I'm not important," she says quickly. "Don't avoid the issue: I want to hear how you got out of your nice little moral mess." Adding wryly: "*If* you ever got out of it."

"Sure I did." He seems disgruntled about her reticence. But she knows it's much better that way, safer, more manageable. After a pause he resumes his talking: "You see, I'd discovered long ago that the one person I could count on in an emergency was Aunt Cathérine. This time she didn't fail me either. Just when I thought I wouldn't ever find a way out, she quietly and generously died in her sleep. Left me everything she owned.

37

The flat in Paris — you must come over soon, it's in the boulevard Malesherbes — and the little villa at Villefranche, and everything she'd inherited from her husband. So *voilà*! And now I've lived here for the last thirteen years and I haven't once regretted it. The mere thought of ever going back to that parochial little world in the bunghole of the world — " He raises his hands in mock defence (beautiful, long fingers, she immediately notices, wondering whether he is conscious of it too).

"And why should you? You have a perfect life. You're famous and everything."

"Famous? Well — "

No, not quite. But with enough success to be content. (Compatriots travelling in Europe regularly look him up: local boy makes good. I'm sure the chap will show us round. You know, all the little offbeat spots ordinary tourists don't know about.)

After a couple of years to settle down he begins to write again. The first of his new novels, written in English, enjoys a measure of success. The second, *Survivors*, fares even better. Then, quite out of the blue, it is discovered by one of the most exciting younger French directors, François Masson, Paul is invited to write the scenario, the film takes Cannes by storm, and suddenly Paul finds himself established. From all over Europe he is approached with offers for new scripts. No single film after *Survivors* provokes quite the same flood of recognition; partly, one suspects, because Masson tragically died in a car accident barely a month after the Cannes triumph. At the same time the event curiously adds to Paul Joubert's reputation. "If only he can find another director like François Masson, his work will come into its own again."

"It's comforting for the ego in a way," he admits, twirling his empty glass between his fingers. "But nobody seems to suspect that I may be losing confidence in myself. I've never been able to finish another novel after *Survivors*. It feels safer to hide behind film scripts."

"Don't exaggerate. It's half-past three in the morning,

which is a very normal time of the night to feel sorry for oneself."

"I'm not feeling sorry for myself!" he denies angrily. "It's the truth, I tell you. *Survivors* wasn't really my success. It was Masson's. Because of his death, it all blew over to me, and I became a scriptwriter." She sees his stubbornness in the way he clenches his jaws. "But I promise you: one day I'll show them. There's a story inside me which I'm going to write, no matter how long it takes. And this one will be a novel, not another film. Films have become a too easy way out for me. And I'm not getting any younger."

"You don't look quite decrepit yet."

"I'm forty-seven, Andrea."

"Some people reach a hundred."

"I'm not counting the years. What bothers me is that, no matter how many years you manage to pile up in the end, it remains a finite number. Even right here, as I'm sitting talking to you, we have two or three hours less left than we had when we started. I'm sure it doesn't bother *you*. Not yet. But for me — " He starts fiddling with his pipe, fussily, nervously. "Before I die I want to know I've at least done something worth while. That's what this novel is to me. Call it an insurance policy if you wish. Does that make sense to you?"

"What's the story about?"

"I'll call it *The Black Death*. You really want to hear about it?"

"Nobody knows where we are right now. For all they care we're lying somewhere in the dark making love. So why shouldn't you tell me about your *Black Death*?"

"Do you know the story of the Black Death in the fourteenth century?"

She shrugs. The thin fabric of her shirt moves slightly. He cannot be unaware of her breasts, small as they may be. "A bit," she says.

He appears to be talking more to himself now than to her. Intrigued, she watches him through the smoke of her cigarette: his head thrown back against the faded green velvet, a greying

39

mane of hair, deep furrows on either side of his mouth, a tracery of fine lines around his eyes, looking through tortoise-shell glasses which both reflect the room and ward it off.

"Within only a few years between one-third and half of the inhabitants of Europe died. Can you imagine? They never even realized what had hit them. Ever since 1345 or 1346 they'd been hearing wild tales of an incredible plague raging in the Far East — but it was so far away, and the stories were so fantastic, that no one really paid much attention. Then, towards the end of 1347, a small fleet of about a dozen Genoan galleys arrived in Sicily from somewhere far away, perhaps the Crimea, and within a few days the people of Messina began to die in their hundreds. Swellings in the groin and under the arms, followed by a brief living hell: black spots appearing on the skin, a violent fever, then a spitting of blood. Towards the fifth day, by which time it seems the body would be pitch-black through putrefaction, death came as a merciful release. When the people of Messina realized what was going on, it was already too late. They forced the sailors back on their doomed galleys and drove them into the open sea. From then on they carried the Plague with them wherever they went, from one harbour to the next, until the entire coast of the Mediterranean was infected. From Marseille it started spreading through France, at a speed, they said, faster than that of a man on horseback. In Germany they later portrayed the Plague as a maid travelling through the air like a blue flame, killing her victims simply by raising an arm.

"In Provence, which is where I'd like to set my story once I get down to writing it, all roads in those days led to Avignon, where the popes had been ruling for the past forty years or thereabouts. And along all the highways and byways of the South, accompanying every solitary merchant or beggar, every pilgrim travelling to see the Holy Father, every whore in search of a few extra francs, came the Black Death. One single flea infested with *Pasturella pestis* was enough." He suddenly looks at her with a wry smile: "Do you realize that up to the present time there are still only five or six areas in the world

40

from which the Plague regularly starts all over again — and that one of them is in South Africa?"

"Doesn't surprise me," she says, her face inscrutable.

He raises an eyebrow, but doesn't comment.

"The Pope himself probably survived only because he isolated himself from everybody else in his huge palace. I suppose isolation was a very natural impulse. Everywhere in Europe people resorted to it, whether they were noblemen or priests or intellectuals or ordinary peasants. The moment someone was infected, others stayed away at all costs, even if it meant closing one's ears to his screams for help. In some places people were sealed up inside their homes and burned alive."

"Was there really no remedy?" she asks, concerned in spite of herself.

"Oh there were innumerable remedies. But it's hard to say whether they were any use. The problem, of course, was that no one had the faintest idea of where the Plague came from. Who would suspect a rat or a flea? To them, it was caused by miasmas in the air, or by invisible evil spirits; it was a visitation from God Himself, to chastise people for their sins, the latest variation of the Deluge. Or otherwise they blamed the Jews for it, or heretics, or any stranger who unexpectedly happened to turn up in their midst. Some tried to take refuge in fasting and prayers. Others went to the opposite extreme of feasting and fornicating, hoping their frenzied excesses would fool the evil spirits. Most people went about in the strangest outfits, trying to cover up the whole body, wearing masks with long beaks which made them look like weird birds, with large crystal eyes. Imagine how those thick lenses must have distorted the world. The beaks were filled with perfumes and oils and sweet-smelling substances to purify the air before they breathed it in. Like the gas masks of the First World War. If you wanted to go on a journey, you would be advised to eat sweet apples, or sprinkle yourself with rose water, or rub your skin with perfumed salves. The more imaginative resorted to mixtures that would have been the envy of any alchemist. A *soupçon* of dried snake, powdered emeralds, figs, myrrh, saffron, and God

41

knows what else. Others did the opposite: inhaled the foulest odours they could find, firmly convinced that these would drive the Plague away. Some apparently squatted on their latrines for days, heads tucked between their knees; and if you look at some of the toilets in the French provinces nowadays, you can imagine what these places must have been like in the fourteenth century."

"And all in vain?"

"Sure. The Plague just went on and on, and even became worse. Moving from the South all the way up to Paris. To England. Germany. The Scandinavian countries. Hardly a village escaped unharmed. You know how close together these villages are. By the time one got word of the Plague it would be ten kilometres away from one's own home. There simply wasn't any time to run away or dig trenches or build walls. You just had to sit and wait, and tremble. 'How shall I recognize the Plague when I see it? How do I recognize a Jew? What does a heretic look like?'

"Sometimes, in the course of my reading through the years, it has seemed to me that this might have been worse than the Black Death as such: not the eggs or apples or carbuncles in the groin or the armpit, not the spitting of blood or the spasms of a horrible death — for all that affected only the body, which has to die some time — but what it did to the mind. The way it warped and distorted the brain, the emotions, one's whole dignity. Making one suspicious towards all other people, even those nearest to one, those one is supposed to love, because their very closeness poses the greatest threat. In the end nothing is too revolting or degrading or excessive to consider. The imagination itself grows weary. One learns not to care. Total indifference settles in. Everything around one is black and transparent with death. And right through the lovely smell of rosemary one recognizes the Plague itself, for everything is infested with it."

"So that's why you'd rather turn it into a novel than a film," says Andrea. "There's no screen big enough for what you have in mind. Even Cinemascope would be too small."

42

He looks flushed. "I've been boring you," he says, offended.
"No. But I couldn't help wondering — "

He relaxes. "I know I tend to get carried away once I get going. I've been living with this for so long. Most of my friends turn tail the moment they see me coming."

"I'd like to hear more," she says quietly, leaning over to stub out her cigarette in the heavy ceramic ashtray on the floor. Her arm touches his knee; she quickly glances in his direction, but he doesn't seem to have noticed.

"All this is just the background of my story," he says. "I got the idea from Boccaccio. In fact, I first thought I'd turn the *Decameron* into a script. That was long before Pasolini did it, mind you, and my approach would have been quite different. All I've retained from Boccaccio is the idea of a group of people, chosen very carefully, of course, who try to isolate themselves from the Plague. I'd place them in Avignon, part of the whole mad merry-go-round surrounding the papal court. When the Plague breaks out, they flee to the more distant countryside, retreating into the mountains — what I have in mind, is something like the Luberon, or the mountains of the Vaucluse, below the Mont Ventoux. Do you know the region?"

"I've been to the Vaucluse."

"Well, that's where they'll escape to. Perhaps 'escape' isn't the right word. I'd like to introduce something of the Pied Piper of Hamelin, you know, who lured away all the children when the city fathers refused to pay him for exterminating the rats and — who knows? — the Plague. And so my little group of refugees ends up in the mountains where there's a very heated debate about how to solve their problems. In the end they decide to have a fortress built in which to hide from the world. Once the job is finished the builders are killed. Not out of cruelty, simply as a sanitary precaution. At this distance the Middle Ages don't seem like a time or a place with much room for sentiment, do they?"

"And once you have them safely tucked away in their fortress, they live there happily ever after?"

43

"All I know for the moment is that there should be two very different phases in their stay: in the beginning I see them as being very pious, leading an almost ascetic existence; but gradually the mood changes. One after the other they proceed to more outrageous behaviour. Like Boccaccio's people they try to while away the time by telling stories. But it goes beyond that: in due course they start acting out these stories, each trying to outdo the others in inventiveness and extravagance. Long after the Plague has ended outside they are still going strong, carried on by the momentum of their own excesses."

"And is that how it's going to end? Or will they start killing one another until there's nobody left?"

"It's a possibility. But for the moment I'm leaving it open. Perhaps it all ends in a sort of Triumph of Death, depending on how the story develops once it gets going. If I'm in a generous mood, or if I feel the characters deserve something better, I may allow them out again. Writing is playing God, after all. So there's the possibility of being reintegrated with humanity, only sadder and wiser, of course. Hopefully, they'll have a better understanding of the world by then."

"So far it's just a general scheme?" she says.

"I know. But I find a scheme important. Can't write without it. And whatever details I invent in the end, these five stages will be there: the outbreak of the Plague; the withdrawal into the mountains and the debate on what can be done; the spiritual phase; the physical phase; and the end, with its panoramic view of the world, or humanity, perhaps of wholeness. Anyway, something to that effect."

"Why five parts?"

"I am fascinated by numbers," he confesses. "I've been amusing myself with sums and signs and stuff ever since I was a kid. You should have seen all the things I persuaded the sergeant's daughter to do, purely on the basis of her birth date!" Adding, when he notices that she is both interested and amused: "Well, you see, five is a perfect figure: the pentagram, the five stigmata, the five members of the body, the five senses; the four cardinal points of the compass plus the centre; the

44

marriage of heaven and earth, since three is the sign of heaven and two that of the Earth Mother. In other words, it concerns the fullness and wholeness of life, health, passion, energy — directed against the total immobility of death. The seed of life and the pus of the Plague. Which is why it also has strong erotic undertones."

"Suits you, doesn't it?"

"What makes you say that?"

She smiles. "Most men trying to pick up a girl come round to that sooner or later, especially after wearing her down with a long intellectual discussion. And even more so when they realize it's almost four in the morning."

"How old are you, Andrea?" he asks point-blank, almost accusingly.

"Nearly a quarter of a century."

"You have no right to be so cynical at your age."

"I don't think I am. I've just got good eyes. My father was a sailor, you see. He could see right through the fog. And I'm his child." She smiles. "Don't worry, you didn't put me off at all." Now she seems grave, knees pulled up against her chest, arms clutching her feet, a frown between the downcast eyes. "There's something pretty unsettling about your story," she says quietly. "I like the idea of all the outrageous and violent goings-on with just the walls of their fortress between them and death. Copulating on black discoloured bodies. 'The seed of life and the pus of the Plague.' But why" — she looks up unexpectedly, disarmingly — "why are you so obsessed with the idea of a scheme, with abstractions and figures, all those fives? It's interesting, OK, but it leaves me cold. If you got a story to tell, why the hell don't you get on with it and concern yourself with the people? They must have been flesh and blood, even though they lived God knows how long ago. They must have loved, and hated, and feared, and got drunk, and vomited and crapped and copulated like real people, not like stupid little numbers."

"Well, I had to start somewhere," he tries to defend himself. "I need something I can hold on to. A plan to keep everything

45

from collapsing. Once I have that, I can start filling in the details. The muscles and sinews and arteries and glands. And you must admit there's something fascinating in the scheme: in one — the light breaking through, illumination, awareness; two — the idea of the echo, reflections, duality, man-and-woman, good-and-evil, life-and-death, whatever; three — the spiritual, the domain of thought, of the mind, of basic principles; four — earth, the human, the tangible, the spatial; five — "

"You've already said that."

Once again that penetrating stare which permits no evasion. And the conversation turns into a duel, a mutual sizing up, an act of assessment, in this defenceless hour of the early dawn, the first light brushing the grey rooftops and red chimney pots of the city outside; when all the usual protections and defences recede: a looking at one another, a very intent gazing into each other, everything reduced to a simple act of exposure: *Look, here I am. Judge me if you wish. Be cruel if you have to.*

She cannot have expected anything quite as cruel as his sudden question, right in the middle of their fencing and thrusting: "Andrea Malgas: what are you running away from?"

For a moment she seems to shrink back, to huddle inside herself. (The spasm of the stomach muscles that greets the entry of a man into one: the sudden twitch as if you've been told some unexpected news. The backyard in District Six, bright patches of washing under the large fig-tree: the sound of her father working his boisterous way home, from street to street, followed by a crowd of children as he makes his way uphill from the harbour like some fantastic rat-catcher, his pockets stuffed with money, his arms loaded with presents, his clothes pervaded by the smell of brine and fish. The late afternoon in the small room behind the hairdresser's. Brian's flat, early daylight on the sheets crumpled and sticky with love: and then the bell. The last long journey through the expanding land. The narrow quiver of the plane. Provence. London. Foggy mornings in Hyde Park. Paris —) Then as she looks straight back at him: "You won't find out by asking."

He knows, she knows, it is not evasion, but the only answer possible; announcing, perhaps, the beginning of a conversation which must inevitably continue through months and years, leading to an inevitable conclusion. All that still has to be decided is the timing of that moment. It may be tonight: it would be easy enough to up-end the old train seat and lock the door. (No need to draw the curtains, this is not the Cape.) Or they can postpone it and decide to wait; there is no hurry, they have time, a lifetime. She stares at him; he stares back. She studies the cheekbones in his lean face, the shadow of beard showing through the skin, the hint of determination in his eyes, the brows meeting above the nose. His hands. The long outstretched legs. Back to the eyes, like the children's game of seeing who can outstare the other. I'm not ashamed to acknowledge my own desire. You can take me now if you wish: only, you're much wiser than I thought. You know very well I am ready to be taken; but it seems you also know that if that happens it would be just as easily finished. (Or is it presumptuous of him to think that this is what she is thinking?)

The sudden sharp morning shout of a man in the street below announces the end of the night, cutting the stare between them. The moment becomes manageable again, at least on the surface.

"Why should it interest you so much," she asks, "to write a story about people telling each other stories in order to forget about the Plague outside?"

"Why else does one tell stories?"

"You've already run away once," she says. (Her turn to be cruel: serves him right.) "Suppose we really lived in the Middle Ages, don't you think it would have been better to try and do something for the sick rather than write stories about them? Burying the bodies. Burning the infected clothes. Spitting that Maid's blue flame right in the face and saying: 'Come on, I dare you!'"

He laughs with a hint of patronizing her. "I don't think you realize how dangerous the Plague is."

"What makes you think I don't know?"

47

"You still look pretty unscathed."

She doesn't respond to that; it's easier to attack: "What do *you* know about the Plague except for what you've read in books?"

"*Touché.*" He stays silent for a while. "But not quite. At least there was one small bit of the history of our time I experienced myself. That was where my obsession with the Plague began. Something which so unsettled me that I've never been able to discuss it with anybody else. Only much later, when I read the *Decameron*, I realized: My God, so *this* is what it was all about — "

"What was it?"

"Hungary, in 1956."

"Don't tell me you were there?"

"No, of course not. It happened just towards the end of my two years' study in Paris. At the time I had firmly decided to stay on for at least another year. Then came the news of the Russian invasion, the tanks in the streets of Budapest. Several of my friends at the Sorbonne went off to Austria to help the refugees. In fact, from all over the world students swarmed to Vienna. My own decision was made when my mother casually mentioned in a letter that a couple of my friends from Stellenbosch University were also on the point of leaving. Aunt Cathérine thought I was mad: it was all right to trek across Europe in search of culture and art, but for God's sake not after blood and war. Still, there was nothing she could do to stop me. In a way, I suspect, she even felt a bit proud of me. Perhaps it confirmed her own romantic impulses. And to be honest, my decision *was* more romantic than anything else. The Great Adventure."

"I suppose it turned out rather differently?"

"The Schloss Judenau," he says, drawing back into himself, as if he's staring through her towards something quite different. "Fifty-odd kilometres from Vienna. I met my old varsity friends in Düsseldorf, and from there we travelled together."

"Must have been quite something."

"It was a different world altogether. Everything white with

snow. More than 25° below. Children skating on the frozen river singing arias from *Don Giovanni*. Some of them were too small to read or write, but they must have been fed opera with their mothers' milk. And then the enormous old castle in that expanse of pure white, surrounded by an empty moat. Every day the ambulances would drive out to the border to meet the refugees as they arrived, most of them more than half dead with cold. They were given brandy first of all. Then we had to bandage their feet. We had blankets and coats and things to keep them warm in a makeshift shelter until it was time for the ambulances to return to the castle. That was where most of us worked, each in command of a group of Hungarian volunteers. Shovelling snow. Identifying refugees. Filling in papers. Above all, there were the clothes sent from all four corners of the earth, whole mountains of stuff that had to be sorted up in the attics of the towers. Food supplies. Some weeks everything went quite smoothly. But after Christmas, and especially towards the end of January, it was hell. A slice of dry bread and a cup of black tea in the morning. Another slice of bread at lunchtime, with a boiled potato and, if you were lucky, a sliver of meat, and tea. In the evenings we were treated to syrup on our bread; and the ubiquitous black tea, of course. Tempers were getting frayed. There were arguments and even brawls every day. Among the refugees, among the helpers, among the different groups and nationalities. Sometimes Hungarian collaborators slipped into the camp, the Avos; on a few occasions they were recognized by some of the refugees. I tell you, then it was hell to pay. Damn near murdered them. Once somebody was actually killed — " He stops, and shakes his head. "But that's beside the point now. I just wanted to give you some idea of what it was like. We had about seven hundred refugees at any one time, sometimes fewer, often many more. Most of the personnel were from Holland, Austria, Germany: the Schloss was run by the Dutch Red Cross. And then the bunch of students, of course. About twenty of us, I think; the rest were sent to other centres."

"You lived in the castle?"

49

"Yes, the whole lot of us, men and girls together in one large round room high up in a tower. As cold as hell. There was only one washbasin, which we screened off with a couple of blankets so that one could have a bit of privacy when one dared to brave the cold water. Some mornings we first had to unfreeze the pipes with blue-flames. In the beginning we were all a bit uncomfortable with each other — the South Africans, one Belgian, some Germans and Dutch and Austrians, three French, and two schoolgirls of fifteen or sixteen who'd run away from a school in Trieste in search of adventure. There even was a genuine Austrian princess, a real blue-blood from the House of Habsburg. She worked harder than anybody else, got up earlier, came to bed long after the others. Gradually we came to know each other. At night it was quite rare for more than half of the beds to be occupied. Even the two schoolgirls from Trieste, scared stiff at all the goings-on during the first week, lost their inhibitions. Towards the end one of them regularly came in behind the screen to chat to me while I was having a wash; even helped me rinse off the soap. Sweet little thing she was, with very small, very round little breasts, straight from a medieval painting. The other one was much more voluptuous. Lise and Helga."

"I can't see any connection with the Plague yet!" says Andrea.

"It wasn't as idyllic as you might think. Even the sleeping together at night was often caused by sheer desperation, just to forget about the horrors and the tiredness of the job. Except for one poor soul, a German, Klaus. He never managed to make it with anyone and night after night we'd hear his little iron bed creak in frustration. For the rest — You know, some of those helpers treated the Hungarians like dirt, like animals. Some of the men took advantage of the Hungarian women. Up in the sorting-rooms one would regularly trap a man having it off with a woman among the piles of clothing. Most of the women had no choice: it was either that or they would be left empty-handed. And the men were bribed with cigarettes to do any favours one required. Try to imagine it,

50

Andrea: after living through hell itself those refugees had finally escaped to the Schloss — and then? All right, they'd made it, they were safe, but that was all. They didn't possess anything. They had nothing to do to keep them busy, to keep them from going mad, except sit around and play cards till the lights were switched off at ten. And there were scientists among them, doctors, lawyers, teachers, highly cultured people, thrown together with the roughest peasants. With us into the bargain. All of us caught up in the same place, with little hope of getting out. For those few months all we knew of life was that small circle in the Schloss Judenau. It came as a relief when one was called up to go to the border with one of the ambulance teams, even though it meant working oneself to a standstill."

"Were you never allowed out?"

"From time to time we had a weekend off. Usually once a fortnight, or once in three weeks, depending on the work. Then we'd leave for Vienna in an ambulance on the Friday, come back on Sunday night, by train, third class, by which time one wouldn't have a bloody groschen left. Not that we got much to start with, about twenty shillings a day, and that was only paid at the end of the month. Most of the guys spent it all on food and drink — towards the end of our stay it was unbelievable, the amount of drinking that went on, just to keep going. Even little Lise. I used to save my money for opera when I had a free weekend. Every show I could squeeze in. And perhaps it's one's defence mechanisms working overtime, but do you know, even today, so many years later, if I think back to those three months in Schloss Judenau, it's mostly music I remember. That's what made it all bearable. The State Opera. The children skating on the frozen river. Whenever I hear *Don Giovanni*, that is the first image the music calls up — "

He is silent for a long time.

"And was that all that happened?" she prods him.

"What do you mean, 'all'?" he asks, indignant. "It was one of the most disturbing experiences of my whole life. *The* most."

51

"That's not what I meant. But what you've told me so far is an adventure story. It's moving, and strange, even shocking in a way. But what did it mean to you? It's as if you're absent from your own story. There must have been something much more personal in it. You were *there*!"

"Everything was personal. To be isolated in such conditions with a crowd of people you gradually get involved with more deeply than with your own family. The most trifling thing can cause an explosion. If someone steals your bread ration, or a few groschen, or pushes in ahead of you in the ambulance queue, or blackmails one of your workers into joining his team, it leads to near murder, I can tell you. On the other hand you also discover what charity really means. Suppose there's an opera you simply *have* to see but you're on duty, and somebody offers to take your place. Or if someone has a birthday and invites you to share a piece of schnitzel."

"And what about your little Lise?"

He smiles. "No need to be jealous of her at all."

"You've got a bloody cheek. Why should I be jealous?"

"I shared my bed with her a couple of times. In a way it was inevitable, I suppose, in that restricted space. And I'm no sexless angel. But I think I really felt more, well, fatherly towards her."

"Which adds incest to injury," she mocks him. But perhaps his words, or something beyond them, have begun to make his obsession more comprehensible to her, even if only provisionally — a willingness, at least, to allow him to persuade her in due course. Yet she refuses to give away too much right now, and all she offers as a comment is: "I do wish you'd start thinking about an end for the story. It's criminal to leave it open like that."

"Perhaps you'll find me a good end one day."

"If you leave it to me, it may not be the kind of end you like."

"I may be willing to risk it," he says lightly.

And then the door to the studio is opened and several people enter, including his girlfriend, a blonde actress, her hair

52

somewhat dishevelled, a smudge of mascara on one cheek, as if she's taken advantage of the night; which forces her on the attack as soon as she sees him: "Paul! I've been looking for you all over the place. And here you're lying behind a chair — "

" — talking," he says calmly, picking up the empty glasses and the ashtray, ready to get up. "No more than that. Have you been hoping for something more exciting?"

"You've had too much to drink again," says the blonde girl, with the smallest hint of a slur in her voice, shaking back her Lippizaner mane. "Well, come on, it's almost day. We must go."

He gets up lazily, tall, shoulders slightly stooped, like a question mark high above her in the grey light from the open window. His back turned to the smouldering actress, he looks down at Andrea. A last attempt to weigh the odds? For should he wish to do so, it is still possible to choose. He knows exactly what is at stake: for the first time in years more than a night is involved, more than a few weeks or months, passing the time, more than relief or passion: a challenge to which the blood responds, a submarine awareness which can neither be denied nor scorned. Perhaps for that very reason — it's so much safer, at least for now — he turns away from Andrea and bows to the girl:

"*Génie oblige.*"

They go out together, followed by the others.

I remained sitting behind the tall green seat, resting my head on the patchy velvet. There was a sudden emptiness in the pre-dawn, a violent awareness of need which both angered and scared me. I didn't want to admit to it. I was ashamed of the desire in my guts.

Much later I got up and went through to the living-room to face the mess. Glasses smudged by lipstick or dull with fingermarks. Half-empty and empty bottles, two of them lying on their sides on a table. Plates exhibiting the remains of food: tattered chicken breasts and drumsticks, limp asparagus, blobs of pâté, salami rinds. Ash on the floor. The carpet crumpled like the skin of a large animal that had died of famine. All the guests had gone. Frank's bedroom door was ajar. I went to have a look, and saw him stretched out and snoring, only partly covered by the spread, his clothes discarded on the floor where he'd shed them.

It is difficult now, so much later, to explain what I felt, or why I was led to do what I did. I undressed in the living-room, neatly piling my clothes on the couch which had been serving as my bed for the past eighteen months (except for the nights I'd slept out), observing myself in the tall antique mirror Frank had picked up at Clignancourt. (A moment, an action, so often repeated in my life!) A very deliberate, meticulous observation. Feeling what? — desire? glee? scorn? detachment? Perhaps it was to see what the stranger, Paul, would have seen had he insisted; had I wanted to. I had. For the first time since I'd left South Africa with Brian, I really wanted to. The few others had been a matter of coincidence, or means to an end; they hadn't touched me, hadn't moved me; in Paris one does as the Parisians do. But that night something different had happened. Paul. I was ready to offer him my life. That might have been the reason why I hadn't invited him when his eyes had asked or challenged me to save him from his filly. Because that was what was at stake: life. And I felt frightened. I'd risked it once; I couldn't afford to do so again. Something, someone had to save me, yet no one else could. And simply by keeping silent, or by turning him down, or by exercising that self-restraint my sister Maggie had always made so much of, was not enough. I had to undo this thing before it could begin.

Turning away from the mirror with its spots and stains where the backing had disappeared, leaving blots and holes like dark patches in the flesh, I went through to Frank's room, and closed the door behind me. Stood with my back against it, looking at him in his sleep.

I said "Frank."

He grunted, but didn't wake up.

54

I pulled the spread from him and stood beside the bed. Confused, he pushed himself up on his elbows, hair half covering his eyes, vaguely chewing his dreams.

"What's the matter?" he mumbled. Then he stared. "Andrea?!"

"You'd better wake up now," I said. "You can have me if you wish."

"Please understand. I've fled from my country, I've run away from Brian. All I have left is myself, this body, and this terrible urge to live."

Four years. It's a strange see-saw they're riding on. Whenever she is "available" he is tied up with a woman. When he is free, she has found someone else. Almost comic. Except that gradually, as the violence of their need subsides, it brings in its wake a curious stability. No demands are made, so there can be no threat. Through the comings and goings of other mates, the two remain steadily accessible to each other as friends, confidants, conspirators.

It's in September of that same year, when Paul returns from his summer holiday with the actress (but now abandoned by her since she's found someone else in Saint-Tropez) that they first see each other again. By this time the rage of summer is over, the immediate fear of involvement past.

"Claire's left me," he announces. "Now we can get on with the talk we had that night at Frank's."

"Where were we? Still in the middle of the Plague, or had we got past that?"

"I think we'd finished that bit." He looks at her intently. "We'd just reached the stage where I wanted to ask you to go home with me. Then Claire interrupted us."

"What a pity," said Andrea. "But just as well, too. Because I might have said yes and just think how that would have carved us up."

"Perhaps it isn't too late yet."

"I'm with Frank now."

"You were with Frank in June too."

"No," she corrects him. "I shared his flat, but he had his own girls and I led my own life."

"And that's changed now?"

"It has. Thanks to you." She moves her empty glass aside. "You can order me another *demi*. And there's no reason why we shouldn't carry on our conversation. I was rather fascinated by it."

The late afternoon traffic of the rue Soufflot comes streaming past them; they're sitting on the terrace of the Mahieu.

"Have you been working on your story lately?" she asks.

"No. Claire was too demanding."

"I didn't know you had problems."

"I don't have problems!" he says, annoyed. "I was referring to the fact that she can never relax, she always has to be seen. And she dragged me along with her. Not a spare moment to write a word. But now I'm free again: except I still can't get anything done, for now I have too much time."

"You ever thought of going back to South Africa?" she asks. "Even if it's just for a visit?"

He hesitates; then says: "No. Never."

"You don't sound very convincing."

A brief smile. "You don't allow one to get away with anything, do you?"

"No, why should I?"

"I did try once," he says with some reluctance. "It was all arranged. Just a matter of catching the plane. Then — it fell through." He changes position, crossing his legs. "Just as well. It would have been an awful mistake. Never again."

"Why are you so terribly anti?"

"I'm not really anti. I just don't feel any inclination." He sips his beer. "It's so much more comfortable here. This is my kind of life, my kind of society. Back in South Africa it's, well, difficult." Another sip, then he nods reflectively. "That's it. Everything is difficult. Everything is trouble. Nothing is straightforward. Trouble to find what you're looking for, to do what you want to do, to be where you want to be. There are always obstacles. Everybody expects you to be brave. To do things. To be energetic. Over here I needn't consider anybody else's expectations. I can afford to be lazy if I feel like it."

"You don't think that's why Claire left you?"

"What do you mean?" he asks, suspicion and irritation in his voice.

"I suppose a woman would be too much trouble too."

He grins. "Maybe." Then he pauses to drink in silence. "Years ago, when Annemarie and I got divorced — I really loved her, you know? But I was terribly possessive. I wanted to organize her whole life for her. I just took over. And gradually, in front of my eyes, I saw her losing her high spirits, all her zest for life. She started nagging, developing all sorts of silly complaints. Even then I couldn't let go. I didn't know how to handle it. But one thing had become very clear by the time we finally split up: never again. Not just because of what it does to me, but especially because of what I do to a woman. It's dangerous for people to get too deeply rooted in each other, expecting and demanding too much."

"Then it's a good thing Claire left. Seems to me you first have to learn how to live with yourself."

"You're saying that from your quarter of a century's profound experience?"

"No. I'm saying it because I still haven't learned it either."

"But you're happy with Frank, aren't you?"

"No one said anything about happiness."

"I know so little about you."

"Maybe I'll tell you some day." She feels an urge to unburden herself, but keeps it in check. One cannot give away too much to another. Not so soon; not again.

"The most important thing for you is to get down to writing," she says after a while. "Will it help if I asked you to start telling me about all those fives again?"

He gives her a searching look to find out whether she's mocking him or not, then eases up and begins to talk about the summer he's just had: it turns out that, in spite of all the upheavals he did have a few days to himself to wander through

57

Provence on his own, mainly in the region of Apt, where he found new ideas for his novel. (It was this excursion, in fact, which decided things for Claire.) "They even have a Wall of the Plague in those parts, did you know?" he says, and a hint of the enthusiasm she remembers from their first long conversation returns to his voice.

"What's that?"

"It's high up in the mountains of the Vaucluse," he explains, "if you drive across the plain from the small red village of Roussillon, past Joucas, towards Carpentras. I didn't go there myself, but it seems there's a little village called Murs in the mountains. Probably named after the wall running right past it, for miles and miles, right through that whole wild region. Built in 1721, they told me, to keep the Plague from spreading into the County of Venasque from the Apt side. I was very eager to go and see it for myself, but because of Claire I never made it. One day — "

" — you'll take me there and show me."

He laughs. "I have quite an allergy right now to taking women to Provence. Somehow it doesn't seem to work out for me."

"Did you know," she says with sudden eagerness, "that soon after the Dutch first landed at the Cape they tried something similar to protect themselves against the dangers of the new continent? When the first stone of the Castle was laid, the Commander, his name was Wagenaar or something, recited a poem specially composed for the occasion. It tickled me so much when I first heard it that I learned it by heart." And as they leave the terrace and head for the pedestrian crossing at the corner of the boulevard Saint-Michel, she declaims:

"Mud walls we had against the Hottentots of old,
Now against all others do these stones make us bold:
Thus we scare off not only Europeans,
But Asians, Americans, and wild Africans."

"Where on earth did you hear that?" he asks, surprised.
"From a historian I once knew."

The lights change to green. She hurries on a few yards ahead of him, but he soon catches up and takes her arm.

"You knew him very well, didn't you?"

"Why do you ask?"

"The way you said it."

At first she doesn't answer. Then, with cool reserve: "Yes. Very well indeed."

"What happened?"

"We left South Africa together."

"All right, I won't pry any more," he says. "Perhaps, one day, you'll make up your mind to tell me."

"Perhaps. You start working on your novel first. Then I'll see if you deserve it."

A playful formula for postponement. But she is amazed, in the following weeks, to see how much he seems to have taken it to heart. For the first time in years he starts making notes for his story again, reading and researching, trying out brief passages, even though most of them end up in the cardboard box beside his antique desk.

Only, by this time the restlessness and irritability she has sensed in him since his return from Provence has begun to affect her too. In the course of the summer she has built up an easy, stable relationship with Frank, neither very exciting nor particularly demanding. Through one of his contacts he found her a new job (having moved into Frank's bed, she has begun to feel uncomfortable in the section of the Department of the Interior where she's been working with Henri: even though — or because? — it was he who arranged for her to get a work-permit):a French firm of importers and exporters, where she is employed as an English translator. But seeing Paul again has unsettled her. Not with the same violence of the first night at Frank's party: just a feeling of uneasiness, a twinge of conscience, perhaps, knowing that her heart has never really been in the relationship with Frank, that it cannot work out in the long run. For his sake — there is no urgency after all — she allows it to drag on for a few more months, before she ends it as gently as she can and moves out of his flat to a room of her

59

own in the rue de Vaugirard.

As if preparing for the inevitable she takes her time to repaint the room, buy a few bits of furniture and make it as cosy as she can before telephoning Paul to invite him over.

There is an almost imperceptible hesitation in his voice before he accepts: "Love to. Do you mind if I bring a girlfriend with me?"

"Oh. I was thinking — " Then, trying to conceal her disappointment: "Of course. Who is she?"

"Margith. She's Austrian. Wardrobe mistress for a film group that's just given me a new commission."

"What about the novel?"

"It'll have to wait for a while. For the moment it's just finger exercises." A chuckle. "Apart from push-ups with Margith."

"You sound very smug."

"I've reason to be. She's been living with me for a month. And she's looking after me very well."

"Well, bring her along, I'd like to meet her."

"You know," he suddenly says in a changed voice, "it's really becoming quite farcical, the two of us."

"Perhaps I'm not the only one who's running away."

A year later, just after he's thrown Margith out (having caught her selling one of his antiques), he comes limping back to Andrea to pour his heart out. "This is the last time, I swear to God," he says. "You be my witness. I'm cutting women out of my life altogether. It's too damn humiliating. One's got to be self-sufficient. I've taken a very deep look into my crystal ball, and what did I see — a series of marvellously shallow affairs with girls who tend to get younger every year. Margith was twenty-three. The next one will probably be nineteen. For heaven's sake stop me when I get to fourteen."

"You've got a cock problem, Paul."

"Aren't you going to help me?"

"No. I've just started something new with the boss in my office. Gérard. I'm not madly in love or anything, but it's serious. I can't hurt him now. His wife died some time ago and he's been through a very bad time. He needs comforting."

"So do I."

"You're not looking for a wife, just a prop to your ego."

The next crisis in her personal life is only indirectly brought about by Paul. It is her mother's death. The event as such comes as no shock: ever since she's left home she has never replied to any letters; and from her family's side the occasional correspondence — brief, conscientious, formal letters from her stepbrother Sonny; a note from her mother; a religious tract from Maggie — soon dried up. There might still be the odd Christmas card, or a birthday card in April, with inscriptions in handwritings she no longer recognized. But it's the way in which the news of her mother's death reaches her, much more than the death itself, that unsettles her. A letter from her sister to her London address, Brian's. He forwarded it to Frank. And since he sees her very seldom nowadays he's passed it on to Paul, who finally uses it as an excuse to come and look her up again.

"Bad news?" he asks, when she just sits there, staring at the single light green sheet.

"Not really." She crumples it and throws it in the corner. "My Ma's died."

He stares at her, unable to say anything.

"It's three weeks already. They didn't bother to send a telegram, and why should they?" She goes to the window and keeps her back to him, looking down into the late afternoon traffic in the rue Bonaparte. It's a month ago she moved here from her room in the rue de Vaugirard; Gérard paid the deposit. "Why should they? We've got nothing to say to each other any more. Ever since Dedda died — " She turns round abruptly: "What do you know about them? What do you really know about me?"

"I've been waiting for you to tell me about them, Andrea. And about yourself."

It is a struggle not to succumb, to let it all pour out, for once. But, as so often in the past, she resists. "I'm too confused, Paul. Give me time."

61

"Why don't you go away for a while? You need a break."

"Gérard can't cope on his own. I told you before he's had a rough time. And now he's bought me this flat and everything."

Taking her by the shoulders, he gently shakes her. "For heaven's sake, Andrea, can't you think of yourself for once? You can't go on bottling it up. Why don't you go away for a while?" A moment of precarious hesitation; then he risks it: "Would you like me to go with you?"

With a wan smile she shakes her head. "No, if I go it must be alone."

Which is how she lands in Chartres. And for the first time, in that darkness under the stained glass, she manages to cry about her people. Not the hopeless rage of loneliness she felt in London, with Brian: but weeping like her Grandma used to cry over the dead, as if she really understands the old woman for the first time. Grandma, the unofficial mourner of District Six. She developed it into a fine art, if not an exact science: so many tears for a child, so many for a man, so many for a woman. (Women were always highest in her reckoning.) So many for a relative, so many for a stranger. Everyone had his place on her scale. If there was a report in the papers about a train crash or an accident in the mines, Grandma would withdraw to weep for the victims. Once she was told about an earthquake in Peru in which ten thousand or more people had been killed, and for a whole fortnight she remained in the bedroom to weep for them. (Afterwards she learned that the figure had been exaggerated; only a thousand or so had died. She just shrugged, and sighed: "It's too late now, my child. I've done my bit. We can all do with a bit of crying.")

Weep for the two old people in the room next door. Weep for Brother Sonny, and Brother Arie, for Maggie, for Boetie. Weep for Ma, for that day in the back room at the hairdresser's, for all the conversations they never had. Weep, above all, for her father, whom she has never been able to mourn because it's been too big for her. Now, at last, it is possible. Her mother's death has swept the block away. Weep, weep. Salt water spilling into your sea, Dedda. Now, for the first time, you're really dead. Now I know it. Now I've finally lost you.

In the sombre, dusty light of anonymous hotel rooms I spent the nights propped up against the large square pillows, making my daily random notes, or reading. Spread across the wide empty double bed of which I filled only a narrow segment, lay the books and papers I'd brought with me. Coulton. Tuchman. Ziegler. Charrière. Bruni. Deaux. Dr Manger. A translation of Nohl. Photocopies of older works, Jusserand, Cardinal Gasquet, even Guy de Chauliac who'd been the private physician of the poor Pope immured in Avignon. On my knees, pulled up under the threadbare brown blanket I take with me wherever I go, lay the opened dark red file with Paul's script, dog-eared and dilapidated by now, the margins filled with lines and comments and exclamation marks or crosses, many passages in the text scored out and rewritten. The constant five-fold patterns which so fascinated him. ("Look, if Mozart could work with threes you have no right to deny me my fives.")

But I was not really reading the script: I was looking right through it, into what I imagined written, in burning letters, in the dark patterns of the wallpaper. (Paul would never have allowed me to stay in such little rooms; he was much too attached to his creature comforts. In July we went to all the best hotels in Provence.)

The seedy little hotel in Chartres where I'd stayed those three days after I'd received the news of Ma's death. When at last I'd shed every tear I had in me, I telephoned Paul from the post office. That was my instinctive reaction: not Gérard, but Paul. For Gérard, I blindly knew without having to reason about it, was past. I wanted Paul to know that I was whole again, that he needn't worry about me. That same afternoon, ignoring all my protests, he came to fetch me in his car. On the way back to Paris neither of us spoke much. But in the evening, after he'd made us something to eat, he put me to

63

bed and sat down at the foot-end, and said: "Right, now you can tell me everything, if you feel like it."

I didn't want to hold back any more. Now I wanted to tell it all: because now that world no longer existed for me, and need no longer be protected. I'd paid my debt to Ma. Whenever I stopped, he would ask something else, he never gave up prodding and urging: "Tell me more. Tell me everything. I want to know. It's no good keeping it all to yourself."

I knew that what he really wanted, what I wanted, was to find an answer, answers, to the question he'd asked me the first night: *Andrea, what are you running away from?* Did my long confession satisfy either of us? In the end one can only invent oneself, as I'm inventing myself here, now; as I'm being invented.

There was no order in what I told him; I simply allowed everything to spill out at random. Gran and Grampa behind the wooden partition in the small dark room they shared with Ma. Dull, indefinite sounds marking the lives of two old people, so close to us, yet so secret, audible but invisible. Bare feet shuffling on the floor. Grampa's cautious measured movements as if he knew he had only so many steps left before death, so they had to be rationed very carefully. Their voices and coughing at night, Gran's robust snoring. In the room on the front porch, Gran's two sisters, the two ancient vultures waiting for her to die so that they could take over the house. When she collapsed one sweltering summer's day, both immediately descended on her, cackling with their toothless mouths, shaking their balding little bird skulls (hardly any hair to speak of, "bum fluff" Ma called it), feeling her all over with their crooked talons. One started praying aloud, as the other tried to pull Gran's rings from her fingers. No use, the joints were too big. In terrible frustration Aunt Joey called out: "Hey, bring me some soap, demmit!" But at that moment Gran came to her senses again and said: "I'm not dirty, Myriam, I just fainted." I swear they're still alive today. Gran too, in spite of her fervent lifelong desire to meet her Saviour. I used to think God deliberately kept them alive for so long, scared of the way in which they'd take over His household if they were given half a chance.

"*They*'re still going strong," I said to Paul, "but Ma died. She never had anything to lose. Except for Dedda, but she never understood him at all. I was the only one who really knew him. And if he hadn't died — Anyway, he won't be in heaven, that's for sure. Straight down to hell, where I'll find him one day, he'll be waiting for me."

"What did you have against your mother?"

"Nothing. Except that she never understood anything — apart from washing and shampooing and doing people's hair, perming and setting and dyeing, and listening to the women talking under the driers: varicose veins and cancer and miscarriages and the church." Even as I was raging against her I couldn't help thinking: Jesus, poor Ma. From the very beginning she'd never stood a chance, for Grandma had annexed us as "her" family, forcing Ma to remain an intruder in her own house. Just because Dedda, her David, had been her favourite child, whom she wouldn't share with any other woman. But also, of course, because Ma had had Sonny, years before she'd ever met Dedda. Ma had come from a good Cape family and she'd been in matric when it happened, so she had to give up all ideas of going on with her studies; and her people had thrown her out. Which was why she didn't mind marrying below herself eventually, with Dedda. And Sonny must have inherited her guilt feelings, for after finishing at Hewatt College he'd gone away from the Cape to teach at Oudtshoorn. I was the only one he cared for, I don't know why, and he was always going on about the need to go to university, never mind the cost, he would pay.

Paul went on asking and asking. I told him about Ma, and how she'd grown more and more withdrawn with time; how, after the day I'd cut my hair, she'd hardly ever spoken to me again. I told him about the others too. Maggie, holier-than-thou but stingy as hell, spending all her money on clothes for herself. Brother Arie, playing the witty coon to the holiday crowd in "his" hotel. Boetie, snarling at everybody ("born

65

political", Ma always said), brooding and vicious ever since the day they'd thrown him from the swings at Sea Point, saying it was for white kids only. The rest of us had shrugged it off, but not Boetie. It kept on burning inside him like a live coal. And once he'd gone to university, it became worse. "Look here, in this country you got Black and you got White. But what about us? What's 'Coloured'? It's nothing, it's neither Black nor White, just in-between sort of, and they're squeezing us from both sides. No use trying to stay out of it. We got to choose, it's either Black or White. And let me tell you one thing, man, you won't see me choosing White."

Ma: "Boetie, you're talking just like those pals of yours again. They're no good, I tell you. Why don't you let them be?"

"It's you who got to let me be. You keep on nagging me all the time and I'm getting blarry sick of it. Andrea's the only one who understands me."

And then my father. I tried to put off talking about him, that night Paul sat with me, because I knew that once I got started I wouldn't be able to stop. The times when Dedda came home, day or night, blown from the sea. One never knew when he would turn up. Sometimes it was after a few months, more often than not a year or longer. But one thing was for sure, one always knew when he was home! Dedda was one of those, when he came in by the door, the whole house would suddenly be full. Usually it was night when he turned up, for he would work his way back from the harbour very slowly and thoroughly, from one bar to the next, disappearing into God knows what sinister joints (the last two on his journey would invariably be the Perseverance Bar in Buitenkant Street, and the Cottage of Content Bar), before he would come bursting through the front door, singing and cursing and laughing. Then Gran and Grampa had to be turned out of their room to move in with us, no matter what time it was, for Dedda wanted the bed, with Ma in it. And some time in the course of the night he would erupt into our room and haul me from my bed in my nightie and carry me on his shoulders through the house to parade me before whoever had accompanied him, including total strangers he'd picked up along the way. Never Maggie, always I. "You stand aside, Maggie, you're a useless *jentoe*. Here's Dedda's child. Come on, Nanna, I want to show you to the people. O sweet Jesus, isn't she beautiful?" His thin, sinewy arms around me. His smell of sweat and drink and male animal, taking my very breath away, until I'd get used to it again and snuggle up against him the better to inhale him. I've never known another person with such a human smell. As if he carried all the odours of his whole life with him. Fish and salt and sea, the sweat of men, cheap women picked up in distant harbours, foreign cities, markets, shops and bazaars, rum and Cape sweet-wine, leather and steel, blood, weariness and joy, exuberant nights and fuck-up days, oh God, my Dedda.

Nanna. The name I'd given myself when I'd been too small to pronounce *Andrea* properly. And, by extension, I gave the name to everything that ever was most my own. My rag doll, eventually loved to tatters. A stray kitten I'd found and pro-tected against the rest of the family. My blanket, the one Dedda had brought from way across the seas and which still goes with me wherever I travel in the wild world, threadbare and stained and worn, but mine. My most beloved pair of shoes, delicate little dancing slippers which Dedda had once brought, much too small for me, but more beautiful than Cinderella's at the ball. My innermost world, my very minest world, has always been a Nanna world. And nobody but Dedda has ever been allowed to call me that.

"Nanna, God is my witness: if I done one good thing in my life it was making you." The day I found him standing at the broken front gate, from where he'd been watching me all the way. "Jesus, Nanna, I never seen anybody walk like you."

"What do you mean, Dedda?"

"Just like I say. The way you walk. A real little *duiker*. A pureblood filly. As if, every time you put your foot down, you decide to step a bit further. Right from the hips. I love that walk of yours, Nanna-girl. But I warn you, if I ever catch a man touching you, I'll throttle him with my bare hands. You'll tell your Dedda, won't you?" A brief, contented chuckle. "But even if you don't, I'll see it with my own eyes. You know, a man can tell from a girl's walk if she's a virgin or not."

A bit uneasily I asked: "How can you tell?"

"A virgin got a special way of walking, that's all. Soon's she's had her first ride, it changes. I can tell from just one look."

Afternoons when Maggie wasn't there I used to walk to and fro in front of the mirror in our room, watching my step. Eagerly. But scared as hell at the same time. Suppose it happened one day and Dedda noticed? What difference would it make to his Nanna's walk?

Only, by the time it happened he didn't care much about talking to me any more. I remember, right at the end, there was the night I also told Paul about: Dedda had come home in the small hours from his drinking; he hadn't been to sea for months. I knew Ma was lying on the big bed next door, waiting; I was sitting at the front window, wanting to see him come home safely before I went to sleep. It must have been a wild night, and Dedda's bladder wasn't quite up to it. He'd barely staggered in through the front gate when he opened his flies. To support his unsteady legs, he groped about him in the dark and got hold of the tap. But I don't think he even realized it was a tap, he clearly didn't notice that in grabbing it he'd opened it so that the water came gushing out. He was just standing there, urgently relieving himself, hand on the tap; and only after several minutes I realized that there was something wrong. Dedda held his stance, and the water went on streaming down. But he was too far gone to notice that it wasn't his. And so he went on standing, very patiently, while the water kept on running as if Moses had been striking rocks again. At long last I heard him heave a terrible sigh. And then he said out loud in the dark: "Oh dear God, if you really want me to piss myself to death tonight, let Thy will be done." It was the kind of night one never forgets: because it was the last.

That's the way he was. Shame upon shame to the family. But to me he was my Dedda. The choicest gifts, when he came home from the sea, were for me: the most extraordinary, outlandish, useless things, porcelain gulls, saris, pictures, drapes, perfumes, anything that looked bright or smelled good. All the others got presents too, of course; he never forgot anyone. When he came home stuffed with money, there would be one endless celebration until the money ran out, and then he would go off again. Ma soon learned to hide some of it to see us through the lean months. He couldn't care less. He was happy when the sun shone, and miserable when it rained. I've never known anyone who was so tuned in to the seasons, to day and night, to rain and shine.

Paul urged me to go on talking, comforting me, steadying me, until in the early hours I was simply too exhausted to go on. Then he made me lie back, and covered me with the old brown blanket. That was another night when something might have "happened" between us. I would have been too tired to resist, had he tried his luck. But he didn't.

Only when he leaned over to kiss me lightly on the forehead, more like a father putting his daughter to bed, I resisted with an urgency I couldn't explain myself. "Please go away now and leave me alone," I pleaded. "I'm not good for people. I'm a witch. Wherever I go I bring bad luck."

But he didn't go. He sat in a low chair near the window to watch over me, because he was concerned about me. When I woke up it was nearly noon, and he was still sitting in his chair, now fast asleep, his chin on his chest.

I got up very quietly and went to make us some coffee. He started up, looking terribly guilty, as I came back with the tray, poured milk for him, adding the two lumps of sugar I knew he took; and we sat drinking without saying anything. The night was still too close, too exposed to be touched by words. I thought: If you choose to talk about it now, I'll understand, of course, for how are you to know, you're a man. But he remained silent, and left soon afterwards with another brief kiss on my forehead. And then I thought: Perhaps it would have been better if he *had* said something to round it off, to finish it all. For now he'd just strengthened his hold on me.

No one after Brian had been allowed to get such a grip on my life.

Within the following week I broke with Gérard, not without several very violent scenes: but I simply couldn't bear his frantic dependence on me any longer, not after the way in which Paul had comforted me that night.

Even so, it still didn't bring the two of us together. He had someone living with him again. And for nearly two more years we went on playing our peculiar brand of hide-and-seek. As if something was deliberately encouraging us to postpone the inevitable.

He took up the research and note-making for his novel again, but it remained in the background, always over-shadowed by film work, and he never actually got round to *writing*. I knew he was scared; through all the years of postponement and dreaming, too much had got involved in it, too much was at stake to risk failure. But I went on nagging him, prodding him; I wanted him to know that I believed in his book, in him. We continued to see each other regularly, but without expecting anything. Each had come to accept that the other was elsewhere involved; in a way it allowed us to be even more open and intimate in sharing our thoughts than we allowed ourselves to offer our partners of the moment. A serene and profound friendship running like a river through both our lives, slowly wearing down obstacles, smoothing the edges of all the headstrong little pebbles in its bed until each found its proper place among the others. It was Paul who introduced me to the photographer Jean-Louis who soon hired me as his assistant; and through him, while Paul was away on a journey, I eventually met the film maker Serge Leloup. (When Paul returned, with yet another shipwreck behind him, Serge and I had just clinched.) And as soon as I felt sure I could trust him with it, I told Serge about Paul's story and introduced them to each other. There was an immediate spark of recognition between them. Paul still felt reluctant about my suggestion that he and Serge turn his story into a film: he'd set his mind on the novel. But I knew very well that, left to his own devices, he would never get anything down on paper and I thought that having broken the ice with a film he might find the confidence he needed so desperately. Serge, I was convinced, was exactly the right person to inspire him. And so, after all those years, it seemed that Paul had finally found someone to liberate his novel for him. For the moment, both of them were still tied down by other projects, but it was clear that neither would rest before the film materialized. And so it began to take shape, until we'd now reached the stage where the script was in its penultimate draft, and I was on my way to Provence to prepare the way for the shooting which was scheduled to begin next spring.

In the meantime relations between the three of us had also changed. Late in April last year, just after my birthday, Serge sent Paul and me to the Loire valley to scout around for a documentary film on the last days of Leonardo which they'd planned to do together. It came just a few weeks after Serge and I had broken up in what could have been a terribly melodramatic scene (I'd caught him in bed with a young cameraman one afternoon when they'd been supposed to be filming a hundred kilometres away); but because both of us had begun to show signs of constraint and irritation recently, it was all settled without too much fuss. The cameraman even came round with an enormous bouquet of long-stemmed roses to thank me for my "understanding"; and I believe if I'd shown interest he would have promptly taken me to bed as well as a further token of his gratitude. So we all remained good friends. Serge's faun moved in with him; and almost relieved I prepared for a new spell of celibacy in my cramped but cosy little flat in the rue Bonaparte. Paul, who'd begun to reconcile himself to loneliness, was working hard, and, for the first time in years, seemed happy and relaxed.

There's something very relaxed in their excursion to the Loire, to the Château de Cloux, near Amboise, where Leonardo spent his last days: as if they're going on holiday, not on a working weekend. Waving at passing cars. Laughing at the

71

silliest pun. They book into the best hotel — separate rooms, as on previous business trips — and spend the whole day working their way through the castle and the village streets. He takes innumerable photographs with his Polaroid; she follows with pen and notebook to jot down particulars. There's barely time to spend over lunch. Avid exploration. Flagstones and early Renaissance walls. Unabashed red geraniums against weathered stone. Sudden views of the Loire. Then the night falls. They change for dinner, drive the twenty-odd kilometres to Onzain and spend three hours over the food in the Domaine des Hauts de Loire. He insists on ordering for both, knowing from past experience the dishes which have earned the establishment a star in the Michelin. After the Pouilly fumé which accompanies the mousse de persil, he impresses her with a Mouton Rothschild to do justice to the main dish. Back at their hotel, when she takes out her key to unlock her door, both suddenly fall silent, as if only struck by it now. "Do you realize," he says, in genuine surprise, "that this is the first occasion in all these years we're both available at the same time?"

"It wasn't other people who've been keeping us apart," she says, not looking at him. "One always has a choice."

"Perhaps it suited both of us. The question is: does it still suit us tonight?"

He pushes open the door. She goes into the room. "You may come in," she says, not daring to look back.

The shock, also the miracle, of a new love. To receive a man, to allow him entry: not submitting to him. Especially if one has contented oneself for so long with substitutes, surrogates, even if the counterfeits were excellent. (Because love itself would have been too dangerous: whatever else happened, one never dared permit oneself to get involved. All that mattered was survival, and this left little scope for the freedom of love.) Now, at last, one doesn't *want* to protect oneself any more. Suddenly there's something, someone, to care for profoundly. Someone for whom one is prepared to put oneself at stake.

72

The completion of circles: everything left open, held in underwater abeyance, patiently preparing itself for this readiness, this availability. At the same time — it cannot be denied — the fear of "history", of the "facts" of love, the inevitable confirmation of the body. Panic (no, that is too extreme: perturbedness, vulnerability) about finality. Each possibility realized excludes others.

Maleness: the fierce, exclusive belief in islands. Shutting out everything for the sake of this instant. Femaleness: the merging of the instant with duration: living with open eyes in the simultaneity of yesterday and tomorrow within today.

"In every moment one lives one's whole life."

"Think of the waste!" Paul exclaims in comic and sincere dismay. "Why on earth have we waited four years? That very first night we should have — "

She puts a finger to his lips. "Don't be such a pig. That's just pure greediness. How I love this furious body of yours. If we'd started four years ago it might have been burned out by now."

"Do you think we can ever get burned out?" he asks indignantly.

"We have a better chance to last now."

"Four years ago I wasn't fifty yet. Now I'm past it."

"Why is it such an obsession with you?"

"It leaves us four years less."

"We've got *now*. I'm happy with that. The rest isn't all that important."

She firmly believes it: the refinement of waiting, beyond all temporary impatience or desire, to allow that first recklessness to deepen into concern, to mature. Nothing is lost, except irrelevance, superfluity. There is no diminution of desire; only added serenity. Nothing needs to spend itself in a day. It may last.

The night is warm and calm. The windows are wide open. The spring air keeps them aware of a larger world outside, even when, after the first celebration, their bodies remain tangled as they go on talking.

"It's the first time in years this has happened to me," she admits, almost shyly. "One gets used to ordinariness. One forgets it can be different."

"The others — ?" he asks.

"They weren't important."

"Tell me about yourself again," he says.

"Haven't I told you enough already?"

"I won't ever have enough of you."

"It's terrible, the way you can go on." She smiles. "But for the moment it makes me feel very safe and protected."

She pulls up the blanket which she has brought with her.

"Why are you so fond of this old rag?" he asks.

"Dedda brought it home once, when it was already second-hand. He used it as a bag to carry our presents in. I claimed it, and it soon became my dearest possession. After Dedda left again, I used to put myself to sleep with it at night, playing with the fringe. I imagined I could smell him in it. Later, when Brian and I left the country, this blanket was the one thing I had to take with me. Nothing else matters quite so much. It's my dearest Nanna."

"You've come a hell of a long way."

Her serious eyes look at him very calmly. "From the moment I set foot in London, after that first trip through Provence with Brian, I knew, even while he was still with me, that I was on my own now. There was no one else. Only me. It was *my* battle. I couldn't turn back." Her jaws tauten. "Not to that place. And yet, to make it over here — I don't know whether you'll ever really understand what it means. I'm a woman. I'm coloured. I'm everything that can be exploited."

"It didn't get you down." There is something almost like awe in his voice, in the way his hand moves across her.

"For one reason only," she insists. "I made the most amazing discovery: I found out that what was most vulnerable in me also gave me a hold on others. I mean men. I could manipulate them. To get jobs. To get a *permis de séjour*. To find a place to stay. To survive." Is she deliberately trying to put it as

74

brutally as she can? — to shock or to test him, to wound herself? With unsubdued rage she goes on: "It was the only way in which I was allowed to fight myself free."

"Surely it wasn't really necessary to fight? Frank cared about you. So did Serge. Even Gérard. And you cared about them too."

"What does it mean, to 'care' about somebody? I needed them, dammit. I was impatient to live. And I didn't have all that many weapons to fight with. I had to use what I had, and it was they who helped me make that discovery. Through them I could find a place to stand on my feet. It was either that, or go under." She looks straight into his eyes. "I'm a cat person, you see? I'll do anything to land on my feet. Does that make me a whore?"

"For God's sake!" he flares up. "You have no right to be so cruel to yourself. I don't ever want to hear you say a thing like that again. Do you think I don't know how much courage it took? And what price you paid?"

"A cat has many lives to spend."

"But not an infinite number. Every time there's one less." His angry, searching eyes cause her to shudder briefly, as if she's cold.

She presses her head against his shoulder.

"I asked you the first time we met, remember?" he says gently. "What are you running away from?"

"I think I can come to rest with you."

For a while he dozes off. Propped up on one elbow she studies his face in sleep. In the dull light of the bedside lamp his features and contours are shadowy, as if she's looking at him through water, in which one face merges with another. Almost resigned, she wonders: Is it really the same thing that happens over and over? The same place one reaches every time, the same face you stare at, sealed in sleep, painfully separate? Over and over. And yet, so different. One changes all the time. Oh sure, one changes.

In the beginning, with Brian: all the passionate absolutism of a first time. (*I can't make love if I'm feeling upset. It's all or*

75

nothing.) One clings to it for as long as possible. Then, slowly, something lets go inside, one's hold isn't quite so determined as before. Compromises? So be it. In order to survive, to avoid unnecessary upheavals. That happy — or terrible? — illusion of youth that the whole truth can be contained in the body of the beloved. Gradually it dulls. One learns to live more easily in one's body, the new shoes do not pinch quite so much as before. It's more comfortable, more comforting too, so much less demanding to share without constantly placing everything at risk. Compassion. Years ago in London, the first months in Paris: the explosive anger if a man refused to take no for an answer. As if one's whole self, one's honour and dignity, were at stake. But gradually it eases up. There's still no need, of course, to surrender simply because a man insists. But it becomes easier both to give and take. (Does one, also, discover in the process that the more readily one makes one's body available, the easier it becomes to withhold oneself? Even from those one loves?) If a man really wants it very badly, and provided one cares enough, why not let him have his way and rid both oneself and him from the urgency of his need? — it even becomes amusing that such a thing can be regarded as so important. It makes so little difference; and it's so much less tiring than a virginal struggle to fight for an elusive honour.

And yet — ! There have been other nights in which she lay looking down at a variation of this sleeping face, thinking with a sense of detached amazement: *How easy for a man to be deluded, to delude himself. Beating about the bush. (Such an insignificant little bush.) No, I don't despise you for it. I don't resent it. It just makes me feel curious — about how it is possible for you to be so easily fooled; how you dare be so content with it.*

So something has changed after all, looking back at it tonight?

Of course. That is why she's been postponing it for four years. To come to know unequivocally the conditions imposed on one, to learn to accept what can be given, and taken in return. With him there is security and a possibility of dur-

76

ation. It's different from her time with Brian. She's grown older. Perhaps the change has involved its share of loss. It's certainly different now; indeed, it's different. Thank God.

In the early hours I also fell asleep; when I woke up, I saw him gazing at me. (My turn; yours.) With an inexplicable sadness in me I half laughed, and said: "Paul, do you realize I've been unfaithful to you already?"

His hand was caressing my breasts, very gently. His breath against my shoulder. "Impossible. Tonight has been the first time — "

"I'm talking of the very beginning, the night in Frank's flat."

"What about it? You know," he said impetuously, "if only I'd known that night that there was nothing between you and Frank — " His hands moved down across my belly.

"After you left, it was already light outside, I went to his room and slept with him."

"I don't understand. How could you? Why?"

"He'd often wanted to, but he was always very considerate. I'd told him the first day I moved in that I would leave if he ever tried to take advantage of me."

"Then why did you go to him that night?" He was caressing my love-hair now. A feeling of warmth in my guts.

"Because for the first time I felt immune. And also because I needed him to protect me against you."

"I wasn't threatening you."

I was wet and open to his hand.

"Oh yes, you were. More than you can ever imagine."

"And I desired you more than I'd ever desired a woman."

"I wanted you. But I was scared. I didn't think I could handle it. I didn't want to go to you just because I was afraid of being alone."

"And now?"

"Now I want you. Come back into me."

"Will you ever be unfaithful to me again?"

"Oh yes, often. But I'll always come back to you."

"How long is 'always'?" A light throb of laughter in his throat against my mouth.

"As long as I love you."

"And if I leave you?"

"I don't think you will. I don't think either of us can do without the other now."

The shock of my breath between my teeth as he entered me. The brief slaking of the interminable thirst. In my mouth the taste of the absolute, as real and warm as the saltiness of his seed.

Hours of talking, all through the following day. His novel, once again; the urge to get those distant months in the Schloss Judenau out of his system.

"You've never told me the full story of that time," she reminds him.

"Yes, I have. Many times."

"Why do you always keep something back? Don't you trust me with it?"

Her grave and sensuous eyes.

"*Must* you know everything?" He smiles, as if he's forced to surrender something of himself; once again.

"There was more to it than you told me, wasn't there?"

"Yes." He leans back against the pillows. She is sitting crosslegged beside him.

"A woman?" she says.

"A girl. One of the refugees. Eva Jelačić."

He shuts his eyes over the memory.

"You still find it difficult to talk about it?"

"I want to, Andrea. I really want to. It's just: there is so very little to tell. It's not a story. Nothing 'happened'."

"But you loved her." (The sudden, unreasonable surge of jealousy!)

"I did." He turns his head to look at her, puts out a hand to touch her knee; watches the sober light from outside brushing her shoulders, her breasts. "Must have been the tremendous pressure we all lived under: the never-ending work, all those different personalities interacting, the strange languages in which one had to try to make oneself understood. So one reacted quite excessively to anything which, under normal circumstances, would be very ordinary. You see, right at the outset I'd had a quarrel with one of the Germans, Brückner, a real thick-skulled idiot who'd gone there with the sole aim of bedding as many women as possible. He always went about boasting of his conquests. At home it had been prostitutes, here it was for free. A bit of blackmail, bribery, empty promises. Even violence, if it couldn't be avoided. The group leader had threatened to send him away. But it was a particularly busy period and we needed every available pair of hands. Then, one day, I caught Brückner — but why go into it now?"

"I want to know."

"Well, he interfered with Eva too. Threatened to confiscate her food rations if she didn't lie down for him. So I thrashed him. From that day, I realized something was developing between her and me. It would be presumptuous to try and define it. We couldn't even carry on an ordinary conversation: I had to make do with the bit of pidgin German I'd picked up in the camp, and she only spoke a few words."

"Did you ever — ?" She hasn't really meant to press him, not quite so crudely; yet she must find out.

"There was only one afternoon, in the clothes-room up in the attic of the round tower, when we were alone for a few minutes. She pressed her head against me. I held her and kissed her. And that was all."

"If you really wanted to be with her, you would have found a way."

"I was very young, remember. I didn't want to take advantage of her in those circumstances. It could wait. One day, when it was all over, we could start a normal life, do the normal things, learn a new language. But right then — "

"So you lost her?"

"Yes. She left."

"Where did she go to?"

He closes up. "All the refugees left in due course. And I

suppose it was better for us that way. It left the dream intact. Who knows, if we'd stayed together, we might have grown tired of each other."

"Cynicism doesn't suit you."

"One tries to convince oneself." A sad little smile. "But because of the whole nature of our love I supposed it spoilt me forever. For years and years after that I tried to judge every new woman in terms of Eva. And of course it didn't work."

She knows she shouldn't ask this; she doesn't want an answer, whether yes or no; but in spite of herself she says: "Does that go for me too?"

"Eva was small and blonde."

"That's not what I meant at all." (So why doesn't she stop asking?)

"Perhaps I tried with you too, but only in the very beginning. Since then — "

"Well?"

"Now you are Andrea. No one else."

"You sure that's enough for you?"

"Do you still have to ask, after four years?"

The days of my journey grew steadily more dank and misty; a musty smell at night when at last I switched off the light, hugging my drawn-up knees in my arms under the old brown love-blanket to wait for sleep to descend, abandoning myself to confused images in which memories of the past merged with moments and incidents from Paul's film script which had become the sign of our relationship. Cracks in the walls of my room; patches of damp or mould. By day, the blurred outlines of crumbling castles and grey villages; deep colours in the forests where autumn was bleeding itself to death; admonitions of approaching winter in the chill of early mornings. I never bothered to buy or read newspapers. Through a Europe old and weary I continued on my aimless way, aware of obsolete possibilities, a past prolonging itself into the present, an absence of urgencies: I was feeling absent myself. I was getting fed-up with myself. At night I missed Paul more and more

80

achingly. Often I would stop in a town on my way, my mind made up to telephone or send a telegram. It would be so easy. But I restrained myself. It was *too* easy. I knew I needed that isolation. When eventually I returned to Paul it had to be openly, unreserved, to give him an unequivocal yes or no. Trying to force the issue would soon unsettle everything. Too much was at stake for me to act impulsively. We'd been happy to wait for four years before. Now, another eighteen months later, surely there couldn't be any need to rush. I needed time for a decision to ripen naturally inside me. In the meantime I could afford to go on wandering for a while. But in the long run I couldn't avoid irritation building up. And one after-noon — the fifth? sixth? — when I suddenly saw a familiar name on a road sign in the mist and rain, like a clear sentence taking shape from a welter of words in one's mind, I simply knew that I'd had enough of aimlessness. It was no longer a diving into myself, but postponement, evasion. It was time I turned back towards more recognizable and basic facts.

Carcassonne, the signpost said. And all of a sudden I was no longer vaguely "on the road": at last I was somewhere again, or at least on my way somewhere. Carcassonne, the warm, walled town where my journey with Brian had ended years ago.

Carcassonne: a word defining the familiar. Or rather, that was what I thought when I arrived there, for I was disillusioned pretty soon. Eight years separated me from my previous visit, and I got hopelessly lost the moment I entered into the maze of narrow streets in search of the little hotel in which Brian and I had stayed. I couldn't even recall the name. Hôtel de la Gare? De la Poste? De Paris? We'd stayed in so many anony-mous and seedy little rooms that distant early summer.

At my wits' end, I finally stopped on a square surrounded by plane-trees. It seemed vaguely familiar; at least not entirely strange. From a couple of old men with blue caps under the canvas terrace of a smoky little café I asked the way to the Syndicat d'Initiative, and went there on foot.

But the morose old man of the Syndicat, clearly annoyed

because I'd disturbed his reading of the newspaper, wasn't very helpful at all. He handed me a brochure with a list of local hotels and their gradings, and paid no further attention to me. Well, I suppose I couldn't expect him to identify the place I was looking for from the few odd particulars I happened to remember — a worn doorknob in the shape of a lion's head with a ring through the nose; a yellow varnished door with a checkered curtain behind the pane; and, yes, geraniums on the window-sills. A blood-red stone staircase leading up to the bedrooms. Ours had looked out on a paved courtyard swarming with cats. A stunted mulberry-tree in the centre. The cupboard door wouldn't stay shut. There had been only cold water in the tap above the chipped washbasin. A faded green bedspread. Brian had wanted to make love, but I'd insisted on first exploring the old medieval city on the hill; and so he was frustrated, and that evening we had another row. Early the next morning we took the train to Toulouse, and from there to Paris; then back to his London. Our interlude was over, our no man's land between Africa and Europe. In London everything would start anew, the two of us openly against the world, scared of no one, ashamed of nothing; we would no longer have to fear a knock at three or four in the morning. And yet I *was* afraid. Not of anything outside, but a terror pointing inwards, right into myself.

Now, back in Carcassonne, I urgently needed to grasp something of that memory again, to reach out towards a long-lost Brian. That afternoon when he'd wanted to make love and I'd refused. As if that trivial moment contained something inestimably important to myself. But now I couldn't even find the hotel with its red staircase and dull green bedspread and mulberry-tree in the courtyard again. No name on the list of the Syndicat rang a bell. I underlined two or three possibilities and went in search of them, but not one of them was the hotel I was looking for. Nowhere a sign to proclaim: *I was here.* (Those words, so long ago, scratched into the plaster of a wall —)

The weather was clearing up. It was still too cool to order

82

something on a café terrace, but in a crammed, smoky little place near the square with the plane-trees I ordered coffee at a small table pushed right against the foggy window; very black, very strong, very sweet.

Perhaps, I thought, the hotel had been closed up, or sold, or demolished. If so, would that have destroyed something vital about Brian and me? Would it deny an ingredient or aspect of our love?

All the places we'd been to, that May and early June. All the way from Nice where we'd dragged ourselves, exhausted, from the plane, directly to the station to catch the train to Avignon, as if something was driving us, hunting us down; as if we were scared to come to a standstill. On the move, all the time, by train or by bus, or hitchhiking, throughout the southern interior. Avignon, Bonnieux, Roussillon, the high regions beyond the Mont Ventoux, then down again to Saint-Rémy and Aix, and all the way to the Camargue and the sea, at les Saintes-Maries-de-la-Mer and Aigues-Mortes. Back to Avignon. From there to Nîmes and Narbonne; then Carcassonne. Five weeks, six weeks, an eternity. An island between two existences: one from which I'd cut myself for ever (that last long journey from Cape Town to Johannesburg, to take my leave of the country, a death watch without end), and a new one which I was as yet too reluctant to imagine or invent.

And now I was back.

Restlessness drove me on. I paid for the coffee and once again went out into the streets in search of the unfindable, concentrating so fiercely on my efforts to retrieve the traces of memory in the world surrounding me that I soon became conscious of a bad headache.

At last, reluctantly abandoning one memory in favour of another, I set out for the medieval city on the hill, crossing the leaden stream with a small stone bridge. At least the walls and fortifications were still up there. Brian and I had meticulously "done" it all, exploring walls and castle on the heels of a guide. Perhaps I would recover something of him back up there.

83

The patchy clouds were dispersing quite rapidly now, unkempt and bedraggled like wool. High up on the hill the late afternoon sun caught the walls of the amber city, designing and revealing the contours of each separate stone. I tried to grope for jumbled memories from the past: Romans — Visigoths — Saracens and Charlemagne, Simon de Montfort and the wars of religion. A never-ending history of blood. And there was something from Paul's papers too: indeed, yes, Carcassonne was where the persecution of the Jews had begun in the time of the Plague. Hurled down from the top of the city walls. Burned at the stake.

There was no one except me at the castle gate and the grumbling guide refused to do the rounds for the sake of a single visitor.

"But don't you understand?" I insisted. "I came here years ago. I just *have* to go in. I'm not asking any favour, I'll pay you well enough."

He merely shrugged, breathing garlic into my face.

"I'll bloody well go and report you!"

"If you wish."

"Monsieur — !" I was ready to do anything reckless. But in spite of my anger I couldn't help being amused by my own urgency. Was it really all that important? What in God's name did I expect to find of Brian and myself inside these massive walls? What did it have to do with the real reasons for my trip to the South?

At the last moment a bus-load of German tourists arrived at the gates and suddenly the guide was all smiles and subservience. The horde paid no attention to me as they swept past me in their Aryan insistence to get there first. And we'd hardly reached the second hall before I began to feel claustrophobic, trapped among those noisy people with their aggressive sibilants. Without asking anybody's leave I turned round and fought my way through them, back to the open space outside, ignoring the angry shouts of the guide concerned about his tip. I ran out of the castle, and through the city gates, and down the hill, across the brown water of the Aude. (The sudden

84

pang of remembering the coke-brown water of the Cape, of Steenbras and Rooi Els!)

Back in the car I consulted the Syndicat's list again, grimly chose the most expensive hotel (at least that would have met with Paul's approval, after I'd let him down so badly the past few days), and drove up to the old city, back to the high walls behind which sat the hotel where I could abandon myself to the attentions of doormen, porters, receptionists and waiters.

I had too much to eat and too much to drink; then sauntered out rather half-heartedly — the walls floodlit, unworldly, like the décor of a film — and soon returned to my room. Arranging the pillows against the head-rest I started paging through Paul's books again. Not very edifying. Johannes Nohl:

It is only the systematic extermination of the Jews which reveals the whole confusion and irresponsibility of those dark ages . . . . The massacres of the Jews in the fourteenth century are so deeply revolting, because the ruling classes, as well as the clergy and the educated classes of that time, were perfectly conscious of the lack of foundation in the accusations brought by the people against the Jews; but from fear of the rabble and still more for the sake of material profit, not only held their peace, but in the most cruel manner participated in the slaughter of their victims . . . . The old myth of the poisoning of wells was first revived in the South of France, and from there spread over the whole of Europe . . . . As early as May 1348 in a town in Provence all Jewish inhabitants fell victims to the rage of the populace. The burning of Jews was particularly thorough at Narbonne and Carcassonne. In Burgundy alone fifty thousand Jews were massacred in the most cruel manner . . . . The legend of Ahasver, the eternal wandering Jew, which originated in the thirteenth century, has always cropped up again in times of plague.

From a "Remonstrance" of the Archbishop of Carpentras in 1721:

85

The public is requested to note that the Jews are enemies of Jesus Christ and of Christians. That they are our slaves . . . . This humiliation of the Jews cannot be termed an oppression by Christians, because they only use just and lawful means to humble them, and because they only wish to fulfil the Prophecies in doing so.

I put away the books and turned off the light. In spite of the revolting reading matter I felt singularly peaceful, as if something had finally been decided in my mind. I didn't want to think anything through any more; I had no wish to resist the inevitable. Sleep came by itself, deep and soothing as the sea, as if I were diving back into familiar pools among the ridges and shoals of fish and gently swaying algae of long ago.

Very early, before dawn, I was awake again, feeling quite fresh and clear. Without waiting any longer, I got up, ran water and took a bath, chose expensive but comfortable clothes for the day — light sweater, shirt and pants — as if it was some special occasion I had to dress up for; then I packed my bag and drew back the curtains to watch the day breaking outside. There was none of the violence of summer left in it; it was much more moderate now, compassionate, touched by grief and age.

Today I would drive right through to Provence. The detours and wanderings were behind me; necessary, but past. It would be pointless to postpone my arrival any longer. Here in Carcassonne I wouldn't find Brian. There was nothing of myself here either. My appointment with myself was in Provence, it couldn't wait any more. Suppose I came too late? Perhaps one was allowed only one such chance in a lifetime.

Carcassonne had marked the end of our trip, eight years before. Now I was on my way from there back to Provence, travelling upstream as it were, against my memories, against myself. Back.

So began the first of my five days. Yet in an unfathomable way the earlier ones seemed to merge into it, drawn into the stream: the way one enters a day with the night's dreams still vaguely in one's mind, unsettling or encouraging.

Narbonne. Béziers. There, unable to resist the temptation (there was no need to hurry; I could reach Avignon in the early afternoon without any effort) I made a final detour, to the sea. The summer beaches all deserted in this late autumn. I stopped at the edge of a promenade, got out of the car and headed for the water. The languid rippling of the Mediterranean, so different from the turbulence of the Cape coast. Would Dedda ever have visited these parts, I wondered? Marseille, undoubtedly. But it would have been good to know for sure.

The sky was still hazy with fleecy clouds, but the sun was beginning to come through quite strongly. On the strangely desolate beach I was alone, except for one old man on a green bench, feeding breadcrumbs to the gulls: he was surrounded by a whole flock of them, screeching and squawking, fighting over the larger morsels. Behind the bench stood a baby's pram, covered with a faded and frayed tricolour. A *clochard*, no doubt, with all his earthly belongings in the pram. Where would he spend the nights, now that it was getting colder? There were no Métro grilles here as in Paris. Perhaps he would soon move inland. But what would become of the gulls then?

As I came past him I heard him muttering something which sounded like an obscenity; and when I looked up, I saw him staring, his small bloodshot eyes burning straight into my crotch. It annoyed me — Jesus, he was so filthy! — but ignoring him I walked on, kicked off my sandals with studied casualness and stepped into the shallow water. I couldn't care less about getting my pants wet up to the knees. It was so good to feel cold water again after all those days of travelling. The gentle subsidence of the sand under my feet. To be here again, to be acknowledged by the sea, the most natural and indispensable of my elements.

Paul had also brought me straight to the sea, last summer, before we'd gone anywhere else: not the same beach, but les Saintes-Maries-de-la-Mer. We hadn't discussed it beforehand, he knew me well enough. Nothing can rinse me quite so clean, nothing frees me quite so effectively from whatever is irrelevant or superfluous, leaving me whole and naked: myself, the purest I, Andrea Malgas. I had run across the sand and splashed in, head first, returning to him much later, smooth and salty and glistening with water. His eyes were hidden behind his sunglasses, the better to relish the view of so many tanned and topless girls. I leaned over him to spatter him with my wetness, plastering a sloppy kiss on his mouth. "Thank you for bringing me, Paul. You're a darling."

"No sweat. There's more than enough here for me to look at."

I removed my top too, not only to do justice to the sun but to bask in his reaction, the satisfying glow of possessive pride in his eyes.

"Yours are the loveliest of all."

"You sure they're not too small?"

"Absolutely. They're a perfect fit for my hands."

Across the red binding of the film script (which he'd refused to abandon even on the beach) I saw him looking at me with unabashed desire; and not without a touch of jealousy, because others were eyeing me with approval too.

He'd often shown something akin to Dedda's possessiveness about me. It hardly suited his sophistication, revealing a boyishness perhaps conditioned by a distant puritanical past, which both amused me and made me love him more: not prudishness, but a certain propriety which he'd carried over from an existence he thought he'd transcended. It had been as impossible for him as for me to break completely free; we would always carry the scar with us. Except that I was perhaps more willing to admit it than he was, having his male pride to contend with. The quiet, private comedy of a male existence: so dignified, impressive, self-assured, convincing on the outside; the inside so uncertain, so easily wounded. The penis his sign and summary. The crude compliment of an erection. So arrogant, so assertive, so forceful: hard as bone to a hand or vagina enclosing it; so soft and vulnerable to a mouth. *Because*

I love you I come to you unarmed, and without resistance.)

That was how I'd come to know him in Paris, once we'd returned from the Loire. That night in Amboise, when I'd said: "You may come in," it had seemed to be no more than the confirmation of what had already existed; we'd known each other so well that it had seemed the most natural thing to happen. Yet in spite of my readiness it had left me amazed: this knowledge and its processes were so wholly different from anything we'd acquired before. *You may come in.* The first shock of recognition in the flesh. The body's impulsive resistance against its own vincibility — and at the same time the terrible urge to be taken. This was quite different from the way in which I'd earlier made myself available to others, whether in play or for relief or comfort: this was an entry not only into my flesh but into my life.

And it caused tension in Paris too. He'd taken it for granted that I would move in with him, in his spacious flat in the boulevard Malesherbes, filled with his aunt's Empire furniture, magnificent paintings, expensive carpets, a somewhat outmoded extravagance in the velvet curtains, the bed with its great canopy and its vignettes and lavish drapings. (Added to this, as unexpected and brutal as a laugh in church: the statuettes and masks from Africa; the Basotho hat and the Ndebele beadwork covering a calabash; the Zulu pot; the long-stemmed pipe from Transkei.)

"No, of course I'm not moving in here, Paul. I've got my own flat."

"But it's all changed now, isn't it? It wasn't just a dirty weekend." Sudden panic in his eyes. "Or was it?"

"No, Paul, it wasn't. But I'm still me, you know. Whatever that may mean."

Absently, I stroked one of his carved African statues, an almost erotic caress. "Perhaps I'm just being silly," I said. "Perhaps it's ridiculous to make an issue of it. That's not what I'm trying to do. But you see, it's the way I grew up and everything. Do you realize, I never had a room of my own before? There was always Maggie. Sometimes Ma slept with

89

us too. Otherwise Gran and Grampa, when Dedda was home. And afterwards there was Brian. In Frank's flat I slept on the couch until I moved into his room with him. Now, at last — "

"I understand, Andrea. But you've fought enough battles in your life. From now on I want to do the fighting for you."

I couldn't help laughing. "That's why I first learned French. When I came over with Brian, we were always together. But sometimes I'd take a stroll on my own, and then I would invariably get caught up in an argument with a shopkeeper or somebody in a market stall. They were always shouting at me because I couldn't speak the language. And when I went back to complain to Brian, he would find it very amusing. 'What do you want me to do?' he would say. 'I can't go back and quarrel with them on your behalf. *I* have no fight with them.' And so I took a solemn vow that I'd use the first chance that came my way to learn French and fight back. As soon as we got to London I registered at the Alliance. It was a battle, I tell you. But eventually I learned to stand on my own two feet."

"There's no need to prove anything to anybody any more, Andrea. I love you. I want to look after you."

"Well, love me then. Look after me. But don't ever try to possess me, for then I'll kick you in the balls."

He made an attempt to laugh, but it wasn't very convincing. "There's something in you," he said, shaking his head, "something no one will ever get tamed. A small, hard, tough stone which no tooth can crack." I don't think he meant it that way, but he made it sound almost like a reproach: "It's something more male than female."

"No, Paul," I said, replacing his little statue in its niche, "it's something human, that's all."

In the end, of course, he gave way. I spent many nights with him, far more than on my own. And often, when we were working in the Latin Quarter or had a meal there, he would spend the night with me. But I hung on to my flat; it was my own, and I was possessive and selfish about it.

Inevitably, it had all led up to the final question, this summer, in the Auberge in Eygalières. And what else could I

90

really answer to it now but *Yes?*

That was the final confirmation I'd come in search of; that was why I was here now. Which was another reason why I had to make the detour to the sea. To cleanse myself and prepare for a new start.

The water was cold but caressing on my calves, a lascivious wetness. On an impulse I turned round to look at the beach. The old *clochard* was still feeding his gulls. Two wanderers were moving very far in the distance. Otherwise the beach was totally deserted. When the old man saw me look round, he shouted another of his obscenities into the wind. A very ancient rebellious impulse sprang up in me. I returned to the sand and, without bothering to turn my back on him, began to take off my light sweater, unbuttoned my shirt, leaned forward to unfasten my bra. The old man was deadly quiet now. As I began to strip off my pants, I could see him getting up and giving a few steps backward, as if he couldn't believe his eyes. There was a flurry of gulls around his head. It gave me a strange feeling of triumph to see how easy it was to rattle him; he no longer was a threat or a nuisance. Now I could forget about him and give myself completely to the sea.

I took off my white panties as well, left all the clothes in a small bundle on the beach, and ran into the water. The cold caused me to gasp for breath, but I went on swimming furiously until I could feel my body heat overtaking the cold. (A little girl, years ago —) Breathless, I turned on my back. A few of the *clochard*'s gulls came swooping down towards me to have a closer look. I raised my head. Far away on the beach I saw the old scarecrow moving, hobbling along like a spider that had lost a couple of legs, heading straight for my bundle of clothes.

"Hey!" I called out. "Leave my things alone! Go away!"

He stopped, shouted something unintelligible, then resumed, much more resolutely than before, his grotesque shuffling towards my clothes.

I began to swim back as fast as I could, but as I reached the water's edge he was already bending over my bundle.

91

"Stop it!"

I didn't fancy the prospect of a tug o' war with the old vulture in my naked state. There was only one other chance and I took it, running swiftly right past him to where he'd left his pram beside the green bench. The gulls which had swarmed down all over it the moment he'd left, flew up again in an angry flutter of wings, screeching indignantly. I hurled myself on to the pram and began to rummage in the junk, praying that this would lure him away from my clothes. Behind me I could already hear him shouting in rage.

Not really knowing what to do next, I stripped the large flag from his pram and began to dry my shivering body; then flung it across my shoulders like a shawl — not that it was much use: from the hips down I was still bare — and threw my weight against the pram to push it away.

My body was glowing from the vigorous rubbing-down; but the air was so cold that I had goose-flesh from head to toe; my nipples were so stiff they ached.

When I looked round again, he was gaining on me, approaching in an unsteady gallop, dropping my clothes bit by bit as he came hurrying on. I pushed on for another twenty or thirty yards to make sure he was far enough away from my things, then let go of the pram, drew the flag very tightly across my shoulders and set off at full speed to retrieve my clothes. My legs were much too long for him; and he was much too old. Before he could do anything to stop me, I'd gathered my belongings and began to put them on, safely out of reach. Just when I was halfway into my pants, he came hobbling back in my direction, so that I had to hop away on one leg as fast as I could, waving the flag at him — more to keep my balance than to taunt him — as if we were practising for a corrida. Some distance behind him the two wanderers I'd noticed earlier had stopped to stare at us; to them it must have seemed like great fun. They even offered amused applause as I desperately tried to retain a last vestige of dignity, hopping and jumping about, trying to fasten my clothes and stay out of reach at the same time.

The *clochard* was shouting at me again, a stream of obscenities such as I hadn't heard for years, always returning to *conasse* and *gonzesse*, with unspeakable variations and embroiderings of the basic theme; and from time to time he would make a half turn to shake his backside at me while making farting sounds with his mouth. For him, it was clear, I represented everything that made a bourgeois Parisienne despicable.

When it finally got through to him that he wouldn't catch up with me, he stopped in his tracks and tore open the safety pin that held his flies together, shaking his shrivelled, discoloured, floppy old prick at me. "*Sale pute!*" he roared with a spray of spittle.

"*Ta gueule!*" I shouted back. And suddenly something tore loose inside me, more exuberance than rage, and I started giving it to him in Afrikaans. "Fucking old cunt-face!" I shouted. "You miserable turd, born from your mother's arsehole because her cunt was too busy!" Reverberating deep inside my head were the echoes of Dedda's cursing when he really got into his stride. The old man stopped in midsentence, gasping for air. For the first time in years (apart from a few occasions at a street market in Paris, right in the beginning, before I'd been fluent enough in French) I fell back on Afrikaans, shouting at the top of my voice, with a gusto I hadn't felt for a very long time, fit to burst my lungs.

He seemed petrified. Shoulders drooping, arms drooping, cock drooping, everything drooping, he just stood there gawking at me as I hitched up my pants which had fallen down again during the shouting match, and zipped up my fly and fastened my belt.

Still clutching the flag in my hand, I ran back to my car. Too late I realized that I'd left my sandals behind, but to hell with them. I unlocked the door and got in, then gleefully turned down the window and waved the flag at him as I drove off. He was faster than I'd thought and managed to grab one end, nearly toppling over in the process. The speed of my take-off caused the faded, threadbare cloth to tear in two. In the rearview mirror I saw him disappear in the distance, waving his arms in rage and despair, his half of the flag still clutched in one hand as I drove off with the other.

There was a curious bitter taste in my mouth, but also an exhilaration in my blood I hadn't felt in years. I threw my head back and began to sing the "Marseillaise".

"A man is a star with five limbs."

"You have six." She bends over to take him in her mouth.

Montpellier. By lunchtime, Nîmes. A cheap, touristy restaurant near the Roman arena where, three months earlier, Paul and I had watched a corrida. No one except one unmistakable foot fetishist paid any attention to my bare feet; and for him I reserved a special kick by rubbing sea-sand from between my toes: I know I have nice feet. Ask Paul. (Frank even wanted to make a whole painting consisting of my footprints on a canvas.)

And then the last stretch to Avignon. By this time the weather had cleared up completely. As I crossed the Rhône (further along the river, the broken bridge of Saint-Bénézet, a chopped-off arm stretching out across the broad stream towards the fortress on the other side, like the old *clochard*'s last futile grab in my direction), it was like a whole flood of transparent new light breaking over me. A luminous landscape, so much like that of the Cape, yet so different. The very similarity confirmed the difference, leaving me, like often in the past, with a feeling of uneasiness, as if I'd been mistaken with something; as if two similar images just failed to fit completely. It was like meeting a brother and sister who look exactly alike: yet they can never be one and the same person, for one is female, the other male.

Following the road circling the medieval city walls, I turned into the rue de la République and concentrated strenuously on finding the right route to the hotel in which we'd stayed in July and where Paul had once again reserved a room for me (even though I was more than a week overdue). A classy, expensive

94

place, as always; and fortunately it had a parking lot for clients.

Still, it was with some hesitation that, suitcase in hand, I went towards the glass entrance. Reluctance. Because of all the memories of Avignon that would never stop haunting me. The first pension where Brian and I had sought accommodation, straight upon our arrival from Nice, from South Africa. A few weeks later, the day of the gypsies — The memory of this very hotel, even though it had nothing to do with the establishment or its staff: after all, what could *they* do about a newspaper report?

In the breakfast-room — glass and chrome, artificial flowers, Picasso prints — Paul sits paging through the newspaper while she is sipping her orange juice.

"I wish you'd put that thing down," she complains. "You're acting as if we're married already."

"Well, well," he exclaims (it's obvious he hasn't heard her), folding the paper inside out. "I see the beloved fatherland is in the news again."

"What's it this time?" She knows it's not usual for reports about South Africa to be published, unless it's bad news.

"Read this." He hands her the folded paper.

Not a very long report, on the foreign affairs page: a baby girl has been found in the veld outside Pretoria, wrapped in two thin blankets and a sheet of brown paper. For a few days she has been cared for very lovingly by nurses in a hospital, but now her future has to be decided and that is obviously determined by her race. *According to a spokesman for the Department of the Interior,* says the report, *the decisive test is the race of the father. The second most important criterion is appearance. In the present case scientific methods have been applied to determine that the child is, in fact, coloured.* These "scientific methods", it is specified, consisted of an examination of a single hair, which was found to be crinkly.

The rest of the report — speculation on whether the child's mother might have been a white girl who wanted to get rid of the baby to avoid possible prosecution under the Immorality

95

Act — does not interest her. It is that single opening paragraph which seems to mesmerize her.

"Forty years ago they also used this brand of 'scientific method'," Pauls says with restrained anger. "Then they examined a man's penis to see whether it was circumcised. Or else they measured noses."

She says nothing. Just remains sitting hunched up as if a live coal is burning in her womb. He's asked her to marry him, she thinks. He knows how much she wants a child. More than anything else in the world, perhaps. But suppose they were living in South Africa now — ? A single strand of hair from a baby's head can decide the whole future. A child, her own: whether he will be accepted as a human being or rejected into a twilight world of half-people, neither white nor black, but something in between, denied, outcast, a stepchild to humanity — all of this will be decided by the big bosses, on the basis of their "scientific methods", applied to one strand of hair from its still-soft head. Rock-a-bye, baby, you sleep in your cosy little cradle, you got nothing to worry about, man, other people will decide your future for you. And if the tree falls, just too bloody bad.

She drops the paper and covers her eyes.

"What's the matter?" Paul asks, startled.

"Let's just get out of here," she whispers. "Avignon isn't good for me."

But I didn't check into Paul's hotel again, after all, in spite of my conscientious decision to atone for the wanderings of the past few days. For I'd hardly stepped into the foyer — glass, potted plants, simulated marble — when a bus-load of tourists came swarming past me, sweeping me aside in their determination to reach the reception counter first. Scandinavians, as far as I could make out. A porter, halfway towards me to give me a hand with my case, stopped in his tracks. Perhaps he'd just noticed that I was barefoot, and wanted to show his disapproval. (Fuck him.) At first I thought I'd await my turn, but after a few minutes I gave up.

The tourists were all elderly, most of them female (there's something frightening about the sheer determination with which such old people pursue their travels, keeping on the move all the time, doing things, proving things, for as long as they possibly can, even when they can barely shuffle along unaided): each with such an air of aggressive self-confidence that no outsider had a chance of leaving a dent on it. Some had their husbands with them, decrepit little grey creatures who had managed, if only just, to survive at the side of their amazons. And this handful of men was completely over-whelmed by the smug tyranny of their frightful wives, who had clearly made up their minds to avenge a lifetime of living as underdogs. With a mixture of condescension and disgust each paltry little husband was dominated by his lady, as if he were a child not yet house-trained. And in the demeanour of each woman I could read the satisfaction (so familiar since my whole childhood in Gran's shadow) of the firm knowledge that the poor creature at her side could no longer be unfaithful, even if he wanted to: not even in her thoughts. Unfortunately it went hand in hand, for her, with a viciousness caused by the knowledge that his inability to be unfaithful was exactly matched by his inability to be a husband to her. Was this the price of ageing — or the inevitable cul-de-sac of marriage? Paul and I in thirty years' time, when I would be sixty, he eighty-two?!

I couldn't stomach it any longer. Picking up my suitcase again I turned round (the porter stood watching me from under his half-mast eyelids, still not moving a finger either to help or stop me), and went back to my car.

On my way out of the town I got lost. Instead of taking the main road to Cavaillon, as Paul had done in the summer, I found myself — after an exasperating merry-go-round — on the road to Arles. After a few kilometres I had to stop to orient myself; for the first time on my journey I took out the Michelin. All right. I could turn off at Tarascon and take the road past Saint-Étienne-du-Grès to get to Saint-Rémy, which was where I wanted to go now. There was a feeling of exquisite freedom in making the choice myself rather than submit to arrangements already made, however lovingly, by Paul. He didn't really figure in it at all. My real appointment was the one with myself, and Avignon would have made it very difficult. Don't ask me why. I simply knew it. I hadn't meant to be disloyal to Paul: after all, I'd tried, hadn't I? And now I was free to follow my own head.

Of course, I didn't know then how soon I would have to drive back all the way to Avignon; I didn't know about Mandla yet.

Mandla Mqayisa. He'd appeared in our lives in the early summer, together with George Tsabalala, a month before Paul and I had left for Provence: they'd been on a trip through Europe to collect money for some liberation movement or other. As far as I could make out, the anti-apartheid people had arranged everything for them, first in London, then Stockholm and Amsterdam, now Paris; and they were still meaning to proceed to East Germany, Czechoslovakia and God knows where else. The decision to turn to Paul had probably been inspired by a UNESCO film against racism with which he'd been involved a few years earlier. He'd often found visitors of that kind on his doorstep. Some of them were chancers or down-and-outs (and not only from South Africa, but from Chile and Turkey and the Philippines and everywhere); others were lovely people. Paul usually approached his contacts at UNESCO or Amnesty International to make sure they would be looked after — his privacy was important to him — except when he really became personally interested in someone.

Mandla Mqayisa was one of those. A striking man — very tall and muscular, the short sleeves of his T-shirt stretching tightly over the enormous, smooth biceps; and young too, at least four years younger than myself, even though he looked older; Afro hair; sardonic eyes which constantly seemed to mock one — yet from the start I couldn't stand him. Not just because of those mocking eyes, but because of his arrogance, obvious from the very way in which he moved, with the leisurely grace and defiance of a lazy young predator, the obtrusive tree-trunk legs inside the too-narrow faded jeans (*see if you can ignore this bulge!*); everything about him which proclaimed: "I am a man. Lie down before me, sweetie, open up."

Personally, I felt much more attracted to his colleague George. He was twice Mandla's age, a thin, small-boned man, with an ever smiling face. Much more reserved than Mandla. He acted almost fatherly towards me, with something dignified and calm about him which made me feel at ease in his company. Unfortunately we saw very little of him: he had friends in the city with whom he stayed, and after the first week or so he had to leave for Berlin and Genève to prepare the way, leaving Mandla behind to finish their work in Paris. So it was mostly Mandla with whom we had to put up.

"Hi, sister," he greeted me, with an African salute to match, the first night Paul brought him back to the flat in the boulevard Malesherbes. (We'd planned a private celebration for the evening: the budget for his *Black Death* had just been approved; and I'd been preparing dinner since five o'clock.)

"I'm not your sister," I replied coolly.

"I see. You're one of those. Pity."

From then on he simply ignored me. Flopped down on the chair I'd come to think of as "mine" (all right, he obviously couldn't have known that), and said to Paul: "You got cane?"

Paul went to the corner cabinet.

"Don't you waste your time with it," said Mandla. "We got a lot to talk about. The lady can serve us."

"This lady doesn't serve anyone," I hit back. I took off the pinafore I'd been wearing in the kitchen, folded it neatly and put it on the back of Paul's chair. Then I picked up my handbag from the telephone table and went to the front door.

"Food's on the stove," I said. "Enjoy it."

I was already on the staircase when Paul caught up with me.

"Andrea, please, he didn't mean to offend you."

"That makes it worse."

"I brought him home specially to meet you."

99

"It was supposed to be 'our' evening, remember?" I said.
"You could have warned me."

"I wanted to surprise you."

"Some surprise."

"But he's a South African."

"You know how I feel about South Africans."

"Mandla is different from anybody else you've met. You
should hear the things he has to say — "

"You're more than enough of an admiring audience."

It didn't help when I learned a few days later, just after
George Tsabalala had left, that Paul had invited Mandla to
move into his flat. The result was that for the following weeks
Paul had to come over to my place when he wanted to spend
the night. (That is, if I felt like it; a few evenings I locked him
out.) Like it or not, I saw more of Mandla. Some of his stories
I actually found interesting, even upsetting; to my own annoyance I sometimes laughed at his jokes. But his arrogance,
especially towards me, remained unchanged. To him I was
just a woman in the background and the most I could do was
to make life pleasant for him and Paul, if they so chose.
Bloody hell.

One evening, when the three of us were together in a
restaurant in the rue du Four, there was a hint of something, a
spark, a brief flash, that shone through his macho attitude.
Paul had absented himself for a few minutes — tobacco?
telephone? toilet? — leaving me alone with Mandla. He was
fiddling with a match between his teeth. I wasn't even conscious of him watching me, until he suddenly asked, his voice
deep in his throat, like a lion growling: "What you doing here,
hey?"

"I live here."

"I can understand why he likes it here" — he made a
gesture with his head in the direction in which Paul had
disappeared — "but how about you?" He moved his hand,
with the soggy match still between two fingers, and put it down
right beside mine on the table. "Sister, you're black. You got
my colour. So what you fucking about here?"

100

"Perhaps I like fucking."

"Tough, eh? Very tough. You can't care less if the world goes to hell."

"What do you know about me?"

"What do you know about *me?*"

We looked in each other's eyes. Neither would be the first to look away. Only, without meaning to, I crossed my arms over my breasts after a while to protect myself against his stare which was stripping every bit of clothing from my body.

"If only you could get to know him better," Paul reiterated, late that night, when we were together in my bed.

"Don't bring him in here with us," I warned him. "This bed isn't big enough for three."

He laughed softly, and gave up. For the time being, at least. But during the days that followed he repeated his efforts to wear down my resistance. I wasn't interested. All I knew, or cared to know, about Mandla was the bare facts, and those didn't divulge much. The University of Fort Hare. Trade unions in Port Elizabeth. Hassles with the Security Policy. Then off to Lesotho and Mozambique. I couldn't care less. I was here; all of that was very far away indeed. And within a few more days or weeks we would be rid of Mandla anyway.

In the last week of June he left; Paul took him to the airport. Just in time, for the whole thing had been getting on my nerves. Not just Mandla's attitude, but the way he treated Paul. Exploited his hospitality, drank up his liquor, never bothered to make his bed or pick up a towel in the bathroom, yet always quick with snide remarks about "bourgeois", "white Liberals", "playing it safe", "living off the system". Worst of all was the way in which Paul appeared to lap it up. He who'd always steered clear of visitors who were too demanding, too passionately committed to causes, seemed to relish the experience of being insulted by one of them. I couldn't understand either of them: neither Paul who just kept on coming back for more, nor Mandla with his fashionable quotes from Fanon and Fidel and Mandela and Sisulu and Slovo and all the revolutionary clichés I'd come to know so well in London,

101

while at the same time he obviously enjoyed every moment of sharing Paul's maligned bourgeois existence. What really got me, was the way they'd clicked from the beginning, two long-lost brothers who'd suddenly found one another in a foreign country — even though each represented to the other what was most repugnant to himself. And it cut *me* out. That I couldn't forgive them.

Soon after Mandla's departure for East Germany, we left on our own trip to Provence. And that was the end of Mandla as far as I was concerned. Paul and I were together again. Once more our happiness was unconditional.

But in the second week of October, without any prior warning, Mandla arrived back from Eastern Europe. It was a double shock to me, not only because he threatened to take Paul away from me again, but because there was so much work we had to do on the still-unfinished script right then. So it suited me very well when I was offered a chance to escape on my own. Apart from all the other reasons, this was important too. And when I got back to Paris in a few weeks' time, Mandla would be gone for good.

Now I was back where we'd been in July. For the first time, on this particular road, I felt in touch with Paul again, as if I were getting closer to him as I drove further. The beginnings of mountains to the right, more pronounced as one approached Saint-Rémy. The inky blue vertebrae of the Alpilles. Black cypresses. The crows of Van Gogh. From the turn-off to Maillane there was the avenue of plane-trees, in summer a tunnel of bottle-green light, now more transparent, more exposed, the few remaining leaves brittle and discoloured. The wheat had long been harvested and the lands were bare and brown, the flowerfields drained of colour. Only the vineyards were bright with the clothes of grape-pickers, and the air was heavy with the smell of new wine.

The summer is a rage and celebration of their love. Among

the ruins and stones of lost civilizations they devote themselves to one another, eating and drinking each other, working together, talking through days and nights, enjoying for hours on end the gastronomy of the South; returning, every time, to a room and a bed which, with an ecstasy directly related to the shortness of their stay, they temporarily, eternally, call their own. In the icy green waters of the Fontaine de Vaucluse they cool the fever raging in their blood; then rush back to the hotel to celebrate that other heat. They trek through small brown hilltop villages — Gordes and Bonnieux, Lourmarin, Joucas, Lacoste, Saint-Saturnin d'Apt — and pick lavender or red poppies in the grass; returning in the dusk with armloads of thyme and rosemary to ward off mosquitoes. They wander through the ruins of old towns — Glanum, Vaison, Oppède, Les Baux — in search of echoes from a remote past: troubadours and story tellers, knights, refugees from the Plague. He takes her to Orange, where his mother's ancestors once lived, the Rouxs, before the wars of religion forced them, like so many other Huguenots, to flee; they attend an opera performance in the Roman theatre still dominated by the imperturbable statue of Augustus Caesar. And deep in the lugubrious mountains of the Luberon — for many centuries, he tells her, a sanctuary for religious refugees — they go in search of the little village of La Motte d'Aigues, where the first Jouberts came from.

An old woman struggling to carry a yellow plastic water-bucket uphill to her house (half the houses in the village appear to be deserted, the grey shutters and doors closed), shows them the way to the graveyard in the valley below. An enormous chestnut tree overhangs a sober war memorial: A Nos Morts; from there a path leads past the *boules* square to the graveyard wall. Two tall cypresses at the gate. Rows of headstones mark the graves, most of them decorated with plastic flowers and bell-jars. Eagerly they hunt up and down the rows, studying inscriptions, the older ones already obliterated by the elements. Rey. Blanc. Cavalier. Couron. Meynier. Reger. Bernard. It's Andrea who discovers, right at the bottom of a

103

row of graves, a tombstone of the Jaubert family (the spelling now changed, but undoubtedly the same name). In a sudden surge of emotion Paul clasps her hand. (In disappointment too, he admits afterwards: for if there really is only one stone bearing that name — with the possibility of a second, but the hieroglyphs on it are almost illegible — there couldn't have been many of his ancesters around. Not that it really matters, she points out: surely one was enough!)

It occurs to him to go to the post office for information; but it turns out to be closed in the afternoon. Frustrated, they go down the narrow main street to a *tabac* with a multicoloured curtain of plastic strips covering the entrance. A row of elderly men leaning on the counter study them in suspicious silence for a long time before one of them deigns to reply. Yes, indeed, there is a single Jaubert left in the village. Jean-Luc. Up there, beyond the chapel. Paul is so excited that he barely takes in the instructions.

They find the stone house on the far side of the hill rising from the old part of the village. A vine at the front door, just like the man in the *tabac* said. And on a rickety chair beside it — a very old black dog, lame, half-blind, at his feet — sits Monsieur Jaubert, shrivelled up like a dried apricot forgotten in the sun. They have great difficulty in making themselves understood as he is almost totally deaf; but in the end there is a general shaking of hands, as Paul concludes a rambling monologue about family ties and the distant past, sealed with a promise to look him up again, next time.

On the way back, Paul is almost too overcome to talk.

"It's so easy to talk about one's 'place of origin' — but my God, suddenly you *get* there, actually to *be* there. That little old man must be a distant relative. It's as if I've only just discovered — after almost eighteen years! — that I really belong here. This is my place, Andrea. It's my world. That's why I had to come back to it. It wasn't just a matter of getting out of South Africa: I wanted to be *here*. It's taken me over fifty years to realize one cannot exist without roots."

She is singularly quiet.

"Why don't you say anything?" he asks, carried away. "Don't you agree with me?"

"If I dare agree with you — what then?"

"Why are you asking it in such a funny way?"

"What does it make *me*? Where do *I* fit in?"

"You belong with me."

"I see. Thy God is my God," she says, very restrained, so quietly that he doesn't notice the bitterness. (Only much later, in remembering, it will strike him.)

And that night in the Auberge in Eygalières, where they have checked in completely impromptu and without luggage, in the beautiful simplicity of the stone room, he returns to their conversation: "This is where you belong, Andrea. Right here, in my arms. With me inside you. Don't you understand? Don't you agree?"

"Say it again, so that I can believe it."

And then, his mouth against her breast, a thin line of spittle like the trace of a snail across her nipple, he put the question, deliberately, lightly, playfully, with all the boyishness she loves so much. And she knows, in the contraction of her womb, in the motion of that secret inner muscle clutching his sex like a fist, how easy and natural it will be to accept, how tempting it is; how nearly unthinkable.

The imposing eighteenth-century château of Roussan, converted into a hotel, where we'd stayed in the summer, had already closed for the winter months, the grey shutters bolted, the large garden desolate among the bare black tree-trunks. Mounds of fallen leaves lay raked together under the trees. It was more than just disappointment: it was the frustration of a cherished memory and of a hope of illumination.

I drove on to Saint-Rémy, and stopped at a few of the hotels where Paul and I had dined before; at last I found accommodation on the far side of town. The building was still fairly new, not the weathered stone of Provence; still, it seemed simple and unassuming, with a long blue swimming-pool covered by fallen leaves, and a wide garden with carefully raked gravel paths. Yes, they could put me up. The moustached *patron* gave me a long, appreciative stare while I filled in his *fiche*. I suppose my hair was still dishevelled after the morning's swim; in the struggle with the old *clochard* I hadn't put on my bra again; and, of course, I was still barefoot. Which all added up to the *patron*'s peculiar interest in me, and his insistence on carrying my suitcase upstairs to the room where he pushed open the shutters — it had a musty smell after probably being uninhabited for a few weeks — and leaned over to test the bed with the palm of his hand (promise, challenge, or threat?); but then his wife called stridently from below and he left hurriedly, clearly flustered, but with enough Gallic presence of mind to offer me a last wink as he went out.

I locked and barred the door, stood at the window for a while to look at the pattern of mottled shadows among the trees caused by the afternoon sun, then turned round to unpack. At last I could empty the suitcase and prepare to stay for a while, not just overnight as in the recent past. A temporary place of "my own" again.

My hair felt sticky from the sea-water when I pushed my fingers through it. I went to the bathroom to run a bath, then spent more than an hour luxuriating in the warm water, tending every finger and toe, washing my hair, before I finally got out and lazily dried myself. On my way to the bedroom to get dressed, I caught a glimpse of my reflection in the mirror on the side wall. Removing the towel from my head, I shook my damp, curly hair in a dark cascade over my shoulders, and stopped to stare at my naked image.

The same gesture, the same experience, repeated so many times, ever since I was a child: back to this body, this mine, this I, every time. Here were my limbs: two arms, two legs, a head. Here I ended, here were my limits.

I stroked my hands down my sides. Breasts, belly, the small sharp ridges of my hips. Loins. How I would love to allow a child to take shape in there. "Allow", not shaping it myself, because that seemed improbable: allowing it by being conscious of it, by choosing the right food, by resting enough,

106

looking after myself, in order to permit and aid this strange growing. A child. Mine. Paul's. A child to still this unnameable need, flesh of my flesh, blood of my own; no longer the fruitless monthly waste. Emerging from my most secret moistest inner darkness into the light. This wound. How penetrable I was. A woman. Would any man ever truly understand it? For them, everything is external, hanging out, rearing angrily upward. But I have to expose myself, made myself available, must allow him to penetrate me, to "take" me. I must be conquered like an old-time town. This breach in my wall. And the fact that I didn't want to be without it, couldn't think of surviving without it, made it so much worse.

Time itself penetrating me, moving inwards, towards life; posing its own severe demands.

Almost detachedly I gazed at myself, this body called Andrea. Each contour and fold, each hair, each separate limb and orifice and pore he had loved, he'd given shape with his hands and tongue, calling it beautiful, thinking it good, like God on the sixth day.

Through his eyes I tried to look at myself: tried to see exactly what he would see, and exactly how.

The others, before him. ("You wear on your face and your body the traces of all your loves, like a malediction." Said who? In what irretrievable night?) And that was what terrified me: how little I belonged to myself; how profoundly I was still dependent on others, always, always. The rough tenderness with which Dedda had tried to make me "his" child. Brian, who'd offered me a new life, then tried to shape me exclusively to his own expectations. And now Paul, finally tempting me with stability, with security, after all the years of wandering, searching, suffering from hunger and thirst and insatiable longing. The others? I might wish to deny or ignore them now, but they had also been there: they'd also had their share of this body. Through them, too, I had lived, had been lived. Nothing in my whole life had ever happened without my experiencing it through somebody else. Not even that: I had to be more specific: not just, vaguely, "somebody else", but: "a man". Every single time. Father, brother, assailant, lover, employer. Dear God, even that morning's *clochard*!

Perhaps it was inevitable? Perhaps the only way one could ever find access to oneself was through another person?

This body standing here, this naked body with her five limbs: this body was willed by me. I wanted her, wanted entirely to possess her, to live my way into her: this was my true "place", as La Motte d'Aigues was Paul's; only more so. She was I. Who was she? This terrifyingly familiar, utterly alien creature, used by so many hands, penetrated by the flesh of so many strangers: why couldn't it simply *be*, wonderful and self-sufficient, just for once, only once. Not eternally delivered to others: but, for once, whole and good and sealed and perfect!

I moved my fingertips across the surface of the body I saw — the thrill of recognition, of joy! — recognizing myself, acknowledging myself, affirming myself; allowing myself the small and precious freedom of doing no more than being there. Simply because I was I.

(But what about the wound? The breach? With the five fingers of my hand I tried to close the lips over their own secret inside being, whole, whole.)

For the moment it was enough. But later? There would always be a later. What, if I went back to Paris — ? What, if I gave Paul an answer to his question — ?

Even then there was this fierce, small certainty of today: this body acknowledged in a mirror.

There was no restaurant in the hotel, so I had to go out for dinner. Another obstacle. I was feeling so content right then, so secure: going out to a restaurant would inevitably expose me to the world again.

I could skip dinner, of course. But I was hungry. The body had its own demands, and could not be denied. The breach was there. So it was easy, really, to use my irritation as an excuse for telephoning Paul.

(Such are the thin edges on which everything is balanced. Suppose I hadn't called him — ?)

The relief when he answered after almost two minutes of solid ringing.

"Paul, my goodness, at last. Where have you been?"

"In the bath." Only then did it seem to strike him who it was. "Andrea! Good God, my darling, where are you?"

"In Saint-Rémy."

"But what are you doing in Saint-Rémy, for heaven's sake? I've been beside myself with worry. Tomorrow I'm off to Strasbourg for the film conference and I'd already given up all hope of ever getting hold of you."

"But we agreed not to phone for a while."

"Why aren't you in Avignon?"

It angered me. "Paul, do you really expect me to do everything you say? I wanted to be alone by myself, and I just wanted to get lost for a while."

"I've already been thinking of asking the police to look for you."

"*That* would have done it."

"But Andrea — !" He sounded desperate. "I'm not angry, darling. I'm not trying to blame you or scold you or anything. But I've been so worried. Don't you realize — "

"There's nothing I should realize."

"Is Mandla with you?" he interrupted me urgently.

"Mandla? What the hell would he be doing with me?"

"Oh no!"

"Paul, will you please get your bloody wits together and tell me what is going on? What's Mandla got to do with it?"

"I sent him down to you. He left yesterday morning on the train to Avignon. I sent you a telegram. Then, last night, he phoned, completely at sea. And again this morning. He'd waited on the station for half a day before picking his own way to the hotel. Only to find that they didn't know anything about you."

"But *why*, Paul? Can you please tell me this, very clearly and slowly: *why*? You know bloody well I can't stand the man.

109

We agreed that I would be on my own for a while. Now suddenly, right out of the blue — "

"Listen, Andrea. I don't want to say too much on the phone. But something really bad has happened. Mandla discovered that his colleague — remember George Tsabalala who came over with him? — well, he discovered that George had been planted by the Security Branch in South Africa to keep an eye on everything. So Mandla had to get out as fast as he could. He was all set to go to the airport when he learned they were waiting for him at the other end. Apart from everything else, he's stone broke as well. George absconded with all the money. So I thought it would be best for him to dive under for a while. Serge was prepared to create a small job in our film project for him. That's why I sent him down to you."

It was too much to digest in one gulp.

"What do I do now?" I asked weakly.

"You must please go back to Avignon. Take him with you when you go somewhere. Find him something to do, just keep him busy. He's feeling very depressed and angry."

"I'm not going to stay in that hotel in Avignon, I'm telling you."

"Well, just go and pick him up then. Take him wherever you want to. I'll phone him to tell him you're on your way. Use the company's credit card. But whatever you do, just look after him."

"Don't you think you're taking advantage of me now?"

"It's only for a few days, Andrea. Please!" Then, a bit too sugary to my liking: "I love you, darling."

"It's a bloody demanding sort of love."

"You love *me*, don't you?" he said quietly.

"Oh fuck you, Paul," I said. "Yes, of course I love you." Adding with a sigh: "All right then, I'll go and fetch him. But you're going to answer for all this, sooner or later."

There were a few of the Scandinavian women in the foyer

again, probably waiting for a bus for an "evening out", when I arrived back at the hotel in Avignon just before eight. I think the porter recognized me — he immediately glanced down to my feet — but he made no effort to approach me. At the reception counter I asked them to ring Mandla; it irritated me that he wasn't in the foyer already. Whether he did it on purpose, I'm not sure, but he kept me waiting for fully twenty minutes before he came bursting from the old-fashioned lift, navy-blue canvas sling-bag over the shoulder. "Bursting" indeed, for his massive body fitted so tightly into that fragile little lift — an up-ended coffin behind bars — that he shot out of it like a cork from a bottle the instant it came to a standstill. Even the old ladies with their peroxide or blue-rinsed hair stopped chattering for a moment and moved closer to the wall to make way for him. An ashtray on a tall stand crashed under the assault of his swinging canvas bag, but he didn't bother to pick it up; perhaps he hadn't even noticed.

The porter still made no move to offer his services. Out of contempt? Or just to play safe?

"You're late," I said coolly when Mandla reached me. "Didn't Paul phone you?"

No sign of remorse in him. On the contrary. "*You*'re bloody late," he said. "You were supposed to be here yesterday."

I glowered at him. "Mandla," I said at last, as calmly as I could, "perhaps we should try to understand one another right from the beginning, I've come to fetch you because Paul asked me to, not because I have the slightest inclination to cart you around, OK?"

"Have you settled the bill?" he asked, not paying any attention to what I'd said.

"Yes. With the company's credit card." I didn't want him to think it came out of my pocket.

"Damn nuisance to move again," he said. "I thought Paul told you to stay here in Avignon."

"I take my own decisions. It would have suited me to leave you right here, but I'll be damned if I'm going to drive to and fro every day to pick you up."

111

I saw his eyes narrowing as he watched me, but for the moment he said nothing. Without waiting any longer he went towards the front door ahead of me. There, with a very deft shrug of his left shoulder, he shook the sling-back into the hands of the porter and said, in English: "Take this to the lady's car." Then he went out without stopping to let me through first.

The car was right outside. I unlocked the doors.

"Will you give him a tip?" said Mandla. "I haven't got anything small enough for him."

Most of the return journey we rode in silence. Only once I made an effort to start up a conversation — to compensate for my bitchiness earlier? or to sneer at his misfortune?

"So you had problems with your friend George?"

"What do you know about it?"

"Paul told me, of course."

"He wasn't supposed to blab about it."

"I had to know."

"You're a woman."

"I see," I bitched back. "And as far as you are concerned a woman is only good for one thing."

He watched me in silence for a while; even in the dark I was conscious of his eyes. "Don't you get any ideas, sister," he said at last. "You're too thin for my taste. I like having my hands full."

"It wouldn't have made any difference," I said, enraged. "I'm sleeping with Paul."

"Paul's white."

"Right. So you don't stand a fucking chance."

Perhaps he would have hit back, but at that moment I suddenly had to swerve to avoid something in the road — a squirrel? a dead rat? — and I suppose he got the impression that I'd kill us both if he made me too angry.

In furious silence I drove the rest of the way back to the hotel in Saint-Rémy. The *patron* was waiting for us (I'd warned him when I left that I would be bringing him another guest); chewing his moustache in obvious resentment, he kept watch while Mandla filled in the card.

When he finally handed over the key he merely grunted: "It's the room opposite yours."

He seemed to be bearing me some kind of grudge, probably piqued by Mandla's presence, which must have put paid to his hopes of slipping upstairs to my door in the night.

Above the staircase, turning left towards my side of the passage I said briefly: "I'll try to figure out something for you to do tomorrow."

"I don't take orders from just anybody." He poked the key into the keyhole and went on fiddling with it for some time, obviously not used to French doorlocks yet. "Especially not from try-for-Whites."

My heart was throbbing in my throat when I closed my door behind me, leaning against it with my back to catch my breath again. I was ready to phone Paul and tell him to get the bastard out from under my feet before there was trouble. But after dialling a single digit I put the receiver back on its cradle against the wall. I didn't need Paul to fight my battles for me. With Mandla I could — and would — fight it out myself.

Gradually my indignation subsided. I also realized that I was still hungry, for in all the commotion I hadn't had time to eat. Taking my keys from my handbag I went out again. On the landing I hesitated for a moment, wondering whether I ought to invite Mandla to join me. But to hell with him. With a feeling of spite I drove off on my own. It was already too late for most of the restaurants in town, so I had to make do with a ham sandwich and coffee in one of the cafés on the boulevard Mirabeau. Reluctant to go back to the hotel room, I took out the small green notebook I'd brought with me and, as on the previous days, began to make brief entries about the day: the journey from Carcassonne (had it really been only that morning I'd left from there?), the preposterous fight with the old *clochard* (the torn flag should still be somewhere in the car, a useless trophy), the return to Provence, the hotel, Mandla.

It was late — most of the clients had already left and the two sleepy waiters were making a very obvious show of stacking chairs on tables and pulling down the shutters — by the time I left. Mandla's door was open when I got back. The light was burning in his room, but there was no sign of him. For a moment I stopped on the doorstep. His navy-blue bag lay upturned on the bed, the contents shaken out haphazardly. A few bits of clothing, the film script in its familiar dark red binding, a couple of books, a passport, small change. I found it strangely unsettling. Could that really be all the baggage he travelled with? Of course, he might have left some of his things with Paul. But even so. There was something terribly spare about his possessions, at odds with the formidable presence of the man. Where would he be going now, after what Paul had told me? Where did he really come from? Who *was* this stranger?

Angrily I pulled myself up short. Why should I care about the man? I would do my duty towards him while we had no choice but working together. For the rest he'd better keep out of my way.

I opened my door, closing it swiftly behind me again and taking the precaution of drawing the bolt shut. Undressed. Put off the light. Then pushed open both halves of the window for the night. I was on the point of turning back to the bed in the dark room, when I heard the sound of footsteps on the gravel in the garden and saw a large dark figure moving on the far side of the pool. He couldn't see me, of course, but I drew aside all the same, conscious of my nakedness. Under one of the tall bare plane-trees he stopped. He seemed to be staring at the pool, perhaps at the reflection of the moon; the next moment I saw him raise his head to gaze up into the sky. I had the wild impression that he might start wailing or barking up to the moon, like some wild animal. But he remained standing like that, head thrown back, quite motionless. Then he sighed. It was more than a sigh: a deep, sorrowful, moaning sound, like the groan of a lion.

I felt terribly naked. The night air made me shiver. I turned away and crept into my bed, drawing up the blankets to my ears to shut out everything outside; and so I fell asleep.

114

I didn't know what time of the night it was when I suddenly woke up again, nor what had wakened me; I had no memory of what I'd been dreaming, except that it had been very confused. And there was an ambiguous sensation when I opened my eyes: as if I'd been underwater for a long time and had just come up for air again — while at the same time it felt as if I was diving into a tidal pool at that very moment, down to an impossible depth. All I recall is the total disorientation with which I woke up. I literally didn't have the vaguest idea of where I was. In my old room in the Cape? But I couldn't hear Maggie or Ma breathing beside me; there was no sound from next door of old people coughing, or sighing, or peeing, dragging their weary bodies to the grave. In Brian's flat in London? The couch in Frank's living-room? Paul's great fourposter? I simply didn't know. I didn't know! I drew in my breath, imagined for a moment that I smelled Africa; quinces, *buchu*, dried fruit, camphor oil, salted fish; briefly, I thought I heard Dedda's voice somewhere. Where was I? My God, where was I? In what times and worlds had I got lost? Where had I come from and what was I doing there? Would I ever be in time for my appointment? Which appointment?

It must have taken minutes before I was able to place my surroundings — the faintest scent of thyme and rosemary and sere plane leaves — remembering the deep lion's sound I'd heard before. Somewhere a beam or floorboard creaked. On the far side of the landing perhaps, where he was still wandering about sleepless? Or was it the *patron* creeping upstairs in his nightshirt to try his luck?

So that was where I was. Africa was unbearably remote. And yet so shockingly close to me. The width of a single passage between me and that dark man.

115

Second Day

❈ ❈

(To try to understand, to grasp. A time; a country. More specifically, a person. A woman. Andrea, you. To seize you "in your own right". But how can I do so other than in *my* words, *my* way of writing and thinking — except when, from time to time, mercifully or shockingly, your own words break into my mind?)

Half an hour for my feet. The dark red nail varnish. Dedda had also been such a one for his feet, enough to drive Ma up the wall. Whether there were people around or not, if he felt like it he would pull off his shoes in the living-room and tackle his feet with scissors and file, thinking nothing of gnawing a recalcitrant toenail with his teeth before finishing off the job with the file. "A man's cock comes first, then his feet and hands. But feet before hands, 'cause you can still go through life without hands. But if you got no feet, you're stuck on your arse." He'd never been reticent about the first of his members. ("Cock needs wetness, otherwise it wilts.") But it was his feet he cared for most meticulously, at least in public: "A man got to look after his feet so's he can get a proper grip on the ground or the bottom end of a bed."

Then my hair. Brushing and brushing until the blackness shone. The pride of my hairdresser mum. A hundred strokes in the morning, a hundred at night. Curls in papers on Saturday nights, for Sunday church. "Doesn't matter if a girl is poor, my child. As long as her hair is shiny. It's a woman's crown. I can give you just one look, and tell you the sort of person you are. If you got no respect for your hair, you don't

116

care about yourself either, and then others treat you like dirt."
Brushing, brushing. Ma and I had never been able to talk
properly. With her brush she was much more articulate than
with her tongue. Thrashed me with the handle if I was
naughty; and if I was upset, she would come and sit beside me
and start brushing, slowly and very thoroughly, until I felt
better. Even Paul knew that if he wanted to comfort me, all he
needed to do was stroke my hair. The end between Ma and me
hadn't come on the day of her death but on the day I'd cut off
my long hair: since then there had been no way left to get
through to each other.

Perfume. Not Paul's choice, for I was still mad at him, but
my own. Subtle but unmistakable, the hint of musk. I was
hoping it would trouble Mandla. It was imperative for me to
start the new day with an advantage, however small; so I
prepared myself in time.

Ever since I'd first become conscious of the advantages of
make-up, after meeting Brian, this had always been the
loneliest time of the day. Confirmation of the need to arm
myself. One day, I used to think, I'd like to be able to do
without it altogether: right now it would leave me too exposed,
like walking about naked in public. (Oh for a beach as desolate
as the one at Steenbras or near Onrust, to walk hand in hand,
unashamed in the full glory of the sun. Sea-birds needed
wetness. A gannet couldn't survive without the brine.) Since
I'd been with Paul I'd become less fussy. In the beginning
there had still been people who said: "What's wrong? You look
different." Then I would hurry home to put on more make-
up. But Paul didn't mind. He actually preferred me without it;
he knew me naked.

But this morning in Saint-Rémy I took great care to prepare
myself for the day ahead. As on that distant journey through
Provence with Brian: then I'd still wanted to impress people,
and I'd had reason to hide myself. Not now. This time it was
exclusively to guarantee my privacy. I was in charge. I meant
it to stay that way.

It was still dark outside when I'd got up. Even after I'd

117

finished my make-up it was too early to go down for breakfast on the terrace. So I used the opportunity to sort through my books and notes. Strange, the feeling of satisfaction it gave me to page through all the horrible accounts of the Plague Paul had sent along with me: perhaps they confirmed the distance between me, here, and that remote, turbulent and terrifying age. It was the same Europe, but how vastly changed. Life was so much more certain and predictable today.

Ziegler:

In the benighted city, where it seemed death to wander abroad, only those servants of death, the grave-diggers, felt themselves free to travel where they would. The rich and privileged fled, the poor remained to drown their fear in looted liquor and die in their hovels . . . . To the casual visitor it must have seemed that society had disintegrated, that the Plague must rage until there is not a home inviolated, not a Parisian alive. If it was not to be the end of the world, it seemed at least the end of the established order.

Jusserand:

Faith disappeared, or was transformed; men became at once more sceptical and intolerant. It is not at all the modern, serenely cold, imperturbable scepticism; it is a violent movement of the whole nature which feels itself impelled to burn what it adores; but the man is uncertain in his doubt, and his burst of laughter stuns him; he has passed as it were, through an orgy, and when the white light of the morning comes he will have an attack of despair, profound anguish with tears and perhaps a vow of pilgrimage and a conspicuous conversation.

I was reassured by my reading, as it drew me back into the world of Paul's script, concentrating and focusing my thoughts, reminding me again of what I'd come to do. After the momentary upset of the previous evening I was once again certain of myself, in sympathy with Paul's characters. How well I understood their need to withdraw from a world devas-

118

tated by the Black Death, to escape from the madness raging outside their walls, within which they tried to adhere to Paul's "reassuring patterns of the eternal complements: heaven and earth, good and evil, light and dark, man and woman, body and soul — " And yet I could not help wondering, as I paged through the script (the end, even at this late stage, left incomplete), whether this was really what Paul had meant to write. Was he being wholly true to his own life, or was there wishful thinking in it? In substituting the film for the novel he'd been postponing for so long, had he yielded to easier ways out, salving his conscience, avoiding what he really knew and perhaps feared? It would help me so much to make up my own mind on the answer I owed him if I could be sure about this.

Yet what right did I have to blame him? What about my own flight, years ago, with Brian? That bleak, terrible last journey through the land —

I was here. Scratched into the gritty plaster, right through the paint, through tendons and nerves, into the mind, it is the one line that stays with her all the way as they drive through the vast land, from the moment Brian picks her up at her friends' house in Athlone (it is just five o'clock; above the hulk of the Mountain the stars are beginning to fade; the sun has already turned and is rising later than before; the first touch of winter is trembling almost imperceptibly in the early light) until, on the morning of the third day, exhausted from travelling and lack of sleep, they reach Johannesburg where they leave the battered old car with his friends and spend the day in a stupor (in separate rooms of course: they cannot take another risk), waiting for the evening plane to Nice.

"It'll be so much easier to fly up to Johannesburg," Brian tries to persuade her before the start of the journey, adding cautiously: "And much less painful."

"I don't want it to be painless." After the days and weeks of being unable to feel, she bursts into tears. "Jesus, don't you understand? It's something I have no right to avoid. I don't want to miss out on anything. I want to feel enough, and to

119

suffer enough, to last me for the rest of my bloody life."

To take her leave. To know exactly what it is she is taking leave of. That, above all. To know. *I was here.*

(And added to that — something she cannot tell him, because he won't understand — the need to retrace, before it is too late, the course of that one journey with her father, either to seal it off for good or to leave it open for ever.)

Cape Town. Whatever is still too dark to see with her eyes she perceives in her blood. The Mountain like a great fortress wall, visible from ever so far away when you approach it from the open sea, her father told her. All his travels across the oceans of the world, as far as Singapore and Hanoi, Japan, India, Istanbul, once Odessa; and Rio, the storms of Terra del Fuego, Santiago. All those names, names. And then, every time, the return; and Table Mountain. Enough to make the hardiest sailors weep with joy. Hurry, hurry, we want to get home. So many who have come from across the sea, Portuguese explorers with the Cross of Aviz on their sails, English soldiers, Dutch merchants. (Even her ancestor Xhorê!) Only she is going off, leaving them all behind.

From time to time, as they drive on, she glances at Brian's sharp profile against the lightening day. For him, it's the first leg of his journey home, back to London. He's just been here on a temporary visit, to finish his research for his thesis on the Khoikhoi. "Your people," he's often remarked, bemused. Not that it is as simple as that! So many different strains of blood running through her veins. Gazing at her intently, as he loves to do, one may suggest: Khoi, indeed, but also, no doubt, Malay slaves (her almond eyes), and Portuguese and Dutch or English. "Who knows, with a bit of luck, the worthy Scot imported by Lord Charles Somerset in the 1820s to improve the slave stock at the Cape, had a go at your great-grandmother too." And certainly darker streams from Angola or Mozambique or Madagascar.

With him beside her it becomes a journey not only through geography, but through history as well; and beyond his knowledge it spills over into a prehistoric world of *Homo habilis* and

120

layers and crusts, of shards and the remains of implements and the fossils of ferns and mighty animals.

Like the first explorers who ventured out from their fort, across the Liesbeek River, from stream to stream, from one mountain range to the next, they proceed further and further from the Cape: their early predecessors in search of the fabled kingdom of Monomotapa, the groping towards something even more elusive as they drive upstream against an entire prehistory, he to rid himself of it, she the better to impress the pain on her mind.

Breaking through the last breach in the Hex River range they enter the openness of the Karoo. The sun is rising. The gentleness of the Boland autumn is left behind, the exuberance of vineyards in the last valleys: here is only unambiguous sun, the harshness of stone, each little shrub doomed to separateness. From time to time an off-white farmhouse in the distance, a few frayed trees, bluegum or poplar, thin cypresses in a small square graveyard enclosed by white or brown walls, the bones inside long since returned to dust. In the whirlwinds which sometimes come dancing towards them, reddish or grey, the remains of ancestors and prehistoric animals are mixed with sand. Here the earth is lean, its ribs showing, the knots of its spine protruding in hard ridges. And the light turns white, leaving no scope for illusion. The sun scorches away all superfluity, burning everything down to the elemental, crude and stark. Earth, water, fire, wind.

There are no thoughts in her. She sits exposed to whatever happens around her, to everything relinquished with the death of her father, everything forever commemorated in the blood. Peeled like a fruit she sits, nerves and senses laid bare in the transparency of grief. Hearing, seeing, feeling, smelling, tasting: everything is immediate, without the intervention of thought. To register. To know.

She sees everything, even what is not visible. The wide landscapes: the plains and outcrops of the Little Karoo with its ostriches and lucerne fields, the green-black darkness of the Tsitsikamma forest, the paler green curves and thickets and the

121

aloe kraals of the Eastern Province, the browns and ochres of the Free State, dung-coloured thorn-trees in Griqualand West, the dried mealie-lands of the Western Transvaal; at last the yellow and white of mine-dumps, a city drifting weightless in the smog. They make no effort to drive straight towards a destination (arrival, in fact, must be postponed for as long as possible), but zigzag as they go, turning off from the main road to explore the veld, making detours to small villages with dusty streets and Dutch Reformed churches, police stations with limp flags in front, general dealers, garages. No detail escapes her. This specific petrol attendant in his army coat and balaclava. This old woman with a bundle of firewood or a paraffin tin balanced on her head. These chickens scrounging in a patchy garden. This rock-rabbit on its hill in the sun. This band of baboons in the Great River Pass. These black children, grey with dust, with their calabash bellies and knobbly knees and snotty noses in front of their hut. This hawk on its telegraph post. This hare squashed in the road.

And she hears the inaudible, all the innumerable sounds of the land. The screeching of a *kokkewiet* to which her father first made her listen. Chirping of swallows gathering on the electricity wires. (They, too, are preparing for a journey.) The clicking of guinea-fowl. A small group of hadedas with their screams of death. The bell of a black cyclist swerving out of their way. Children shouting as they wave, baring their white teeth in laughter.

The smell of dung or thornwood fires. Dust. Dog-piss bushes. Acrid Karoo shrubs. Bruised leaves. In the Eastern Cape, rain. Bitter aloes. Mealie stalks.

Tastes: thorn-tree gum. The *putu* porridge simmering in black three-legged pots. (In the very early morning, as they pass a row of labourers' cottages in a farmyard: a string of salted herrings, mouth-watering *bokkems*.) *Snoek*. Dried ribs. Lucerne leaves. Red earth.

She touches whatever they pass on their way, feels herself rubbing against everything. The grittiness of stone. Basalt and sandstone, ridges of lime. The brittleness of *gnarra* leaves.

122

Labourers' huts plastered with red clay. Dung floors. The worn wooden handle of a bucket. Wind in her hair. Specks of rain on the road to Queenstown.

All this she sees and hears and smells and tastes and feels: as every single thing, each separately, shouts out at her in the great silence: *Remember me! Remember me! I was here!*

In a little Free State *dorp* where they stop for petrol, while he is in a café next to the garage to buy them chips and tins of Coke, she watches a small girl with plaited hair coming past, a loaf under one thin arm, barefoot, sobbing. It shakes her. Why is the child crying? What has happened? There she's walking, not even aware that someone is looking at her. Not realizing that my image of this village will forever include her. I don't even know the name of the place. But I do know about this child, although half a minute ago I wasn't aware of her existence. As I sit looking at the crying girl, a police van drives past very slowly, obscuring my view for a few seconds; when it is gone, the child has disappeared. I shall never see her again. She may be killed in an accident this afternoon; perhaps scarlet fever will carry her off this winter; she may die in childbirth one day; in fifty years no one will remember her any more. Except I. I have seen her. Her existence has been burned into me.

And not hers alone. Each little shrub along this road, each blade of grass, each stone, each shadow, each drifting cloud, is known to me. I have become responsible for their existence, even though they are unaware of me. And if I do not remember them, dear God, if I don't absorb them into myself: who else will ever know that they've been here?

In taking leave from it, she draws the whole land towards her. The land itself, alive beyond its people and animals and shrubs and trees, beyond farms and villages and townships and cities: the land in its immobility and eternity, looming behind its many events. Now and then Brian says something, tells an anecdote, makes a remark. Do you know what happened at this spot? Expeditions. Frontier wars. Here the Xhosas died in the great famine following the prophesies of Nongqawuse.

123

Somewhere on these plains children picked up a bright stone that turned out to be a diamond. Here's the Big Hole where people from all over the world arrived like locusts to seek their fortunes. Here's the Witwatersrand which lured the *uitlanders*. Here Boers and British fought a battle; here women died in a concentration camp. All of them gone now. The land remains.

Something drives them on. They dare not stop anywhere to spend time together; not after what has happened. Only in Grahamstown, where he has a few academic friends, he manages to persuade her to spend the first night. She withdraws from the strangers: a gaunt man with a reddish bald head and bad breath; a plump woman with uncertain features, as if someone had tried to fashion something from a lump of clay and then abandoned it. The men sit talking shop all evening. Frontier Wars, causes of the Great Trek, relations between Black and White, the Afrikaners. She finds an excuse to go to bed early. It is still dark when they set out again. For another full day and night they continue, except for a few hours in the early evening spent in uncomfortable "rest" beside the road: he stays awake on the front seat while she sleeps in the rear; then they change places. Both are still sleepy when they drive off again. But she forces herself to stay awake throughout, exposed, suffering. Until at last they arrive at his friends' home in Johannesburg, where they collapse in their separate rooms, too exhausted to sleep.

And then the plane. So this, she thinks as they go through one control post after the other, this is the outcome and final goal of it all. So many aeons of blind evolution, of forging ahead in the dark, developing from amoeba, via countless forms of plant and animal life until *Homo sapiens* emerged: followed by thousands of years of civilization, spreading from the Nile Valley and Mesopotamia and China and India, to develop from savage to twentieth-century man, from troglodyte to inventor of satellites and projectiles; a thousand years in which the Khoi left their footprints in the dust of what had been inland seas; three hundred years of Whites. After disputes

124

and treaties, war and annexation, heroism and cowardice, this is where we are now. And what is — for us — the sum and summary of it all, the culmination of our brand of civilization? Not prosperity, happiness, fulfilment, not power or contentment, not war or peace, but only this: that he and I are forbidden to love one another; because he is white and I am brown. Driven out. Like victims of the Plague.

With the other passengers they walk out across the tarmac to the waiting plane with its blue-and-green lines on the tail. The ground is covered with asphalt, but below it she senses the earth, acknowledges it: one day, long after the present generation has passed away, grass may be growing here again, nourished by blood. This remains. Even after she has left, it will remain.

With one foot on the bottom step of the stairs she stops, suddenly unable to move, unable to persuade herself to lift the other foot from the ground. She looks back. The sunset is an obscene and bloody spectacle through the smoke of the city. Somebody behind her impatiently pushes against her. Hurry up, lady, you're holding us up.

I was here.

For the first time she realizes just how tired she is.

I stacked all the books and photocopies on the dressing-table and took only the film script in its dark red binding downstairs with me to the breakfast table.

The *patron* came out to serve me. Croissants, rolls, a bowl of chocolate. He seemed more subdued than the previous evening.

"What about your friend?" he asked as he took the small plate heaped with sugar cubes from his tray. "Isn't he coming down to breakfast?"

"He's not my friend. Just a colleague. I really don't know whether he's still asleep. And frankly, I don't care."

Light returned to his bedroom eyes. His whole drawn face changed; he even winked at me as he went away. Not that it

125

was much use to him: through the kitchen window, I noticed, his wife was keeping a very close watch.

Mandla only came down a quarter of an hour later.

"You didn't call me."

"Of course not."

Unasked, the *patron* brought his breakfast, including chocolate.

Mandla pushed it aside. "I'll have coffee."

The *patron* raised his arms and looked at me as if expecting me to intervene, but I just shrugged and began to page through my script, making no attempt to translate for them. They could muddle through on their own.

When the man finally left with a great show of frustration to fetch the coffee, Mandla said: "Why didn't you tell him he could stuff his bloody chocolate?"

"It was yours, not mine."

He changed his angle of attack: "What's that you're reading that's so fascinating you can't even talk?"

"Paul's script. I thought you'd recognize it."

He shrugged, pushing his chair back in irritation. Before he could return to the attack, the *patron* arrived with his coffee, making a point of spilling some in the saucer.

"Is it necessary," Mandla asked after the man had gone at last, "is it really necessary to waste so much time and money on making a film about some damn plague that happened thousands of years ago?"

"Hundreds."

"What's the difference?"

"Paul thinks he's got something important to say."

"Paul, Paul — !" He made an angry gesture with his arm, nearly knocking over the precious cup of coffee. "There he's lying in Paris between his fine sheets smelling his own arse. But you're *here*. What makes you go to all this trouble for a thing like that? Haven't you got more sense?"

"Mandla, if you really find Paul so awful, why don't you just drop him?"

He sneered. "What makes you think you'll understand?"

126

"Try me."

He broke off a chunk of bread and stuffed it in his mouth, staring straight at me without talking, chewing all the while, then washing it down with a large mouthful of coffee. Across the rim of the thick white cup his eyes never left me.

"Why don't you answer?" I said. "Because you're feeling guilty?"

He went on chewing very slowly, deliberately, staring at me, moving his eyes from my face down to my breasts. In an instinctive, protective gesture I raised my arm, then resisted the impulse to cover up; but I couldn't help hunching my shoulders just a bit. He put another piece of bread in his mouth, slowly raising his eyes back to my face.

"What were you doing in the garden so late last night?" I asked, trying to force him to answer.

He raised an eyebrow. "You were spying on me?"

My cheeks were stinging. I'd taken a false step, I realized. But now I was forced to fight back: "Playing the peeping Tom, were you? Did you think I'd leave my light on?"

"If I want to look at you, I'll do it openly," he said bitingly. "I don't spy." He took another mouthful of coffee, then filled up his cup again. "I'm not like you."

"Why are you pestering me like this?" I exploded.

"Perhaps, you'll see yourself one day like I'm seeing you, then you'll understand."

"How do you see me?"

"You're not safe."

"You take a lot for granted."

"One learns not to trust just anybody."

"You obviously had a good shock." I couldn't restrain my glee.

"Five months," he said suddenly, with unexpected vehemence, putting out his hand to take a roll from my basket. He broke it in two with a single deft jerk of his hands — a young dog playing with an old rag — and put one half in his mouth. "Five months," he repeated, his mouth full. "And wherever I went, the moment they heard where I came from

127

and why I was there with the anti-apartheid crowd, you should have seen them: all those girls just falling on their backs for me. In London. In Stockholm. In Amsterdam. So blonde, you'd think they'll break if you touch them. Properly begging me, I tell you: *Give it to me, baby.* Just so they could brag about it afterwards: *I fucked a freedom fighter.* You know what I did, every time? I'd pull out and let them lie there, thrashing and moaning, and I'd wank off all over their tits and faces. Take that! That's what I think of you randy white bitches." He pushed himself up on his arms, his muscles bulging; the table wobbled. "You think any one of them cared a fuck about me? Come again."

"Is this supposed to be an answer to my question?" I hit back, hard, and below the belt. "Or is it just your way of bragging?"

"You haven't asked a single question yet that deserved an answer."

"Well, what are you going to do now?" I asked sharply. "Now your little bubble's burst. Or are you planning to be a film star?"

"Fuck films. I thought Paul told you. I'm just diving under for a while. That bastard, George — if ever I lay hands on him! You heard the whole story? Came all the way with me. Pally-pally with the whole lot, knew everybody by their first names, introduced me to them, the works. I already had my bags packed to go to the airport, on my way home, when Jacques turned up. One of our French contacts. Told me George had been seen having a meal with one of the embassy people."

"It's an occupational hazard, isn't it? If you insist on doing this sort of work."

"You spend five bloody months with a guy. He's your passport, he's your dictionary, he's everything to you. He's just as black as you are. And then he goes and does a thing like that. They paid him. And he took it." He leaned forward on his massive arms, but he was looking right past me. "*He took it*, I tell you."

"And now you'll have to find a new toy," I said, more viciously than I'd meant to. His anger had upset me; but I'd be damned if I let on.

"Toy?" he stormed at me. "What are you trying to say, man?"

"Every man needs a toy. Have you never watched boys playing?"

"I'm serious, damn you!"

"Don't you think boys are serious too?"

He sat down again, glaring at me as if he couldn't make out whether I was talking shit or groping for the truth. With all his heavy, unformed violence he sat opposite me; and I suddenly found, to my dismay, that I had to suppress a ridiculous urge — dare I call it "maternal"? — to comfort him, this man so much bigger and stronger than I. Like one day, years earlier, when a gang of bigger boys had taken Boetie's soap-box cart and beaten him up when he'd tried to stop them; and when I heard about it I immediately ran to give them hell (Jesus, they would have killed me!), so that he had to give me a bloody nose to stop me from getting involved.

"What we doing today?" Mandla suddenly asked — not, I think, to change the subject and certainly not to make peace: it sounded more like an ultimatum than anything else.

"We're going to Avignon. I've got to check on a few of the rooms in the papal palace for the film, so Serge can start negotiating for permission."

"To Avignon?" he asked, stunned. "Then why didn't we stay there? Can't you use your fucking head?"

"I didn't want to stay there."

"Why not?"

"None of your business. Those walls oppress me. I prefer Saint-Rémy, it's much more open here. And I like the Alpilles. The mountains."

"I already *was* in Avignon, then you came to drag me off."

"Look here," I shouted at him, "for all I care, you could have stayed there. It's Paul who thought you'd shit in your pants or something if I didn't come to hold your hand. I hope

129

you don't think I like having you around."

"That makes two of us." He got up slowly, the lazy, ominous movement of a large predator; once again. "Let's go." He'd cut himself off totally now.

I closed the hard binding of the film script with a sharp clap, took my keys from my handbag and walked to the car, not bothering to see whether he was following me; but with the uncomfortable feeling that he might suddenly jump on me from behind.

As he got in, he noticed the torn French flag which was still lying crumpled on the back seat.

"Well, well," he sneered. "I didn't know you were so attached to the place that you carry its flag around with you. Do you fly it from your window at night? Or do you sleep under it?"

"I took it from a tramp," I said, realizing too late that this made it sound even worse.

Mandla slammed his door.

Neither of us felt like talking, which suited me. Almost mechanically I pushed a cassette into the recorder and turned up the sound. Reggae: Bob Marley. Surrendered myself to the irresistible rhythms, both sophisticated and very primitive. Only after a while I discovered that Mandla was also listening, drumming lightly with his fingertips on his knee to keep time. And as I had no intention whatsoever of pleasing him, I promptly ejected the cassette, clenching my teeth, and exchanged it for Mozart. One of the horn concertos.

He looked at me sharply, obviously annoyed. "What kind of shit is that?"

I leaned back, satisfied. "My kind of shit." (Witch!)

Neither of us spoke soon after that brief exchange. I kept my mind clear of thoughts, concentrating on the road, trying not to see anything on either side. It was bad enough that we were on our way back to Avignon. With Paul beside me I could endure the town. But something of my early shocks, with Brian, would always haunt me. Perhaps because it had been my very first experience of Europe: because we'd barely landed at Nice, after our sleepless night on the plane and the days of travelling through South Africa, when Brian had rushed me to the station to catch a train to Avignon, his favourite town.

They get off at the station and lug their two heavy suitcases (everything she possesses, everything she has dared to bring along, is crammed into her single bag) through the ugly building to the street outside. Opposite them are the city walls with their square towers, very obviously restored and rebuilt in places. It's the first time in her life she's seen anything like it (Carcassonne still lies ahead).

"I can't believe it, Brian," she says.

"Impressive, eh?"

"No. I find it a bit ridiculous, really. Those walls couldn't have kept out much."

"It was in the Middle Ages, remember," he says. "In those times they could keep out anything that threatened them."

"But why should people close themselves in like that?"

"If they hadn't, they would all have been killed. They didn't have much choice. And there was a lot they had to defend: the Pope and his whole court."

"Let's go and find a place to stay."

From a porter he gets directions to the Syndicat d'Initiative; and after working through the list of hotels and the assortment of pamphlets, they head for an address that seems likely to suit Brian's budget, staggering through the streets with the heavy luggage.

It turns out to be quite an attractive pension, just inside the city walls. And the wiry middle-aged lady who receives them (black dress, white pinafore, grey bun at the back of her head, half-moon spectacles) appears very cordial. Until, without any warning, she seems to change her mind about them.

"Two rooms?"

"No, only one," says Brian.

The thin lips are pressed together very firmly. "Sorry, I have no place for you."

"But Madame, you've just told us — "

131

"Please go," she says, her mouth puckered like an anus. "I don't put up people like you. This is a decent place."

The old, familiar, numbing terror taking hold of her. Surely it's not possible! They couldn't have come all these thousands of kilometres just to meet with the same rejection as before.

Even Brian, usually keen to avoid a fuss, is clearly so taken aback that he cannot keep his cool. "Madame," he says, his voice trembling with anger, "do you realize we've come all the way from South Africa? And now you tell us — "

"I don't care where you come from," says the tough little vixen. "You're not married and I'm not going to let you share a room."

Still half dazed, they go down the narrow stairs. It's only when they reach the street again, in the bright May sunshine, that they start laughing. First Brian, then Andrea (she takes longer to shake off the numbness). Putting down the heavy bags on the pavement, he leans against the front wall of the building, howling with laughter.

"And I thought — " she says, "I thought it was because of *me*. I thought — "

"We'll drink to her health tonight," he says, wiping away the tears. "Don't ever underestimate the free French. It's obvious that there are still many Protestants around here in the South."

"Now we still don't have a place to stay," Andrea reminds him.

"There are several more possibilities on this list. But they're all outside the walls."

"Suits me," she says, bracing herself to pick up the dark brown suitcase again.

Only a few kilometres from Saint-Rémy, where the landscape begins to open up, we passed a cyclist, a man in a blue T-shirt, with a yellow line down the side of his shorts and a number on his back. Blue cap almost covering his eyes. His whole body leaning forward, tail up, sinewy legs pedalling like mad. I couldn't help chuckling. Because in July, when I'd been there with Paul, we'd come across a cyclist just like that on every single one of our drives, riding as if he had death itself breathing down his neck. We hadn't caught on immediately: it must have been a week or so before Paul suddenly said: "Darling, haven't we seen this bloke before?" And again the following day. Then we started noticing. It couldn't have been the same man all the time, obviously not. But to us he was the same. And Paul, ever ready to turn anything into a story, began to give his imagination free rein. "You know, Andrea, if ever I have a chance to write a comedy, this will be it." — "What on earth can you do with a guy like that?" — "There's no end to what I can do." And then he started spinning it out: a cyclist from the Tour de France who gets lost from the crowd one day in a heavy fog in the mountains, the Mont Ventoux or somewhere, and then starts pedalling like hell, like some kind of Flying Dutchman, in search of his team. Over all the hills and dales of France he pedals on frantically, but everywhere he comes, he finds that the Tour has passed by already; and then he's off again. In due course he rides right out of time and space, through the centuries, one mad chase, no longer with any tangible destination, just for the sake of riding, just to keep going. Paul turned it into a wonderfully complicated story, adding to it every day, devising a history and a family and a career for his cyclist, thinking up all kinds of twists and turns and climaxes. Why did it come back to me now? Just because that madman had become such a feature of our summer trip? All I know is that, on the morning Mandla and I drove to Avignon, the cyclist came as a curious relief: an object to focus on, a person on whom I could concentrate all my anger, a lightning conductor. At the same time there was something reassuring about his presence: if he was still around, hurrying on towards God knows what appointment — with a team? an organizing committee? a winning line? himself? — it meant that I still had some grip on the summer, on Paul, on the reason for being there myself that day.

Not that the thought of Paul was much comfort. As I drove

on, I could feel the resentment against him building up steadily. He should have known better. He could have saved me from this. (He could have saved us both!) If I, and my decision, were really so important to him —

It confirmed my loneliness. But even that was not just painful: there is reassurance in the discovery that one *can* make it alone. And like so often when this thought got hold of me, I struck up a conversation in my mind (if Mandla hadn't been there I would have spoken aloud) — with a man I'd never known, a man long dead, yet more real to me than many of my friends. Because in my thoughts he'd gradually become mixed up with Dedda? Or because he filled such a primitive need in me: a kindly spirit for moments of faith, hope, and love; an evil one for a bad conscience; a lover for the nights without a man? Xhorê, my ancestor, whom I'd come to know so late in my life, through Brian.

— *Grandpa Xhorê, today you got to help me, they're* sukkeling *with me again.*

— *So what's the matter, Nanna?*

— *I got a right to be alone for a change, haven't I? These menfolk, all mucking about looking for history, why can't they let me be? I'm happy to stay out of it. I don't want to get mixed up in it.*

— *History turned its backside to me too, you know. One can't always choose it to be the way you want.*

In the year 1613 (right, Brian?), in May or thereabouts, the captain of the English ship the *Hector* took on board two men of the Khoikhoi at the Cape. Nobody is quite sure how he managed to persuade them. Did he use force? Made them drunk? Lured them on board with copper wire and beads and, undoubtedly, tobacco? Whatever happened, by the time the two came to their senses again, Table Mountain was disappearing in the distance, its dark head morosely covered in its turban of fog. One of the two died very soon, "out of pure spite", the English said. The other one endured. That was my old Grandpa Xhorê. For six months they kept him in London, in the home of, as far as I remember, the Governor of the East

134

India Company, treating him like a tamed monkey, with a copper chain round his neck, and buckles everywhere, and the smartest clothes, feathers in his hat and all; taught him to speak English too. But Xhorê was as headstrong as any mule. Instead of appreciating what they were doing for him, he would just lie on the floor day after day, moaning in his broken English: "Xhorê home go, Cape go, home go." In the end his good masters got so sick of it they put him on a boat back to Cape Town. And no sooner had he set foot on his own shore, than he tore off all his new clothes and copper orna-ments and changed back into his old sheepskin *kaross*, and his prick quiver, and hung his customary dried guts around his neck, and rubbed *buchu* and sheep's fat into his body, and ran off. Like a dog returned to his vomit, the English said, and a swine to his wallowing in the mire (II Peter 2: 22).

So ungrateful! The first thing he did was to warn his whole tribe that copper was dirt cheap in England, so they had to watch out for visiting sailors and merchants, offering to barter their sheep in future. That was gratitude for you.

But a strange thing happened: the English had hardly set sail again, when Xhorê started longing back. From time to time he would put on his copper armour and parade before his people; and he tried to furbish his house like an Englishman's. All they did was to laugh at him. He didn't seem to belong anywhere any more. And the end was predictable, I suppose. One day a Dutch ship weighed anchor in the bay, there was an argument between them and Xhorê's people, he wasn't treated with the respect he felt he deserved, and so he refused to supply them with the fresh provisions they demanded. Right there on the beach they hanged him: the Dutch didn't take kindly to a cheeky *hotnot*. And ever since Brian first told me the sorry tale, one thought kept niggling me: when they'd finally hanged him, had he been wearing his copper armour, or his skins, or both? It would have made a difference to know for sure.

You should never have gone back, Grandpa Xhorê. (Rather stayed on your precious English carpet crying your heart out?)

135

Brian always used the story as the introduction to a new tirade about exploitation. It surprised him that I just wanted to find out more about Xhorê himself. (How old was he? was he married? did he have any children? where did his tribe live, or did they migrate with the seasons? was there really nothing more written about his stay in London?) "It's not really important, Andrea. All that matters is the incident, the case history. A classical demonstration of culture conflict. We know nothing about the man — nor do we need to."

"I have to know. What if he really was my ancestor?"

"That would be pretty far-fetched. I was just joking."

"To me he's just as important as Sir Francis Drake is to you." He used to derive so much perverse pleasure from telling me how he'd traced Sir Francis hidden somewhere behind an unofficial branch of his family tree. That was why the Cape had such an attraction for him, he would joke, this most stately thing, the fairest Cape in the whole circumference of the earth, etcetera. Perversity, I said, because Brian himself was very much working-class, and proud of it; he'd "worked himself up", his father had been a plumber. His mother had had a better education and was a teacher. There was nothing he was quite so vitriolic about as the British class system; but when he'd drunk too much — which was his weakness — he regularly held forth about his one ambition, to become a don at Oxford. Oh well.

I loved Brian. Else I wouldn't have allowed him what I did. Perhaps, if I were to meet him again now, I would feel the same soft spot for him (only, I would know better than to yield to it): Brian with his thin body and angular cheekbones, the light in his eyes, his jacket sleeves always too short, his long hands: I was fascinated by his hands, the nails bitten to the quick, the prominent knuckles, the bluish veins on the back. He looked the way I would imagine a medieval monk, just as hard and thin, with that fierce look in the dark eyes set in his very pale face; and I was in love with his voice, so much deeper than one would expect from a man with his frail appearance. Perhaps that was what first made him notice me:

136

the way I could listen to him for hours. I was so hungry for everything he could introduce me to. History, his passion for facts, his crusades for great causes. His love of music. Mozart. He made me read, he made me listen to records right through the night. And the way he had of moving from an intense discussion or a long session of music straight into making love. Meeting him, one would never expect such an erudite, "abstract", ascetic man to be so passionately involved with the physical.

The wonder of his body when he took me. The extremes in him, also in his lovemaking: tenderness enough to make me cry; and then that violence, that savage fury with which he could devastate me, splitting me, impaling me. A demon inside him, something that just had to spend itself. Which was exactly what happened later: as if the body were too frail for the fire consuming it. An unbelievably destructive urge, as if he could murder me with love. But in the end, I think, it was himself he destroyed.

At the Cape I'd only glimpsed the edges of it, suspecting very little of how far, how deep, it really went. But what happened to us seemed to remove the lid. For a while he could still control it. On our long journey through the land, after it was all over, he hardly ever spoke, just sat beside me very pale and tense, smoking and smoking. But here in Provence it broke out.

In the years to follow she will not remember many particulars of the journey with Brian and most of her memories will blur together in water-images. Behind the tourist attractions on their journey runs the constant undercurrent of "their" lives, private and painful, which they prefer not to discuss, intuitively scared of what may be brought to light. They wander through the unseasonal, excessive heat of early summer, exploring castles and cathedrals, walls and ruins: drink pastis on café terraces in the shade of plane- and mulberry- and chestnut-trees, study inscriptions on tombstones in windblown

137

graveyards surrounded by black cypresses: often skip lunch in the afternoon the better to indulge in the joys of southern gastronomy in the evenings — pâté, crevettes, aïoli, bouilla-baisse, ratatouille, stuffed tomatoes, lamb in thyme or rose-mary, cassoulet, veal in mustard sauce, fillet in cherry vin-egar, fruit in armagnac. (Only sometimes, without warning, she shocks him with violent, vulgar cravings for hamburgers, for chips with loads of tomato sauce. Many years later, even after she has met Paul, she will still occasionally yield to these urges for forms of food he finds revolting.) They spend their days in ancient towns with Roman ruins — arenas, temples, aqueducts, theatres — and remains of the wars of religion. But behind it all, untouched by what occurs on the surface, exists a precarious "we" conscious of an equally precarious "ours".

Brief moments. Something she will only try to define long after it has happened: she's sitting on a terrace watching him choose postcards from a swivelling stand outside a news agency. A lock of hair over his eyes, as usual. The thin freckled arms, peeling from too much sun. The pale blue shirt which she washed the previous evening. And the sudden discovery: There you are, my life is linked with yours, yet what do I know about you? As you're standing there, at this moment, I don't even know what it feels like for you to be standing there. (And the converse is just as easy to imagine: Brian leaving their room early one morning, returning with milk and bread and cheese to find her still asleep, which allows him undisturbedly to gaze at her: one elbow thrown across her forehead; the sensitive, slightly lighter hue of the skin on the inside of her arm; something like a flush darkening her cheeks; the curve of her shoulders; the eyes closed; the sheet which has fallen away from her, leaving the small high breasts exposed; the almond colour of her skin. Everything so intimately known to him, yet so remote in her sleep, so wholly strange, unknowable; making him feel an intruder into her privacy simply through being there.)

One of the few occasions when the ridges of their private

existence emerge above the surface of their days, occurs in Montbrun, the small brown village on its hill on the far side of the Mont Ventoux. As if a tide has receded suddenly, leaving the submerged rocks exposed. It takes something very banal for it to happen. (Admittedly, there's been an earlier warning in Roussillon.) They are spending a few days in a hotel on the outskirts of the village, set among large shady trees surrounded by lavender fields and plains sprinkled with red poppies. A small dark room, with cold water only, and water-pipes which start humming and throbbing at odd hours, which gives them the feeling of living inside a huge church organ. But to them it is "home", a small space into which they can withdraw at night after each exposure to a sweltering day. Then, one morning as they come out for breakfast, the old widow in black who runs the place, awaits them in the passage with a summary instruction to pack up and go, as the room has been rented to other guests.

"But Madame!" says Brian. "You said we could stay for a week."

"Sorry, the room was booked long ago," says the old crow, her voice leaving no doubt about the finality of her decision.

Livid, yet containing his anger, he goes back to the room. Andrea follows him as far as the door.

"What are we going to do now?" she demands.

"No choice. We'll just have to shake the dust of this bloody place from our feet."

"Do you think it's because of me?"

"For heaven's sake, don't always bring that up," he says, annoyed. "This is Europe, not South Africa."

Her dark eyes are smouldering, but she controls herself. "What other reason can she have?"

"She probably found people who are willing to pay for full board. We're only taking bed and breakfast, you know. She's obviously a penny-pincher."

"Are you going to let her have her way?"

"You don't want me to make a scene in a hotel passage, do you? One has one's dignity."

139

"What dignity will you have if you just give in to the old bag?"

"Andrea." He sighs. "If one has to have a fight about something, at least make sure it's worth while. Not over any bagatelle."

"You call it a bagatelle for us to be thrown out like two lepers?"

"Oh, come on — "

"Aren't you going to answer me?"

"Why don't you start packing, then we can clear out."

"You can bloody well do the packing yourself." She goes out in a huff. The old woman is still hovering in the passage, no doubt to make sure they won't slip out without paying. "Bloody old cow!" Andrea snarls at her, in Afrikaans.

She goes outside to wait for Brian, settling on the steps at the front door, keeping her back very rigid.

After a long time he emerges, struggling with their bags and an assortment of loose things draped over his shoulders; one glance tells her that he is in a foul mood. Behind him she notices the old *patronne*, muttering half audibly to herself.

"So where are we going now?" asks Andrea, not getting up yet.

"I don't know. Perhaps another hotel up in the village."

She makes no attempt to give him a hand, but marches off ahead of him, leaving him to lug the heavy baggage up the steep incline.

Fortunately, as it turns out, there is another place to stay, high up on the hillside. The Hôtel des Voyageurs. It has clearly seen better days, the paint is peeling, the sign at the front door faded; but the people seem warm and friendly, and it is cheaper than their hotel down in the valley. Not that this makes much difference to their mood. She follows him upstairs to a large grey room, where she unpacks their bags in silence while he sits down at a rickety little escritoire and starts writing furiously.

"What are you writing?" she asks after some time.

140

"A letter to the old witch. To tell her what I think of her manners."

"You're very brave," she says.

He flares up. "What do you mean?"

"Why couldn't you say so to her face?"

"It'll have more effect this way."

"Oh really?"

"Andrea, why don't you just leave this to me?"

She gasps in anger. Without even trying to say anything, she stalks out of the room, down the stairs, through the narrow streets, right out of the village. Over the sharp ridge of the hill covered in green grass and red poppies, past the hollow walls of the half-restored old castle on the summit, and down the other side. Only when, much later, there is a violent roll of thunder does she discover how far she has strayed. The whole sky is covered in clouds. Before she has covered a hundred yards of the long way back, the storm breaks out over her.

Her first impulse is to start running, back to the village on its distant hill; but soon she realizes that it's useless. Whatever she does, she will be drenched by the time she gets there. The rage begins to ebb from her, giving way to a different kind of liquid fire burning in her blood, an exuberant joy about the rain that penetrates her clothes, causing her jeans and blouse to cling to her, plastering her hair against her cheeks and forehead, running abundantly into her mouth. Throwing her head back, she swallows the rain, standing like that for minutes on end, until she feels quite dizzy. At last she begins to walk on again, very slowly now, as if trying with each step to spread roots into the soggy earth. After what seems like hours, soaked to the skin, she reaches the hotel entrance, where she makes an unsuccessful effort to shake the worst wetness from her before taking off her shoes to run upstairs.

"What on earth has happened?" Brian asks, dismayed, when he sees her. "Look at you!"

"I'm wet, I'm absolutely drenched. It's wonderful." But her teeth are chattering from the cold. She struggles to undo her buttons and take off her clinging clothes to rub herself with a

141

skimpy, threadbare hotel towel until her whole body is glowing. Without more ado, she crawls into the big bed, naked.

"Aren't you coming to warm me?" she asks provocatively, then watches him undress. His angular body, like a monk's; with the erection that has never ceased to amaze her because it seems so extravagant compared to the rest of him. All his pent-up aggressiveness he vents on her, while outside it rains and rains; later the ceiling starts leaking, dripping right on their bed, so that he is forced to jump out and open an umbrella over them.

"That means ten years' bad luck," she says, laughing. "That's what my Ma used to say. But rather this than getting soaked again. Come, hold me."

Later, while he sleeps, the weather clearing up outside, she sits up in the bed, the ridiculous red umbrella still open overhead, an obtrusive flower blooming in the drab grey room: she stares at his sleeping face, the somewhat spoilt mouth and the angry lines beside it smoothed in rest. How easy it is for him, she thinks. For him everything is fine again. I've opened my legs for him, I've groaned under his attack, and he is satisfied. But I — ? However little has been said between us today, something which has been threatening us for a long time (Avignon; Roussillon . . .) has finally shown itself and has been acknowledged. An animal has bared its teeth to us.

The worst is that, for that very reason, she feels a greater need of him than ever. It may be provisional only. But there is an urgency and a violence in it which upsets her more deeply than before.

When they go outside in the late afternoon, enjoying the spectacle of the drenched world shimmering in the last sunlight, they discover a circus which must have arrived in the rain; a tent is being pitched on the muddy square behind the hotel. Men with bare torsos are driving iron pegs into the soggy ground. On one side is a row of cages, surrounded by a horde of village children pestering the animals. A single lion with tufty mane and a toothless mouth, its haunches patchy with a

142

skin disease, lies motionless on its pungent damp straw, staring in total apathy at the gang of jeering children who are pelting it with twigs and stones: no hint of majesty in the great head, only a terrible weariness, an expression of blank amazement in its yellow eyes. (Where in Africa did they find him? Would he still remember anything at all? How long ago has he given up resisting?) A skinny jackal. A scabby wolf with one wounded eye swarming with flies and bluebottles. Two timid monkeys, their thumbs chopped off, poking their maimed little hands through the mesh of their cage like tiny beggars. One of the boys has got hold of a spiky length of wire with which he pokes them in the ribs to provoke a reaction; when he jabs too hard, they utter small whimpering sounds, but that is all. A wild boar on its knees in a small enclosure, digging for truffles among the turds and tufts of wet straw.

"Shall we come and look tonight?"

"Shit," she says. "Let's go."

And that is the end of the brief let-up in their day. That night, after dinner, and after she has once again submitted to the vicious affirmation of his manhood, she has to press a hand to her mouth and bite into the palm not to cry out, not to vomit. Not because of him — dear God, what does she have in the world beside him? if he were to leave her here, what would become of her? she cannot even speak the language — but because of everything she can no longer control. Because of herself, forced to lie there spreadeagled under him in a strange bed. Because of the day's sun and rain. Everything forever lost: two old people shuffling in a room next door, the clang of a chamber pot; her mother's hairbrush; her brooding brother; her dead father; a long-lost Xhorê grovelling on an English carpet.

Long after the din of the circus has died away, after Brian has contentedly drifted off into sleep, in the dark night where nothing stirs any more, she suddenly hears, very close by, the deep throaty groan, a sound which she has never heard before in her life but which she recognizes without fail. Not a roar; the old lion is much too far gone for that. Just a groan. But in that groan such awful futile power that it draws tears from her. Africa, Africa!

Unremitting tourism. After that experience we never stayed in one place for too long again. One learns. *Keep on moving, don't ever stop, or you'll be overtaken.* A series of small, cheap, stuffy rooms in the too-early heat of the South; sometimes rain or the Mistral forced us to stay indoors, cornered in our cages, leaving us only one desperate way out. Except that I grew very skilled in the art of avoiding Brian's overtures — without making it too obvious, of course, as I didn't want to wound him unnecessarily. Through his aggressiveness and his increasing recourse to drink, I could see his own helplessness. He found it just as impossible to cope as I did; his expectations had been thwarted as much as my own. It made me panic. If I couldn't depend on him, who else was there?

Hence the unremitting element in our days. Leaving no stone unturned, visiting every museum or church on our way as if our lives depended on the accumulation of irrelevant new knowledge. And Brian was never content with superficiality. Every available historical fact had to be dug up, even if it cost hours of sweating in obscure village libraries or Syndicats d'Initiative. To *know*, to find out. In which year this ruin had originally been built, when it had been restored, what notable events had taken place in it. I could scream in frustration: but for the sake of keeping more or less intact what little we had left, I also threw myself on facts and objects. Town after town was "done" by us; and evenings he would spend more hours to make notes of what the day had brought to light. (Had I taken my cue from him?)

Roughly in the middle of our trip, when we were in Saint-Rémy, my period was supposed to start. But it stayed away. (I wasn't on the Pill yet and had to rely on foam, since Brian couldn't stand rubbers.) At first I didn't tell him, just counted the days while I rebuffed his amorous attempts more and more brusquely, which made him tenser and more intractable than ever. When I was eight days overdue, just after we'd reached

144

Aix, I finally told him. He reacted very impulsively:

"Then we'd better go to London as soon as possible so that you can have something done about it."

The worst thing I myself could think of right then was a baby; but his reaction made me wild. "Don't you want my child then?"

"But we can't cope with a family right now, Andrea."

"In South Africa you couldn't stop talking about the sons and daughters we would have."

"Later, Andrea. Once we're settled in. As soon as we've had time to sort things out. Not now." Adding, with almost pathetic eagerness: "Are you quite sure?"

"I can count." I drew a deep breath to keep calm. "But I suppose there are doctors in Aix too."

"Yes, but — " He checked himself. "Andrea, please don't misunderstand me. Good heavens, I love you. Why do you think I brought you with me all the way? It's *you* I'm thinking of — "

"That's not the impression I got just now."

He came towards me and gently pressed his palm against my stomach. I drew back as if a snake had bitten me. "Don't touch me! If you want to do something for me, then go find a doctor. But keep your hands off me."

He was ready to snarl back at me, I could see that; but thank God he didn't. That same afternoon he took me to a doctor. Because I couldn't understand French, Brian had to stay with me all through the examination. I'd always thought I'd love to have him with me if I gave birth one day, but this examination was different. Only once before in my life had I felt so humiliated: that night in the rooms of the District Surgeon in Cape Town. No matter how well I knew Brian, how many times I'd put my body at his disposal — and he was such an intrepid explorer! there was no nook or cranny he didn't know intimately — I couldn't bear lying there like that, stripped from the waist down, knees drawn up for the doctor to peer at me and poke his gloved fingers into me, while Brian tried to translate as clinically as he could.

145

It turned out to be a false alarm. Two days later my period began, a regular flood that simply went on and on as if to wash my very womb from my body, every last hint of what might have been a child or seed of Brian.

Strange — or wasn't it? — that throughout that week he was closer to me than even in the first days of our love, more attentive, more considerate, ever so gentle. (And God, I did love him!) He allowed me, almost forced me, to stay in bed late in the mornings. Brought me fresh fruit. Planned our route in such a way that it would not be too tiring. Small attentions which made me love him and loathe him in turn. I wasn't sick, for God's sake! There was nothing wrong with me. Unless my very femininity was an affliction.

It was a time when I became more vulnerable to the landscape as well. Previously it had been no more than the intermittent space between one town and another. Now, perhaps because we found ourselves in the Rhône valley and among the Alpilles, I became enthralled by the earth itself. When we travelled by bus, I would insist on getting off at every village; if we hiked, I would ask the driver to stop after a mere kilometre or two, often to Brian's great embarrassment. I simply had to get out into the open, to wander about, to sit on a stone or lie in the grass, to stare at everything, to listen to the insects in the shrubs, to smell, to breathe. In an inexplicable way I felt at home there. The landscape was so like the Boland, so familiar, as if I'd grown up in it. The colours of vineyards and wheatfields and mountains, the ploughed soil. The signs of irresistible fertility in the earth, in spite of the harshness of the landscape: nothing gentle or superfluous, everything essential, male, muscled, bony, tough.

At the same time it was different from the landscapes back home. The sound of the cicadas was different. The light was different, more fluid, like honey. But the difference went beyond that. Even now I can only be very tentative about it: a feeling, perhaps, of something so ancient about the earth at home that human beings still seemed irrelevant, accidental. On that journey through the land with Dedda — the silence of the Karoo, a silence of total innocence — we were an almost obscene intrusion in that arid world. Here in Provence I was just as conscious of primitive earth, except that here the sense of age derived from man's experience of it. The signs were everywhere — Ligurian, Celtic, Phoenician, Greek, Roman, Gothic, Frank: Brian dutifully explained the lot to me — the traces of our own antiquity. Here people had not just co-existed with the earth but rooted themselves right into it. The very faces and bodies of the peasants resembled stone, weatherbeaten olive-wood, flint and grit. (Perhaps the Khoikhoi had been like that, those men-of-men to whom old Xhorê had belonged. "My" people? But they'd all died. They'd been exterminated from the world. And those who came after them were still strangers to the land.)

Sometimes, when we were in the veld like that, people would come past. An old man on his bicycle. A young farmer on his tractor. A couple of women working on the land. Invariably they would greet us cheerfully, stop to exchange a few words with Brian. Then I had to keep in the background, of course, as I didn't understand a word of their tongue. And in the long run this was what most upset me: it confirmed to me that it wasn't my land at all; I remained excluded, branded as a foreigner. Before I could hope to regain a sense of "belonging" I would have to learn the language.

As soon as we got to London and settled down —

This urge, too, began to drive us on. This, and everything happening underwater between Brian and me. More and more, once we'd found a place to stay in a new village — all those similar, oppressive little cubbyholes — we'd set out on separate walks: he invariably in search of historical buildings, I heading for the veld beyond the houses of the town, the sensuous certainties of stone and red poppies. When we got back to the room our lovemaking would be more savage than before, furious couplings in dingy little hothouses, as if to prove in the marks left by teeth and nails that we still had a hold on something more and more elusive, a more innocent happiness.

147

Innocent! But everything in the early days of our love, back in South Africa, had branded us as guilty. And yet there had indeed been this wild innocence about it, at least in retrospect. Now it was changing. We were two raindrops on the windscreen of a moving car, driven together by the wind, trembling but together; the moment the speed decreased, they would flow apart in separate tears. Only by moving, by desperately accelerating, was the violence created which could keep them together.

"Why did you bring me to Provence?" I sometimes asked him. "Why here?"

"I thought we would be happy here."

"But why here, Brian, and not somewhere else?"

"Because it's so far away from everything. It's like an island. Nobody expects or demands anything from us."

"Will we always be on the run like this?"

"We're not on the run, for Christ's sake!" Then he would pour himself another drink — he had developed a habit of bringing bottles back to the room — before repeating very emphatically: "Of course we're not on the run. Hell, we're just taking time off to find our feet again. A brief rest before we go to London and get on with our life together."

"You have a strange idea of taking a rest."

"Andrea — " Through the alcohol the pain in his eyes was very naked. "We're happy here, aren't we? Tell me you're happy."

Sometimes I obeyed, for his sake, even though despising myself for it. Sometimes it was for my own sake too, because I didn't know what I should have to face if I denied it. On very few occasions did I have the nerve to go on nagging him:

"Why *did* you bring me here, Brian? What is it in Provence that draws you to it so strongly?"

"Because I know it. Because I've been here before. Because I've been happy here before."

"On your own?"

"Why do you ask? Of course I was on my own."

"You sure you were on your own? Every time."

148

One evening, near the end of our journey (although we were still unaware of it), back in Avignon, I managed to drive him far enough: because this time my own despair was deep enough to force him over the threshold of himself. Or perhaps it happened simply because he'd had even more to drink than usual.

A calamitous day, from the outset. All night a terrible quarrel between the *patron* of the pension and his wife has kept them awake until the small hours (voices shouting and cursing, bottles breaking, furniture knocked over, like some nights when her father was home, especially if the old people tried to intervene); and when she gets up that morning she finds the toilet blocked. When she goes to complain about it — Brian is too immersed in his pamphlets and brochures, preparing for a new excursion — the *patron*, sporting a black eye and red scratches all over his face, immediately becomes aggressive; all the more so because he has to speak English to her: "You womans always put the bad stuff down the cistern, yes? You not read the notice on the door. Then you ask *me* to fix it!" — And when they finally set out on their excursion, through the nearest gate into the city, away from the main thoroughfares to the smaller, more "colourful" district below the papal palace, they are overwhelmed by the sordid, noisy life of the back streets. Old women in black shawls installed in front of their houses, crocheting or sewing; a sturdy young woman squatting on her doorstep, cutting her toenails; small boys screaming and running about or scrambling up broken walls; dogs crapping in the street. In yet more remote corners they come across dark-skinned gypsies — sly-eyed men; women aged before their time, draped in garish rags; incomparably beautiful half-naked children — skulking like barely tamed animals in portals and corners, biding their time to dart out like rats to beg from passers-by. If one happens to pass in a group, they duck out of the way; if you're on your own or one of a couple they swarm all over you. Upset and depressed by them, Andrea urges Brian to take her away from there, and

149

they make their escape from the oppressive stench and darkness of the back alleys to the openness beyond the walls, on the banks of the river. But there something even worse happens, when a gypsy in the shadow of the wall loses his temper with his wife and attacks her, dragging her from behind a row of rubbish bins to start thrashing her with the buckle end of his broad, studded belt. Gasping from shock, Andrea screams at the man to stop, but he pays no attention. She grabs Brian by the arm: "Stop him, for God's sake! Stop him, he'll kill her."

"It's no use trying to interfere with these people, Andrea."

"Would you rather write him a letter afterwards?" she snarls at him. Without waiting for an answer she rushes towards the gypsies and tries to pull the woman away from the man. The only reward for her trouble is a blow from the belt on the side of her face. Stunned, she reels back. Before she can catch her breath again, the gypsy woman turns on her with her long nails. Frantically trying to duck away, she catches sight of Brian approaching gingerly, shouting at them to stop. In his voice she recognizes not only anger, but fear. She fully expects the gypsy to have a go at Brian, but to her amazement she sees him recoil. In cringing servility, the habit of generations and centuries, the dark man cowers before the European, although there is no mistaking the hatred gleaming in his eyes.

"Come," says Brian, pulling her away with him.

From a distance she looks back and sees the gypsy once again raising his arm with the heavy belt, and the woman shrinking into a wretched bundle at his feet to await the blows.

Overcome by rage and hopelessness, Andrea bursts into tears.

"That's what you get for your trouble," says Brian, still panting from the effort and with shock. "You won't eradicate evil from the world like this. Don't you understand?" Almost fearful he brings his fingertips to the oozing wound on her cheek.

"No," she sobs, slapping his hand away. "And I swear to God I don't *want* to understand either."

150

"Come on, now. Please." Dumbly, he tries to comfort her with an arm round her shoulders, but she shakes it off.

Afterwards (it will take her mind off the experience, he assures her) there is the interminable journey through the palace of the popes, caught in a throng of jostling, sweating English tourists; a few times Andrea feels almost overcome by claustrophobia, but no escape is possible. With the best of intentions Brian is clutching her very firmly to his side. Once inside, one cannot turn back: the only way is right ahead, at a pace determined by the flock of sheep they're caught in, accompanied by the drone of the guide's voice, his quips and jokes as worn as old shoes. She gives up trying to resist, surrendering herself to the headache throbbing behind her eyes as they shuffle along from one room to the next, some bare and lifeless, inhuman, uninhabitable; others with the remains of wall paintings and the depressing signs of past splendour, now peeled and irrelevant, conveying absolutely nothing to her.

Lunch is yet another disaster. The food they are served is not what they have ordered (it's at a cheap restaurant terrace on the place de l'Horloge) and when, in spite of Brian's attempts to avoid a scene, Andrea makes a fuss about it, the waiter turns nasty and begins pointedly to ignore them, so that it is past three before they can set out again. Brian is adamant: they must cross the river to the Fort Saint-André even if it gives them blisters on their feet. All she wants is to be left alone; but after what has already happened he regards neither the town nor the pension as safe for her on her own. So she has no choice but to go with him.

That night he very steadily and deliberately drinks himself into a near-stupor.

"You must be mad," she says at last, making no attempt to hide the bitterness in her. "Don't tell me you're enjoying it — whatever you may have found in Provence before." She pauses for a moment, then pounces. "You weren't alone, were you?"

"Why are you asking me that again?"

151

"Because I don't believe you. You had someone with you, didn't you?"

"Oh, Christ — " Like fish in murky water his swollen eyes stare at her through his glasses. "All right, then. I had someone with me. A woman."

"You could have told me earlier, Brian."

"I didn't want to hurt you."

"Was she really so important to you then?"

"Every time one thinks it's important." It lashes her like the gypsy's belt.

"And every time you are mistaken — ?"

"That's not what I said."

"But it's what you're thinking."

"Andrea, what the hell is up with you?"

"I don't know. And that's the truth." She moves her glass, half empty, away from her. "I just don't know at all. Only you can tell me. And you don't want to. All you can do is to make me feel second-hand."

And now I had returned to Provence. This time on my own; in July with Paul. How come we all return so constantly to the graveyards of our past loves? To try to undo what had happened, what had destroyed the first innocence?

My God, I couldn't claim innocence, not even when it had first begun.

And yet we'd tried. We'd tried so hard, so terribly courageously, each for the other's sake; but each for himself, herself, as well. Keeping up at least the pretence of wholeness until at last, after Carcassonne, we'd set off for London. Only after the end of that summer had I dared to admit the falseness of it — and then not because of something that had happened to Brian or myself, but through an insignificant little report in a Sunday newspaper. Two children in Provence, a boy and a girl, had caught a cicada and set its wings alight. With no bad intentions; just because. Because they were children, because the cicada had been there. And then they'd let it loose with its little wings aflame to see what would happen. It landed in a

152

wheatfield, which caught fire — it was just a week before the harvest — and thousands of hectares of fields and forests were burned down.

Destructive memories. Made possible — no, unavoidable — by this return to Avignon; by Mandla's presence next to me; by my resentment against Paul. Hence the curious impression, as we drew closer and closer to the lovely town about which I still felt so apprehensive and ill at ease, that these were not "memories" at all coming back to me across the space of years, not evasions or day-dreams, but something happening to me *now*, at *this* moment, part of *this* day's passions and revolt: extensions and additions, a necessary supplement.

"If you and Paul want to muck around with this thing, it's your own business," said Mandla. "But don't try to draw me into it. It's not my scene."

We were in the high gardens of the papal palace. I'd left the car in the underground garage on the square in front of the fortress and took the steep zigzag road up the hill, ostensibly to give him an idea of the lay of the land, but mainly because I hoped the view would ease my own feelings about Avignon: it *is* a beautiful place. The fascinating panorama of terracotta roofs and chimney pots, the grey and ochre walls, the matt surface of the swiftly flowing Rhône below, the colossal palace directly underneath, dominated by the tall white statue of the Virgin. And, from the belvedere, the undulations of the Provençal landscape. To the north, the crags and folds of Montmirail and, more to the right, the high bald summit of the Mont Ventoux; further to the east, the mountains of the Vaucluse and the Luberon. And then, but obscured by mist that morning, the Camargue and les Saintes-Maries-de-la-Mer (the sea: inescapably, miraculously, always the sea); further away, Marseille. Where the Plague had begun in the fourteenth century. And in the eighteenth. Brought there, time and time again, from the high seas by merchants and sailors from distant lands: every time they would plant their black

153

seed on the coast, leaving it to spread inland throughout the whole known world.

We walked through the high cool gardens, drank Coke on the terrace beside the pond where enormous indolent fish poked their heads from the water to be fed; then passed the swans on the steep stone staircase to the very top. Depositing Paul's script and my pile of books on the wall to give my arm a rest, I briefly — and coolly — explained to Mandla what we were supposed to do.

"Do what you like," he said. "Just leave me out." Then turned his back on me and went over to the far side of the lookout to stare into the distance, in the direction of the invisible sea. (He too? It caught me unawares. But I would be damned if that would make me relent.)

"You didn't come here to sit in the sun watching the women work in the mealie-lands, you know!" I snapped. "Paul sent you to help me."

"That doesn't mean it has my blessing."

"I don't want your damned blessing. But you needn't try to pick quarrels all the time." Angrily I rearranged the pile of books, then made another effort: "Look, I can understand that you got a scare through what George did. But somehow you've got to make a new start — if you have any hopes of surviving in Europe."

"What makes you so sure I want to survive here?"

"What else? Don't tell me you're planning to go back after what's happened?"

"Of course I'm going back. As soon as I can. There's nothing to keep me here. The only place I can go back to is Azania. That's where I belong."

"You won't convince me with that sort of rhetoric."

"What you so conveniently call rhetoric is my fucking life. Can't you accept that?"

"We're *here* now," I said, more urgently than I'd meant to. "That land you're talking about — it's like a sunken ship. It's like Atlantis. It's gone down for good, it's buried under the sea. We've managed to get out. We very nearly drowned, but

154

somehow or other we got hold of bits of wrecking or something and got washed out in a new country. Now we're here."

"You talk just like that book of Paul's. What's it called? — *Survivors*. Don't you have any thoughts of your own?"

"As it happens, it's exactly what I *am* thinking."

"You forgetting one thing," he said, not looking at me, still staring towards the invisible coastline.

"What?"

"Azania hasn't sunk. You can try to wish it away, but it stays right there. You hear me?" This time he swung towards me. "*It's right there.* So it's no use pretending it's different."

"What difference does it make? Is there anything you or I can do to change things?"

"Don't tell me you're really happy to stay here — with Paul and his stories! — while your country is going to hell?"

I could feel the blood draining from my face, but I kept my cool. "Mandla," I said, "it's eight years I've been away now. Please don't think it's been easy. Especially in the beginning — But I've taken my time to look at it from all possible angles. For days and nights on end I walked through the streets of London, thinking and thinking and thinking until I thought I'd go mad. I listened to everything the South African exiles had to say — all the stuff you repeated to Paul in Paris — and then I began to think all over again. I tell you, I nearly went crazy. And there was only one thing that stood out for me, one thing of which I'm still absolutely sure; and that is that as I stand here in front of you, I have no hope in hell of changing anything about it."

"And so you try to ignore it? You think you'll get rid of it that way?"

"I have no choice, Mandla."

"Of course you got a choice!" He was so angry, I thought he would hit me. "Don't try to make it easier for yourself by lying about it. You got a choice, Jesus Christ. Even if that's the only fucking thing you got, I tell you, you got a choice."

I shook my head fiercely. *For God's sake, stop it. I don't want to listen any more.* Wasn't that exactly why Paul's

155

question had so scared me as to become the main reason for my finding myself here today, in this high wind above the city of the popes?

"You got a choice!" he cried again into the wind.

"No," I said numbly. My mouth felt dry.

"Aren't you a human being then?" he said.

"What's that got to do with it?"

"If you're a human being, you got to choose. Take away a man's choice, and he's no longer a man. Then you can do anything to him." He snorted with disgust. "That's what they did to my people. Made them believe they had no choice. And that's why I cannot stay here. They need me there."

"You're mad," I whispered. "You're out of it now. You can stay out."

"I tell you, that's why I got to go back. Right, I got out for a while. But only because I *could*. What about others who're not so lucky? What about a farm labourer, or a man on the mines? He doesn't even know he's got a choice. Which is why I must go back there, so's he can know."

"All you can do for him is to make him more miserable."

"You rather want me to shut up?" A brief hesitation before he spat it out: "Like you?"

"I told you there's nothing at all I can do."

"Anything's better than shutting up. Anything! You think by staying silent about something you can bury it? All right, so for a while no one sees it any more. But it's not a funeral, it's planting a seed, and it starts growing. I tell you, man, it just keeps on growing all the time until it's all over the place. And you thought you could bury it by keeping your mouth shut."

"What is it you want to do, Mandla?" I asked, not knowing whether to cry or to laugh. (How many countless others had I heard in London, talking just like this, using these same rousing clichés? until it literally made me sick. *Mandla*, I wanted to tell him, *I've also read those books, you know. I also know Fanon and the rest. Brian saw to that, all right. So what? What happens after the volcano has spewed out its fiery words?*)

156

"Even if you just shout or wave your arms. Just keep on challenging them. Keep them on their toes. Hell, man, if they try to step on you, don't make it easy for them by lying down!"

The anger had left me, leaving no more than a dull feeling of nausea. I picked up my books again and turned away with a weary little laugh. "I can see you have what it takes to stir up the crowds," I said into the wind. "I'm sure you must have been a great success in the trade unions. But I'm not innocent any more. I cannot get charged up by anything any more. Nor *for* anything."

"Pity," he said in a low, angry voice. "It's a real pity. I thought there was still some hope for you."

"My only hope is to stay where I am, Andrea. I can never fit in there again." Subdued and sad, Paul stands looking through a rainy window. (What is the occasion? What has prompted the discussion? She will be unable to recall anything about the circumstances, later, except the conversation itself; and the rain spattering against the glass.)

"You told me once that there *was* an occasion when you thought of going back," she insists patiently.

He looks round at her, trying to probe her with his eyes. (That first night he didn't know her well enough, perhaps didn't trust her yet. Today?)

"Only once," he admits reluctantly. "It was one of those decisions of which one only realizes afterwards that the whole course of one's life was changed by it."

"Was it long ago?"

"Quite a few years. Just before I turned forty: I think that had something to do with it, in fact. It came soon after the filming of *Survivors*, when I was still on the crest of the wave. Invitations from all over the world. Conferences, congresses, symposiums. Offers from every conceivable company. But all the time I knew something was gnawing away at me, inside; a depressing feeling of dissatisfaction. Not only because I knew very well that my success was really due to François Masson; and not just because of the accident that killed him so soon

157

after the Cannes Festival. I suppose it had a lot to do with the 'romantic agony' of early middle age, when one suddenly begins to have doubts about things like 'art' and 'action'. I think it was Lamartine who said: 'It's not enough to be the first poet of one's generation: one must also be its first man of action.' Something to that effect. There I was, a writer, and famous too — while back home my country was slowly going to pieces. It was as if *Survivors* was beginning to come true right there in terms of my own life — "

"Like *The Black Death?*" she asks, knowing it will provoke him.

"*The Black Death* is different, Andrea. My God, surely you don't think — "

"So what did my middle-aged romantic do about it?" she asks serenely, with such irresistible warmth that his anger subsides.

"I had two good friends in Amsterdam at the time, Afrikaner expatriates. Both of them much younger than I, in their late twenties. One of them, Dirk, was involved in a kind of agit-prop theatre group; Johan was an academic. Both were very passionate in their beliefs, very active in the anti-apartheid movement and things like that. Mainly as a result of *Survivors* I became something of a father figure to them. Days and nights we spent discussing the involvement of the intellectual. Between the two of them something was hatched; they even got the blessing of the ANC. A plan to slip back to South Africa and start paving the way for more white involvement in the liberation movements. The first trip was intended as a sort of reconnaissance to establish contacts, that kind of thing. I was persuaded to join them. I felt guilty about remaining on the sideline as a mere spectator. Also, I knew I was getting older and I hadn't ever really achieved anything."

He returns to the window with its watery patterns, his back to her, a bluish line of smoke from his pipe.

"Why did it fall through then?" she asks.

"Everything was planned to the last detail. Then one of those ridiculous mishaps took place which can alter the whole

158

course of events: on the evening I was supposed to travel to Amsterdam to join them, I got caught up in a traffic jam and missed the plane. The next one was too late to catch our KLM connection to Johannesburg. So they had to leave without me. I never slept a wink that night. Probably had too much to drink too. Anyway, I just realized very acutely how outrageous the whole thing was. We three utter amateurs — "

"What happened to them?"

"The Security Police awaited them at the other end. They'd known all along. Followed them for three or four weeks wherever they went, made notes of all their visits and phone calls and contacts and negotiations, then caught all their fish in one net. Dirk and Johan both broke down at the trial. Tearful confessions from the dock and pleas for forgiveness. So they were given the minimum sentence. Five years. After their release they both came back to Europe, and ever since then they've been attending every congress and gathering you can think of, to parade their miseries in public and cash in on interviews."

"*You* would never have recanted!" she says.

Paul looks at her, pipe clenched between his teeth. "I was just lucky, my darling: I was never put to the test. In a way, of course, I've never forgiven myself for letting them go on their own. For not trying harder to stop them. At the same time I cannot tell you how relieved I was to have learned my lesson in time. Since then, I've reconciled myself to the fact that every person has to do in his own way what he believes in." A pause; a small puff of smoke. "That's why *The Black Death* is so important to me, see? It must be the final proof — not so much to others as to myself — that I'd made the right choice after all."

"I know you have, Paul," she says fervently. "I believe in you, don't ever forget that. In London I saw enough people just washed out on the shore. Not even 'survivors' — just flotsam and jetsam."

In London she moves into Brian's small basement flat in

Islington, which has been cared for by colleagues during his absence in South Africa. Almost a year of impressions upon impressions which she will only be able to start sorting and interpreting much later. The feeling of security which goes with moving into "his" city, into "his" flat, temporarily subdues the unhappiness and turbulence of Provence. For the moment their love is less precarious, less desperate. The eagerness with which he introduces her to his way of life reminds her, quietly amused, of a child's excitement over a new toy. He encourages her to read and read and read until she feels dazed. It revives, for her, the voracity with which she discovered the world when she first went to university. He takes her to concerts. To the theatre. Overwhelms her with books and records. Mozart, Mozart! (Now and then, when he has to work in the evening, she slips out to a jazz concert, telling him afterwards that she's been to a movie.) She insists on attending classes at the Alliance. But she needs work too, to earn her own money, too proud to be supported by him. When he finds out that she's got a job at a hairdresser's he is flabbergasted. "Why not?" she asks. "I tell you, I'll do anything. I'll work in a massage parlour if I have to." A violent quarrel. After which he makes sure he finds her something more to his taste, a part-time typing job in the administration of SOAS; when she gets bored with that, he manages, through friends, to find her a place at a travel agency.

At the same time she keeps house for him. While he's working, she tidies the flat, rearranges the furniture and the pictures (mainly prints of Klee, Hockney, Sutherland). He complains about the changes, but she laughs it off, nestling against him, covering his face in fluttering little kisses, or placates him with food — all her grandmother's recipes.

Only occasionally, very seldom, when she is alone, or at night after making love (now more perfunctorily; she's on the Pill; it's all safe), she rediscovers something still tugging at her, deep down. God knows, she doesn't want to be ungrateful; she knows he has to work very hard and she doesn't want to upset him unduly; she owes so much to him. But slowly, slowly, in

160

spite of herself, her resistance is eroded. The London weather doesn't make things easier either. The greyness, the low clouds, the damp days. Not the Cape rain where one can see the Mountain turning green through the drizzle, but a monotonous depression that frays the nerves. The Thames, black barges booming or lowing in the fog. Hyde Park in the mist. A longing in her guts that wears her down and makes her physically ill. Endless bouts of crying and crying, no more passion or rebellion left in her; an existence as monotonous as the rain. "But what's the matter?" asks Brian, desperate. "You don't want to go back, do you?" She stares at him, unable to grasp what he can possibly mean. "Of course not. I never want to set foot there again. But I'm homesick all the same. Oh my God, Brian, I'm so terribly homesick."

With the best of intentions, thinking that it will comfort her, he insists that she meet "the South Africans". The mere thought is enough to make her sick with fear again. But he's got it into his head that it is the only remedy for her depression and refuses to take no for an answer. He'd met some of them even before leaving for South Africa; most of them have been in London for many years. Now he begins to look them up again, attends their functions, every demonstration arranged by them. "We can't hide away now, Andrea. It will be playing into the enemy's hands. The only way to make sense out of the awful thing that's happened is to *use* it, to make sure it doesn't just go to waste."

"I can't expose my hurt like that, Brian. You can't do it to me."

"The world must *know* about it."

"Do you think the world cares a damn? How can we expect the world to pay attention to us?"

"Then we must *force* the world to take notice. Open its eyes if it cannot see. Shout in its ears if it tries not to hear. Stuff it down its throat if it cannot swallow."

"You sound like someone from the SB."

"Andrea! You don't know what you're talking about."

"Don't I?"

161

"Come on, now, or we'll be late." (He cannot stand being late for anything.)

One by one she meets his crowd. In the beginning she still tries to distinguish names and faces; gradually they simply blur into a grey mass. Jackson, blind in one eye after his detention. Harry, who had to swim through the Caledon River to escape to Lesotho, the SB on his heels; before his wife and children could follow their car was blown up. Rachel, who still has a husband on Robben Island. Lifebuoy, who spent eighteen months in detention. Sipho, with the long scars on his back. Noni, whose child was shot dead in her arms. Abe. Cedric. Jason. Sophie. Nomosi. Names, names, names. Each with a story of suffering and horror.

"So what do you think of them?" asks Brian.

"My Ma once told me of the time she spent in hospital after my brother Sonny was born. The ward was overflowing with patients, some were lying on mattresses on the floor. The nurses were too busy to handle it all. The patients spent their time telling each other about their complaints, each trying to be bloodier and more scary than the others."

"Andrea! These people have gone through the most appalling experiences, and you poke fun at them?"

"I'm not. Brian, you don't understand." She wants to shake him in desperation: "You don't understand! I'm shocked by everything they told us. But it just makes me feel sick. I can't handle it, there's nothing I can do about it."

And the more she sees of them, the less she can cope with it. Always the closely-knit group, the same faces, the same stories. Each time a newcomer arrives everything is taken out and polished and brought to light again. Over and over. Not to extract anything from it, not to do anything with it: just the stories for their own sake, interminably.

When they question her about her own experiences, she becomes evasive: "It was nothing. Compared to you, I was lucky."

"Andrea, you should have *told* them!"

"I have nothing to brag about."

162

"Is that what you think of them?"

"No, Brian. It's what I think of myself." For the first time she loses her temper: "And of you, if you go on like this."

"Are you trying to tell me — "

"Yes, I am. You're turning what has happened into something cheap. It was ours, it was private. It burned inside. It was hell. Now you're going round boasting of it."

She feels an urge to say: *That's what you did to me once, in Aix, remember? I won't expose myself to be examined like that again.* But she holds back, sparing him the extremes of her own hurt.

"You don't understand," he sighs, wretched, confused. (Always the same desperate accusation, sometimes he, sometimes she: *You don't understand. You don't understand.*) "It's not just a matter of talking. We're *doing* things. Next Sunday there's a big demonstration in Hyde Park — "

"You're writing letters again!" she snarls at him.

He stares at her, uncomprehending.

"What did you do over there, in South Africa, while you were there, when everything happened?"

"Did you expect me to defy them? You know what would have happened then. Not just to me, but to you. I tried to protect you."

"The way you protected me in Montbrun? And the day in Avignon, when the gypsy hit me? Once it's all over and done with, you have a whale of a time writing letters to record your protest."

"Andrea, if that is what you think of me, I have nothing more to say to you."

"I haven't had anything to say to *you* for a hell of a long time."

It hits them both like an electric shock.

Without a word he goes out, not even bothering to slam the door.

When he comes home, late that night, staggering on his feet, she meets him at the door and leads him to bed, undresses him and makes him lie down, creeps in beside him,

163

pressing herself against him, whispering: "I'm sorry. Brian, I'm sorry. Brian, I have nowhere else to go." Loathing herself for it.

The next time it happens she doesn't apologize again. Soon after Christmas she moves out of the flat; one of her colleagues at the travel agency has found a room for her; other acquaintances offer their help with furniture and things. The first few nights she cannot sleep at all. Twice, three times she packs her bags and goes as far as the front door, resolved to go back. But she doesn't.

(Grandpa Xhorê, Jesus, you got to help me now.)

After a few weeks she discovers that she is still breathing. She is alone, yet nothing has happened to her. Her father was right, after all: "You're a cat, Nanna-girl. You're your Dedda's child. You'll always land on your two feet."

She can even risk seeing Brian again, now on her own terms. A few times he comes over to spend the night. If she feels like it, she lets him in. Once she turns him away. It makes him so furious that he nearly breaks down the door; but the next morning he writes her a note, a very loving note. It angers her, but she forgives him. So they'll be able to work it out, after all. She has survived. She will. She has work to do.

We had work to do. I led Mandla back down the steep path winding down from the Rocher des Doms, and into the streets: was it to annoy him, or simply to postpone the visit to the palace, that I insisted on taking a walk through the town first? A way of steeling myself by exposing us to so much I'd found painful in the past? Perhaps a necessary act of preparation: an attempt first to recover something of what Brian and Paul had dutifully, enthusiastically, tried to "teach" me about Avignon, and in the process to submit Mandla to something akin to my own earlier unhappiness? Layer upon layer, I began to peel the city off in my mind. The Auenio of the Celto-Ligurians, the fortified mercantile city of the Romans, the walled fortress of the Middle Ages, safer and more impenetrable than any other town in Provence, the place where Petrarca had fallen in love

164

with his Laura (that, too, had inevitably found its way into Paul's script!), and then the Black Death in which Laura herself had died. All my efforts were in vain. Mandla was, quite simply, bored; and his apathy was aggravating. Would Paul really appreciate, I wondered, what he was doing to me? Of course it was unfortunate that Mandla had landed in a cul-de-sac in Paris: but others could take care of that, not I. The anti-apartheid organizations and Amnesty International and God knows who else had arranged his trip for him and looked after him on his way, so surely it was their responsibility, not mine. Not Paul's either: and since he'd chosen of his own free will to get mixed up with it, he could get out of the mess by himself. It was no concern of mine. Honestly, he was being just as selfish and unreasonable as Brian had been when he'd tried to force me to meet the expatriates. In London it had ended in a break-up, as Paul knew only too well. I'd often told him about it, and he'd made it very clear that he regarded it as most inconsiderate of Brian to have behaved like that. (Adding with his roguish little smile: "But in a way I suppose I must thank him for it. If you hadn't left him I may never have met you.") What obtuseness, then, had caused him to behave with just as little sensitivity? Had Mandla made the least effort to be co-operative, even to feign interest, I would have forgiven him — but now he seemed bent on conveying to me that I either left him cold or, worse, unbearably annoyed him.

By lunchtime I had taken a very cool, deliberate decision. For Paul's sake I had tried to work with him, and it had failed. From now on I would do my duty towards him — no one would be able to blame me afterwards for being unreasonable — but no more than just my duty. And partly to "punish" him I didn't take him to a restaurant for lunch, but bought some fruit at a market stall, a baguette in a bakery, and pâté and a bottle of wine at a food shop. We sat down on a flight of steps on the square in front of the papal palace to have our frugal meal. I discovered too late that I'd forgotten to buy glasses or paper cups, and it grieved me to have to share the bottle with Mandla, taking turns to swig from it like God knows what good

165

pals (or, worse, a loving couple), but I denied him the satisfaction of seeing me abstain.

The paved square was quiet in the lunch hour, unlike the place de l'Horloge lower down, which we'd crossed on the way. Small clusters of pigeons were pecking crumbs from the paving stones. Two ice-cream vendors hung limply over their carts. A few tourists, most of them elderly, were waiting patiently for the palace to open. No sign of the summer throngs that had overrun the place during the July festival. And in this quiet emptiness the massive building had a strange air of irrelevance. Awe-inspiring certainly, but with an oppressive feeling of hollowness, as if it were no more than a façade, the décor for our film. Stupendous, colossal, magnificent. But quite empty, resonant as a skull. How the Mistral would howl past those buttresses and towers in winter.

It was difficult, on that serene autumn day, to imagine the city of Paul's scenario. Admittedly, he'd telescoped its history, introducing both earlier and later centuries into his image of the chaotic fourteenth; but this was understandable, even indispensable for the mosaic of impressions he wanted to convey. Avignon, the freetown, where anyone who paid his bribe was allowed to settle — Jew, gypsy, criminal — immune from prosecution. The tavern and brothel of Europe, the haven of troubadours, monks, whores, deserters, academics, pickpockets, hired killers, madmen, magicians, alchemists, layabouts, quacks, cabbages and kings. And behind the proud walls defying the carousing world outside? — no devotion, no world-forsaking godliness but a wild assortment of hard-drinking cardinals, lecherous archbishops, self-indulgent priests, voluptuous courtesans, outrageous actors and musicians. And right in the centre of it all, His Holiness himself. During the time of the Black Death it was Clement VI, the wealthy nobleman who ruled — his mistress at his side, the beautiful Cécile de Commingues — over the whole Western world, turning his court into the most splendid in Europe. Luxuria, superbia, avaritia, gula and all the rest. (Paul took such delight in rolling the names from his tongue.)

Clement VI, scholar, aesthete, grand patron of the arts.

And then the Plague arrived from Marseille.

Tuchman:

> Although the mortality rate was erratic, ranging from one-fifth in some places to nine-tenths or almost total elimination in others, the overall estimate of modern demographers has settled . . . . around the same figure expressed in Froissart's casual words: "a third of the world died." His estimate, the common one at the time, was not an inspired guess but a borrowing from St John's figure for mortality from plague in Revelation, the favourite guide to human affairs in the Middle Ages.
>
> One-third of Europe would have meant about 20 million deaths. No one knows in truth how many died. Contemporary reports were an awed impression, not an accurate count. In crowded Avignon, it was said, 400 died daily; 7000 houses emptied by death were shut up; a single graveyard received 11,000 corpses in six weeks; half the city's inhabitants reportedly died, including nine cardinals or one third of the total, and 70 lesser prelates. Watching the endlessly passing death carts, chroniclers let normal exaggeration take wings and put the Avignon death toll at 62,000 and even at 120,000, although the city's total population was probably less than 50,000.

Guy de Chauliac:

> In Avignon the contagion was so fierce that not only by watching with the sick but even by simply looking at them people seemed to catch it; the result was that many died without anyone to look after them, and were buried without priests to pray at their funerals. A father would not visit his son, nor the son his father. Charity had died . . . . Even the doctors did not dare to visit the sick for fear of becoming infected themselves.

Petrarca:

> Avignon is a sewer in which all the effluence of the world is

167

gathered. God is held in contempt, money is revered, both Divine Providence and human laws are trampled underfoot. Everything breathes the Lie: air, earth, houses, and especially bedchambers.

This was the kind of world from which Paul's small group would try to escape, lured away by their Rat Catcher; this was what they would have to defend themselves against in their fortress in the mountains — knowing only too painfully that nothing could be guaranteed in advance. For one of the most terrifying aspects of the Plague was its unpredictability: while some communities were wiped out entirely, in others there would be hardly a single death. In one abbey half the monks would die, the rest remain unaffected. Some doctors working with the sick and the dead day and night escaped unharmed; yet nuns who never set foot outside their convents would die. There were castles in which every living soul died except for the guards at the gate, the only ones exposed to the deadly miasmas in the air. Boccaccio's ten beautiful debauchees survived; so did Paul's group — provisionally, at least; some, of course, were destined to fall victims to their own excesses.

In this formidable palace before us, Clement himself had taken refuge, surrounded by his exotic frescoes and tapestries; and comforted by his lovely Cécile with her exquisitely depilated, smooth, and fragrant body, the lips of her vulva painted as scarlet as her mouth.

Tuchman again:

Helpless to alleviate the Plague, the doctors' primary effort was to keep it at bay, chiefly by burning aromatic substances to purify the air. The leader of Christendom, Pope Clement VI, was preserved in health by this method, though for an unrecognized reason: Clement's doctor, Guy de Chauliac, ordered that two huge fires should burn in the papal apartments and required the Pope to sit between them in the heat of the Avignon summer. This drastic treatment worked, no doubt because it discouraged the attention of

168

fleas and also because Guy de Chauliac required the Pope to remain isolated in his chambers.

What an imposing, powerful, yet helpless man. His efforts to stop the excesses of the Flagellants; to put an end to the persecution of the Jews when they were universally blamed for the Plague. All in vain. The Black Death could not be averted either by violence or mercy (just as it made no distinction between rich or poor). And what could even a pope do in isolation? Promulgate Bulls? Like Brian who used to write his letters after the event; or to strive for justice in South Africa once he was safely back in London? No way, Brian. No way, Your Holiness. I stared at the picture of Clement's papal coat of arms which Paul had pasted inside the binding of the script: it was to become a motif in the film. The red shield and its three golden keys: the two fighting eagles on either side. Crowned by the towers of a castle. And below, the rather secular motto: A *Bec et Griffes*. But how effective could a beak and talons be from behind the thick walls of this palace? (What was the alternative? — to venture into the world and physically confront Evil, at the risk of being infected oneself? In which case the world would have been left leaderless.) Clement VI: the pathos of the intellectual. He really deserved a film in his own right. God's representative on earth; powerful enough, in a manner of speaking, to command the world itself to stand still. Only, the world has a nasty habit of not listening. So the only way to conquer it is to paint wonderful scenes from that very world on one's walls and rule over an empire of images. (At least he had his Cécile too; perhaps he ruled over her. The thin man with the big cock.)

Mandla paid little attention to what I read or told him about the history of Avignon. From time to time, obviously resentful, he would take a book I practically forced into his hands and skim through a passage. Otherwise he sat staring into the distance while I tried to explain Paul's view of the town. Not that he could look very far, for the paved square was closed in on all sides. The palace opposite; behind us the ornate façade

169

of the National School of Music; to the right, the back of the buildings looking out across the place de l'Horloge; left, the Petit Palais and the rocky hill of the gardens. The only possibility of a panoramic view, between the Rocher and the museum, was cut off by tall ornate railings and a large gate.

He seemed to be waiting for me to lose my self-control again, but I'd be damned if I gave him that satisfaction. Once, when he began to whistle casually through his teeth as I was reading a passage aloud, I nearly reacted. But sensing that below his feigned nonchalance he was ready to pounce, I swallowed the bitchy remark I meant to make. Instead, leaving the book on my knees, I opened my handbag, took out my cigarettes and lit one. Inhaled, then blew the smoke out very slowly.

Mandla was still looking away into the distance. But he'd stopped whistling. After a few seconds he said in a hiss: "I can't stand women smoking."

I struck back immediately: "Oh really? You're very quick to squeal about being oppressed by Whites, but who are you to complain? You treat women like dirt. Don't you think that's just as bad?"

"Put out that thing," he said curtly.

"I won't." I inhaled again, very slowly, then blew the smoke right at him.

He got up so quickly that I started. For a moment I thought he was going to hit me. Then he grabbed the cigarette from my hand — a movement as quick as that of a cat striking at a mouse — and hurled it away. He was still not looking at me.

His action left me speechless, and more helplessly furious than I'd been in a long time, even with him. My hand, I noticed, was trembling as I took the packet from my handbag again, and I had to flick the lighter three or four times before I was able to control the small flame.

Now just you try again, I thought, my whole body tense.

To my surprise he only uttered a brief snort through his nose before he turned away to walk across the square, a slow

170

aimless movement. I went on smoking angrily for a while, until I felt calm enough to pick up the book again, my heart still pounding fiercely in my throat. It took a long time to unwind, but at last I was composed again. Occasionally I glanced up from my book to watch him as he paced to and fro, from wall to wall, the familiar feline grace in his movements. At the railings of the gate to the gardens he stopped, clutching the bars with his hands, his head pressed against them for a moment. Then he let go again to resume his lazy pacing, as if he felt closed in even on that wide square. And a strange thought occurred to me: it wouldn't surprise or shock me if he were to raise a leg and pee in each of the four corners to mark off his territory like a lion in a zoo.

At the top of the wide stairs leading to the main entrance of the palace a small crowd of tourists had begun to move. It was time for the afternoon's first conducted visit. I picked up my books and gave a few tentative steps in Mandla's direction: he was ambling back towards the railings. But as if he were aware of my approach, he stopped before he got there, and turned round. I beckoned to him. With an unusually subdued air he came back.

(How little, how almost nothing, I knew of him!)

Fortunately there was only a handful of visitors, not the stampeding hordes of my previous visits with Brian and Paul. We entered through the tall portals — above, the mitre and keys and shield of the popes, dominating two kneeling (vanquished?) figures — bought our tickets and followed the guide across the large courtyard to the consistory. (The courtyard, I decided, would do well for one of our early scenes; if the builders and restorers could be persuaded to remove their scaffolding.)

While the guide was delivering his commentary in a not altogether unpleasant recitative, Mandla took up position — legs akimbo, hands on his hips — in front of the row of papal portraits on the northern wall: the expression on his face inscrutable — cynical? curious? mocking?

I went over to him as the others moved into the chapel

171

opposite the entrance. "What do you find so fascinating?"

"Just wanted to have a look. There's something very similar in the faces of all rulers, have you noticed? After some time, even the brighter ones get a dumb kind of look. The smugness of power."

"Not very surprising," I said, with just a touch of spite. "This lot wasn't painted before several centuries later. By the same painter. And the same model posed for them all."

"Wouldn't have made much difference anyway. Dress them in suits, stick carnations in their buttonholes, add a South African flag or an ox-wagon in the background — and you'll still recognize them."

It was time to move on: with such a small group the guide obviously did not want to tarry too long. Through the gallery below the cloister, and upstairs to the top floor of the Old Palace. The vast Banquet Hall, resounding with our voices and footsteps, emphasizing the emptiness of the great stone shell. The kitchen of Clement VI with its enormous open hearth: this would be quite spectacular in the film, if one could revive the large burning fire, the perspiring cooks, the endless flow of dishes — plumed pheasants, exotic game, suckling pigs, calves' heads, whole lambs roast on the spit — the masticating jaws of the ruling class.

"Now watch," I whispered to Mandla as we passed through the State Chamber, moving out from the stern solidity of the Old Palace into Clement's own wing, more graceful, more airy, more aristocratic, altogether more pretentious. Here were the most beautiful of all the rooms, in which Paul's film could capture the great man trapped in the centre of his empire. The bedroom with its blue tempera walls covered in an intricate filigree pattern of branches and leaves and unexpected yellow- and red-breasted birds: the heavy ornate beams on the ceiling; the anomaly of cold grey flagstones on the floor. After that came the study, the "Chamber of the Deer", its dark walls decorated with scenes of hunting and fishing, and almost surrealist white hounds; coloured tiles on the floor, squares of green and brown and amber, interspersed with images of

172

outlandish fish, eagles with outstretched talons, lascivious pigeons and mythological animals.

Next came the Great Chapel, the only room in the whole palace which suggests, mainly because of the high grey arches, an air of sanctity. Remarkable resonance: every sound, even the smallest whisper, is echoed ten or twenty times. ("So that latecomers can still hear the first part of the service," quipped the guide, like his predecessors in July, and eight years earlier: was there no escape, ever, from echoes of the past?)

On our way downstairs to the Great Audience Hall, I stole a glance at Mandla, but his face conveyed nothing. As on the previous occasions I felt both impressed and downcast. And it came as a relief, after pushing our way through the Guards' room and the vendors of postcards and souvenirs, to return to the uncomplicated autumn sunshine outside.

From one of the ice-cream carts I bought two cones. We sat down on the same steps as before to eat them; it was a relief to put the books down for a while. Two small children were chasing pigeons across the square while their mother kept watch beside a pram; she was pregnant again. Would my children, Paul's, also be running about like this in a few years' time, perhaps in the Jardin du Luxembourg or the Tuileries gardens of a Sunday morning? I couldn't make out whether I felt depressed or happy at the prospect. Yet only a few days ago, during my anonymous, underwater journey, I'd felt my womb burn with desire. Had something been displaced already? Was it merely my temporary grudge against Paul for violating my independence? Or was something more profoundly disturbing taking place inside me? It was like diving in the pools at Onrust when the tide came in: suddenly the water would be disturbed by foam rushing in, obscuring the transparency of the green water, causing one to lose all sense of direction. Not for long. But it would be enough to cause a hollow feeling in one's stomach, an awe for the force of the sea. A few times I'd even wondered, quite ridiculously: suppose the tide swept Dedda's body into these pools: suppose I met him under the water — ?

173

"You got what you were looking for?" Mandla asked beside me, leaning back on his straight arms, staring up at the sky, far beyond the towers of the palace, where everything was a limpid blue, without a trace of cloud.

"I wasn't looking for anything in particular. I just wanted to check on the rooms and halls we can use."

"You're looking for something besides that."

"I've got what I wanted." (Really?) After a moment, before he could react, I asked: "I hope you were suitably impressed?"

He shrugged. "Why bother to make a film out of it?" This time he turned his head to look at me, a suggestion of sympathy in his eyes, as if I was to be commiserated with.

"It's important to Paul. Ever since I first met him — which was five years ago — he's been obsessed by it."

"Why do you care about his obsessions? Paul is impotent."

It stung me. (Was it impossible, then, to have an ordinary conversation without offending either of us?) "You can leave that to me to judge."

"I'm not talking about what he's like in bed," said Mandla. "I can't care less about that. But Paul used to be different, I can see that. Now he's lost his grip."

"Paul is barely fifty. He's just getting into his stride."

"Films!" He got up impatiently; for a moment I thought he would resume his pacing of the square, but then he turned back to face me. "You know, I was curious about this film thing in the beginning. Never seen it from close by before. Paul introduced me to his crowd, especially the last week or so. I couldn't believe it. It felt like I was a healthy person who suddenly woke up in a madhouse. No matter how much you bash against the walls, no one pays attention."

"Have you ever considered that, to me, *your* world looks pretty mad?"

"Well, I'm not shut up indoors the way they are. I'm outside. No matter if it's ground or shit I'm stepping on, at least it's out in the open. I see people. I talk to them. I rub shoulders with them. If I scream, they hear me."

"Perhaps it's just your own voice echoing in your ears."

174

He ignored the remark. "That film crowd," he said, shaking his head again. "Sometimes I sat there for a whole night listening to them talking, arguing, carrying on. All about films. Whether the focus in this cut is OK. Whether the script-girl's made a balls-up. Whether this shot should have been two frames longer or shorter. Talking about every bloody film ever made in the world, as if their lives depended on it." He slapped his open right hand against the biceps of his left arm. "And the worst thing is that for them it's true: their lives do depend on it. Outside that studio or set the world can go to hell: the whole of Paris can be blown up, they don't care. Famine, massacres, torture, oppression, you name it: no matter what fucking obscenity happens outside, they just don't care. As long as they can go on faking their films. That's what it is, I tell you. Fakes. Paul showed me himself, he was bloody proud of it too: there was one film for which they needed a sunset. So for more than a week, every bloody day, they shot a sunset. But it didn't work. Didn't look right. So? — in the end they just faked the whole thing in the studio, with filters and coloured discs and cut-outs, the lot. Nothing can lie like a camera. But it's fine with them. As long as they can fake it, everybody's happy."

"You're being very unfair," I said (hating myself for it, for why should I come to Paul's defence?). "Some of their films are shown all over the world. Thousands of people see them. And in the process they learn to take another look at themselves. Slowly, very slowly, but very surely, some of the wrongs in the world may be cleared up."

"The black children in my country who go about with their bellies swollen from hunger," he said, "they're not hungry from a lack of films or books or concerts."

"And you think if you give them food that'll solve everything? You think all one needs is food to eat, and a blanket, and a roof over your head, and a job to do? Come off it. You can't be so naïve."

"You want to feed a hungry man a roll of celluloid," he said. "That's what I got against it. And then you talk about

175

listening to echoes of your own voice! — the only sound you people can still hear is the noise of your own films. No voice from outside can get through to you any more." Once again that penetrating stare right into my insides. "Right now, as you're sitting here talking to me, you don't hear me. You've lost the use of your ears. You stay here for a little while longer and you'll be just as impotent as Paul."

"You don't have to draw him into it."

"Oh yes, I have to. For you keep on hiding behind him."

"I'm not."

"He's just a good excuse to you, Andrea. And you must learn to do without it."

"What gives you the right to judge my life? It's got nothing to do with you."

"It has," he said quietly.

"Why? How? Can you tell me?"

"Because of this!" He grabbed me by the wrist, so hard that it hurt. But I refused to let him notice. "Paul's white. You're not."

"Shame," I said. "Have you become so twisted by apartheid that you're talking just like them? Can't you see anything but black and white in the world?"

"You talking just like a White now," he sneered. "It's only Whites can afford to forget about colour. To pretend they forget. It's a luxury, man. It's not for me. I can't, I tell you. You understand that?"

"This isn't South Africa. Why can't you get it into your head? This is Europe, it's France. Here I'm not black or white or green or purple. Here I'm a person. I'm a woman. The rest doesn't matter. That's why I left there. And don't think I'll allow you or anyone else ever to infect me with it again."

"Who's infected?" he shouted. "I? Or you, playing the European? Speaking French and all. But that's not what you really are. I refuse to believe it."

"And what are *you* doing here then?" I asked. "Also needed a breather, did you? Who paid for you? Who's carting you from one country to another?"

176

"You call this a breather?" He snorted. "I came to collect money. We need it for our struggle. And I told you before, I'm going back as soon's I can."

"Your struggle will long be over," I said, "when Paul's film will still be shown around the world."

"His precious little film about the Black Death? The Middle Ages? A bundle of fucking happy-go-luckies from God knows how long ago? Well, let them show it then. Perhaps Europe will like it. They got nothing else to keep them busy. Everything's second-hand here. Even shit and death you've turned into culture. You've forgotten what it means to live."

"You think the Black Death belongs to the past?" I asked. "You think it was just something from history, all over and done with?"

"Listen, man, in the Eastern Cape, where I come from" — his voice had changed, it was much deeper now, as if he was talking only to himself — "there was another outbreak of the Plague last year. At Koega. The same Plague you're making your film about. There's nothing you can tell those people about the Plague: they lived through it. Some of their own children or mothers or fathers or friends died of it. Not acting dead in front of a lot of cameras and lights. I'm talking about real death."

"But there are other people in the world who don't know about it. Perhaps, through the film, they'll begin to understand."

"The film won't teach them a thing about death or the Plague. Just about films. Of course, you'll probably all get stinking rich out of it."

"Paul has enough to live on," I said, piqued. "He's not making films for the sake of money."

"So what's he do with the dough?"

"He ploughs it back into something new."

"I see. One film, and then another, and another. Like wanking off. And when's he going to find time to start living?"

"Films are his life."

"True's God?" he asked in contempt. "If that's so, then

either he or you or both of you must be fucking hopeless in bed."

I had no answer to his elusive arguments any more; I simply didn't have enough hands to keep on warding off all the attacks.

"If you can't do anything but insult us — " I said.

Mandla heaved a sigh and turned away with a gesture of dismay; but then came back. "Is that all you can see in it? Insults? If I tell you that Paul is impotent, I'm not trying to insult him. Perhaps I'm trying to say: What a fucking pity." Once again he changed his angle. "Did you know Paul also gave us money?"

"What?"

"A shithouse full of money. And I took it, because I knew he meant well by it. Anyway, we needed it. But I almost felt sorry for him, you know. Because he really thought I wouldn't see that he was just trying to buy off his conscience. Now *that* was an insult. Except, I took it from him, because he doesn't know what he's doing any more. He's" — he seemed to be groping for what he wanted to convey — "he's like an electric toaster or something that's not plugged in any more. There's no power coming through. He thought if he plugged in with you, he would get charged up again. Meantime, it seems to me, you were thinking just the same from your side. That's why you making me so the hell in."

"Well, if you pretend to know all about electricity,"I said, "where's the bloody hole to plug into?"

"There's no lead in the world that's ten thousand kilometres long," he said. "When you left, didn't you bring a kettle or an iron with you?"

"Why?"

"Because if you did, you would have noticed that South African plugs don't fit in the holes they got over here."

Turning round abruptly, he walked away from me; but there was nothing hurried in his stride. It was the same loping motion of before, almost weary, yet with a suggestion of subdued violence. I stared after him as he ambled on, back to

178

the iron railings on the far side of the square; then my eyes left
him to gaze higher, to the summit of the Rocher des Doms, an
urge inside me to be back there, in that high pure wind; but I
already knew that today one couldn't see the sea.

Turning away from the pond in the green gardens of the
Rocher des Doms where they have been feeding the fish —
looking back, she notices the voluptuous, romantic nymph in
the middle of the sluggish green water still dancing on her
pedestal, unmoving — she and Paul stroll to the belvedere at
the back from where one can look out over the terracotta roofs
basking in the July sun. While he is studying the orientation
table, looking for landmarks in the distance, she moves on,
down a brief, wide flight of stairs to a lower level, where she
stops in the searing heat to stare over the low grey wall. An
unexpected, very small movement catches her eye. Below her
is a tall, stark building with barred windows. A prison? Must
be: over the front gate, where a group of heat-dazed people
stand waiting at a bus stop, she can make out the inscription
Maison d'arrêt. A faded tricolour hangs limply from its post.
The whole building — surrounded by high walls topped with
barbed wire — appears uninhabited. But what could have
drawn her attention then? Straining her eyes, she catches
another slight movement in one of the windows. It is difficult
to distinguish anything in the pitch-black shadow behind the
dazzling sun: a man changing his position? an arm waving
half-heartedly? As she stands there staring intently into the
glare, a small piece of white paper comes darting from the
window, through the bars, rocking and swaying on the currents of air before it is caught by a blast of heat that sends it
high into the sky, spiralling, fluttering this way and that, until
at last it disappears into the dark chasm of a distant street.
      When they come to the bottom of the hill again, much
later, she persuades Paul to make a long detour behind the
palace, through streets they have not visited before. But
nowhere does she recognize either the street or the building

she has seen from above. From time to time she stoops to pick up scraps of paper at her feet, but it yields nothing.

"What are you looking for?" Paul asks, bemused.

"Nothing," she says evasively.

"I can see you're looking for something."

"I tell you I'm not," she cuts him short. "Come, let's go back. I'm tired."

Paul, I'm so mad at you. And I miss you so.

Instead of taking the short-cut back to Saint-Rémy, I chose the road to Arles and then turned from it on the route past Les Baux. Mandla didn't seem to mind; he probably didn't realize what I was doing. There was something more relaxed about him than before, but perhaps it was just a brief respite before the next attack, allowing me to catch my breath after the last tirade. But I refused to be mollified, and kept very much to myself. My safety was at stake now. He'd begun to threaten my wholeness. His aggressiveness had upset me much more than at first I'd dared admit.

Yet what had really happened? On the surface it had been such an ordinary day. An excursion to Avignon. An hour in the high gardens above the Rhône; a walk through the streets; a visit to the papal castle. And the conversations on the open square. Was that so disturbing?

Still, it was no use trying to play it down, to underestimate it. Something had happened; was happening.

And it was so unfair of him! He had no right to confront me so brutally.

You got a choice.

Hadn't I come to Provence precisely because I'd believed in that possibility of choice myself? Then why should I blame him for reconfirming it?

But the choice he'd talked about was something different. Much more invidious. Inside me I was aware of a terrible emptiness expressed in flesh and bone. And it had been this emptiness to which he'd addressed himself.

180

The "appointment with myself"?

So be it: but then I had to be involved as I was, and nothing but myself, Andrea Malgas. Nanna. I. Why should he want to deny me that by keeping me enmeshed in the web that bound me to others? — Dedda's daughter. Brian's girl. Frank's *petite amie*. Paul's mistress.

I didn't want to be anything but me; approachable only in terms of myself, not through outsiders.

Or was that indeed out of the question, and had he sensed it more lucidly, more uncompromisingly than I? Could one know anyone, anything, except in its relations to other people, other things? — the apple in its relation to the tree, to the stone inside, to the taste in my mouth, to the challenge of the Serpent, Adam's outstretched hand, the crunch of the teeth in its moist wet flesh? Nanna in relation to her love-blanket — her father — her lover — her image in a mirror — a tattered French flag on the back seat of her car — a cyclist beside the road — the enigmatic expression in the dark eyes of this big, silent man beside me?

Hadn't I glimpsed this myself, the previous evening, looking at my reflection in the mirror? And wasn't that, ultimately, the true meaning of "choice"? — to choose between one's relations to others and one's responsibility to oneself?

Even so! Surely I had made my choice the day I'd left South Africa, hadn't I? Hadn't I? Why dig up everything anew then? Old bones were smelly, of no use to anyone.

I had to pull myself together. Hell, he didn't have a hold on me. He was, at most, an obstacle; I would be granting him too much by admitting that he'd upset me. The worst I could reproach him for was that he'd caused me some uneasiness, that he'd been responsible for my feeling of resentment against Paul for sending him to me. Because on this journey, above all, it was necessary to be absolutely clear about my attitude towards Paul, an unquestionable lucidity.

In a more insidious manner, too, he had disturbed things. The fact that Paul had given him money — *a whole shithouse full* — had a direct, and urgent, bearing on my own decision

181

about the future. His colleague George would undoubtedly report at home the names of all who'd contributed to the "cause". What would happen to such a person should he ever try to set foot in South Africa again? Surely it was a germ that would infect anyone who came into contact with him. Undoubtedly his wife.

Except, I passionately thought in an impulse of defiance, except if I did say yes to him; if we did get married as soon as possible: then the choice would be made for us, it would be beyond our reach; then we could regard it as concluded, and get on, as best we could, with what remained of our lives. Of course, that was precisely what I had been fearing most: yet, in the circumstances, even this might be preferable to Mandla's cruel alternative.

What irony, though, that his attempts to test my love for Paul hadn't brought Paul to the foreground of my thoughts, but Brian. It seemed absurd: Brian belonged to a past long since written off. Unless it really went beyond Brian too: to the acknowledgement that the failure of our relationship had not been his fault alone, but the result of a lack in myself.

Even then it was past! Or did one's early loves remain latent in one's blood, incubating, biding their time to erupt in a deadly boil? And not only one's loves, but everything one had had; everything one had dared to be.

For how could one really tell when a thing was over? One might firmly believe it to be finished while it was still going on, or assume it was going on when it had already ended. That first time I'd come to Paris, without Brian: what had I known, then, about things past?

Brian is caught off-guard by her announcement. "I can't possibly go to Paris with you, Andrea. You know I have a deadline for my thesis."

"I never thought you'd come with," she says calmly. "Brian, you seem to forget that I'm standing on my own two feet now. I didn't come to *ask* you — I'm *telling* you."

He gives a small, bitter smile. "It's easy to forget, especially when you're standing so close to me." He puts out his arm — he's sitting at his untidy desk in the small Islington flat; she stands beside him — and in an intimate gesture touches the inside of her thigh.

"Brian — ? She gives him a probing look. "Do you blame me very much? Do you think I used you?"

"I never want to hear that word again," he scolds her. "Neither of us could foresee what might happen while we were still there, right in the middle of everything."

"No. Let's not talk about it. We've decided never to regret anything, haven't we?"

"It was worse for you than for me. You lost everything."

"Don't say that!" she protests. "What is 'losing'? What is 'winning'? So what if it was painful?" She shrugs. "It's painful to be alive. You can't have one without the other."

He moves his hand up along her inner thigh until it brushes her groin. With his top finger he starts caressing her, more soothing than provocative, moving it gently across the ridge of her sex. For a moment she yields to it, closing her eyes, rocking her body. Then, leaning over quickly, she kisses him on the forehead — his hair is already thinning at the top, she notices with a mixture of sympathy and aversion — and moves out of reach.

"Who are you going to Paris with?" he asks, making an obvious effort to sound as neutral as possible.

She smiles. "You needn't fear a week of unbridled passion. Bill and Harriet invited me to go with them. It won't cost me a penny, for we're going in their car and we'll be staying in a flat of friends."

He relaxes. They're two of his closest friends, Bill a music tutor at Trinity College, Harriet a translator for a publisher.

"If Harriet hadn't gone too I might have felt worried," says Brian, pulling a face. "But I know she keeps a peeled eye on him."

Not that the peeled eye turns out to be much use. On only the second day in Paris, while Harriet is off to a publisher to

183

pick up a book for her London employers, Bill comes to Andrea's room: they've arranged to go to the Louvre. Instead of waiting at the door he comes inside, closing it behind him. A banal little scene from which, a year or so later, she will be able to extricate herself with a laugh or a quip; but right now she is unprepared for it.

"But—what about Harriet?"

"Come on, sweetie, save us the sermons."

"Bill, I'm not going to — "

"Don't tell me it hasn't been in your mind all along. Your face is more revealing than you think."

She tries to get past him to the door, but he cuts her off, laughing.

"Come on, Bill!"

He takes her by the arms to kiss her.

(Grandpa Xhorê, are you going to let the bastard rape me?)

Knee in the balls. And as he doubles up, she is already through the door, on her way to the bathroom where she locks herself in, ignoring his furious knocking and shouting. When Harriet returns in the afternoon, her things are already packed.

A very impulsive, exaggerated reaction, no doubt. And where can she go to? She has very little money with her. For an hour she wanders through the Jardin du Luxembourg, sitting down on a bench from time to time to try and think it out, but it's too cold to stay in one position for more than a few minutes; she has to keep moving. The gardens are white with snow; stark black trees in empty space. Each twig encased in a transparent sleeve of ice. The small tracks of birds in the snow. That is what finally brings her to a standstill, catching her breath in her throat: even the birds have left their footprints, a delicate tracery of cryptograms in the white: *We were here.* Spellbound, she stares at the tiny marks, slowly raises her head to look beyond the bare trees and grey buildings. If even the birds can leave footprints, why not she too?

In the early dusk she is driven from the park with the few other remaining loiterers: the gates must be locked for the

184

night. But it does not upset or alarm her. On the contrary, it rekindles in her the very old urge to survive.

She has three or four addresses Brian has given her. The thought of having to ask strangers for favours repulses her, but he made so much of the fact that they were old and trusted friends —

No answer at the first two places — one of them not far from the gardens, near the Gare Montparnasse; the other at the opposite end of the city, below Montmartre. Night is deepening around her. On a late Métro she ventures back to the Panthéon, spends a whole hour trying to find her way to the rue Mouffetard, where at last, on the third floor of a dilapidated old building, she drops her rucksack from her weary shoulders to knock on a dark green door that bears a card with the name, Frank Wilder.

The man with paint marks all over his grey sweater glares suspiciously at her until she mentions Brian's name. Then his eyes light up; so much, in fact, that it worries her.

"I have nowhere to stay," she says. "I hope you can help me. Only, I want to make one thing very clear before I come in: I'm not going to sleep with you."

Was it perversity which had drawn me, from the beginning, to the ruins of Europe? Not walls, but broken walls, as if I felt more at ease, even safer, among them than within the protective enclosures of castles and fortresses? From the very first time, when Brian and I had gone there in a rattling yellow bus — nearly suffocating in a cloud of blue smoke as we crept up the last steep incline — I'd been enthralled by Les Baux. My feeling had been enhanced by the few days Paul and I had spent, in July, in the relaxed comfort of the Mas d'Aigret below the summit, where late in the summer evenings one could lie on one's back in a bright blue pool watching the sunset behind the enormous walls far above. (A flock of pigeons fluttering down from the cliffs to drink the water that had splashed from the pool.) Afterwards there would be dinner

185

on the terrace — rabbit in mustard sauce, lamb with rose-mary, a Provençal entrecôte — with a view across the wide plains below the dark spine of the Alpilles: the red quarries opposite, the vineyards of Sainte-Berthe and the Mas de la Dame; in the distance the power station of Cavaillon; and high on the hill behind one the tragic ruins of the once impreg-nable fortified town. Les Baux had survived enemies, sieges, traitors, even the Black Death itself (see how well I remember, Paul!); but then came the wars of religion. The Protestants were driven out, the castle and the houses of noblemen razed to the ground. And yet these remains moved me more than the well-preserved papal palace of Avignon. There was no oppressive limitation imposed on space on this high ridge, but total surrender to the horizon: the humility of ancient walls which had once again come to terms with tough grass and shrubs, olive-trees, vineyards and cypresses, thyme and rose-mary. Brown lizards rippling among the stones. The wind moaning through the empty eye-sockets of windows and doors and the honeycomb pattern of dovecotes in a stone wall, or round the tumbled corners and remains of staircases leading nowhere.

To me it seemed the ideal place to end Paul's film. This was what would remain of the fortress once the debauchees had left. If it opened with the palace of Avignon, surely these crumbling walls should have the final word. Not melancholy, or just a hint of it; but the reassurance of stone upon stone. The very graffiti on the broken walls were in keeping with the rest: even the most humble people (or especially the most humble?) had been unable to resist the temptation. And dare I confess? — the first time I'd been there, while Brian had gone off somewhere else, I'd found a secluded corner below the Saracen Tower and, with a rusty nail, had carved my own marks into the stone. It was just where a built-up wall joined the natural surface of the cliff, high above the plains that opened underneath like Paarl Valley. The rough outline of a heart, and within it my name, ANDREA. I wasn't sure whether I should add Brian's, and before I could make up my mind, I saw him coming back. As guilty as a schoolchild caught red-handed I threw away the nail.

In July, back at Les Baux with Paul, I'd tried to find the spot again without telling him what I was looking for. In vain, of course. Too many years and marks and other hearts had come in between; the distortions of memory. Yet I continued fervently to believe it was still there, to prove that in an obscure way I'd had some share in the long history of Les Baux.

Now I was back, which in itself confirmed a kind of freedom. Nothing had forced me to return; it had been my own choice. (And to hell with Mandla.)

Although it was past the tourist season the parking areas were crowded with cars and buses. No end to the throng of visitors in a place like that. That was the only thing I regretted about returning to Les Baux: we would have to make arrangements well in advance to have the village cleared for a few days if we decided to do any shooting there. It was like a crowd at the scene of an accident, all of them jostling and straining to see the corpse. Not quite as bad as in summer, but frustrating enough. I could see that Mandla was also irked, perhaps even more than I; but he didn't say anything.

In order to withdraw for a while from the busy streets so that I could discuss with him the film scenes I had in mind, I took him to a café terrace and ordered two beers.

"What exotic country does the lovely lady come from?" the young waiter tried to chat me up.

"From Paris," I said laconically. "Now cut out the shit and bring us the beer; I don't fall for amateurs."

"What did he want?" asked Mandla as the youngster withdrew with a flustered apology.

"Oh he was just taking a chance."

"You seemed to put him down all right."

I smiled. "How else do you think a woman can survive in this place?"

For the first time I sensed a shift in his attitude. Nothing as positive as appreciation yet: but at least a move away from complete contempt.

"You're very fluent in the language."

"I saw right at the beginning that I'd be asking for trouble if I wasn't. A girl with a foreign accent — " I shook my head briefly. "Frank thought I was just being otherwise. But he soon found out."

"Who was Frank?"

It was too late to retreat now. "A painter. Put me up in his flat when I first arrived. An Englishman. Terribly British. And the more he ranted and raved against the English and their bourgeois ways, their lack of imagination, you name it, the more English he became himself. A very good painter he was; still is. But he felt he was being stifled in Birmingham. France was the only place where one could really be free, he used to say; free to discover who you are. He made a very tough impression, but deep down he was a romantic. And he was very kind to me. Poor thing, fell for me boots and all. Yet he never tried to force himself on me. We had an arrangement, you see: 'good friends', nothing more. Sometimes I wished he wouldn't really take it so seriously, but he was too much of a gentleman."

It had clearly been more difficult for Frank than for me. He'd made it very obvious that he desired me, which had given me a new awareness of myself in a way I'd previously experienced only with Brian. Not "lust"; not "power". But a pure, keen, positive knowledge. Perhaps I should have allowed him to share it with me, but I'd been too scared that it might complicate our relationship. It was so much more manageable that way. Manageable — ! where, previously, I would have plunged in head first. But for that very reason I had to be more cautious now.

Learning French well enough to be absolutely fluent in it had been part of the process. In the beginning, Frank had found it funny, or exaggerated, or charming; discovering how serious I really was, he'd flippantly said one day: "There's only one way of becoming fluent in a language: you must get you a French lover."

He was taken aback when I took him at his word and, after

188

carefully looking through all his friends, chose an architect. "I want to learn French properly," I told Stéphane. "Will you become my lover? Frank assures me it's the only way. I know you have an *amie*, but it needn't interfere with your relationship at all."

In a way Frank had been right; in another, completely wrong. My French improved beyond comparison. But I hadn't been prepared for all the emotional complications when Stéphane's girlfriend left him and threatened to commit suicide and God knows what else. Worst of all, he got it into his head that he wanted to marry me; and when I refused, he flew into such a rage that he assaulted me. I had to spend a few days in bed; and Frank was so furious that he went to give Stéphane a thrashing. Unfortunately, he also got beaten up and then I had to get out of bed to look after *him*.

"So that's how I polished my French," I told Mandla. "Only, in the process I discovered that men can be difficult."

"*Men* can be difficult?" With a disdainful, incredulous snort he got to his feet. "Let's go. And please warn me in time if you get the urge to learn Xhosa."

My face burned. "I assure you it's one language I haven't the faintest interest in."

"Just as well," he snapped. "You won't ever need it over here."

Over the green cloth of the round café table we stood sizing each other up. I couldn't make out what he was thinking; and I preferred not to know. I was angry, all right: mainly at myself, for being foolish enough to drop my guard, allowing him a glimpse of myself he should have done better without. In future I would have to be that much more careful.

We went back into the narrow streets of the restored village, still resounding with people talking every language under the sun. Before the afternoon got completely off its tracks — already I could see a small muscle flickering dangerously in Mandla's jaw — we had to get out of the herd: even though, ironically, other people offered the best guarantee for our own anonymity. At least I felt equal to him again — rather his frontal attacks than the slow erosion of my resistance by the buffeting crowd.

Fortunately we found a few quieter spots once we'd left the main shopping area. Below the church I led him to a small look-out protected by a low stone wall.

"That's the Valley of Hell," I told him. "It doesn't need much imagination to picture devils dancing about down there, does it?"

"A very fertile hell," he said, pointing at the vineyards and orchards in the narrow valley, the red roofs of the luxury homes and hotels which had appeared in recent years; the aquamarine patches of swimming-pools. "But then, I suppose hell must cater for so many different tastes these days."

"We can have dinner down there tonight," I proposed impulsively. "The hotel over there. Paul took me there one evening in July. The food is out of this world."

He stared in silence at the wonderful scene below us, a hint of cynicism in his face.

"What's the matter?" I asked.

"Just wondering," he said moodily. "If that is hell down there, what's heaven look like? You see, I've always prepared myself for hell, thinking it would be the one place Whites would stay away from. Now they've taken that over too. That's what Group Areas do to people."

"Let's go up to the Old Town. I'm not sure if it qualifies for heaven, but at least it's higher up."

We paid the entrance fee inside the museum at the gate. St Peter must have been off duty; for the time being he was replaced by an old witch with broken teeth and two large hairy moles on her chin. Up here, at least, there were fewer people than in the streets below. The silence of stone, of emptiness and wind. An endless panoramic view to all sides. One could almost believe in the legend of the three Magi passing this way on the road to Bethlehem, leaving their precious gifts behind: Caspar's gold in the rage of the sun; Melchior's incense in the rosemary bushes; Balthazar's myrrh in the bitter smell of cypresses. Tranquillity. Even if it was a delusion: for the lords

190

of Les Baux had all been killed simply because they'd dared to be Protestants, in opposition to the Catholic king.

"You like it?" I asked Mandla.

He shrugged.

"You must feel *something*."

"Why must we wander about here like baboons looking for scorpions among the stones? There's no scorpions here. Everything's been tamed. There's death in this place."

"Think of the incredible town that once stood here. Look at those walls, built right into the cliff. Try to imagine — "

"Why? We got nothing to do with it."

Suddenly it was very important to me to convince him. "Do you realize, this used to be a palace as big as the Pope's in Avignon. All the most powerful kings in the world visited it. From Spain, France, England, Poland. Even emperors from Byzantium. This court was more splendid than those of Paris or Aachen. All the troubadours of Europe flocked to it. There was singing and dancing, poetry, anything you can think of."

"No wonder it went down the drain. All they still needed was film festivals." Picking up a small stone he flung it into the distance. It struck the cliffside, shot out across the precipice, disappeared into the void below. "One day all the white cities of Azania will look like this," he said, almost with glee. "Better warn Paul to get his cameras ready in time."

"It's easier to destroy a city than to build one," I taunted him.

He didn't seem to hear. Without explanation, he suddenly asked: "Have you heard about the Afrikaner farmers getting out of Zimbabwe after Mugabe took over? — before leaving, they would bring in the bulldozers to level their farms, leaving no house or shed or hut or lavatory standing. To make sure the kaffirs wouldn't get it."

"What makes you think of it now?"

"Everything makes me think of it." For a long time he was silent. I saw his face changing: nothing clear-cut or defined, just a hint of a cloud passing over it, a dulling, a blunting; a new cautiousness.

"It's not the first time I've stood looking at a place like this," he said. "Only, the last time it wasn't stones and walls. It was corrugated iron, and planks and cardboard, sheets of plastic. It was pots and pans and beds and blankets. It was people. Children. Women. Old men with stick-legs."

"Where was it?" I asked.

The day of the bulldozers. Coming all the way from Port Elizabeth. Great yellow monsters, escorted by phalanxes of police vehicles. Men in camouflage uniform. FNs. Dogs tugging at their leashes. The people take care to keep out of the way, retreating among the houses. Small brick houses most of them, but very straight and clean and proud, each with its vegetable garden: lettuce, beetroot, carrots, onions, a few mealie patches; here and there a peach-tree. All the signs of a settled community. The children have stopped playing; now they're standing at a safe distance to watch, their noses runny from the winter cold; last night's frost still covers the hard soil where scraggy chickens are scratching; a sow is suckling her litter. The women keep together in a huddle of blanketed bodies, suspicious and alert, a few still balancing tins on their heads, or carrying babies on the back. Some of the older men remain stubbornly seated in the sun in front of their homes, pretending not to mind, fiddling with a pipe or whittling away at a piece of wood, staring vacantly into the distance. Others approach cautiously, dragging their feet. Only one man risks it a little way ahead of the others, on his head an old hat with a small guinea-fowl feather in the greasy band; his jacket tatty, his thin goat's beard proudly stuck into the wind.

"You've been given sufficient warning," announces the officer in charge. "You knew we were coming to clear up today."

"This is our place," says the gaunt old man standing in front of his people. "We live here. Our fathers and mothers lived here, and their fathers too. The white people gave this place to our ancestors. They got a letter from the big Queen across the sea, telling us we can always stay here."

192

"You're being given another place in exchange. In the Ciskei."

"I know. You took me there the other day to show me," says the old man. "There's nothing there. Just the bare veld. Not a town, nothing. Not a tree. Here we have our ground, we have goats, we're farming all right. We not bothering anybody."

Talk, talk, talk. It's been going on for months. For years. The foremen have even gone to Cape Town to see the Government. The Minister came to have a look. But the decision has been taken and cannot be changed. The white people need this piece of ground for their own farmers. So today it's the end of arguing, they've brought the bulldozers.

The people are timid; only the other day, not quite two months ago, when another settlement was cleared up, the people also got together like this: and then, without any warning, the police started firing, killing the leader who was trying to calm the others down, to persuade them that talk would save them. So today they won't easily risk it again.

Some of the women begin to cry as the first row of houses is bulldozed. They are herded away. The Administration Board men try to carry out furniture from the houses before the bulldozers approach, but some of the house-owners lose their tempers: they won't be thrown out just like that. So they drag their things back into the houses. The police are getting annoyed too. After a while the bulldozers start razing the houses with the furniture still inside. After all, the people have been warned to clear out their possessions in time; no one can say this has been unexpected. There's only one mishap: a young woman comes running from a farm shop where she's gone to buy samp and beans, arriving just in time to see the bulldozers bearing down on her house. The police try to scare her off with their dogs, but she doesn't seem to be conscious of them, heading straight for the thundering yellow machine. The only way to keep her away is by locking her up in a police van, where she goes on screaming hysterically, banging against the metal sides. Only afterwards they discover what she's tried to convey to them: she left her baby in the house.

193

Now he lies buried under the rubble. (Tonight on TV the Minister will personally express his sympathy with the next of kin, adding that the authorities have done everything in their power to persuade the people to move out in time; the possibility cannot be excluded that the woman deliberately left the baby in the house to provoke an incident: even so, His Excellency will give the unconditional assurance that the bulldozing of the houses has been done with the greatest possible care; in fact, with compassion.)

The old man who has been leading his people now stubbornly takes up position in his door. "I'm not going away. My grandfather built this place with his own hands."

They have no choice but to remove him too, for his own safety. As he refuses to walk, they have to drag him away forcibly. Even after they've thrown him into the van he tries to jump out again; they have to slam the door on his hand. By nightfall, after all the houses have been bulldozed into the earth, the police vans drive away. The women and children are left among the mounds of rubble: something unforeseen has gone wrong with the arrangements and the trucks summoned to transport the people to the Ciskei haven't turned up. But they're bound to arrive in the morning. A night in the open won't harm anybody, except possibly a few children who may die of exposure, but that is neither here nor there. How can the Government be expected to foresee that it will be raining in the night?

"My parents were there too," said Mandla. "I heard about it in King William's Town the next day and immediately arranged to go to them. But when I got there they'd already been taken away in the trucks. Only the rubble was still lying there. Even that was cleared up and levelled later: fertile soil for the white farmers who'd been eyeing it for years."

"What became of your people?" I asked.

"We were kept away by the police from where they were dumped, near Peddie. It was three or four days before I managed to slip through, with two journalists. They tried to

194

keep the Press out, you see. The resettlement camp wasn't quite ready for the people yet. A few rows of wooden huts. For the rest, tents had to be put up. Even then a number of people had to sleep in the veld for some time. And it was raining for days on end. The whole place was one swamp. In the first week eight or nine children died, and a couple of old folk. Later it got a bit better, especially after we took the story to the newspapers. Only, both the journalists who went there with me were picked up. Fortunately I got warned in time, so I managed to stay out of the hands of those Special Branch *Boere* for a while."

"And your parents?"

"They just had to fend for themselves. I took them blankets and food and stuff, but it wasn't easy with all the police around. They were among those who had to spend the first week in the open. Afterwards they were given a tent, and three months later one of the wooden huts. But by that time my father was sick already. My mother tried to help, but what could she do? There were no doctors. Once a week a mobile clinic, but there were so many sick people, the nurses got impatient. They said my father was just putting on. He lasted till Christmas, but in the first rains after that he went down." He was silent for a moment; then he added grimly: "Perhaps it was better that way. The really unlucky ones in that camp were the ones who stayed alive."

"You've never told me this before," I said.

My remark seemed to hit him like a blow from a sjambok. "Why should I? You're pretending to be white. You're on their side."

I went on alone, up to the highest, farthest ruins, a wing of the old castle leaning against the sheer cliff.

Don't be so sure, I should have liked to tell him.

When I looked back, he was still standing where we'd been, on the ridge far above the rest of the world, in the wind which was beginning to increase.

195

I must have been about nine or ten when a group of school-children went to Cool Bay for a Sunday-school picnic. On New Year's Day we usually went to Kalk Bay, by train; but this was a special occasion. They'd hired a bus for us, a green one. It was so full, some of the children had to sit in the aisle and on the steps in front. We were in high spirits, singing at the top of our voices, fit to burst the bus. As we drove through the Strand the thing broke down and we all had to get out. While the driver and the teachers in charge were repairing it — just a matter of changing a wheel, if I remember correctly — most of the children quietly sat waiting on the low stone wall between the road and the beach; but a few of us risked it out on the sand. We'd been told very emphatically to stay away from there, but who could resist those green waves coming in towards the fine pale sand of the beach? There must have been six or eight of us; but I was the only girl. I'd always been a tomboy.

I'm not sure any more exactly how it happened: I presume some of the white bathers summoned the cops. Most people would have ignored us or been content to shoo us away, but somebody must have complained, for all of a sudden the cops were there, with a dog.

The boys took to their heels, but I first stopped to watch, afraid that the dog might grab one of them; this gave the constables a chance to cut me off from the bus.

I heard the others shouting as they waved their frenzied arms: "Come on, Andrea! Andrea, run! Run!"

I made a dash for it, but not towards the bus: anything to stay out of their hands. So I ran straight into the sea. Most of the white people were killing themselves laughing at the stupid little *meid* running into the water, clothes and all. I paid no attention. My legs thrashing and churning, I began to swim. Dedda had taught me. My ears were humming, I could hear myself sobbing in fear, but I never let up, just went on swimming and swimming, swallowing gallons of water as the great waves broke and foamed over me. I knew I was going to die. Before the day was out they would be dragging my body

196

from the sea. Let them. For sure's hell, they wouldn't get me alive.

In the end a man caught up with me from behind and brought me out. Must have been a white man; I was already too far gone to notice or to care. By the time we reached the beach the police had already left. I heard voices exclaiming: "Shame, poor little thing!" But there was one voice, a woman's, I would never forget: "What's the bloody little *hotnot* doing on a white beach anyway? Would have served her right if she drowned."

The Sunday-school crowd took me over from my helpers and carried me back to the bus. I was allowed a whole bench of my own to lie on. The wheel had been changed, so we set out for Cool Bay again. When we got there I was feeling all right again. All the same, I stayed out of the water all day, just sitting on the warm white sand outside the cave they called Dabad's Hole, looking at the others swimming and cavorting about.

What's the bloody little hotnot *doing on a white beach anyway?*

I didn't try to fight it. I simply couldn't understand. That was the first time. Afterwards, I got wise.

Ma: "No use kicking against the pricks, Andrea. The law's the law. It's the will of God and we got to abide by it."

Dedda would never have taken it lying down like that. But he wasn't home then; and when he finally came back again it was many months later, by which time the hurt had begun to heal.

Only the scar remained.

I thought that even the scar would disappear in due course. But that afternoon at Les Baux I discovered, aghast, that it was still smarting, like an old wound in rainy weather.

Quite aimlessly I wandered about among the ruins. Looking for what? Nothing, really: I was simply trying to stay away from Mandla, knowing it would be difficult to look into his eyes again. Perhaps it wouldn't have surprised me at all to look up suddenly and see somebody coming towards me: not another

197

person, but I myself, one of the many selves I'd thought I'd shed along the way. The Andrea Brian had known. Paul's Andrea. Defined by the man at her side — whether in rebellion against him, or in the surrender of love. And today? I couldn't describe it yet; too much had begun to change in the course of a single day. I could only go on wandering. And perhaps, precisely because I wasn't looking for something, I suddenly came upon it. Honest to God: against a stone buttress, hidden in a deep corner below the Saracen Tower, a dark spot reeking with urine, there was the faded, uncertain outline of a heart enclosing my name.

No, no, I must be honest: I cannot swear that it really was the right place; and the marks were much too faded, like a very old scar, to be deciphered for sure. It might have been my imagination. But that was what I *willed* to be there, what I wanted to read on the stone: ANDREA. For I needed the reassurance of knowing that I'd been there before; that my surroundings were not altogether strange; that I was not really so utterly alone.

After a long time I went back; Mandla was on the far side of the narrow plateau, near the cliff looking out over Maussane. He didn't say anything about my staying away for so long. I came up beside him to look at the sunlight diminishing over the landscape, the shadows expanding, light shrinking, space retracting.

Inside me something was blindly struggling. Revolt: but against what? A dull ache revived by the unwanted memory. Something Dedda had said, laughing but at the same time concerned about me, when after his return I'd first told him of my swimming out to sea. "Nanna," he'd said, shaking his head, "You're a wild, wild one. Nothing will ever tame you. What'll become of you one day? You always want more than you got a right to."

"What about yourself?"

He'd just laughed again, slapping my backside playfully.

But now, standing on this high cliff among these ruined

walls, so far removed from the world below: what *had* become of me? Had I indeed been tamed? Had I lost something along the way, something achingly important, a wildness without which life was not really life any more? Had it already been lost on the day I'd carved my name into the stone: had that been a cry of despair, or affirmation? And if I were to repeat the gesture today: what would it be?

Grandpa Xhorê: is it you I've lost?

And was it truly irrevocable, or could something still be done?

At Mandla's side I stood looking out into the failing light of the autumn day. The two of us, cyclists lost from our race.

Was I already aware of it then, and was that what made me breathless with excitement and fear: of time running out, of days diminishing: of something urgent and indispensable that had to be attained, but with less and less time in which to find it?

I was conscious of a heavy weariness inside me as we walked down the incline towards the town. The old woman at the gate was annoyed because we'd kept her waiting, and snarled at us as we came past; I didn't bother to argue. I wasn't really feeling like dinner in the Val d'Enfer any more — I'd much rather return to my room, and pull the love-blanket over me, and go to sleep — but I felt I owed it to Mandla after denying him his lunch that afternoon.

In retrospect, it now seems to me he must have felt even less inclined to go to a luxury hotel; but I suppose he was being considerate to *me*. So in a sense we both deserved what happened.

We drove down the steep hillside into the shadows of the narrow valley; I missed the signpost the first time, so we had to turn round at the bottom and drive back again. The hotel was open, the lights were burning, there was a line of sleek, shiny cars in the parking lot beside the large, coldly gleaming swimming-pool. The terrace was deserted; the autumn evening was much too chilly to dine outside, as in summer.

199

At the reception desk I asked for a table. The girl paged furiously through her notebook for a while, then apologized and went through to a room at the back where I could see her conferring with a stocky grey-haired gentleman. He leaned far back on his chair to look at us. Then he rose and came to the front desk. A very formal little smile.

"I'm sorry, Monsieur-dame, but you didn't make a reservation, and unfortunately we have no empty tables."

"But — " I checked myself immediately, gave a brief nod, and motioned Mandla to follow me.

At the entrance we had to step aside for a smart-looking elderly couple, a lady with tinted hair and a string of pearls, a bald gentleman in a striped suit. Mandla went out. I held back for a moment, perversely I suppose, and heard the gentleman ask for a table at the reception desk; watched as they were escorted to one of the many empty tables. Only then did I follow Mandla outside.

"What's the matter?" he asked.

"You saw for yourself, didn't you?" I said fiercely. "They're full." I didn't look at him.

"Like hell they're full! Was that what he said?"

"Let's go, Mandla."

"Did he insult you?" he asked in sudden quiet rage.

My lips felt dry. "No more than he insulted you."

"I can't care a damn about me, I'm used to it. But I won't let him walk over you."

He tried to push past me. Almost in a panic I grabbed his arm and held him back, a strange dizziness in my head. "There's nothing we can do about it, Mandla. And he wasn't rude or anything."

"I'll fuck him up properly."

"What's the use of making a scene? That won't make us any more acceptable to them." I took a deep breath. "We're too black for them."

A brief if still grudging smile. "We're sure in this together, sister."

We went back to the car. I avoided his eyes. My nerves were

too raw to face him. We're sure in this together. For the first time, and fatefully, I knew it was true. Perhaps I'd known it all along. It wasn't him I'd been fighting so desperately but this knowledge which, once granted, meant that nothing could ever be the same again.

We drove back in silence, he and I together, away from the darkening Valley of Hell.

Third Day

❁ ❁ ❁

I woke up early, missing Paul. The previous night, because I couldn't sleep — and how could I, after what had happened? — I'd stayed up late, making notes, although I hadn't really been conscious of what I was writing. It had simply been something to keep me busy. After midnight I'd gone to the door and cautiously opened it. Like the night before Mandla's door on the other side of the dark landing stood ajar. But I didn't go nearer; I knew the room was empty. Once again he'd gone out into the night, somewhere among the dark trees in the hotel garden. The knowledge of his being there was both disturbing and reassuring.

Although I was still not relaxed enough for sleep, I put off the light and lay bunched up under my brown blanket, stroking with one hand the frayed edge as I'd done so often, over so many years. Everything I'd ever been was preserved in that worn, much-loved old rag, even though the knowledge was hardly inspiring.

It was a restless night, the wind tugging at the open shutters, rustling in the vine outside and in the dry leaves of the plane-trees around the pool. In the cypresses the sound was different again, a spare funereal whisper: not just moving air, but a ponderous presence. Once, when I'd been ill as a child and Ma had come to me in the night, I'd said: "The wind's got a cold too, Ma. Listen, you can hear it sniffing." That was the kind of night it was, my own restlessness tuned in to that of the wind outside. Whatever was happening or moving out there — that dark shape on its lonely rounds — was repeated inside me.

In the end I did fall asleep. And in the heart of my sleep I

202

knew I heard — or dreamt — a sound which I wasn't able to identify, although it moved me to the bone. Like the whining of a baby. With a feeling of emptiness and panic I woke up. Outside it was still dark, and very quiet. Yet I knew the sound had been there, familiar and old, unbearably sad. I drifted off again, this time into an uneasy slumber full of dreams and half-finished memories, feeling alternately hot and cold, aware of a searing unquenchable need, only partly sexual. Paul must have been at the root of it all, for when at last I woke up I began to grope for the body I expected to find beside me — but he wasn't there.

Unable to contain my need of him, I sat up, grasped the telephone and began to dial him. I could hear it ringing at the other end, but there was no reply. A surge of jealousy hit me in the stomach, causing me to feel quite nauseous — was he sleeping out? with whom? how dare he? — before I remembered that he'd left for Strasbourg the day before to attend his film conference; it would be a few days before he returned to Paris. Making no attempt to replace the ringing telephone, I remained quite still, unable to move, trembling in the early morning chill, taut with rebellion and disappointment, feeling the light perspiration of sleep turning cold on my shoulders and between my breasts; delivered to the unbearable silence around me.

Inside me was the aftermath of the shock with which one is left when awakened by the shrill of an alarm — or a doorbell — at an untimely hour of the night: quaking with unnecessary fear, a tightness in one's throat and in the pit of one's stomach which stays with you all day, leaving you with a sense of unfulfilment, of being in search of something you have never had, perhaps the other half of the dream left unfinished by the interruption.

At last I forced myself to go to the bathroom and open the taps, just to set myself in motion. In my mind an underwater knowledge of the weight of a past accumulating from day to day, a millstone round the neck. (Now, in retrospect, there is an added perspective: not only of the past which is extended

203

unbearably every day, but of the future diminishing correspondingly. That morning, of course, I had no inkling of it yet. (Would it have made any difference had I been able to look ahead and realize how finite the remaining days had become: five — four — three — two — one — ? Oh Paul, you have infected me!)

Frustrated, I reclined in the bath, trying briefly to slacken my need of Paul with my own hand, but giving it up almost immediately. I might succeed, for a while, to assuage the desire searing my body, but not the sadness, the ache of missing him. So the body had to be endured. With an old, stubborn practicality — inherited from Ma? — I started soaping myself; then shaved my legs, trimmed my pubic hair. Brian had wanted me to shave there too, the mound a gently rounded shell for the hollow of his hand: he'd always wanted me naked, defenceless, exposed, the better to possess me. At the Cape I would have done it for him, of course, and eagerly too. But not in London. It had led to one of our worst quarrels. Just too bad: I wouldn't allow him, or anyone else, to dominate me so totally any more. Such a pity it was: for in the beginning he'd been so gentle with me, so infinitely patient, so caring and concerned.

There was nothing exceptional about the way I'd met him. The University of Cape Town had telephoned our office for a temp in the Department of History; their secretary had taken ill or something. I hadn't been in the pool for long, only about a month, having just completed the secretarial course I'd taken after dropping out of university. Earlier that year we'd been kicked out of our house in District Six to make way for the Whites who'd decided to start developing it for themselves; and so we'd moved out to the Cape Flats, to the wind and dust of Bonteheuwel, far away from everything; and our world had been turned so upside down that I'd lost all interest in lectures, even though I'd known it would hurt Dedda. (Had I known that he was to die so soon, would I have carried on for his sake? But just as these five days in Provence I'd had no way then of knowing what was still to happen.)

204

After a couple of weeks the History Department's secretary was back at work, but by then I'd already started typing Brian's research material on the Khoi (he'd been working on it for a year or more, and he was eager to get it all sorted out so that he could start writing up his thesis) and the prof asked me to stay on for that.

It often meant working overtime, the two of us, and inevitably we got to know each other better. In the beginning I didn't feel anything special for him; but I enjoyed listening to him. Once he got going he could keep me fascinated for hours. That was when he told me about Xhorê; and that, I think, was what first hooked me. With no ulterior thoughts, of course. He was an Englishman from London, he was white; there were no points of contact between his world and mine. (We couldn't even talk about films! — there was no relation between the flicks he went to see and the spaghetti Westerns on show at the Globe.) All we could share was his work. Xhorê. Everything he told me about the Khoikhoi, "my" people, as he playfully referred to them, and of whom I myself knew so little. Otherwise he'd tell me about England, about Europe. At school I'd always loved history and geography, and I'd continued with these subjects at university; through Dedda I'd lost my heart to whatever was far away, and on my bedroom wall I had a large map of the world on which I could trace his fantastic voyages. Yet I'd never thought of Europe as an accessible place, not for me. If I ever went there it would be with Dedda: that was what he'd always promised me, but ever since he'd lost his interest in life and stopped going on his trips, that prospect, too, had faded. It was only with Brian, through his endless talking, that Europe acquired a sense of reality again. He knew it well; it was "his" world; to him it was the most natural thing imaginable to say: "One day, as soon as I've finished my research, I'll go and show you everything. Right?"

Then I would laugh, light and carefree. "Sure." It cost no effort to agree; not for a moment did I think it could be for real.

205

He never crowded me, never made me feel imposed upon. All he did was slowly to open his world to me in such a way that, imperceptibly, it began to cross the horizon of my own. I could talk to him about what, before, I'd been able to discuss with no one but Dedda: and ever since the day at the hairdresser's that had also come to an end. Brian became a means of escape from the new bare-brick house on the Flats where we were living now, where there was no chance of taking root, where there was nothing I could call "mine" any more. The move from District Six had left us all shattered, Dedda more than anyone else. So I suppose it wasn't strange at all for me to work longer and longer hours, leaving me that much less time to spend at home.

Sometimes, usually when I'd finished a new section of work, Brian brought me flowers. Perhaps I was obtuse, but I never noticed anything special in the gesture, even though he made a point of choosing the flowers he knew I liked best of all: white gypsophila, so delicate and tiny, the flowers of the poor and the old, little girl's flowers. (That was before the interior decorators discovered them, of course, promoting them into something rare and expensive.)

After the university closed down for the long vac we spent even more time together, just the two of us in his office, working, talking. I was actually dreading the prospect of ten days' leave from just before Christmas until after Second New Year's Day — and all the more so because Dedda had, at long last, decided to go on a trip again: on a fishing trawler this time, along the West Coast, as far as Walvis Bay, which would keep him from home for weeks. In a way it was a good thing, as his presence had begun to lie very heavily on the family. But his absence might be even worse. The rest of us never got along well when he wasn't there. Constant fights between Ma and me; or between me and Maggie, because of her knees-together brand of piousness; or her and Boetie; or Gran and everybody else. And then that wretched little bare-brick house too, exposed to the basking sun and the fury of the Southeaster in December and January.

The first few days after Dedda had left I was particularly depressed. Brian must have noticed, for he kept on asking what was wrong. I avoided direct answers, trying to keep it to myself. Dedda was nobody else's business. The third or fourth afternoon after he'd left I was working even later than usual. Brian had gone into town earlier and I wasn't expecting him back. A depressing day: miserable outside, my own mood uneasy, patchy; it was only a few days before my period. I was missing Dedda; that morning there'd been another explosion at home. Normally I could get it out of my system by working, but the typewriter was giving me trouble — one of the keys constantly got stuck. Just after a new mistake had forced me angrily to tear yet another sheet from the machine and hurl it into the wastepaper basket — "Oh *fuck* you!" — I heard a sound behind me and, swinging round, saw Brian standing in the doorway.

"Oh I'm sorry, I — I wasn't expecting you back."

"And I wasn't expecting to find you here. I've just come to pick up some books. You should have gone home long ago, Andrea, it's nearly six."

"So what? There's nothing at home for me."

"Come on," he said firmly. "I'll take you back."

"Never. There's a bus."

"Why are you always so evasive? It's no trouble, really."

"It's out of your way." I knew he had a flat not far from the university, below the railway line, in Rosebank.

"I've got nothing else to do. Honestly, I'd love to take you."

"No." I got up, covered the typewriter, put away the paper and his files, and picked up my handbag.

"What if I insisted?" He was standing right before me. For the very first time it struck me that he — that I — Even today I find it difficult to spell it out. There was nothing definite or tangible about it: just a shadow which had finally, and very suddenly, emerged from a deeper layer of my mind. And which I would have preferred not to admit.

"No, Brian."

The merest touch of his hands on my arms. "Andrea,

207

please?" — as if I would be doing *him* a favour.

I should have liked to. Fifteen or twenty minutes by car instead of, possibly, an hour's wait at the bus stop followed by an interminable journey in a jostling, sweating crowd. And it had been raining intermittently all day. Also, his mere presence was, well, comforting. More than that. Especially after the long depressing afternoon. But I still resisted.

"Thanks, Brian. It's very kind of you. But I'll manage. I'm used to it."

"How about just going for a drive then? You need fresh air."

I couldn't help laughing — he was so transparent in his male resolve not to give up — and I was getting tired of refusing just to be difficult. Whom was I spiting — him, or myself? My stubbornness changed sides: *Why shouldn't I? It's been a hell of a day. I need a let-up. And I can look after myself.*

"If you're sure it won't take too long."

A boyish smile. "Come on."

In his battered old Volkswagen we drove towards Wineberg. It was long past the peak hour and the traffic was easy; it was still drizzling, very lightly, an intimate isolation from the world, making me feel extraordinarily cosy and protected.

"Where are we going?"

"You have any suggestions?"

"Will it take too long to go to the sea?" I knew I was being reckless, but the feeling of being cut off from the ordinary world in that gentle fog affected me like strong sweet wine.

The beach at Muizenberg was deserted. How strange to find myself there, with him: on that stretch of sand with its "Whites Only" notices. As if his presence suspended whatever normally threatened or diminished me. An improbable freedom, guaranteed by the endless fog enclosing us. The drizzle had stopped, but the clouds were so dense that it was impossible to make out where the sea ended or the sky began. A grey eternity obliterating all colour, all sound, except from time to time the screeching of invisible gulls. A delicate lambent mist against our cheeks. Carrying our shoes, we strolled on barefoot, not very far, I think, although it felt like miles. The soughing of the sea; the cool moist sand touching the sensitive hollow of a foot. Once or twice, quite unintentionally, a brief brushing of arm against arm. We didn't embrace; we didn't even hold hands, just kept on walking in the pure, pure breeze.

At last we stopped, small clouds of breath escaping from our mouths. I was glowing inside, which made me all the more conscious of the chilly air. In spite of myself I shivered.

"Are you cold?"

Impulsively putting his arms around me he drew me close to him. He didn't try to kiss or caress me; just held me very tightly. I briefly surrendered myself to the awareness of his body, then firmly pulled away; he immediately let me go.

"Andrea — "

"We must go back now, Brian. It'll be getting dark soon."

"I wanted to — "

"Don't say anything."

On the way back he again tried to persuade me to let him take me home, but I was adamant. As far as the bus stop, all right, but no further. Even that was more than I should rightly allow—but after our walk together along the beach, and that feeling of wholeness in the mist, I was prepared to grant him that.

When we stopped, he leaned over as if to kiss me, but I got out quickly. "Thank you, Brian. See you again tomorrow."

"You *sure* I can't take you home?"

"I am."

It was more than a wish to hold back in the face of something I dared not yet acknowledge: it was also a final assertion of independence, a refusal to owe anybody anything.

On the way back I managed to keep my thoughts in tight control, paying scant attention to what was going on around me. Which might explain what happened. By the time I got out of the bus to walk the last few hundred yards, very reluctant indeed to reach home, it was already getting dark. As I made a wide detour to avoid a muddy pool in the road, a police van came past from behind, driving very slowly, brist-

209

ling with constables in uniform. They stopped opposite me. One of the men (blond, crew-cut, square face) poked his head through the window and called out: "I say, lovely long legs you got, hey? Looks like they're meeting somewhere. How 'bout it?"

Staring straight ahead, I marched on.

"The *meid*'s putting on airs," I heard one of the others say.

The van was moved into gear again, driving at a walking pace to keep abreast with me.

"Check those tits," the man at the window said again.

It went on like that for a few minutes and I knew I was going to lose control if it continued for much longer. To get out of their way, I suddenly ducked into a narrow muddy lane behind a row of houses and ran to the next street. A minute later they were beside me again.

"Pussy doesn't like us, it seems."

"Go to hell!" I shouted at them.

That really set them off. Their remarks grew more and more smutty and direct. A few more times I tried to make an escape, but every time they caught up with me. Soon, they were deliberately trying to cut me off, no matter which side of the road I walked. Until I got so furious that I scooped up a handful of mud from a pool and flung it at them. But it missed the van, drawing a roar of laughter from my tormentors. This time they gave me a handicap of twenty or thirty yards, then suddenly, revving like mad, they came charging right at me. I jumped out of the way, but not quite fast enough to avoid the spray of muddy water thrown up by the tyres, soaking me to the skin. Without stopping, they drove off, having had their bit of sport for the day. And I was left covered in mud from head to toe.

It would have been easy for Brian to react by saying, the following day: "You see, you should have let me drive you home." But he didn't. He was livid, insisting we should go to the nearest police station to lay a charge.

"There's nothing one can do about it," I argued. "It's not important anyway. It's the sort of thing they do every day."

"I won't let them get away with it!"

210

Et cetera. Deep inside, it did cause a glow of gratitude to see him getting worked up like that on my behalf. But I never thought it would go any further. It was only a week later when, worried by his tense, pale looks and his efforts to avoid me, I asked him point-blank, that he reluctantly came out with it: on the day I'd told him about my experience with the police he'd gone to Caledon Square to report the incident to the most senior officer he could get hold of.

He'd been convinced that it would have some effect, as the man had appeared very sympathetic. But the only result had been a visit from the Security Branch at his flat in Rosebank. Five men had appeared on his doorstep, showed him a warrant, then proceeded to turn the whole place upside down without offering any reason or explanation. It had lasted until well after midnight. They'd been extremely polite, while methodically and with great thoroughness they turned the flat into a rubble heap. After looking through all his notes, strewing the papers over the floor, they'd confiscated a few books, giving him a receipt for them; and at long last they'd left. At the door the commanding officer had looked back, the shadow of a grin on his face: "Mr Everton, you're just a visitor in this country. I have no quarrel with your work. But if ever you feel tempted to poke your nose into what doesn't concern you, you may be in for a surprise. And by the way, if I were you I'd watch out for coloured girls. It's just a friendly warning. But I do hope you will take it to heart."

"But what on earth has the SB got to do with it?" I asked, dumbfounded.

"That was what I was wondering myself. Good heavens, I have nothing to hide. But if they think I can be browbeaten like that — "

"Brian, it's no use." Without thinking of it I took one of his hands in both of mine. "I told you not to interfere."

"Those hooligans insulted you!"

"What's that got to do with you?"

Very quietly, his lips barely moving, he said: "More than you may think."

211

Once again I turned down his offer to take me home. In fact, I was even more emphatic about it than before. Because now I knew what I hadn't dared to admit a week earlier. That there was more between us than working together, talking, sharing sandwiches at lunch.

We continued to hold back. Struggling, fighting, resisting: not each other, but ourselves. We were frightened. Yet there was a kind of electricity in our fear, a heady feeling, as if in a strange way life had suddenly become worth living: because we *knew* we were alive; and there was no way of telling whether it would last, or for how long.

Still nothing "happened". For a whole month. And then Dedda died.

It's Maggie who phones her at work with the news. Washed overboard by a wave. At least, that's what the men on the trawler reported. No one else was harmed. Normally Dedda, hardened old sea-wolf, would never have allowed any wave to get the better of him, no matter how freaky it was. Normally.

She sits motionless after Maggie has rung off. She doesn't cry. Impossible to cry over her father. It isn't he who died: it is she, something in herself, something that has made and kept her human, something that has made her aware of what it means to be alive.

That last night she saw him alive: when he came and leaned on the water-tap outside. *(Let Thy will be done!)* And the next morning, a few hours before he went down to the harbour, she'd found him in the lounge with his bottle of cane. Three flying geese against the wall. *The Lord is my Shepherd.* The calendar with the still-life of flowers.

"Andrea?" Brian comes towards her. A hand on her shoulder. She doesn't know where he comes from. The Lord must have sent him.

"Brian, he's dead. My Dedda."

He doesn't say a word. Quietly, calmly, he removes the sheet of paper from her machine and puts it with the others in the green file. Draws the pale grey cover over the typewriter.

212

Hands her her handbag. Together they go down to his battle-scarred car. It's obvious that he isn't taking her home — he wouldn't know the way, he's never been there — but she makes no attempt to stop him. Leaving the city behind, he drives across the Flats in the direction of the Strand. Where the bus broke down when she was a child. (Behind the deepest row of waves, in a dimension beyond time: a skinny little girl swimming for ever through the green turbulence.) He drives on, oblivious. Past Gordon's Bay, round the edge of the mountain, high above the tranquil blue-and-green of the bay. The tracks of the wind on the dark water. On the far side, rising from the afternoon haze, the bluish smear of Table Mountain and the tongue of the peninsula all the way to Simon's Town.

At the mouth of the Steenbras he stops at last. It's a weekday, there's no sign of other cars or people. She hasn't the faintest idea of how he's come to know the place. They go down the slope under the bridge, following the red footpath that runs between milk bushes and proteas. The shrubs exude a smell of semen, a warm, bruised odour. On a small patch of sand among the rocks they sit down. She stares up at cliffs covered in lichen, grey and orange and pale green. The bright Coke-brown of the water. The waves of the incoming tide thundering against the promontories at the mouth and sweeping up the river. An hour. More. Her body leaning against his.

The sun is moving over to the horizon. They are still alone and undisturbed.

In the first cool of the approaching sunset she gets up, kicks off her sandals and moves away from him to a large rock where she can sit with her feet in the water. After a while he follows her, pulls her to her feet, holds her against him. There is a shallow cave scooped from the high cliff behind them, only a few yards from the water. Rather smelly, but that she remembers only in retrospect. For the moment it doesn't matter. The weight of his lean body. The feeling of rings rippling in a pool as he moves into her. Grains of sand on her back and buttocks, afterwards.

213

Only then, in the descending dusk, do they start talking. She tells him about her father, anything she can think of. The last deep red of the sunset is still discolouring the sea when at last they put on their clothes again and prepare to leave.

The silence of that return trip. The heaviness of knowing: *Now it's happened. Now it is a fact.* A knowledge which, if he were just a man, she just a girl, a woman, would have been grave and complicated enough to come to terms with; how much more so now, with this frontier crossed, this no man's land surrounding them. All the normal reflexes and defences have fallen away; the world has become an alien place in which she no longer readily finds her way, in which her customary reactions are no longer adequate.

One thing she discovers for the first time (no, there has been one other, earlier, occasion): not only the existence of her own frontiers, but also the exhilaration of finding that they can be crossed, to venture ever more deeply into this new territory. And whatever happens, nothing can be excluded in advance any more. Whatever lies ahead, she has chosen it; chooses it now.

As they come to a standstill in the street in front of her house — potholes, stones, suspicious dogs, dustbins — her mother and Boetie appear in the open front door.

"It's me, Ma," she says. "You needn't have worried about me. A friend has brought me."

Boetie: "My God, Andrea, the man's white!"

The previous evening, back from Les Baux, I'd brought the torn French flag to the room with me to get it out of Mandla's sight, and left it in the bathroom. Now I found myself standing on it as I dried myself after the bath. The wet imprints of my feet deepened the colours of the faded old rag: red, a dirty white, dark blue. There was no reason why it should have upset me to see my soggy footprints marking it like that, but it did. Anxiously, I plunged the flag into the bath to soak it completely, obliterating all traces of myself, then looked round in some uncertainty. I could dispose of it in the small bin in the corner, of course. But what would happen if someone found it? Ridiculous as it might seem — who on earth would care about a thing like that? — I didn't want to be implicated in any way. As if it were some piece of vital evidence that had to be destroyed, I bundled the wet rag into the bottom of my cupboard before picking my clothes for the day.

Mandla was already waiting on the terrace when I came down with my pile of books and notes and maps under the arm, my face carefully made-up against the onslaught of the new day.

"You're early," he said as I sat down.

"You're even earlier."

He shrugged.

"Did you sleep well?" I asked, rather formally.

"No. And you?"

"Me neither." I would have preferred not to have to admit it; in a way it made me more vulnerable. Yet there was comfort in discovering that I was not the only one.

It was still too early for breakfast. Unfolding the yellow map, I began to plan a route for the day. The obvious place to go to was Apt, after Avignon the most important town in Provence we intended to include in the film. But as I straightened the Michelin on the table my eyes fell on the circle with which, in July, Paul had marked La Motte d'Aigues, the village of the Jouberts in the Luberon mountains, only a few centimetres to the south-east of Apt on the map. And immediately I knew: yes, we would go there too. Not for any particular reason. As far as I knew the place hadn't had anything to do with the Plague. But it was Paul's town of origin, that little dot on the map. And, illogically perhaps, I felt I owed it to him to go there, a small pilgrimage to the place where we'd found the last wizened little member of the tribe in July. Was I feeling guilty about the day before — my resentment and rebellion, my conviction that Paul had been unreasonable in saddling me with Mandla? What a visit to La Motte d'Aigues might do to change or improve matters, I couldn't tell. Perhaps, if I'd been successful in reaching him on the telephone that morning, I wouldn't have felt the need to go. Now it was irrepressible. And anyway, there was no reason why we shouldn't just go there to enjoy ourselves. Mandla also needed some relaxation, I thought, to alleviate this heaviness, this wordless depression in him. For I found it more disturbing than before; even if it wasn't really my responsibility, at least I might do something to lessen it. A sombreness unto death.

"I'm sorry about last night," I suddenly blurted out, glancing up from the map, my finger still pressed on the circle indicating La Motte d'Aigues.

"You shouldn't have stopped me."

Feeling bold in the light of a new day I dared to challenge him: "Would you really have beaten him up because you thought he insulted me?"

"He insulted us both," he grumbled, refusing to take the bait.

I kept a straight face too. "I suppose I've forgotten that such things still happen."

"You have no reason to worry about it," he said. "You're a woman. They'll still make allowances for you." Adding, almost reluctantly, his face expressionless: "And you're beautiful. So they can try to take their chances with you."

"It's not easy to take advantage of me," I objected. "I don't allow them to."

"You needn't. It's enough for them to think they can. With me it's different. When I'm with you, I stand between you and them: they feel threatened by me. The 'dirty nigger' must be kept out."

"Why do you say that?" I asked, indignant.

"Because I got reason to." For the first time he appeared eager to talk. "I already told you: wherever I came, I was bowled over by their hospitality. As long as my hosts were with me. The anti-apartheid people and suchlike. Because then they opened doors for me. Everybody knew who I was, where I came from, and that made all the difference. Especially the women — I told you, didn't I?"

216

"You did." I was perturbed by the memory. "No need to repeat all the gruesome details."

"The blonder they were, the wilder they acted." Once again the ugly, angry grimace; and suddenly I realized: no, this wasn't bragging, he wasn't trying to make a show of it — on the contrary. It was precisely because he found it so perturbing that he had to talk about it.

"Sometimes I thought I'd rather be insulted than to have them throw themselves at me like that, you know," he resumed after a pause. "Not that I liked the insults. One night in Amsterdam — " Another long pause. He seemed reluctant to go on. "I went out for a meal on my own," he said at last. "Just a sandwich on the Leidse Plein. I was invited to a party, but I cancelled it. It was just people, people all the time until I no longer knew if I was coming or going. So that night I took off and went out on my own, with no chaperone to guard me. It was a wonderful feeling of suddenly being free again. I felt like bursting into song or doing something outrageous, but of course I didn't. The Dutch are such a bloody smug nation, I didn't want to upset them. Anyway, when I wanted to pay for my beer and sandwiches I discovered I didn't have enough money. Left my wallet in the hotel. I called the waiter and explained to him what happened. Told him I could be back in ten minutes. But he immediately became nasty and called the manager. This man lammed right into me, calling me a 'dirty nigger'. I offered to leave my watch with them as a guarantee until I brought the money. He just went on calling me names. I said he could send the waiter with me to make sure I don't abscond, but he refused to listen to reason. So finally I got mad too and grabbed him by the front of his shirt. In a jiffy the whole café was on top of me. Just as well somebody called the police, else it could have been a proper fuck-up."

"Did the police let you go?"

"Not a bit. Started yelling at me all over again. Then bundled me into a car, and off to the station. When I tried to explain to the constable next to me where I came from, he really exploded: 'Why didn't you stay in South Africa then?

217

There they would have kept you in your place.' On and on it went. After an hour or so at the station they finally allowed me to phone my friends, and they came round immediately. Quite a commotion, as you can imagine. Official apologies from the police, the lot. But it was too late, as far as I was concerned."

I felt sick, but tried to talk it down; which made me even more dissatisfied with myself. "Mandla, but it could have happened to anybody. The man thought you were trying to cheat him, that's all. It's got nothing to do with race."

"'Dirty nigger'?" he asked testily. "I was quite prepared to accept that he got mad when he thought I wanted to take him for a ride. But 'dirty nigger'? That was the first thing he said, you see. Straight from the guts, a reflex. Not 'bloody thief', but 'dirty nigger'. That wasn't the only time it happened to me either. And Holland wasn't the only country. What hit me was that I came here to look for support, expecting people to care for our struggle. All the hospitality, the back-patting, the money — was it just to salve their own consciences then?"

"There are people who care," I answered, but without daring to look at him.

He went on as if he hadn't heard me: "Yesterday, when you told me about the Jews in Avignon, and how they got blamed for the Plague, and how even the Pope couldn't help them — I mean, hell, if *he* couldn't do anything, then who could — ?" (And I hadn't even realized that he'd been paying attention after all!) "You know, when I was in East Berlin in August, you should have seen how royally they treated us, simply loaded us with money. But *why*, d'you think? Just to get rid of us again as soon as possible, I tell you. So that we could go and do their dirty work for them: throw off the yoke and bend our necks for the new bosses. And then they talk about freedom! I met several African students over there, just back from Lumumba University. And what they told me about how they were treated in Moscow by the very people who were supposed to train them for revolution! — just the same kind of racist

218

bastards you find anywhere else." He shook his head slowly, sadly. "Even George's stab in the back was easier to take than that."

"Paul has a theory about it," I said quietly, knowing it was up to me now to lighten the black heaviness of his mood.

"Everybody's got theories about it," he snarled. "What difference does it make to *me*? I'm not a fucking theory."

"The way Paul sees it," I went on, grimly determined to get through to him, "is that we're making a terrible mistake by regarding 'civilization' as the natural condition of people. We've barely had time to get used to it. If you look at us in perspective, it's only yesterday we started developing from the state of animals. So we're really no more than an aberration, a mutation, something unnatural. Our whole civilization is unnatural."

"What about it?" he said roughly. "I could have told you that long ago."

"I know. But try to think of racism in the same way. We regard it as 'uncivilized', but actually it's part of our natural condition to resent and hate and persecute whatever looks different from ourselves. It threatens us. It's something we've got left over from our animal state: and only here and there you'll find exceptions, individuals or societies that have progressed a bit further. The rest is still 'on the road'. People must be given a chance to come to terms with it first before they can start thinking about the next step forward."

"And in the meantime it's all right for them to trample on me? Did you like being thrown out of that smart place last night? Oh, they were very civilized about it, I know. But what it came down to was that we were thrown out, plain and simple."

"It was just as bad for me as for you, Mandla. Perhaps even worse."

He stares at me in silent defiance.

"Paul once said: 'In the Middle Ages people who had the Plague were isolated or ostracized. They were supposed to be possessed by evil spirits, so the victim was often killed. Today we no longer kill people, we try to heal them.' He's absolutely convinced of it, Mandla: you can't get rid of racism by treating it like the plague: the only way is to regard them as sick people who have to be healed with patience. Until at last we'll all have grown out of our mental Middle Ages into a slightly more civilized future."

"You allow yourself to be convinced by him?" he asked. "Why? Because you cannot look truth in the face? Look, instead of swallowing Paul's little theories about racism: suppose it isn't a sickness but some kind of wild animal? You can try to tame it. In the end it may eat from your hand and lick your face. But one day it sees its chance to tear you to pieces."

"Dogs were also wild animals once," I insisted. "Today they're domesticated."

"And that comforts you? That makes you believe *all* animals can be tamed? Even if it's true, even if they'll all be domesticated in a hundred or a thousand years from now: what about me? what about me, here, today? I'm not looking back over a thousand years, Andrea. I'm right here, now. I'm burning *now*. I'm being torn to pieces *now*. Don't try to comfort me!"

Perhaps it was a good thing that the *patron* chose that moment to bring our breakfast. (He'd remembered from the previous day: chocolate for me, coffee for Mandla.) But it didn't calm Mandla down; he was quiet for only a few minutes. Then, throwing his croissant down onto his plate, he got up.

"Aren't we doing anything today then? Why don't we get going?"

"It's too early, Mandla. We can look at the map together just now and plan something. Sit down and finish your breakfast first."

"There's no time to eat." But then, changing his mind, he sat down again. "I'm fed up, Andrea. Look at me, eating this fine white man's food. Look at the hotel I'm staying in — " He waved his arm towards the large stone building as if he would like to demolish it. "And all the time I'm lying about

220

here — there's those people over there: *they* got no time to rest."

"Is there someone waiting for you?" I asked.

"They all waiting." Then he grasped what I had meant. "No. Of course not. I'll make sure there never is anyone again."

"So there was someone?" Why did I keep nagging? It had nothing to do with me; it might be safer not to know.

"OK, so I had a woman," he said unexpectedly, as if to challenge me. "We weren't married, but we were together. Ntsiki. She was carrying my child. Three months, then the *Boere* picked her up. Not because of something she did, you understand: actually she was always trying to hold me back, scared something would happen to me. We often quarrelled about it. You see, I didn't want to tell her what I was working on, it's not a woman's business." (I was ready to interrupt, but restrained myself. This was no time to argue about a thing like that: he probably wouldn't even realize what had upset me. What he expected from a woman was compliance, subservience.) "Right, so the *Boere* took her away. Trying to get at me through her. They thought she would talk." A flash of pride: "They didn't know Ntsiki. For two months they kept on with her. We never even knew where they were holding her. If somebody took her food or clothing, they just said: 'She isn't here.' It turned out to be King William's Town, but that we only found out afterwards, when she came back."

"And the child?" I asked, my lips dry; my scalp felt taut.

"For months they held her," he repeated, staring straight in front of him. "That Boer's name was Willemse. They called him 'Spike'."

"Why?"

He glanced at me, his eyes narrowing. "Just because." He slowly clenched and unclenched his hands as if they were numb.

"And the child?" I insisted. I had to know.

"No, after they got the child out of her, they let her go. They had nothing against her."

221

I could feel my lips moving. I wanted to say something, but nothing came through. I drew my arms together across my belly.

It took some time before he continued: "Afterwards her father came to fetch her. They were Transkei people, and when they heard about what happened they said she had to stop living with me in Port Elizabeth. I went after her to bring her back, but her brothers chased me away with knobkerries. That wouldn't have stopped me, except that she said in front of me she couldn't take it any more. She never told the *Boere* a thing about me, but all the same she couldn't go on. Perhaps, if I could have spoken to her alone she would have said something else. But I suppose it was better for me too, that way. I loved Ntsiki, I was going to marry her. But how could I do that to her? If they hurt her like that again, it would be the end of me. Also, if I went on with my way of life, working for the unions, getting in trouble with the police all the time, and *impimpi* everywhere — the spies, the informers, people like George — how could I survive if I had to worry about a wife and kids? If you're in a struggle like that, you got to make up your mind. It's all or nothing. The struggle itself becomes your wife and kids. You're not a private person any more, because everything that's private they can touch. It's the balls they can grab you by. So you must make sure they get nothing to grab. And you must be hard, else you don't last. You're like a naked man running in the dark. If you stop, they catch you. It's just running, running all the time. That's why you got to be free of wife and kids. And after Ntsiki left, I swore I would close that part of my life up forever. One got to be true to one's name."

"What has your name got to do with it?"

"When I was born, I was my father's first, and things were hard for them right then, so my father said: 'This son must give me my power back, so we can stand on our feet again and walk through the world in pride.' That's why he called me Mandla. *Power. The strong man.* I got to survive. But I can't do it here. I'm losing all my force here. And over there — " He shook his head. "What am I going back to? I know I got to. I must. But

222

what am I going to *do* there? You think I want to go back to kill, to hunt and be hunted, to help soak the earth in blood?"

"Is it really all that's left?"

"That's what they heading for. And it's all their doing." Deep bitterness was burning in his voice. "Nine wars it cost them to get us where we are now. Do you know the Eastern Cape at all? Its aloes and thickets, its euphorbias, the deep kloofs of its rivers, and the ridges of its mountains. Why are those aloes so red, d'you think? It's blood. Why do the bushes grow so thick there? It's because their roots go down to the blood of all the warriors who died there. If you're alone on a mountain late in the afternoon, at sunset, you can hear them coming up from the shadows, all the great men. Hintsa. And Ngqika. Kreli. Sandile. Makana. Wars and wars and wars, all because of this land which once was ours. At night, in the moonlight, their spirits wander about. All the thousands who died, their feet black with blood. And they won't ever rest before they got a place of their own. Nine wars there was, the last of them just a hundred years ago. Now it's getting time for the tenth. And this one we not going to lose." Adding, so softly that I could hardly hear him: "*Nkosi sikelel' iAfrika.*"

The gloominess, the silent deep restrained violence of his voice, made it difficult for me to speak for some time. Yet I had to persist, to persuade not so much Mandla as myself: "There *must* be other ways too, not only bloodshed."

"Don't you think we've tried other ways? Don't you think *I* have?" For a moment I thought he would elaborate, but I suppose he didn't trust me quite enough for that yet. All he said, was: "It's not we who wanted it this way. They left us no choice."

"And now you must go on, whatever the cost?"

"Well, if you got to die — " He reflected for a long while. "At least you have the choice what you want to die for. As long as you can do that, you haven't lost."

"Have you talked to Paul about this?" I suddenly asked, as if that offered a way out.

Mandla gave a short laugh. "We hardly spoke about any-

223

thing else, these last weeks. Paul understands my feelings."
And then: "But what's he going to do about it? That's what
worries me."

"Paul has a conscience."

"I shit on his conscience. It's what you *do* that counts.
That's all. When it comes to the last trench, he's still white,
and I'm black. We can never look at anything the same way.
He's living in luxury."

"It's no fault of his."

"I'm not talking about money. I'm talking about being
white. He can afford to be liberal."

"Why are you telling me all this?" I asked, rebellious.
"Don't draw me into it." Why was it suddenly feeling like
pleading? "If there really is to be a war, then keep it between
yourselves. I'm neither black nor white."

"Right, so you're in between. It means you got to choose."
(Boetie!)

"I've already made my choice. Hasn't Paul told you?"

"I know why you left the country. But there must have been
a time when you could have gone back if you wanted to."

"I didn't want to, that's all."

If a prisoner escapes from his jail, can anything persuade
him to return? Brian had made it inevitable for me to run
away, all right: but I'd known very well — if not at the time
then afterwards — that he had been no more than an opportunity I'd grasped because life had already become unbearable.
Eventually something just snaps. Then it's past. Which was
why I'd proceeded deliberately to cut myself off from the
country. Now I no longer *wanted* to know what was happening there. It was no longer necessary. In fact, it could only
threaten me, gnaw at my security. As long as I continued to
cling to the past I could never be free.

"You can't expect me to go back," I said as calmly as I
could. "What shall I do there? What *can* I do?" I became more
aggressive. "It's men who made history, not women. Black or
white, they were all of them men. It's men who've been
making war, ever since the time of the Bible. Just look at all

224

those lists: so-and-so begat so-and-so. And such-and-such begat such-and-such. Father and son, father and son, all the way. You've kept us out of it. Now you can clear up your own mess."

"The greatest event in the history of my people," he said quietly, "was caused by a woman. When the spirits spoke to the girl Nongqawuse and told her that the people must kill all their cattle and burn all their wheat and wait for the day when the sun would turn back to the East from the middle of the sky, the day all the ancestors would rise again so that the dead and the living together could drive the white men into the sea — "

"No spirits ever spoke to me."

"I'm speaking to you."

"I prefer to stay out of history."

I didn't want to argue with him. Even when he was excited or eager I could feel the weight of his sorrow; the previous day I'd been too dumb to understand. Now, having become aware of it, I felt the dark need to know more. Even so, he shouldn't expect me to give up everything just like that.

Perhaps, I thought, it would help him compose himself if I could persuade him to resume his more personal memories. I wanted to *talk*; not to be "addressed": that put me on the defensive, even scared me off.

"How did it all begin, Mandla?" I asked him deliberately. "What triggered it off for you?"

For a moment he seemed perplexed. Or perhaps he was, once more, sizing me up.

"It was my father," he said at last. "But how can I make you understand about a father and his son — ?"

"I know what my father meant to me."

"When I was a child we were poor — I tell you, man, we were dirt poor — but my father was my father. No matter if his pants were patched, never mind the tear in the seat, or the tattered old khaki hat on his head, to me he was a giant, greater even than Makana. No one could walk through the veld like he did. No one was so tall and straight. No one could

225

hunt like him. No one could talk the way he did. And because I was his only son he always, ever since I was very small, spoke about the things we'd be doing together, the two of us, once I was grown-up, a man like him."

He remained silent for so long that I had to prod him: "What happened then?"

They arrive at the butchery together, the father and his son, both of them grey with dust, for it's a long road they have behind them, several days' walk from Port Elizabeth. Usually they come in to town once or twice a year: just before winter, and again before Christmas, with some money they've saved, and skins and eggs to barter, a few chickens, and a goat or two if it's a good year. When several people club together it's possible to rent a donkey-cart. But this time, because of the bad drought, it's only their family, so they've had to come on foot. Now their few things have been bought and sold, the womenfolk are off to Pep Stores for clothes, and father and son have come in search of meat: soon they'll be on the road again. The butchery is so crowded that the boy — not used to white people and very young, only about ten or so — hesitates on the doorstep while his father goes inside. From the door the boy watches a small herd of red oxen approach, followed by a child with long thin legs, switch in hand, his only clothing an old tattered jersey full of holes that hangs down to his knees. A car that has just pulled out from behind the butchery hoots impatiently; the little herd-boy rounds up his oxen against a fence, anxiously trying to get them out of the way. Their eyes white as they bellow in fear and rage, some of the animals rear up in the herd, half climbing on the bodies in front of them, making thrusting movements with their massive loins as if, castrated or not, they're eager to cover everything in their way. It takes a while before the herd-boy can control them again and pursue his dusty journey in the direction of the abattoir.

A commotion inside the butchery attracts the attention of the boy on the doorstep. Anxious and curious, he edges past the screen-door. Some of the white people in the shop, it seems, are annoyed by his father's efforts to push past them to the counter. It's only when the butcher — a large man with a bald head and a red moustache, freckled arms the size and shape of a leg of beef — shouts something about a "bloody kaffir" that the child realizes it's serious. He keeps one hand on the handle of the screen-door, just in case. The butcher comes from behind his counter. The other Whites move aside, turning their backs, chatting away, pretending not to notice what is happening behind them. Now the big man has grabbed his father by the shirt-front, shaking him like a dog playing with a sack.

"Can't you see there's a separate door for Blacks? What are you doing on the white side?"

"Sorry, Master. I didn't know. I won't do it again."

"The hell you won't. Think the place belongs to you? Getting bloody cheekier by the day. I've had enough of your shit, you hear?"

"I said I'm sorry, *Baas*."

"Shut up!" The man slaps him in the face so that his head jerks back.

The child at the door is edging out of the way. Behind his father and the butcher he sees the row of bloody carcasses suspended from their hooks. Yesterday, no doubt, they were still alive, like the red oxen of a little while ago.

"Get out!" shouts the butcher.

The child trips over his own feet in his hurry to get out first. From a safe distance he sees his father bundled right through the frame of the screen-door; the butcher's voice comes bellowing after him from inside, followed by a roar of laughter from the other customers.

Behind the butchery a black delivery man appears pushing his bicycle, the front basket piled high with neat brown-paper parcels of meat — slaughtered, chopped into bits, weighed, sorted, manageable.

The man rides off. It's only the two of them now. But they do not walk together. The son keeps a few yards between him

227

and his father, refusing to look back even when his father calls out at him. He never wants to look in those eyes, that face, again.

The night Dedda came home so drunk that he had to support himself on the garden tap as he tugged at his flies, I quietly slipped back to bed in the end, not knowing whether I should laugh or cry. And the next morning I had to get up early to do some shopping before going out to UCT to work. On my way to the kitchen to make coffee I found Dedda sitting at the dining-table, his nearly empty bottle of cane in front of him, his eyes red and swollen. He tried to say something but had trouble controlling his tongue. It was obvious he hadn't been to bed at all. On other nights, if he came in so late, he would sleep it off immediately, even if it took the whole of the next day; but that night he'd stayed up.

Through painful screwed-up eyes he gazed at me as if he had to wade through many memories before recognizing me; even then he stayed silent.

"Morning, Dedda," I said. "Can I bring you some coffee?"

"What d'you mean 'morning'?" he mumbled. "It's still night."

It was no use arguing. I went to make coffee and came back to have mine with him, but he didn't touch his; from time to time, with a great effort, he would unscrew his bottle to take another swig, then fumble to put the cap back on again, staring fixedly at me as if he couldn't fathom my presence at all.

Once he got to his feet, stumbled across to the window and stood there staring out, his eyes more closed than open. "What d'you know?" he mumbled. "Just look at the sun coming up. And for what? Can you tell me for *what*?"

Then he returned, resuming his alternate staring and drinking. We were in the same room, but not together at all.

There we were, the two of us who usually, even when he was far gone, talked nineteen to the dozen: this time we couldn't think of anything to say. It quite unsettled me. Not

228

because he was so drunk; not the fact of our silence, but the discovery that we found ourselves in two wholly separated worlds. To me it was morning, the beginning of a new day; for him it was still last night. We were sharing the same space, but our times were different. And although we could see one another there was no conceivable way in which we could bridge that gap in time to touch each other.

Why did it unhinge me so?

Perhaps because it was the last time I saw Dedda alive. That same afternoon, before I came home from work, he went down to the harbour to join his trawler to Walvis Bay; and it was on the way back, six weeks later, that the wave washed him from the deck.

"It wasn't the day the bulldozers came to demolish the houses and the people were taken away on the trucks to the resettlement camp that I lost my father," said Mandla. "It was that day in the butchery. There are many ways to cut out a man's balls. And it wasn't just what they did to him, but doing it in front of me, that got me. I was his son. I saw it all."

I couldn't restrain myself. With a slight movement of my hand I touched his. He didn't react. But he didn't push me away either.

"From that day," he said, "all I wanted was to get away from home, so that I needn't look into my father's eyes again. I always wanted to go to school. There was a small farm school near our place, but one didn't learn much there. And that's how I got to Port Elizabeth. My mother had a sister living there, in New Brighton, and I went to live with her family. Because of the school, but also to get away from my father."

The little house in New Brighton overflowed with people. The woman, his aunt (I can't recall her name), had a large family: apart from four or five children of her own she also lodged her husband's sister and her two children; and because she was a generous person she'd allowed several acquaintances to put up a shack of corrugated iron and cardboard in her backyard, a small square of eroded, hard-baked red earth where her chickens scratched about in the daytime and slept in the carcass of an old car at night. She also kept a shebeen, and in the evenings the living-room was filled with chairs; in the kitchen the bottles and cartons of drink were unpacked, and all through the night there would be a coming and going of guests. Which didn't make it easy for Mandla to get on with his studies. The paraffin lamp in the room he shared with all the other children — all of them sleeping on the floor, as the single bed in the corner was for his aunt and her husband — was needed in the living-room; so he had to make do with a candle. Many nights, when he fell asleep over his homework, the wax would smudge his books, which meant a hiding at school next day. The school itself was just as crowded. If one didn't arrive well in time, the only place to sit would be on the floor or on a window-sill. Prefabs under corrugated iron; no ceiling. In summer it was so hot it made one dizzy; in winter the wind swept right through the place. But he persisted. He wanted a proper education. It was like a physical hunger inside him. Only with an education, he believed, would he be able to put his father behind him. The memory of that day in the butchery urged him on.

He was fortunate in finding a friend who helped him along: Vuyizile, the principal's son, who regularly brought him books he'd borrowed from his father. Anything on a printed page they devoured, no matter what it was. Vuyizile wanted to go into the church, his whole family was devoutly Catholic. Mandla hadn't made up his mind yet about what he would like to become. A teacher, perhaps. Or a lawyer. As long as it were a career in which he could go on reading.

He did well. But in what would have been his final year at school, the "unrest", as it was called, broke out, starting in Soweto and rippling right through the country. Everywhere, in New Brighton too, schools went up in flames. For days and nights on end, for weeks, there were the sirens of ambulances and police vans and the fire brigade. At first Mandla tried to keep out of it, determined to prepare for his exams. But it was impossible to stay at home while the townships were in turmoil. And his aunt was getting difficult too, because with police swarming all over the place she had to discontinue running her shebeen for the time being. Tempers were frayed.

One morning — all the schools that hadn't been burned down had long been closed — he was poring over his books in the bedroom when his aunt sent him out to buy bread. He protested. She flew into a rage: "You think you can just lie on our necks like this? What's this shit with the books all the time? You getting too white for us, I see!" By the time he ran out, slamming the front door behind him, he was in a foul temper.

Not far from the shop he noticed a crowd. It turned out that a police van had got stuck in a ditch; a group of school-children, seeing the acident, had assembled on the scene, jeering and ululating; panicking, one of the constables had fired a shot into the air. Instead of scaring off the children it had drawn yet more people to the scene, and by now the mood was turning sour. The police shot a way open through the crowd and made their escape to the shop a block away. Somone unscrewed the lid of the fuel tank and dropped in a match. Black smoke was still billowing from the wreck when reinforcements arrived: seven or eight armoured vehicles; men in camouflage suits, armed with automatic rifles. The crowd broke up in consternation. Mandla also ran away as fast as he could, but he stepped in a hole or on a loose stone and lost his balance; and the next moment he was bludgconed to the ground with the butt of a rifle.

"Leave me alone!" he screamed. "I wasn't fighting, I just went to buy bread!"

But the police paid no attention and dragged him back to the nearest van. Together with scores of others he landed in the cells.

He was lucky. For weeks and months special courts sat to process the detainees. Most of Mandla's friends, children of fourteen or fifteen, all those who couldn't afford legal advice, were sent to jail for years; several went to Robben Island. But Vuyizile's father, spurred on by his son, hired a lawyer and that speeded up Mandla's case. After only two months in detention he came to court; and thanks to the lawyer and the testimony of Vuyizile's father he was set free.

He immediately left New Brighton and went back home, refusing to have anything more to do with school. He'd got fed up with the hopelessly inferior education they'd been giving him anyway. Vuyizile came out to their settlement several times to try and persuade him to come back, but Mandla stubbornly refused. Just as stubbornly, Vuyizile proceeded to supply him with books again. New kinds of books. He hadn't known that such things existed in print; unable to control his appetite, he fell upon them as if physically to devour them. All the while Vuyizile went on nagging: no matter how bad the education was, it was still better than nothing. For months Mandla continued to resist, but when Vuyizile passed his matric at the end of the following year and started talking about going to university, he made up his mind: all right, then he would do so too. He also wanted to go to Fort Hare.

By that time his aunt had already moved out of New Brighton to a new township they'd opened between Zwide (rows upon rows of small identical boxes on the plains), the salt pans and the Chatty River. The people also called it Soweto, like the one at Johannesburg. A bare, barren stretch of earth, but his aunt thought they'd have more space there. Only, there were so many thousands of others who thought the same. Overnight the shacks began to sprout like weird unsightly growths. First a wooden framework fastened with wire and driven a few inches into the stony ground. A few cross-beams. Then the holes would be filled in: a doorframe, old windows "picked up", if you were lucky, in a scrapyard or at somebody's back door, corrugated iron, wood, hardboard, even cardboard if need be; with sheets of black vinyl or blue plastic, even yellow Checkers bags ripped open. The roof would be held in place by stones. Here and there taps were installed, surrounded by mudholes in which the smaller children spent their days. Clusters of toilets, each straddling its own hole; and if that began to overflow, the rickety structure would simply be moved elsewhere. Clouds of flies. Thin, ribbed, scavenging dogs. And all the time the people continued to pour into the place, month after month, year after year, like an infestation of rats. Dusty roads gradually turned into ditches. In the open patches among the shacks, rubbish dumps grew into small mountains, smoking day and night, in which old women and *kwediens* dug and burrowed in search of something edible or useful. Donkey-carts piled high with children and junk moved to and fro between Soweto and the white suburbs.

On one side the graveyard was also expanding steadily. Rows upon rows of small red mounds. Iron posts or wooden spars bearing heart-shaped boards. Names and dates. Ages: three months, four weeks, two weeks, six months, eleven months, eight days, twenty days. All the children. Gastroenteritis. Cholera. Measles. Whooping cough. Kwashiorkor.

In the midst of it all Mandla resumed his studies. At night with the candle beside him, in the stuffy but tidy little room with its chintz curtains while the men were drinking next door in the living-room, where the crockery was neatly displayed on the dresser against the plywood wall and plastic flowers stood stiffly in empty green bottles. By day he went to school, now more secretive than before, but more conscientious than ever. If Vuyizile could make it, there was no reason why he shouldn't. Another year and he'd be at Fort Hare. Then everything would change for the better.

Although it was I who had urged him to talk, I was almost relieved when he stopped. I had no defence against it.

"Why are you telling me this?" I asked again.

"Somebody got to know. Anything can happen to me. No matter whether it's now, or in a year, or in ten years. Then somebody got to know about it all."

Without saying anything more, he got up and went into the hotel. To pick up something in his room, or go to the toilet? I didn't know. I stayed behind, depressed. What did I really grasp of it then? How could I guess at what was already in our

233

midst, that heavy, unavoidable presence? His rebelliousness I could understand; the spurts of passion with which he grasped at certain ideas; even the occasional despair. But not the profound, submerged thing.

To counter my own depression I began to page through the books again, opened the map, a green smudge over the remains of our breakfast.

Paul. Even more than before I missed him.

"Aren't you expecting too much of your film, Paul? Can it really be so terribly important?"

"You know it's not just a film, Andrea. It's a way of trying to get a grasp on life again."

With sudden revolt I'd asked: "And you see me as part of that grasp?"

"No. You're part of life."

The Plague which broke out in Marseille in May 1720, spreading from there throughout the whole of Provence, has been regarded by some historians as the worst of all time, more destructive than even the Black Death of the fourteenth century. On the Saturday of 25 May, Marseille was still in the throes of its exuberant festivities in honour of Mademoiselle de Valois who'd arrived there on her way to Genoa where she was to marry the Prince of Modena. Dancing in the streets, a fair, cannon shots, unbridled gaiety. Towards evening, a boat from the East, the *Grand Saint-Antoine,* arrived from Smyrna and Tripoli and Cyprus and cast anchor in the port, loaded with cotton, silk, muslin and other materials. There were a few ill sailors on board, but Marseille was justly proud of its sanitary facilities, and the boat was promply placed under quarantine, the ill taken to a hospital. Everything appeared under control. Except that one of the stricken sailors, a Turk, handed his dirty clothes to his wife when she came to visit him in the hospital. She took the bundle to a laundry in the rue de l'Échelle. The laundrywoman died. Overnight the Plague was let loose in the city as if it had been lying in wait in the dark for years; by the

234

end of August a thousand people a day were dying in Marseille. From there it spread across the whole of Provence.

A remarkable twist to the prehistory of this outbreak has been recorded by Artaud. Twenty days before the arrival of the *Grand Saint-Antoine* in Marseille, at the time when no one on board had as yet fallen ill, the viceroy of Sardinia (a man, interestingly enough, with the name of Saint-Rémys), had had a most unusual dream, a nightmare in which he'd seen himself stricken by the Plague and his whole state wiped out by it:

Under the onslaught of the pestilence social forms disintegrate. Order breaks down. He witnesses all kinds of moral deviation, of psychological problems; inside himself he hears the murmur of his own bodily humours, torn asunder and entirely undone, turning heavy and changing slowly into carbon. Is it too late to cast a spell on the Plague? His insides destroyed, his organs pulverized and burnt to the very marrow, he still realizes that one does not die in a dream, that one will continue to function to the point of absurdity, to the negation of the possible, to a transmutation of the lie from which truth can be refashioned. He wakes up. Now he will be able to get rid of all the rumours he has heard about the Plague, about the miasmas of a virus brought from the East.

The very next day the *Grand Saint-Antoine* arrived in the harbour of Sardinia and requested permission to land. But the viceroy refused and the boat was forced to turn back to the open sea. His subjects were incensed by this inhumanity, this act of pure madness, because at that stage no one, not even the captain of the vessel, had the faintest idea that the Plague was on board. Only twenty days later —

However familiar I already was with all these texts I went on paging through the photocopies of the Artaud in a mixture of revulsion and fascination, waiting for Mandla to come back. The terrifying description of the disease:

235

Before any physical or psychological illness becomes obvious, the body is covered with red spots which the patient only discovers as they turn black. Before he can recover from his shock, his head begins to boil and grow unbearably heavy, and he collapses. He is overwhelmed by an atrocious fatigue, the fatigue of a central magnetic suction as his molecules are split and drawn to their destruction. His bewildered body fluids, shaken up and in disorder, appear to race through his body. His stomach contracts, it is as if his insides want to burst out through his teeth. One moment his pulse slows down to a mere shadow, then starts galloping to match the churning of his internal fever and the derangement of his mind. This pulse, beating as precipitately as his heart, intense, heavy, thundering; this red and burning eye which turns glassy; this gasping tongue, swollen and enormous, at first white, then red, then black, as if carbonized and cracked — everything announces an organic tempest beyond comparison. Soon the body fluids begin to search for an escape, like the earth tormented by thunderbolts or a volcano under the pressure of subterranean storms. In the centre of each spot a burning point is formed, and round these points the skin begins to blister, like bubbles forming under a lava skin; surrounding the bubbles circles appear of which the last, like the ring of Saturn enclosing its incandescent planet, indicates the limit of a bubo.

The body is covered with them. But just as volcanoes have their places of preference on earth, these buboes tend to concentrate in certain parts of the body. In the groin, in the armpits, in all the precious spots where the active glands faithfully perform their functions, the buboes appear through which the organism rids itself either of its internal putrefaction or, as the case may be, of its own life.

Two organs, especially, are singled out by the Plague, as Artaud sees it: the lungs and the brain, the only two organs that can be directly controlled by will and consciousness. We can master our thoughts as we can our breathing, accelerating or slowing them down — unlike other bodily functions like the circulation of blood, the digestive system, etc. *The Plague, then, seems to manifest itself in those parts of the body . . . . where the human will, conscience, and thought are expressed.*

As soon as Mandla returned to the terrace we set out together. Just as well, for the *patron* was beginning to make very obvious his irritation about my open map which prevented him from clearing away our breakfast things. I wanted to confer with Mandla about the route, but he wasn't interested. For the first part of the trip, in fact, until we reached Cavaillon, he didn't speak at all; merely grunted when I said or asked something. Was he regretting the way he'd opened up to me earlier, trying to distance himself from what he had confided?

The long avenue of plane-trees continued for many kilometres, now more exposed to light than in summer, offering a view of harvested fields and autumn vineyards, the summer's sunflower fields turned bare and brown.

Just after the first turn-off to Eygalières we passed the cyclist again, head down, tail raised like a target, sinewy legs thrashing, on his way to God knows where. I remembered the old story Paul had once told me, of the caliph or sultan who had an appointment with Death: because he misunderstood the message, expecting Death to turn up in his own city at nightfall, he hurried to Isfahan, very far away. Where he arrived just in time for the true appointment. Who knows, perhaps this poor creature lost from the Tour de France, was also hurrying towards a meeting with whatever he was so urgently trying to avoid.

I was tempted to drive to Eygalières, the small brown village among the olive-trees where Paul and I had spent a single night in the beautiful old stone Auberge (the almost medieval simplicity of the wide red bed and the flagstones in the bedroom; the leaves of elm and acacia outside the window; dinner in the courtyard where a row of old washing slabs — or slaughtering stones? — stood against the wall among old-fashioned hay-forks and wooden rakes and an enormous iron spring-trap, its jaws locked in an ominous grin). The serene chapel of Saint-Sixte on the road to Orgon, where the victims of the Plague had been nursed at a safe distance from the village. We would undoubtedly use the chapel in the film, a shelter for the refugees on their long journey (on their way out of the turbulent world or on the more subdued return?). But the memory was too intimate to share with Mandla: it belonged exclusively to Paul and me. The love we'd made that night: his indefatigable virility, his control, his intuition about my body. And in the course of it he'd asked the question which had now sent me back to Provence. No, I wasn't ready yet to return to that inn and assume my full responsibility for that unforgettable night.

(*"How I love this furious body of yours."*)

Was it a way of being unfaithful to Paul not to take the detour to Eygalières? Evasion; a lack of loyalty? (*I shall always come back to you.*) Or, on the contrary, an urgent desire to preserve something intact?

After Cavaillon the landscape changed. At first an untidy stretch with ugly modern buildings and factories on either side, interspersed with thickets of reeds. Then one entered the long plains, pale ochre, with the Luberon mountains to the right, dark and brooding even on a light summer's day; and on the left the tumbled range of the Vaucluse. The transparency of autumn. At home it would be spring now. (I was startled by the thought: not just by the idea of spring, but by the discovery that I'd thought of it as "home"!) The sudden, brutal seasons of my land. No gradual transition from winter to spring, like here; nothing of the gentleness with which a seasoned lover like Paul would initiate a virgin, but an angry violation, a ferocious affirmation. Excessive, overwhelming, bringing with it the smell of dust corroding the sweetness of blossoms; the certainty of merciless sun, of new drought, of brittle yellow grass. A climate of extremes; a barely curbed violence hovering, always, just below the surface. And the curious thing was

238

that, as we proceeded through the landscape, that absent spring was more real to me than the slightly hazy autumn through which we drove. An awareness of savage life refusing to be thwarted or ordered, struggling against predictability and the eventual security of death.

All the strategies, all the incredibly complicated plans and schemes and arrangements to spend some time together and evade the world. Going up Table Mountain in separate cable cars, wandering about for hours before meeting, "by accident", at the appointed place. (Only, on this particular day, there are so many tourists on the Mountain that they find nowhere to hide; and in the end, to avoid suspicion, they have to return, frustrated and depressed.) When she goes to his flat in Rosebank, she gets off the bus several stops too early to shake off possible spies, then boards the next bus. Earlier, they used to work together all day without giving it a second thought; now fear has seeped in. They take turns to wander through the building at irregular intervals so that no one will become suspicious. On the few occasions when she allows him to drive her home, he drops her a few blocks from her house so that his car will not be noticed.

Not that her younger brother is fooled by it.

"What's the matter with you these days?" he confronts her one Sunday afternoon. "You can't sit down for a moment. You got an itch in your arse?"

"I'm bored."

"Looks like you're waiting for someone."

"Who can I be waiting for?"

"Who's the man who brought you home the day Dedda died?" The question is like a blow in the solar plexus; she has to restrain herself from doubling up.

"He's a — he's just someone doing research at the varsity. Been working on it for over a year. I'm typing his notes."

His aggressive dark eyes. "He screwing you?"

"You mad or something? What makes you think such a thing?"

239

"I was just asking."

In spite of herself, she turns away. "What's it to you what I do or who I do it with?"

"A white man! Aren't you ashamed of yourself?"

Stung, she swings round. "Why should I be ashamed? Is it a sin to love somebody? What about you? You've been sleeping around ever since you were fifteen. Don't think I didn't notice."

"I keep away from Whites."

"Brian didn't do anything to you, Boetie. Leave him alone."

"Why d'you think we are living here on the Flats in the wind and the dust? Who threw us out of District Six? Who took away our right to vote? Who fucks us around from the day we're born — ?" In the violence of his frustration he spits on the floor. "Who makes all the laws? Can't do this, can't do that — ? Come on, I'm asking you."

"Brian is English. He's got nothing to do with it."

"You think he'll take you to England with him? Or has he just found himself a bit of brown ass to keep his cock busy? Yes, *Baas*. No, *Baas*. Please fuck me, *Baas*."

"Boetie — !" She comes up very close to him, trembling. "I'll kill you."

"Have a try."

When they were children she could dominate him as she liked; he's two years younger. Now he is a head taller.

"What d'you think Dedda would have said about it?" he taunts her.

"Jesus, that's below the belt," she whispers. "I thought you had more in you than that. Leave Dedda out of it. I'm the only one in this house who ever understood him. You were always otherwise. So keep out of it."

"I wish I could," he snaps. "You're the one who draws everybody else into it. One can't stir a finger anymore, 'cause we're being watched all the time. Because of you."

"Nobody knows."

"Is that what you think?"

"What are you scared of? You got something to hide then?"

Less than a fortnight later there's a knock on the door. In the small hours of the night, just after four. The gentle balminess of September in the air. A whole bunch of men on the doorstep. They've come to search the house from one end to the other, as the family sits herded together in the living-room. Grampa, short-sighted and toothless. Gran, large and flabby in her night-dress, like a shapeless feather mattress hung over a chair. Ma in curlers, thin and frightened, convinced that this must be the prelude to the Last Judgement. Maggie, her dressing-gown buttoned to the throat. Boetie, brooding in the corner. Andrea in the silk gown Brian has given her for her birthday, last April: chin up, her back straight and defiant against the wall.

In Boetie's room they find (or at least, that is what they report) the books, the pamphlets, the stencilled sheets. No one in the family has had an inkling of it; Andrea certainly not.

Two of the men escort him out. At the front door he tears himself away from them and comes running back to Andrea: "It's all because of you!" he hisses.

They come back to fetch him; this time with more force.

The other men — four or five have remained behind — take their time to tidy up.

"And so they should," Gran says loudly, seething. "Blerry impertinent they are. Got no manners."

Only when they prepare to leave the officer in charge, the one who showed the warrant as they first came in, turns to Andrea. "Will you come with us, please?"

Her heart contracts.

"Now what's she supposed to have done?" demands Gran.

"Just routine," says the man. "It shouldn't take long."

"Why can't you talk to me here?" asks Andrea, controlling her voice with some difficulty.

"We prefer to do it there. Then we don't disturb anybody. Will you please get dressed and come with us?"

"You think maybe I'll seduce you like this?" But she returns to her room. Maggie, suddenly tearful, wants to go with her; but they restrain her.

241

Just after nine the next morning she is home again, still in time to get to work without having to think of embarrassing explanations.

After that the strategies become even more elaborate. For Brian's sake, mainly. As for Andrea, there's something almost reckless in her attitude. Certainly defiance. *You think you can tame me so easily? It's just for his sake —*

The clandestine weekday trips to Onrust; to Steenbras. Once or twice, when some of his colleagues are away, they borrow a house or a flat for a night or a weekend, spending hours to make sure they get there separately, and unnoticed. Never a message on the telephone. Never a letter, not even a note.

A feeling, nevertheless, of slowly suffocating. For no matter how careful you are, you *know* you're being watched. You just know it. In the most innocent gesture or manoeuvre something suspicious can be detected. How much more so in what is *not* innocent! A growing desperation. And yet, at the same time, a singular, excessive elation: *We're alive! Oh God, it's so terribly dangerous, the abyss is so deep, we're dancing on the most precarious of ropes: but we're alive!*

Now and then an instant of despair, especially in him: "Andrea, I can't do this to you. It's so humiliating to live like this. I love you, I'm not ashamed of it. I want to show you to the world: 'Look at her, this is the woman I love!' "

"Finish your work first, Brian. There'll be enough time later."

"I can't expose you to so much danger."

"Then leave me."

"Andrea, how can you say a thing like that?"

"Well, stop complaining then. I love you. That's all I want for now."

"I want you, don't you realize that?"

"You've got me."

"How can I have you if it's a crime just to hold you in my arms?"

"I can take it."

"Andrea, Andrea — "

"Don't talk so much. We have little enough time together. Hold me."

Duration is unthinkable. A single lapse of concentration: one night in his flat, in the rambling old building set deep in a garden bordered by tall fir-trees. Redbrick below, cream above. Noisy water-pipes. The smell of damp towels. Floorboards moving under one's weight. Disembodied radio music behind walls. A sheet torn in the violence of their lovemaking. An uncontrollable fit of laughter. Then the depths of a satiated sleep. And, like an alarm clock in the middle of the night, the banal shrilling of the front-door bell.

"Brian, who can it be?"

"Don't worry, it's all right. Relax. You stay right here. I'll be back."

The dumb contractions of her heart.

In a daze of sleep he struggles into his dark blue gown and stumbles to the front door. Deep men's voices erupting into the room.

"Don't move. Stay where you are."

Camera flashlights blinding her, over and over.

She presses the torn sheet against her breasts. Somebody grabs it out of her hands. More flashes.

"Not a stitch!" Laughter.

"Check the sheets."

"Bring them along."

The bare bulb of the charge office. (Outside, the blue lamp.) Worn brown woodwork. Ink stains on a blotter. A notice-board with sheets of paper pinned to green felt. Brownish files with pink ribbons. A round tin filled with pins and paperclips. Full names. Address. Age. Race.

The worst — the worst, by far, of all — is the surgery of the District Surgeon. A grumpy, mumbling, middle-aged man, annoyed because he's been awakened from his sleep following an over-indulgent evening. (Stale whisky on his breath.) Teeth discoloured by nicotine, like the second and third fingers of his right hand, the fingers he sheaths in a rubber glove to poke

243

into her. Her vagina distended by the cold metal speculum. The thin wood spatula. "We'll need a smear." The matt light on his bald head. Long grey wisps of hair wiry from sleep.

"Jesus, you people."

With his back to her he stands scrubbing his hands vigorously for a long time, as if he's been infected by her.

The dull pain caused by the rough examination. (The next day: a hint of blood in her panties.)

Brian has gone. They've taken him away while she was with the doctor.

"I'm not going to a cell like this. I want to get dressed first."

Two constables take her back to the flat building in their van; in the early dawn the customary cream has turned a vulgar pink. They go inside with her. One remains in the living-room — last night's plates and the wine bottle and glasses are still there: they were in such a hurry to get to bed — while the other escorts her to the bedroom.

"Get out, I want to change."

He grins.

She holds the lapels of her dressing-gown very tightly together.

"Why are you covering up like that?" he asks. "You don't have any secrets from me, do you? How about it?" He presses a cupped hand to his balls, shaking them.

She stares at him in silence. Then doubles up without warning and starts vomiting. On the floor, and on a corner of the blue bedside carpet. All the remains of last night's meal, which she prepared for Brian and herself. Mushrooms. Bits of meat. Carrot. Everything turned sour, and green with bile.

The road to Gordes branched off to the left. We drove uphill to the little town growing right out of the mountain in the morning air bitter-sweet with cypresses; from the bottom of the slope, the darker smell of olives. On the far side of the narrow plain, below the Luberon range — a massive, sleeping animal — were the dark red cliffs of Roussillon which Brian and I had

244

visited eight years before. We'd roared and rattled up the hill in an ancient bus all the way from Apt. The village had been one of the most delightful discoveries of our trip; like an entranced Hansel and Gretel we'd wandered hand in hand through the ochre caves. I'd rubbed the fine red dust into my face, redder than any Indian's, hiding behind the pines to scare the passers-by. Brian had been terribly embarrassed by me, but nothing could dampen my high spirits. Suddenly, quite unexpectedly, it had begun to rain, a heavy thunderstorm which rapidly turned the entire mountainside into a liquid mass: and because of the red-and-yellow ochre, the earth seemed to change into blood and honey. Drenched, we ran back into the village, my face and hair stained with the brightly coloured mud; as far as we went we seemed to leave a spoor of blood. No wonder the *patron* of the small hotel where we tried to find lodging promptly threw us out. By then we were already so thoroughly soaked that we simply sat down on a glistening wall beside the village square to wait out the storm — an end which came just as abruptly as the rain had begun. We ran downhill from the village, into a pine forest, where in a secluded spot we took off our clothes and spread them out on the branches to dry while we stood in the sun, shivering lightly, trying to warm ourselves. I pressed myself against his thin white body: "Hold me," I said, but he only embraced me very briefly, clumsily, before he moved away again, afraid that someone might see us.

"What does it matter if they see us?" I asked.

"I feel too exposed like this."

"I'll cover you."

"Andrea, don't be silly."

"If we were at the Cape now you would have made love to me."

"Just because we had to use every possible opportunity."

"Now I disgust you. You're ashamed of me."

"For heaven's sake, stop it! Before you make me say something we'll both regret."

"Are you scared then?"

Suddenly, disarmingly: "Yes. Because sometimes I get the impression that you're no longer the person I once knew."

"Perhaps you've never known me after all. Did you really love me, Brian, or did you just use me to hit apartheid below the belt?"

I fully expected him to strike me; I was stunned by my own audacity. But worst of all was the silence that followed, in which neither of us was brave enough to risk being the first to apologize.

That night in Montbrun, where we'd hitchhiked in the afternoon, I repulsed his efforts to soften me up. He became angry. "In Roussillon, right there in the open, all you could think of was to make love. Now that we're safely surrounded by walls — "

"It wasn't in the open, it was in a dense forest. Here I feel suffocated. The room is too small."

"Are you blaming me now because I can't afford anything better?"

"I'm not blaming you for anything, Brian. Just leave me alone, please."

Eight years later, when Paul and I had come back this July, we'd also visited Roussillon: part of my attempt to return to as many of the places I'd been to before as possible — even though I hadn't told him about it, not wanting to hurt him. (Would it have hurt him? I'm sure Paul would have understood only too well.) It had settled like a fever in my body, this urge to delve into the past. Looking for — what? I couldn't even define it. Except that it had been something lost along the way, something of tremendous importance. A form of innocence? No: rather a sense of originality. Only once in life can one love so absolutely. So wildly, so demandingly, overwhelmingly, cruelly, beautifully.

I couldn't find the spot in the wood again. Somewhere, I'd thought illogically, I would suddenly come upon us again: breaking through a ring of pines I'd immediately recognize the place, and find two young people there, he white, she brownskinned; and who knows, perhaps this time they would be

246

making love. But the wood had been deserted, except for the birds — and, of course, Paul and me.

"Looking for something?" he'd asked at last, amused and quizzical.

"No. Let's got up to the village and have something to drink."

Even the hotel where we'd been thrown out so unceremoniously I couldn't locate with any certainty. Yet, in the course of our summer trip, I *had* occasionally recognized something to which I'd reacted with the familiar shock in the guts, even though, most of the time, it was very elusive: the movement of chestnut leaves, the swinging skirt of a passing girl, an old man on a doorstep, the dilapidated notice-board of a third-grade hotel. In my mind it was possible to retrace at least some of those early steps: here this had happened, there that — But I could no long *grasp* it. Everything had changed. (Even the sun: from late spring to midsummer.) Shops had closed down, pensions had disappeared, old buildings had been demolished or renovated beyond recognition, revels had ended, people had died. I, too, was different. Here I was back, with Paul. Like him, at least in part, I "belonged" here now. I could speak the language. I could find my own way. I was more or less independent. Hopefully something in me would never be completely tamed, but at least that terribly distant spring had passed forever. The savage romanticism, the oppressiveness of small hot rooms, two bodies wrestling or lying apart in apathy. The awful, exposed hurt. The anguish about what was past, about what might lie ahead. Past, past.

We didn't spend much time in Gordes. (In July Paul had had trouble dragging me out of the alluring little shops: the silversmiths, the joiners, the candle-makers, the honey vendors, the potters, the sellers of small jars of citronella or lavender to keep away mosquitoes, the weavers; I'd even, in spite of the midsummer heat, bought myself a multicoloured woven mohair coat for a winter about which I couldn't even dream as yet.) Back down the sweet-smelling slope, into the open plains among vineyards and olive orchards and the bare fields where lavender and wheat had lain so unashamedly in the sun. In the distance ahead the plains ended against the sheer cliffs of Lioux, unless one turned off to the right, towards Apt, as we planned to do. But first, after Gordes, there was the small hamlet of Joucas on the summit of one of the foothills of the Vaucluse mountains.

It had been a good day when Paul had first taken me there. And the luxurious Mas des Herbes Blanches — an access road lined with purple lavender; honey-coloured stone, terracotta roof, tall cypresses, a crystalline swimming-pool; an incomparable meal on the terrace — had so charmed Paul that we'd stayed on for several days. Also, it was the ideal place from which to drive into the mountains to see the Wall of the Plague or whatever remained of it, high up in that wilderness, beyond the village of Murs. Except that we'd never got as far as that on the first day, having spent too much time on the terrace and in the pool. "Tomorrow," we'd promised ourselves. And then again: "Tomorrow. Most certainly tomorrow." Yet something had always held us back.

How he'd been questioning me again, that day on the way to Joucas! Irrepressible, like a boy whose curiosity has no end.

"What more can I possibly tell you?" I'd laughed at last. "You almost know me better than I know myself by now."

"I want to know everything. About all the years before I met you."

"Are you jealous?"

"Not of Brian, not of other men, if that's what you're thinking. But jealous to know that so many people shared something of you of which I know nothing."

"It's not important."

"But what you are now is the outcome of everything you've ever been, Andrea."

"You may not approve of all the Andreas I have in me. I warned you long ago. Some of them are nasty, bitchy, screwed-up, hungry, destructive."

"I want them too."

248

"You're too inquisitive. Sometimes you scare me. I need breathing space, Paul."

"I don't want to smother you. I just want to know everything about you: the way I know your body."

"A lover doesn't really know the woman he loves. Not even her body. Especially not her body. You only see what you want to see; what you desire."

"Do you mistrust me then?"

"No." I'd kissed him on the cheek. "On the contrary. You make me feel very good. You make me feel a woman, a person. But please don't ever turn me into a story. I'm not a story, I'm me."

"That's what I'm trying to grasp. The *you* in you."

"Let's play hide-and-seek then."

"Are you daring me?"

"Perhaps."

Then we'd arrived at Joucas.

On the road to Joucas Mandla took something from his pocket and held it to his mouth with both hands. For a while I couldn't make out what he was doing. Then a low, windy, droning sound insinuated itself into my mind, a monotonous, disembodied, strangely familiar sound that disturbed and moved me, because it was the first time in years I'd heard it again. A sound that didn't pass through the ears, but was absorbed by the body itself, trembling in the very marrow and the blood. The sound of a *trompie*. A Jew's-harp. It was like a sound from a dream already forgotten. And as it came back, it suddenly revived the dream as well. (Last night!) I couldn't even remember exactly where I'd heard it before. Not with Dedda. He'd had a mouth-organ. Perhaps it was the mere gesture of the two cupped hands held to the mouth, rather than the sound as such? But there was something about the sound too. I knew it. A sound from the nights and dreams of my childhood. One of Boetie's friends perhaps? A neighbour? Someone passing in the street very late at night, from one lamp-post to the next, hands cupped against the mouth, murmuring this sad, plaintive, tuneless little tune. Warm summer nights in our small stuffy room, the shuffling sounds of the old people next door; Maggie and Ma in their beds, the sea in the distance: no audible sound, just a presence. The foghorn moaning in the dark. And the first discovery of latent pleasures kindled in oneself, a new awareness of the body, perspiration, tensed muscles, the intimate smells of oneself. And that eerie sound somewhere in the large, hollow, fertile shell of the night.

That one journey with Dedda, in a borrowed old jalopy, through the enormous land. Nights under the stars, with the glow from the lights of a distant town against the sky. Wind. Space. And once again that sound from God knows where; some nameless, invisible wanderer in the night perhaps. In the Karoo, or on the bare plains of the Free State, the Highveld. Dedda and I: and that sound. Never connected with a person or a name, just the sound as such, as if it were the land itself that moaned in sleep, a plaint from all the blood and violence and meekness of its timeless times. Wind keening through the bones of the veld, through brittle peeling layers of stone, through tumbleweed and Karoo shrubs and the dried stems of aloes, sisal plants, euphorbias. Your very own voice, Grandpa Xhorê, lamenting through the ages and refusing to be comforted.

"Where did you find it?" I asked Mandla when at last I could speak again. (Joucas to the left, brown walls and discoloured roof-tiles on its small outcrop of sun-scorched rock.)

He went on playing for some time as if he hadn't heard, his body swaying gently to the rhythm, a motion much too big for the cramped space of the car.

"My *trompie*?" His voice caressed the word. "I didn't find it. You might say it found me. It was while I was still living at my aunt's place in New Brighton, soon after I first got there. She'd given me a hiding and I was feeling as miserable as hell. Felt like running away, except there was nowhere to go. A windy August day. It was still cold, there was frost in the mornings, and a thin wind cutting right through one. Papers, tins, all

250

kinds of rubbish in the streets. A few donkeys. Dogs sniffing my legs. So I just wandered about, feeling sorry for myself. I stumbled over a stone and fell, skinning my knees. That was the bloody end. I just cried and cried. Then a police van came past. They were always on their rounds, day and night. You never got away from them. There was a man in the back, like a monkey in a cage. Must have been on their way to the charge office, except the cops generally didn't like to go back with only one at a time, so they were cruising about looking for others. I pressed myself against a redbrick wall. The man in the back, the monkey, called out to me. I was scared to go nearer, but he kept on waving at me while the van stood idling on a street corner and in the end I slinked up to him. "Hey, man, take this," the man said and he shoved the *trompie* through the wire-mesh of his cage. I waited till the van had gone before I picked it up from the dust. That's how I got it. It dried my tears for me. And I've never been without it since."

He began to play again. At the crossroads we turned off towards Apt.

"I brought it with me," he resumed. "And when I play on it I feel I'm holding it all right here in my hands."

He didn't explain. It wasn't necessary. I knew exactly what he was holding, tasting: the bitter shrubs and sweet muscadel, the pervasive smell of buchu and aniseed, the tang of salt in the sea-wind, the shriek of gulls, kiewiets, hadedas; sunsets, nights, bare plains, mountains, bleached bones. Africa. Mine. His.

Why, I suddenly thought, could we not stop talking about that distant place, those remote times? And yet it should not surprise us. What else did we have to talk about? It was so much more real than today, than Europe, here and now. Neither of us was really here.

Fort Hare is not the place he has imagined. He's been lured by the names. Open-mouthed he used to listen when Vuyizile's father spoke about them. Z. K. Matthews. Jabavu. Mda. Mandela. Sobukwe. Dennis Brutus. Mugabe. Of course he

251

had to go there! But it has become a different place altogether. In the beginning he is not yet so aware of it. Everything is too new, too strange. There's so much to learn, so many new faces, so many books, enough to make one's head turn. He is happy just to be near his friend Vuyizile again. But slowly an oppressive feeling begins to filter into him. "Watch out what you say, and to whom," Vuyizile warns him. "Before you know where you are you'll be picked up." "But I haven't done anything wrong!" "No need to. They're scared. Give a scared man a gun and he fires right into the crowd."

The first skirmishes of the new year are caused by something quite insignificant. Complaints about the food. A sit-in at the principal's office brings in the police, who arrive with dogs and sjamboks and batons and tear-gas and automatic rifles. Lectures are suspended for a week. Immediately after the resumption of classes there's another incident. One of the white lecturers reports to the Security Police on some of his students; when he is confronted with the rumour he admits it without any hesitation: "Of course I did. National security is more important than a bunch of agitators. They're not even properly out of the bush yet, and already they're trying to dictate to us." This time one of the university residences is extensively damaged and several cars burnt out. The campus is closed down for a month.

What triggers off the next round of conflict is unknown even to Mandla. There are rumours about a mass demonstration, but he keeps to his room, preparing for a test. Only afterwards does he learn of a message sent to all the residences that students not presenting themselves for lectures at a given hour will be suspended. Very few students have received the message; Mandla certainly did not. The first he hears about it is when he is summoned to the registrar's office where he is ordered to pack up and leave the campus within an hour. Many others find themselves in the same predicament, and after comparing notes they decide to approach the principal to state their case: all they want is a chance to carry on with their studies; not one of them has been involved in the demon-

252

stration. But the principal refuses to see them; instead, the police are called in again. They are all bundled into vans. Halfway to the Hogsback the police turn off the road into the bushes, let the students out one by one and thoroughly beat them up. Afterwards they are driven to King William's Town and dumped at the station, with stern orders to catch the first trains home.

This time it takes all Vuyizile's persuasive powers to convince Mandla that he should try again next year. Vuyizile himself, keeping out of politics altogether, is still as firmly resolved as ever to finish his theological studies.

But less than three months into the new academic year, without any prior hint, it is Vuyizile who packs his bags to clear out. Mandla is flabbergasted. As soon as he can scrape enough money together he goes to PE for a weekend to see his friend. But Vuyizile refuses to say anything; he doesn't want to discuss Fort Hare at all.

Deeply depressed and frustrated, Mandla goes back. Only a few weeks later trouble breaks out again. This time two of the white lecturers unexpectedly side with the students, but they are summarily discharged. Mandla too has had enough; no one will see him at Fort Hare again.

It takes many days of nagging and threatening and pleading before Vuyizile is at last persuaded to talk. All right, he admits, it was the SB who called him in and asked him to spy on his classmates and report anything "untoward". They specifically referred to Mandla: after checking his record for the previous year they'd decided he should be watched. Vuyizile refused. He had no desire to get drawn into politics. He was a Christian, he told them, he wanted to go into the Church, and he couldn't square a thing like that with his faith. They offered him money, a staggering amount. He refused. They warned him: something could happen to his father or other members of his family. Under the strain he broke down and began to cry. "Go home," the captain told him, with a show of sympathy. "After you've cried your heart out, give it a think and then come back to us. We'll be waiting."

253

It was then that he packed his things and went home.

Two months later his younger brother Khaya is picked up with a few other youngsters: they tried to steal pigeons from a white man's backyard in Newton Park, it is alleged. They're kept in a cell for two weeks. Afterwards the others come home with reports of how Khaya was beaten; how the police hammered his head against the wall until he dropped. On the day he is finally set free, just after he is returned to his home, he has a fit and dies. The District Surgeon signs a death certificate announcing death from natural causes. An autopsy is not regarded as necessary. (It is ordered only after the Press has got hold of the story, but it seems that nothing can be proved unequivocally. And the Medical Council finds no reason to act against the District Surgeon.)

All these years Vuyizile's father has avoided controversy, concentrating on his schoolwork. Now, after the death of his child, he can no longer suppress his feelings. Many people from the townships come to talk to him. A protest meeting is organized for the Saturday evening, in his school hall. But that morning the principal is picked up by the SB. He is only detained for a few hours, but when they return him to his house the officer hands him his banning order. Five years. He cannot attend the evening's meeting. The order also prohibits access to any educational institution, so he can no longer teach. A week later he receives his discharge from the department. His wife, a social worker, is also fired: the authorities can't afford employing a person whose husband is suspected of underground political activities.

"Why you looking at me like that?" asked Mandla. "I haven't even started. Wait till I tell you about the people who were inside. In the Red Hell in North End. Or in Pretoria Central. Or on the Island. You know nothing!" He brought the *trompie* back to his mouth, then changed his mind and said: "I hope you don't think I'm telling you this to turn Vuyizile or me or anyone else into a bloody martyr! There was nothing exceptional in what happened to us. Multiply us with a hundred or

254

a thousand or a million if you wish. We're not exceptions, I tell you. That's what happens to anyone who refuses to go on saying: Yes, *Baas*. What I told you about my father in that butchery — you think that was something special? Of course it wasn't. I told it to you because that's what happens to all of us, all the time. And if sons go on seeing their fathers humiliated for generation after generation, then one day you're stuck with a race of slaves. Not because the white man oppresses us, but because we allow him to cut off our balls. And it's only now, in my time, now that we've seen Mozambique and Angola and Zimbabwe, that we're beginning to discover it needn't be like this. We can say No. We got a choice. We have learned, at last, to hate. That's why 'seventy-six happened. And the white man saw it too, and took fright. That's why. For every day he tries to postpone the explosion he brings it one day closer."

"Is that the only end you can foresee — an explosion?"

"There's been too much blood already. It can no longer be avoided."

"Then the only way to stay alive is by keeping out of it," I said. "Like me."

"You call this life?"

I didn't look at him.

"Is it because of Vuyizile that you became involved?" I asked at last, staring straight ahead at the road.

"It's not because of anyone. It's because of myself." He was beginning to turn defensive again.

I wanted to keep him talking. "What happened to Vuyizile?"

"He's not there any more."

"You mean he's — ?"

"He disappeared, that's all." He was silent for a while. "They came to pick him up one night. That's all we know. Six months or so later they said they'd released him, he was no longer in their hands. But he never came home. In Parliament the Minister said he had reason to believe that Vuyizile had fled to Lesotho. But I know he didn't."

"How can you be sure?"

"If they'd released him, he would have let us know. His parents. Or me. We were like brothers." He shifted his legs in the small space of the passenger seat. "Anyway, I also went to Lesotho later. And I know for a fact he never got there." He looked at me. "And Vuyizile wasn't the only one who disappeared after being picked up in the night. It's the sort of thing that happens, that's all."

"And then you — "

"Vuyizile opened my eyes. Just like him, I thought at first we were trying to solve moral problems. He showed me that it was something else. It's political problems. That means we must look for practical answers, else you've had it."

All the curbed, defeated *impis* of history, I thought: and still the fire was raging. It struck me that, perhaps, Nongqawuse hadn't failed as everybody had always thought: they were in too much of a hurry to draw their conclusions. One day, in our own lifetime perhaps, all those dead might yet rise from the hard earth red with their blood, rise like aloes flowering in winter, and come back. That Tenth War of which Mandla himself had spoken.

Did he guess what I was thinking? Suddenly, without looking at me, he said: "Something is going to happen. It must. Everything cannot have been in vain. All the burning inside, the suffering, the blood: one can only bear it if you believe it's the price of a better world. All the victims. The men. The women. The children. One day it's got to make sense. And it will."

He brought the *trompie* back to his mouth, cupped his hands and began to play. I had to clench my jaws not to cry. My God, I thought: you spoke of hate today. But this is love. This is the sound of love, a love as terrible and immense as death.

It was Sunday, market day in Apt; and it took us half an hour from the outskirts of the town to the centre, the traffic was so bad. My nerves were raw by the time we finally found a place to park in a junkyard far above the river, almost out of town again. Neither of us really liked the thought of facing those crowds. But we were there and might as well make the best of it. In a way it suited my purpose too, because the heavy traffic made it impossible for a vehicle to get near the market, which meant that the streets were completely at the mercy of pedestrians, as it must have been in the Middle Ages. The paved alleys, barely a metre or two wide, all the way from the river to several blocks past the cathedral, were brimful with people. Townsfolk, but mainly country people, peasants from the plains and the mountains; some must have come a very long way indeed, father, mother and children, to buy and sell at the market. Sausages, cheese, poultry dead and alive, charcuterie, bags and bundles of herbs; vegetables, late-summer fruit, grapes already redolent of wine; earthenware, wood, leather, cloth, shoes, fish, mussels, eels. There were priests and nuns, and prim-and-proper men in grey suits, and farmers with dung on their shoes, and gypsies with copper earrings. Street musicians — cither, flute, fiddle; and one little old man with a cassette recorder round his neck: while it blared out martial music he beat out the rhythm on a drum on his belly. Bewildered, thin, scraggly Black Africans — from Senegal? Gabon? the Ivory Coast? — selling crude ornaments, leatherware, shells, beads, ostrich eggs, copper trinkets, fake or real ivory, displayed on reed-mats on the ground at the feet of the trampling hordes. Most people made a detour to avoid them, keeping them at a distance as if there was something bizarre about them, like the circus at Montbrun, years ago. All that was missing was the children tormenting the monkeys and throwing stones at the scabby lion.

"God, take me away from this place," cried Mandla almost in despair. "I can't take it."

On the other side of the cathedral the streets were not quite so busy. We sat down on the stone wall of an ancient fountain. Children were playing around us, but that didn't upset us.

"What are they doing in a place like this?" asked Mandla

257

angrily, as if I were personally to blame. "Those Africans with their cheap trinkets?"

"You know how it is. They were lured to the metropolis. Now they have to fend for themselves."

"Slaves!" he cried. "Everywhere in Africa people became free — politically. Nowhere economically. That's something else Vuyizile taught me. That's why we started the trade unions. I mean, look at those people. Still slaves. Nothing has changed for them. Can you see why it makes me so mad?"

"They were free to make up their own minds," I reminded him.

"They may think they're free. But what else was there for them to do? In their own countries everything's been broken down. They have nothing left. They got the smell of the masters' food. Now nothing else can satisfy them."

"Like my Grandpa Xhorê," I said softly. "You're right, nothing has changed."

"Who's your Grandpa Xhorê?"

I told him.

He didn't respond. He took out his *trompie* and started playing again, very subdued, but with a hint of silent rage. Some of the children stopped to watch and listen, but no one risked it too close to us. Perhaps they could sense that he was different from the ones in the market: that his attitude was deceptive; any moment he might jump up and pounce on his prey.

Just for the sake of doing something, and giving his mood a chance to subside, I began to page through my books again, in an attempt perhaps to rediscover through words, and through Paul's film, the town around me; as if my eyes were too sensitive to stare at it directly.

Where this gay Sunday market was under way, the Plague had raged at its fiercest, time and time again in history. (And if the streets had been as busy then as now, how easy for a handful of rats to spread their invisible destruction!) All the statistics were in Bruni. 1348, the Black Death. Then again in

258

1399, and in 1427, and in 1588; and at last the worst epidemic of all, in 1720–1.

A cruel malady [*Bruni quotes one eighteenth-century doctor*] which cannot be healed by anything, which is contagious, and for which the only two remedies are fire and flight.

As a result, everything had to be purified:

Nothing escaped the careful examination of doctors and consuls. Even the homes of the ravens [*undertakers*] and perfumers did not escape the cleansing fire; all the clothes and rags in the possession of a junk dealer, the widow Daudré, as well as those of one Pierre Premier were destroyed. The precautions were intensified when one visited the home of one Meissard, a locksmith, where the Plague in Apt had started, rapidly killing seven or eight people. There the dose of perfume burnt was doubled, even though all rags and furniture had been destroyed at the time of the first fumigation . . . .

Apart from the perfumes used to disinfect houses, enormous quantities of vine shoots were burnt in the town, as well as aromatic herbs, thyme and rosemary, stripped on a grand scale from the neighbouring hills. On street corners large barrels were placed, filled with vinegar, in which linen, paper and registers were plunged. One has difficulty to imagine, today, the odour pervading the whole town, both sweet and bitter, which could be smelled "a league away."

By one o'clock the streets were emptying rapidly as the market crowds overflowed into the restaurants. As on the previous day in Avignon (could it really have been but a single day ago?) we bought cheese and wine and bread at the market, and ate it in silence on the fountain wall, offering the remains to the pigeons who could barely wait their turn. How different, I thought, from my visit with Paul: then we'd had a leisurely meal on a terrace overlooking the river and our only reason for annoyance was the slow service.

259

If he'd been here today, would he have been able to find us a table? What a ridiculous thought. It was neither Mandla's fault nor mine that the Sunday crowds had overrun all the restaurants. First come first served. And yet I couldn't help feeling rejected. Yesterday it had been our own choice — mine — to have a picnic lunch; today it was different. Today I should have liked to spend a good two hours over the meal. Oh well, it just couldn't be helped. Perhaps we could make up for it in the evening, somewhere else, not in this town where one could still imagine the smell of aromats wafting through the hazardous streets.

On the first corner, on our way back, the Africans had just started rolling up their mats and packing away their unsold wares (had they sold anything at all?). Seeing us approach, potential customers, one of them impulsively held out a pair of fake ivory bracelets to us, his teeth exposed in a dazzling white grimace in his black face; his eyes yellowish, ringed with red. But when he saw Mandla he hesitated, grinning more broadly to show his gums too, and remained frozen in that attitude, the bracelets still dangling from his outstretched hand. And when I looked back from the next corner, where we had to cross the narrow bridge over the sluggish river, he had still not moved. Only the grimace had disappeared. What I could see on his face, even at that distance, was — I think — naked hate.

Hate in Boetie's eyes peering through the wired glass. His face vague, distorted by the glass as by water. The face of a corpse. During the past seven months, since the night they'd taken him away, his brown had dulled into ashen grey.

"What are you doing here? I'm on the other side now. We no longer speak to the likes to you."

"Boetie, I've come to say goodbye."

"You bloody well said goodbye long ago. You just didn't know it then."

"I'm going away with Brian. The magistrate gave us six

months, but the people from the university gave evidence, and the British consul too, so they suspended it. As long as we leave the country."

"Yes, why not? Nothing is keeping you here."

"Don't talk like that, Boetie. Don't you know — "

"What? You burned me. So why come back? You enjoy seeing me here like a baboon in the zoo? You think I'll do some tricks for you?"

"Boetie, you're my brother. Jesus — !"

"One wouldn't say so. It's because of you that I'm here."

"You can't blame me for it."

"You could have kept that white man out of your cunt." As crudely and cruelly as he could.

"I love Brian. We're going to get married over there."

"You don't care over how many bodies you step to get there, do you?"

Her eyes are burning; the tears of helplessness and rebellion distort his face on the other side of the pane even more. "Don't let's part like this, Boetie. Jesus, can't you see how it's hurting me?"

"I know what it feels like this side. I can't care a fuck about yours."

"I hoped you would. I don't know what to say. You've always been different from the rest of us. Angrier. More stroppy. More difficult."

"Because I couldn't stand the way you all just took things lying down. Dedda — "

"Dedda's dead. Leave him out of it."

But he went on: "Dedda could never care a shit about anything or anyone, as long as he could go on whoring and roaring in his own way. The world could go to hell for all he cared."

"I'm not going to let you talk about him like that. What do you know about him? What do you know about me?"

"I know just what you told me: that you're fucking off with your white lover. You think you can shake us off like dog-shit from your foot? But watch out: you'll be taking our stink with

261

you. It'll keep you awake at night so you can't sleep. It'll always be in your nose until you're all burnt out. You hear me?"

Helpless, she turns away from the small window, but she cannot leave him like this. His furious dark eyes seem to suck her back. Only ten minutes, they said, as a special favour, for he's not entitled to visits yet. The ten minutes must be nearly over. And then — ?

"If you'd only try to understand!" she pleads, cut off from him by the impassive glass.

"I don't want to understand anything. You're turning your back on us today. You're leaving. You don't want to be bothered with us any more — "

"I have no choice. Else we had to go to jail for six months."

"I'm going to be here for five years. For what? Because they pretend they found a few books under my bed when they came to check up on you. Jesus, they should have taken you to a vet. That's what they usually do with a bitch in heat." His helpless hands fall against the glass. "But go, by all means. You think you can just pack your suitcase and fuck off — What's the blarry matter with you? Listen, man, if you got an itch in your arse, you damn well take it with you, no matter where you go."

"I don't want to listen to you any more!"

"Then don't. Go away. Who asked you to come anyway?" He drops his clenched, manacled fists. Shocked, she sees his face contort. He begins to cry. "All these years I've been thinking you're the only one in the family who's different. You're not nevermind, you're not don't-care. You got it in you. I always thought one day the two of us — Then you fell for the first white prick around. Oh my *God*, Andrea! And next week they're taking me to the Island. I'm scared!"

The guard standing beside him moves away from the wall against which he's been leaning all the time: because the time is up, or because Boetie has said what he wasn't allowed to reveal?

"Come on, time's up. We told you it was a special favour."

262

"Andrea, you must come back. One day you and I — "

"Hurry up," says the guard.

The sun is blinding when she comes outside. The high rump of the Mountain. The impossibly blue sky above. The foliage of the oaks just beginning to turn yellow: it's autumn. In the air a premonition of a cold winter ahead: but she won't be here. She is heading for an unseasonal spring.

She doesn't want to think about what he said. Never, never will she permit herself to think of it again. What's happened has happened, and now it is past. For good. (As past and gone as you, Grandpa Xhorê?)

All that remains to be done is the ride down to the harbour. She's already bought the wreath; it lies on the back seat of Brian's Volkswagen, waiting to be tossed on the dirty, oily water of the docks. There is no grave to welcome it, mercifully perhaps. A grave would be too small for Dedda; the sea is wide. *(Will you shake me off too, Nanna? Or will you remember?)*

Brian gets out of the car when he sees her coming down from the prison. His eyes are quizzical, but she avoids them. He holds the door open for her, but she is reluctant to get in. The ugly building keeps her in its spell. Is this really a cheap way out, as Boetie said — running away? Would it have changed anything at all if she were willing to face purgatory like him, perhaps in the same building (or do they send women elsewhere?). Would it have changed anything for herself? Changed: even though it may not have been easier, then at least a little bit more understandable?

Through the window she sees the wreath on the back seat.

How she would like to talk to Brian, but when she glances furtively at him, he seems strange, remote. Are those the eyes in which she could once drown herself, the face that breathed against her? Is that the body, now hidden in shirt and brown jacket and jeans, she's given herself to, unquestioning and without restraint — the body she chose above father, mother, sister, brothers, predictability and safety? He's the only one she has left now. Her future carries his name. But it is her own she is looking for. A *Nanna* lost in dark water: a snorkel has become clogged, the air has been cut off, she is left floundering all alone in an underwater world where she will never be entirely at home.

It has been like this ever since that night in the doctor's surgery (his breath; his eyes behind the spectacles; the light on his bald pate): the constable cupping his balls in his hand; her stomach retching. Then the cell.

Only for a few hours, but because the bare bulb was left burning there was a sense of timelessness. Sleep was unthinkable. For a long time she sat on the edge of the narrow bunk. Then she began to pace from wall to wall, from steel door to high barred window, from toilet to washbasin. Somewhere far away in the building, a woman was screaming hysterically. A door clanged shut. She heard, or thought she could hear, footsteps, a distant murmur of voices in the hollow corridors. Then silence, except for the continuing screams of the woman. Drunk? Mad? Giving birth? In pain? Or sheer perversity?

Only when the door had been closed behind her did it really hit her: all contact with the outside world was now cut off. What happened out there was irrelevant here. What might be immensely important there could cause no stir inside. Even sound acquired a different meaning. And for how long would it go on like this? (No: that was not what worried her. A lifetime, years, months, days, it made no difference. She was here now. She knew about it.)

They brought her food. A metal plate; porridge with milk and sugar. Two slices of brown bread with a lump of butter on top. A mug of coffee. But she left it untouched on the floor just inside the door. Eating would make her vomit again.

She returned to the bed and lay down, knees drawn up protectively against her body: but nothing could exclude the memory of what had happened. The doctor. She could not seal up either her body or her thoughts. The dull ache inside. His fingers in the red rubber gloves. The black bristles on the backs of his hands. He'd stood washing himself at the basin as

264

if he would never be able to rid himself of her smell and her slime. Now she felt infected by *him*. Never had she been so totally exposed before. Nor so lonely. Not even the thought of Brian offered any comfort. On the contrary. Even the sound of his name made her feel nauseous.

Once again she began to pace to and fro, trapped like an animal in a cage. (*Jesus, Nanna, your way of walking*. Would Dedda notice the difference today? Now, for the first time, I'm no longer a virgin. You thought it would make a difference? Not even Brian made a difference. Only this. This is what it means to be raped. From now on I'll always walk differently. I'll never catch up with myself again. Somehow I've now escaped from myself.)

In the wall above the washbasin words had been carved through the paint and gritty plaster into the bricks underneath. The codes and curses and alarms of her predecessors, all sharing this cell with her now:

Cunt is king
Nearer my God to Thee
S.J.B.
14.3.71
Help!
Kilroy

Others she could no longer decipher.

But there was only one she really noticed. The others she might imagine afterwards, on the basis of probability: this one was carved right into her nerves.

I was here

The door was unlocked. She was summoned. Someone had paid her bail.

She gets into Brian's car and they drive down to the harbour with the wreath. The gulls are screeching as they swoop across the oily water.

I'm scared of the final Yes, Paul. For your sake too. However much you've asked me about myself over the years, what do you really know about me? I told you I was a witch. I destroy

265

whatever I touch. Behind me lies a trail of destruction. Surely it is no coincidence that they give hurricanes the names of women. Warning: Andrea is on her way. What I wish I do not do. What I do is not what I want.

It was the most difficult part of our route that day, from Apt, past Céreste, into the heart of the Luberon, through oaks and broom and pine forests, past Vitrolles with its burnt-ochre wheatfields and bright vineyards, to La Motte d'Aigues. From the names it was obvious that this was Huguenot country: a road branching off to La Bastide des Jourdans; an estate called Les Roux.

"It's understandable why the Huguenots should have taken refuge in these mountains," I told Mandla as I stopped for a moment after a hairpin bend on the slope above Vitrolles — the sudden piercing scent of the pines — to catch my breath and wipe sticky strands of hair out of my eyes. "First the Cathars, later the Vaudois, then the Huguenots. Out there on the plains. Out there on the plains everything is exposed, but who will ever find a fugitive in these mountains?"

"They'll find you if they want to. One can never get away altogether." His face expressionless, he sat looking at the scene below us and I couldn't make out whether the ambiguity had been intentional.

"They must have had an unshakable faith," I said, trying to steer the conversation away from more ominous reefs. "Imagine going on and on like that, against all the power of kings and cardinals and armies."

"That's exactly what makes one go on."

I didn't reply, but the restrained way in which he'd said it moved me inexplicably. Why? Just the impression, the feeling — dare I say it? — that he was a believer in his own way. Not in any conventional sense of the word, of course. But with a fervour in him that might burn its way through whatever obstacles appeared in his way: and no matter how much he himself might be conscious of the flaws in whatever he was

266

involved in, it made no real difference. His faith would carry him through.

Or perhaps what moved me most profoundly was not just the perception of that furious faith in him, but the intimation that in this foreign land he might have reached the end of his road after all. Which might be the real explanation for that deep gloom in him: the discovery, undoubtedly for the first time in his life, that his faith alone was no longer enough. Not this time.

And there was something else too: the shadow of that faith in myself. For I know there was a time when I'd also experienced it. A fierce pagan grasp on God. Dedda had had it; he'd passed it on to me. That was why I was able to acknowledge it in Mandla. But what had become of mine then? When and how had the flame been quelled? (Or was it no more than a brief eclipse?)

All I know is that on that trip through the mountains I became aware of fear. Something was approaching which I could no longer avoid — something from which I'd deemed myself free for many years. Had it really been "freedom", living in seclusion as I'd been doing? Oh easier, undoubtedly, after the tumult of earlier years, especially the time I'd been with Brian. But free? — no. A postponement, no more. Deep inside me it had been prepared; it had been lying in wait all the time. Now everything was once more at risk. And would I have the courage, this time, to prevail?

Perhaps that was not the right question. One can endure almost anything. One can survive. But everything that happens leaves a scar. Everything brings one that much closer, not simply to one's own individual death, but to death as such. And that was different, a momentous certainty.

We drove past the co-operative cellars into La Motte d'Aigues. A heady, pervasive odour of new wine. Past the *tabac* with the brightly coloured plastic strips in the doorway, where three months earlier Paul and I had enquired about Monsieur Jaubert; following the steep alley uphill into the old part of the village, oleanders and geraniums on either side of the street, to the small square in front of the chapel at the top. There we left the car and went down the other side of the hill on foot, to the small stone house with the vine at the front door where we'd found the old man in July, sitting on his rickety chair, with the old blind black dog beside him. The last of Paul's clan who had survived the centuries.

But the house was deserted now, the small windows closed up with wooden shutters, the door locked and barred. Nobody opened when we knocked. There was no sign of the decrepit old dog either.

"Oh well, it's Sunday," I said as airily as I could. "I suppose he's spending the day with relatives. Perhaps he went to church in one of the neighbouring villages."

"This house has been standing empty for a long time," Mandla said, unperturbed.

I could see it too, of course, but I didn't want to give in so easily. Stubbornly I took him back to the *tabac* with me, facing the stares of the old men at the counter who abruptly ended their raucous conversation to watch us. I'm sure they were the exact ones who'd been there on the day Paul and I had entered the place.

"Old Jaubert? No, Mademoiselle, he died a month ago. Poor thing, he was getting on, you know, and there was no one to look after him — "

We left, I didn't say anything. Mandla also sat quietly beside me, not even bothering to play on his *trompie*.

A few kilometres from the village, on the road to Cucuron, we passed the Étang de Bonde. On the far side of the lake, near the narrow strip of beach, I impulsively parked the car. The place was deserted. Without trying to explain anything to Mandla, I got out and walked uphill through the bush, to the rocky summit, into the yellow glare of the late afternoon sun.

So he was dead. The last of the Jauberts. I felt inexpressibly sad, for Paul's sake. Quite illogically, of course: the old man hadn't really been related to him any more. Even the spelling of his name had been different. And La Motte d'Aigues would remain Paul's place of origin whether there were other

268

Jauberts or not. But what did it have to do with logic? Death had intervened. Something to hold on to, I felt, had been removed from Paul's grasp. (Or did it pain me because it was I, much more than he, who needed something to grasp right then?) Part of his own solidity had been relinquished. As if even a thing like that had implications for the two of us: for our future, for the question to which I still owed him an answer.

I saw Mandla coming through the trees. At first he seemed to be heading past me, then changed his direction and made straight for me. I didn't want him there, not then. I needed to be alone. Couldn't he have sensed it? I resented his obtuseness. Surely he could have granted me those few precious minutes of solitude.

The sun was right behind him. I watched him as he came up towards me, pushing his shadow ahead of him: a large, elongated shadow moving across stones and shrubs and broken stumps, unstoppable.

I turned away from him. Perhaps, if he saw my back, he would realize that I wanted to be left alone.

As I turned I could see my own shadow in front of me, splashed on the ground, reaching from my feet to a distant ridge of white rocks. As if I'd never noticed it before, like a child making silhouettes on a bedroom wall, I moved my arms and watched my shadow mimic me.

The strange discovery: *I have a shadow!* It's mine, exclusively mine. I claim it. It's mine. Look at me standing here, being here. I have substance enough to block out the sun and cast a shadow. My own.

There was no "point" in my shadow, obviously not. But simply standing there, being there, in that late sun, in an alien landscape which soon would be nothing but shadow, I was aware of a new strength, a new certainty growing in me. I and my shadow: what a long way the two of us had travelled together. District Six. The streets of Cape Town. Hand in hand with Dedda. Downhill to the Gardens. To the Museum. Up the Mountain. Our trip through the land. My shadow on the barren earth and the scrub of the Karoo, in towns and cities. A network of routes through Provence. London. Paris. And now here, in these mountains, today.

I hadn't come all this way just to be a woman who could get what she wanted by lying down for some man or other. I owed my shadow more than that. I couldn't spell it out as yet, but I knew there had to be more to it than that. Perhaps I wouldn't miss my appointment after all.

He approached from behind. I could hear his sand-shoes crunching on the gravel. I no longer wanted to exclude him: he was no threat to my solitude anymore. I saw his shadow flowing soundlessly past me. He stopped behind me. His shadow completely covered mine.

What was this urge really, ultimately? — this overwhelming need to reach out and touch someone, something, a substance, to acknowledge that you wanted to go on together, all the way, to the end. The end of what? There was the earth, there was heaven and hell, there was life; there was truth. There was, perhaps, even death.

I didn't speak to him. I couldn't. Not then. I walked past him, alone, back through the bushes to the car, a small white speck against the dull grey sheet of the lake.

We took another road back, passing along the south of the Luberon, over Pertuis to Cavaillon and Saint-Rémy. There was no special reason for the detour; I simply felt a new route — one I hadn't travelled before, not even with Paul — would be good for us both.

What had become of my idea of a "pilgrimage", a sincere gesture of contrition towards Paul? Perhaps more than I could grasp at the moment. What is judged in the end: the act, or its motivation?

We were both silent. He took out his *trompie* again. The dull melancholy sound came almost as a relief. Our talking had reached a point beyond which, for the moment, words could not proceed. I was thinking of what I'd entrusted to him, especially about Brian; those last anxious, hectic months in South Africa. (And also of what I was still keeping to myself, what I still *had* to keep secret, not for his sake but for my own.) The landmarks and interiors of his world which he'd discovered to me. Both of us had become very vulnerable.

Yet it had also armed us, in a different way. What I'd told him about myself, what he'd trusted me with, had been nothing as sentimental as a confession. Each had invented himself, herself, to the other anew. It had indeed become necessary for both. Together, we'd reinvented that distant land, giving it new shape and meaning.

For the moment there was much we had to digest first, each separately. Not history. Not biography. But whatever we'd dared to invent or acknowledge or affirm about ourselves. To remember; to remember irrevocably. So that neither would be free of that knowledge again.

Only, time was so short. So much shorter than we thought.

In Saint-Rémy we went to a restaurant. I think it irritated him to spend so much time over dinner; he wanted to get back to the hotel. Which was precisely what I wanted to postpone by lounging in that charming old dining-room of the Castelet des Alpilles, all plush and velvet, where Paul and I had had so many of our meals in July.

At last we went home.

(Home?)

We took our keys from the pigeonholes behind the counter (the *patron* and his wife had already retired to watch television in their living-room behind the glass door: one could see the flickering reflection of the screen on the small panes through the lace curtains.)

As I unlocked my door upstairs, Mandla was behind me. I turned towards him to say good night. It was like the afternoon when he'd followed me up the hill. He said nothing. In the dull light of the landing he was very large and dark. He followed me across the threshold into my room. I didn't try to prevent him. But he stopped just inside the door.

I didn't dare look at him again.

"Andrea — ?" I heard his voice behind me, a deep growl, barely audible.

271

Crossing my arms over my breasts I kept my back to him. "Are you afraid?"

I nodded.

"Of me?"

I turned round slowly. "No. Of myself."

He stood staring at me in silence for a long time. Then, with the hint of a smile — it was too dark to see for sure, the only light was the dull glow from the landing — he said: "Good night. Sleep well."

From the door his shadow fell across the whole length of the floor, grazing the opposite wall.

"Good night, Mandla."

I closed the door after he'd gone out. Without turning on the small bedside lamp — there was some light from the lamp above the hotel entrance outside — I stripped off the bed cover and folded it very meticulously. Then undressed and went to have a bath in the dark.

Only after that could I face the light again. I put it on and, still naked, sat on the bed to make my haphazard notes about the day. Then I got up to brush my hair in front of the mirror. Ma would have been proud of me.

The movement left me glowing with warmth. But as I sat down on the bed again, paging aimlessly through Paul's books and notes, still reluctant to yield to sleep, I realized it was chilly. For a while I resisted, then I went to the large rustic wardrobe to get my gown. On the bottom shelf, with the washing I'd still meant to do, lay the crumpled, torn flag. Surprised, as if seeing it for the first time, I picked it up and held it in my outstretched arms. An odd assortment of stains and smells. Tobacco, smoke, wine, those I could recognize. But the rest?

Poor old sod. I'd been bloody unfair to him. Had it really been necessary to taunt him like that?

The dull red, the dirty white, the faded blue. A sudden lump in my throat. This France which I'd come to love so deeply, to which I'd grown so attached: what did it really mean to me? Sanctuary, refuge, asylum, safety, security? Love — ?

272

Frank — Gérard — Serge — Paul; the other more anonymous ones, the casual intruders in my life. Was it quite
inevitable, even to keep me in touch with the country, always
to need a man as go-between?

Was there not something desperate in it? Undoubtedly.
From the beginning. Ever since the first night when I'd said to
Frank: "I hope you can help me. Only, I want to make one
thing very clear before I come in: I'm not going to sleep with
you."

Conditionally. Every time. To maintain my "integrity". To
survive.

And for that reason, if I really dared to face it squarely: even
now no more than a guest, a traveller, an adopted child, in
transit.

(Paul — ?)

What was here that I could truly call my own, so indisput-
ably my own that I could place my life at.stake for it? So
wonderfully my own that I would be prepared (as Mandla
might say) to die for it?

Almost with compassion I spread the damp tattered flag over
the foot-end of my bed, inadequate protection against the cool
of the night. Naked, I got into bed, put off the light and
remained sitting, propped up against the large square pillow,
waiting for my eyes to get used to the half-dark.

Far away in the night I heard again the low, muted sound
that gave me goose-flesh: a sound against which neither
blankets nor flag could protect me, leaving me totally vulnerable: the sound of Mandla's *trompie*.

Fourth Day

✺ ✺ ✺ ✺

It is the closest they have ever come to the reality of the
Plague. On their way back from La Motte d'Aigues that
afternoon, Paul turns off the main road from Cavaillon to
Saint-Rémy to take the detour past Eygalières and the serene
little chapel of Saint-Sixte of which he has spoken so often. It
comes as no surprise to her. Wherever they've come or gone
on this journey, he has made a point of deviating from the
more predictable routes. This is one of the hottest days of the
whole searing summer, and as soon as they enter the village
Paul stops under a shady tree in front of the Hôtel de Ville and
takes her to the nearest café terrace for a cold drink. Afterwards, revived but still perspiring, they saunter up to the oldest
part of the village. Inhabited four thousand years before the
Romans, Paul tells her. (She accepts it without a murmur, as
she submitted to Brian's teaching years ago. Men and facts.)
High on the white hill, walking round the small eleventh-
century church, Paul discovers to his delight that the badly
restored stone building has been turned into a somewhat
haphazard village museum, much of which is devoted to the
Plague. There is even — a discovery which sends a shudder
down her spine in spite of the stifling heat — a table stacked
with human skulls and bones, discoloured and decayed, some
still bearing a crust of earth, like large potatoes freshly dug up:
almost all of them, according to the hand-written poster above
the table, found in a communal grave of the victims of the
Plague of 1720.

Refusing to go near the macabre table she moves away, past
implements and objects from the neolithic age, to an

274

exhibition of photographs and posters on which, in copybook writing, teachers and pupils have recorded the history of the village. Seated on a stone step beside the exhibition of skulls Paul opens his small green notebook and, almost unable to contain his excitement, begins to jot down facts and comments while she continues to work her way through the rest of the museum. When she has finally completed her circle through the small building and returns to the entrance, he is still writing feverishly. From the open door she looks out over the burning, hazy landscape. Stone and shrubs. The plains covered in olive-trees. The earsplitting sound of the cicadas. Here in Provence their sound is different from their strident screeching at home: it is more like geese cackling very loudly; whole trees are vibrating, pulsating with it.

She looks back and sees him standing beside the long table, a brown grimacing skull in one hand. He smiles when he notices the revulsion on her face, strikes a theatrical pose, and declaims: "Alas, poor Yorick!"

"Put down that thing, Paul."

"He's been dead a long time, my love."

"He died of the Plague. He can still infect you."

"After so many hundreds of years? Come and have a look. Try to imagine — "

"I don't want to. This isn't a story, Paul. These people really lived. They're really dead. How would you like someone to stand holding your skull like this one day? You should have more respect."

"You're just being superstitious, Andrea." But he does put down the skull with the others, where it remains grinning up at them with a very superior, defiant, knowing look.

"Let's go back. This place gives me the creeps."

"Incredible. All this on one day: first La Motte d'Aigues and old Monsieur Jaubert, now this."

She cannot shake off the feeling of horror, almost begrudging him his enthusiasm. But as they reach the doorway, ready to stride out into the fury of the sun, he stops for a moment to take off his glasses and, in an old familiar gesture, wipe them

275

with the tail of his shirt: and the sudden vulnerability of his naked eyes both disarms and appeases her, like so often before. Defenceless, he needs her now to protect him against the world, and possibly against his own impulses. On their way downhill she allows him to chatter in boyish excitement; once she even presses her head playfully against his shoulder.

Back at the car he notices the beautiful weathered stone wall of the Auberge to the right of the square and impulsively they go through the large arched entrance to look at the courtyard. Oleanders and geraniums and petunias in stone pots. A few rows of tables in the shade of a great elm with a dark, gnarled trunk.

"Let's stay here for the night," he says spontaneously.

"We have no luggage with us."

"We don't need anything, do we?"

In the night, one of their most intense ever, while he is making love to her, she is suddenly gripped by an almost paralysing fear: *My God, with these same hands, only a few hours ago, he handled the skulls of people who died from the Plague!* The curious thing about it, however, is that, unlike earlier in the museum, she is not repulsed by it: in the very terror she discovers an abandonment and a lust more ferocious than she has ever known before. And later, half waking from a deep sleep of utter fulfilment and hearing, vaguely, a rustling somewhere in the dark (undoubtedly the leaves outside, she realizes in the morning), she thinks, almost with resignation: of course, what else? — it must be a mouse, perhaps a rat.

That night I was actually awakened by a gnawing sound, something familiar from my childhood, like a mouse or a rat under the floorboards. But as the sleep receded I realized it was something quite different: something or someone at the door, trying the knob. It was both locked and barred; far from being afraid I felt vaguely amused, touched by pity: what on earth was Mandla trying to do? But I shook it off. Mandla would never creep back so furtively. He would knock openly, or call out, or even break down the door to take what he wanted.

276

Perhaps it was the *patron* with his sad moustache, cold-shouldered by his mousey wife and now taking a chance with me? (How hard to be a man, always driven by one need or another. How precarious a man's self-esteem, all six inches of it.) After a while it stopped. I got up and moved soundlessly to the door, but there was nothing; so I went to the bathroom and then returned to my bed. For a quarter of an hour or so I lay waiting for it to start again, but all was quiet. Perhaps a rodent after all? I abandoned myself to incoherent thoughts, and to sleep.

Remarkably refreshed I woke up in the morning — that decisive fourth day — my mind tranquil, my body at ease. Not passive. A feeling, rather, of readiness, of being prepared. (But for what? I couldn't tell. And perhaps it was just as well.)

After my bath I spent a lot of time on my make-up. Not more than usual, I suppose; but, if I must be totally honest, with a different aim from that of the previous day. Grooming my eyes and mouth, eyebrows, cheekbones, fingernails, toes, was not so much to prevent the world from looking in too readily as a concession to vanity: I *wanted* to look beautiful today. I felt beautiful. I wanted to be acknowledged as beautiful, the way it used to be when Dedda had been home. (On that trip of ours through the land it had made him so mad if I claimed the rearview mirror of the borrowed van; and then he'd always scolded me in mock rage, but Jesus, so proud: "Hell, Nanna, you looking grand.")

As I was opening the door to go out, the telephone rang. I was so preoccupied, already anticipating breakfast with Mandla on the terrace downstairs — and, at least initially, the line was so bad — that I didn't immediately recognize the voice.

"Andrea? Hello! Hello?"

"Who am I speaking to?"

Other voices intruded; then, suddenly, the line was clear and I realized it was Paul.

"Good God!" he exclaimed. He was trying to make a joke of

277

it, but the real horror in his tone came through. "I can't believe it. Have you already forgotten my voice?"

"Hi, Paul." In spite of myself I felt cagey. (But why? The previous morning I'd been so miserable when I couldn't reach him.)

"Darling, are you all right?"

"Of course. I'm fine."

"You sure?"

"Why shouldn't I be fine?"

"You were so upset the other night when I told you about Mandla. I was wondering — "

"The first day was hell. We went to Avignon. You know I've never felt at ease there. We quarrelled all day."

"I wish I didn't have to do this to you."

"It's all right now. Yesterday was much better. Maybe I was wrong about him after all."

"I told you so!" (All men should wear this as a slogan on their blazers.)

"It's just that I never had a chance to find out much about him before. He's not exactly forthcoming, especially where women are concerned."

"Don't underestimate him." There was an airiness in his voice which sounded just a bit too strained to be convincing. "I hope he hasn't tried anything with you yet?"

It annoyed and provoked me. "I can look after myself, Paul."

"I was just concerned about you."

"I understand more about him now." But I had to add: "I'm not sure how he feels about me. Even when he starts talking, like he sometimes did yesterday, he doesn't give away any secrets."

"Just like you?"

"We went to La Motte d'Aigues," I said, ignoring his pointed question: he couldn't really have expected an answer. "Your Monsieur Jaubert is dead." Adding lightly, but not without a prick of deliberate malice: "Now you're all alone in the world."

He was silent for a moment. Then, almost coolly: "I hope *you* haven't forsaken me yet."

"All these questions. I told you I was fine. Where are you phoning from?"

"Still in Strasbourg. I hope to be back in Paris by tomorrow night. Then I'll phone again."

"If you want to."

A pause.

"Andrea, is there something wrong?"

"Of course not."

A gentler tone in his voice: "Have you made up your mind yet — about us?"

"Don't ask me yet."

He was too wise to insist; and his tact was comforting. He knew my moods and attitudes so well. What more could one hope for in marriage? Or was that what still caused me to hesitate — his very predictability, his security, his concern and gentle care?

"How are you getting on with the Plague?"

"We're going to the Wall today."

"Well, I envy you. I'll never forgive myself for not going there. We were so close. Now you'll have to look for my part too."

"Mandla will be there to help."

"Do you see any hope?"

I misunderstood his question and felt apprehensive. "What hope?"

"For our film, of course. Have you found some good spots?"

"Too many. But you know — " No. How could I tell him about the doubts I was beginning to feel? I knew how much it meant to him. (But why must a man always be so ready to put himself at stake in his work? Why this insistence on living externally, through projections, signs, oblique references? Or was my resentment unfair?)

"Are you beginning to lose confidence in me?" he asked softly.

"Not at all. It's just, you must admit, a tall order to spend

279

one's time and energy working on a film while life is flowing past all around one. Your Middle Ages seem so far away."

"You've obviously been listening to Mandla."

"He's not necessarily wrong."

"To me 'my Middle Ages' as you call them, may be more real than today's world. I feel more at home there, even in spite of the Plague."

"Because you're scared of facing today?"

"Why do you say that?"

"It was just a question."

"Mandla seems to be doing more harm than I expected." He obviously intended it frivolously, but it sounded resentful.

"How's your conference going?" I asked, hoping the interest would comfort him.

"Exhausting. But exciting. A few of the Swedes have really set things alight with their ideas. I can't wait to see you again. I've got enough to tell you to keep you awake for a night."

"I hope you're not just going to talk all night."

"Wait till I lay hands on you again."

"I may beat you to it," I laughed. "'Bye, Paul."

"I still wanted to — " Disappointed, but loving: "'Bye, darling."

I put the telephone down. The conversation, light-hearted as it was, proved more unsettling than yesterday's frustration when I couldn't get through to him. (Perhaps it *was* a matter of "getting through"?)

Mandla was no longer in his room when I knocked. He was already outside on the terrace, wearing a blood-red T-shirt, with the same faded jeans and sand-shoes as before. I could see him studying me very thoroughly, approval in his eyes. But he didn't say anything.

"Slept well?" I asked as neutrally as I could.

"Not bad. What were you doing at my door in the night?"

"I?" I was quite taken aback.

"Weren't you fiddling with the knob?" Mocking: "You shouldn't have given up so soon."

My face was glowing. "You've got a cheek!" Then,

280

remembering the disturbance during the night, I frowned. "There was somebody at my door too. I thought it was the *patron*." I gestured towards the fat man with the moustache and the long white apron, approaching us with his loaded tray. "At least I'm relieved to know it wasn't you."

"You didn't think I would — " He sounded indignant, then saw the humour in it and pulled a face. "Must have been somebody who lost his way or walked in his sleep." With exaggerated emphasis, in an atrocious accent, he turned to the *patron* and said: "*Merci, Monsieur.*"

"*De rien.*" The man grinned with unsuspecting benevolence. "*Bon appétit, Monsieur-dame.*"

"Paul phoned just now," I said, stirring my chocolate. "Sent you his greetings."

"Hm." His mouth was full of bread. "Did he say anything — ?"

"No. He only spoke about the film."

"He would."

"You mustn't judge him too harshly, Mandla." (Oh God, why this eternal shifting of loyalties?)

"I'm not judging him at all. He's beyond my judgement."

"You got along so well in Paris."

"Of course. He's first-class. And he helped me a lot. But does that make any difference to what he is?"

"You mean, white?"

He didn't answer directly. "You ever thought how weird it is? — if a White South African wants to have a normal conversation with a Black, it's easier for both to come to Europe. Over there it's just not possible."

"Have you tried hard enough?"

"When were you there last?" A cut with a sjambok.

"Why did you really come to Europe?" I asked after a long pause. "I want to know."

"You know already. We needed the money."

"Just money?"

He shrugged, his face inscrutable.

"Money for what?"

281

"Everything costs money. It's the only language they understand in Europe and the States. I told you before: we have no illusions about morality. Neither has the West. Their only concern is to back the winner. Ours is to make sure we're the winner. We have one advantage, that history is on our side."

"You're very confident."

"I am. Ever since I discovered how scared the *Boere* are. And a scared dog always bites. He doesn't understand reason."

"What makes you so sure they're scared? They have all the power."

"I've seen it with my own eyes. Many times. But there was one day I'll never forget. They came to bulldoze another squatters' settlement, just beyond Greenbushes outside PE. As usual, they waited for winter: in summer it's no use, you see, the people don't mind sleeping in the open. This time they really went for broke. Confiscated all the food and medicine the Black Sash and Women for Peace sent to the squatters. Fenced in the whole place with barbed wire. Then they moved in. They were used to squatters running away from their dogs and tear-gas and guns. But that day something else happened. The people drew back as the police approached; but then suddenly they began to move forward. The *Boere* started firing into the crowd, but the people just kept on coming, right into the bullets. OK, in the end everything was razed to the ground and the people were forced to flee. But I tell you, some of those cops and Board chaps were shitting in their khaki pants that day. Scared of that pack of starved people who suffered so much that they didn't care any more. They had nothing left to lose. An army of the sick and the poor, rejects, scum, people with death already in their eyes, some of them no more than bones with flaps of skin around them, half-rotten people. But people all the same. People, I tell you, with hate in their eyes, the most naked goddamn hate I've ever seen in this world. And that was what scared the men with the guns. They got scared of the living dead. Scared to face their own guilt. Scared of themselves. Because what they saw that day, if you ask me, was their own death coming towards them.

They never thought it could happen. They couldn't believe there would ever be an end to their power. That one day the last human dregs of the world would stand up to their guns and say to them: 'Now you've gone too far. Now we rise up. This is the beginning of the Tenth War.' That's what I saw that morning, the little bit I could see through the tear-gas, before I had to turn tail too, with Vuyizile and the others from Pebco and the unions."

I finished my breakfast in silence. (How deceptively peaceful the beginning of the day had been!) Afterwards, without any argument or discussion, we drove off. I hadn't planned any details of the trip. I knew what destination I wanted to reach, as I'd told Paul, for that was the one place I'd been heading for, inevitably, since the day I'd left Paris; but the detours we made were unpremeditated.

The plane-trees lining the road to Cavaillon appeared even more ragged than the day before. Ahead of us, the smoke of the power station at Orgon. The sun struggling to break through the haze.

"If one didn't know better, it would look like a township there in front of us," Mandla suddenly remarked. "Those early mornings. When you get outside, the night's smoke would still be covering the place, a thick black bank. Candles or gaslight in the windows. Voices. The streets still empty. The sun has a special way of rising there, you know. Shining on broken bottles and corrugated iron, a red patch in the fog."

Was it my imagination that I heard him say: *That's hell for you: but it's beautiful in its own way; it's mine?*

"People everywhere. The houses standing shoulder to shoulder, each of them jam-packed. You can never get away from the sound of people in that place. Not even at night. Especially not at night. You're never alone. And when you come back in the dusk, looking at the first smoke from all the open fires, there's something swelling in your heart. *My people*, you think. In these shacks and shanties we're born. In impossible places in this smoky dark we make love, we make children. In these holes and hovels we laugh and cry, we bind

283

up our wounds, we get drunk, we learn our lessons. All of us. My people. Here we die countless forms of death, none of them strange to us. Far away from the white man's cities. They keep us out of sight, because they're scared of us." He suddenly fell silent, as if angry about what he'd given away. But then he continued in his low, dark voice: "Then we go to bed. One goes to bed early if there's nothing but paraffin lamps or gas. Except weekends, then it goes on forever. Everybody together in one house, such a crowd it seems the walls are bulging. Drinking. Talking. Making music. Laughing. You know, if I live to be a hundred, I'll always remember the way those people laughed. No matter what happens, they're laughing. Because they're not scared. They got life on their side."

"You used to tell Paul about the meetings you held at night," I said, trying to recover what I'd missed in Paris.

"Yes, hell, those meetings. The unions. That was something else." He grinned with something like secret satisfaction. "You see, when I left Fort Hare, the older unions were already going strong. But most of them were run by old-time White Liberals, by intellectuals. Never got through to the grass roots. And they mainly concerned themselves with the factories: wages, working hours, that kind of thing. But there was something else coming up just then. Black Consciousness. And when the Government decided to legalize the unions, there were more and more people saying: 'You can't cut a man in two, leaving one half on the job and the other half with his people. The two halves belong together.' Right, so the struggle started: against FOSATU and that lot, the ones who got registered and said they were going to improve our working conditions from the inside, through negotiation, through bargaining and so on. We said the hell with it. By registering you just give the *Boere* a better hold on us. That's when the meetings got going. We first tried to take over NAAWU, but that didn't work. So we started something else. You should have seen it, the night MACWUSA got off the ground. Hell! Just after I came back from Fort Hare for good. It was Vuyizile who took me to that meeting; he was with Pebco then. Eight

284

thousand people, I tell you. From schoolchildren to old men on sticks. You never seen such a thing. They even had a praise singer there. We sang freedom songs. In between there were speeches. It went on for hours. 'Comrades! We shall overcome, from the Cape to the Limpopo!' That sort of talk. It felt like a new sun rising. But that was only the beginning. Because then the troubles started. The back-stabbing, the infighting, all the shit. Some wanting to talk, some wanting to negotiate, others wanting to boycott, still others wanting to break down everything. Travelling to and fro all the time, night after night. From PE to Uitenhage, to King William's Town, to East London. Even Cape Town and Jo'burg. Some of us hardly had time to get on with our jobs in the factories in the daytime. Otherwise we'd work all day, go to bed early, then get up again at three or four. That's when we had the real meetings, in the deep of the night. It was never safe, you see: the *impimpi* were everywhere. From the day MACWUSA started, we had the *Boere* on our backs. Offering us unions with one hand, taking away the leadership with the other. Time and time again they came in to take our chaps away. Except, every time a man was picked up, there were two new ones to take his place. It went on and on like that, night after night. And at daybreak you would stagger out to see the sun rising again, all red in the smoke, and you would wonder whose blood would be shed that day. But there was something you knew above all: one day, when it was over, that blood would not have flowed in vain."

In the beginning the bosses do not take them seriously. If a labourer doesn't do his job to the satisfaction of the foreman, he is summarily fired. No cheek from you, kaffir. Fuck off, and don't nag me about signing your *dompas* either.

But then, one morning, the factory yard is deserted. No one has turned up for work. Hours later the union leaders arrive and ask to speak to the bosses. The bosses are busy. All right, then we'll talk tomorrow; in the meantime the work can wait.

285

"Don't bother to come back at all," the workers are informed. "There are more than enough jobless in the Eastern Cape, we can easily hire replacements."

But word has already done the rounds: anyone offering himself as a replacement is in for trouble. One more week and the factory has to close down altogether. This time, when the men arrive for discussions, the bosses are not quite so busy as before. Only, the unions are more adamant in their demands now. What they want is so much per hour. And what about pensions? What about insurance? And of course, the sacked man must be taken back.

Impossible, say the bosses: they cannot allow insubordination.

Well, just too bad, then we don't talk any more.

That's when the police arrive. If there's any possibility of a demonstration, they appear immediately. If all is calm, they come in the night. Four o'clock, that's the hour that suits them best: a pestilence that walketh in darkness. One by one, two by two, in fives, in droves, the men of the unions are taken away. MACWUSA's men, the GWU's, SAAWU's. Outside the unions, too, they get picked up: the people of Pebco or the BPO. That's how Vuyizile disappears.

Meetings, meetings all the time. Every night. There are mornings when the sunrise is bloodier than on others: mornings when a count has to be taken: How many have been raided last night? How many carted off? How many got away?

No matter. There are new ones. We're more than they. In the end we'll still outnumber them.

The bus tariffs are increased. All right, the meeting decides, so the people will walk. Let the buses die of famine. Get up earlier, two o'clock or three o'clock if necessary, to walk the twenty or more kilometres to work; and back in the afternoon. Keep the buses empty. Strangle them slowly. We have legs, our feet are used to walking on the bare earth, we don't need to ride. For the weak there are cars available; for pregnant women, for the old. Pirate taxis. Even some Whites offer private transport, to make sure the buses stay empty. The

286

police are there too, stopping the cars and the walkers, carting them off in vanloads. A lot of bloody agitators, that's what they are, Communist infiltrators, ANC agents. Waylay the taxis, beat up the drivers. Take the Whites to court. Barricade the roads.

But the people go on walking.

After four weeks the tariffs are lowered a bit. Not all the way, but it's something. "The whole situation will be thoroughly investigated," promises some spokesman or other. Many of the people feel they must go on walking, but others have grown weary. The strike peters out. Victory? Defeat? Not an easy question. At least the people have shown their power. And there are too many of them to be eradicated: there isn't enough place for them all in jail. Next time the bus companies may have to think twice. Just like the factory bosses. They, too, have felt the first brush of fear.

It remains difficult. Even more difficult if you have to spend half the night reading just to catch up and stay abreast. Books on trade unions are available in the libraries. But there are others as well, banned, but doing the rounds all the same. Cleaver. Malcolm X. Stokely Carmichael. There's Marighella and Fanon. There's Slovo. There's Biko. Where do the books come from? No one says a word: they're just there. Crawling from the woodwork and the wallpaper when it gets dark.

Some nights there's a show. If the weather is good it takes place in the open air; otherwise they find a beer hall, a community hall, a church, anywhere. A group from Joburg's Soweto. Mdantsane. Or right here from New Brighton or Kwazakele. Put on a play. Get the people together. Gone in the morning, disappeared into the smoke. Next week, next month there's news about the author being picked up: he's in detention, where they keep him for six months; when he is let out, he's sick and shivery. But his play is still doing the rounds. It brings the people together. A strange thing about it: no one in the audience cries or draws in his breath because of the terrible things presented to them. They're laughing. Laughing their heads off when the *Boere* arrive to pick up a man or put the electrodes to him or pull the wet bag over his head. Slapping their thighs when one gets knocked down. Rolling in the aisles when one is hanged. The laughter is infectious; it soothes the pain. And come to think of it, it *is* funny, isn't it? — that the *Boere* can do such things to people without realizing it's going to happen to them too, one day. It's bloody funny. You can kill yourself laughing.

Afterwards you go home, with all your people, and the heavy night is loud with laughter and sound; and in your guts you feel something which isn't always easy to grasp, something without a name as yet, but which may, perhaps, be called freedom.

Only, later that night people are picked up and taken away again. For the bosses are scared of laughter. And tomorrow morning there will again be the silent roll-call to find out who — who — who

And one night they come for Mandla too.

We crossed the Durance, almost dry after the summer, and drove into Cavaillon, the traffic slowed down as always by a convergence of trucks and other heavy vehicles crawling in to market. The first town of the day, and in my imagination I could see the black flags hanging limply as of old, here as in all the other towns and villages of the South, signalling from afar to any intrepid wayfarer: *Stay away, the Plague is in our midst.* The air so thick that not the slightest fluttering is visible.

"Didn't we pass this place yesterday?" asked Mandla. "We're not taking the same road, are we?"

"Only as far as Joucas."

"Is that the only way?"

"No, we can turn off here." Actually it suited me too. Travelling this way the day before, on my pilgrimage of contrition to La Motte d'Aigues — and what had I gained from it? — had made some sense; today it was difficult to explain even to myself what shift had taken place. "We can take the northern road, past Carpentras."

288

It would not be without risk, skirting so narrowly a route once travelled with Brian, to Montbrun. But of course we didn't have to go all the way; not all the way.

I waited for him to resume, but he didn't. Perhaps he, too, had come too close to something still exclusively his own. (Would he have shared it with Paul? Their relationship was becoming less and less understandable to me. If one could call it a "relationship": yet in Paris the impression had been unmistakable. Unless it had been no more than a signal of distress, something dangerous and urgent: what desperation had driven him to open his heart to Paul?)

Carpentras offered a welcome escape. It had nothing to do with my work. It was an extra. We could pretend to be tourists. And suddenly I was looking forward to it, even bearing in mind the warning of Avignon two days before. We left the car on the square at the entrance to the old town, where the streets become too narrow and congested for easy traffic. On a nearby terrace we had coffee — the early haze was clearing up; it was turning into an exceptionally fine day — then took to the streets. In July, at the height of the summer festival, Paul and I couldn't get through to the courtyard of the Palais de Justice where he'd wanted to show me the old Roman triumphal arch. This time we were free to go.

On our way, as we passed the crumbling façade of the Église Saint-Siffrein, I took Mandla to the northern entrance, the Porte des Juifs, which Paul had shown me in July: in the Middle Ages Carpentras, always a centre of commerce, had been in the forefront of the persecution of the Jews, he'd told me. And this entrance bore witness to it: one Good Friday the Jews had burnt an effigy there; the reprisals had been predictable. What Paul hadn't noticed — curiously enough, for he seldom missed anything — was the large stone ball surmounting the archway, covered with rodents. Mandla immediately pointed it out.

"Is that why you brought me?"

Even when he showed me I didn't immediately catch on. "What?"

289

"You always see the Plague in everything. Isn't that the earth, swarming with rats? Do you think they tried to protect themselves that way? Or was that what they thought of the Jews?"

"What if it has no connection with the Plague at all?" Why did I so stubbornly hold out? Paul would have been delighted to learn about it. Note, note. All he'd told me about had been the relic inside: the Holy Bit, he'd said, welded from two of the nails of the Cross that had landed here somehow or other after the mother of the Emperor Constantine had brought it from Jerusalem. Unfortunately the Bit was sealed up in a box, a real little Pandora's box it seemed, and kept behind opaque glass, so that one had to accept it in good faith. Which I hadn't been able to muster, I'm sorry to say; and so the Bit hadn't meant a thing to me, although he'd assured me that through the centuries it had regularly been paraded through the streets to ward off (guess what?) the Plague.

I had no desire to go inside. Much to my surprise Mandla went ahead (I'd dutifully told him about the box), while I waited in the sun outside. In a way I felt cheated by that emblem above the Jewish Gate: I'd come there to get away from predictable encounters with the past, not to be reminded of my work (or of Paul?). To breathe freely for a change. To show Mandla something which had nothing at all to do with the film; perhaps to prove to him that I was not entirely beyond redemption. (The Bit didn't really matter, it was invisible.) But I should have known better. We were still in Provence.

He made no comment when he came out. Together we went on to the Palais de Justice. The triumphal arch, dwarfed by the large buildings surrounding it, was unimpressive. Couldn't have been much of a victory it celebrated. The decorations were almost completely worn away and one could barely make out the two main figures under a banner, one in a tunic, the other in what looked like an animal skin. Probably a Gaul, a barbarian. The other a Roman officer? (Or were both of them prisoners? Perhaps it didn't make much difference.)

"Well now!" Mandla laughed, an unexpected carefree tone

290

in his voice, as if the sight of the arch liberated something inside him. "What do we have here? Master and servant? Or Christian and Jew? Or Catholic and Huguenot? Or White and Black?"

The fact that he'd turned it into a joke make me cautious about responding too readily.

He persisted: "Have you noticed the way they always come in pairs? The one can't do without the other."

"You think it's funny?"

This man in his tunic — this barbarian in his skins. For the sculptor who'd fashioned them from the lovely honey-coloured Provençal stone, or for the commander who'd commissioned the work, it must have been a proud job. To the greater glory of Rome. At the expense of the barbarians. Could it ever have occurred to that centurion, or whatever he'd been, that one day, two thousand years later, two barbarians would come to look at his emblems long after Rome had been buried under its own ruins? Would they have been more wary had they been able to look ahead? Or would they have chopped and chiselled away all the more frantically to get the job done before the next victory? The spears and slings of the Gauls against the sophisticated techniques of Rome; the assegais of Blood River against the guns of the Boers.

Perhaps, even then, they had felt a tinge of fear. Perhaps that was why.

(But what about the two of us in Carpentras today, exiles in a strange country: were we not frightened too?)

We returned through the cool judicial building with its colourless light, back to the square and the streets outside. The mist had cleared up completely, the sky was a translucent blue.

A Saturday morning under the fig-tree in the tiny backyard: she's standing with a mouth full of washing-pegs, taking pieces of wrung, wet clothing from a yellow plastic bucket to hang them on the line. In a street far away she hears the bugle of her Dedda. Through the green leaves she stares up, head thrown

291

back, into the tremendous blue of the sky, a blue so uncompromising that it brings tears to her eyes, so violent that it makes her insides ache. An instant so naked that she knows it will take a lifetime to come to terms with it. A pang of hunger, an impossible thirst, a flame, a joy, a sadness so unbearable that she clenches her hands, feeling the nails cutting into her palms. For the sheer blueness of it. Because there's no end to it. And because of this washing hanging here at this moment, this fig-tree growing here, that bugle blaring, announcing the arrival of her father; because she is here. Because she's *here*.

"That's the worst of the Plague," Paul had said, "however much of a cliché it may be: that one tries to deny what one doesn't know. That what you know nothing about you cannot accept as true."

I lingered in the doorway of the Palais de Justice in Carpentras until my eyes had once again got used to the disinterested light of the square outside, looking at Mandla as he went on ahead of me, into the sun. As on previous occasions, only in a different frame of mind, I studied his body in motion. The movement of his muscles through the thin shirt, the large shoulders, the tendons running down his back, the relaxed biceps, the contraction of his buttocks as his legs swung effortlessly: a liquid, a languid, feline stride. Impossible to deny him. There was something so inescapably *true* about him as he walked across the square. Who would dare not to acknowledge him? (I had, a mere two days ago!) He was no prisoner of Rome or anything else. He walked as if he ruled over the place, as if he was proud to be seen there. What had happened to him to turn him into the man he was? To prevent him from becoming something else? I was overwhelmingly conscious of his manhood, his youth — he was younger than I! — and something else besides: a wisdom, a freedom, a dark fire latent within him, a readiness, a heaviness, defiance, pride. He stopped and looked back towards me.

"Aren't you coming?"

His face. The weight of his brows, the line of his jaw. God, the man was beautiful. He could have been a centurion.

"I'm coming."

Without waiting, he went on, taking from his back pocket the *trompie* and bringing it to his mouth to play, swinging his hips as he went, his body swaying to the rhythm of a dance. People moved out of his way as he approached, some looking back self-consciously after he'd passed: as if they daren't quite admit that the tune had charmed them; apprehensive, the way one is reluctant to tease a lion even when it appears to be in a playful mood. Also: as if they somehow disapproved of what he was doing, blaming him perhaps for daring to play and dance when there were so many more important things to be done (buying a kilo of tomatoes, or a chicken, or a bottle of olive oil). Even the gendarme on the corner, where the narrow street broke into the square, flattened himself against the wall as Mandla passed; and only when he felt safe again did he explode against a pedestrian who'd dared to cross in front of an approaching car.

"And now — back to work? Back to your Plague?" he asked as we got into the car.

"It's Paul's Plague, not mine." My voice sounded more emphatic than I'd meant to.

"Oh?" He chuckled, putting away his little harp.

"Look, why don't we go up the mountain first? There's lots of time."

"What mountain?"

"The Mont Ventoux. Where the wind is born. One can see very far from up there. On a clear day you can even see the sea."

"That's what you said in Avignon too."

"On a clear day. Then it was hazy, remember."

"All right, let's go then. I haven't seen the sea for a long time now."

"Was that in PE?"

He looked at me, then nodded. "Yes in PE." Then he opened up again: "At Swartkops. Sunset, when the tide is low;

293

the sand goes on forever. It's dangerous, but it's a good feeling."

"I used to go to the sea with my father. Later Brian took me; after Dedda died."

"He got drowned, didn't he?"

"How do you know?"

"I think Paul mentioned it."

"I'm not sure whether he drowned. A big wave washed him overboard, they told us. But they never found his body. Perhaps he's still swimming. He was mad about the sea."

"Suppose he comes back one day, then you won't be there."

"Jesus, Mandla, now you're fighting dirty."

"I'm not fighting."

"What are you doing then?"

He didn't look at me, and when he spoke again his voice was dark: "It was you who said he might still be swimming."

I kept my eyes on the road: downhill out of the town, with the blue folds of Montmirail showing up to the left, on our way to Malaucène where one turns off to the Mont Ventoux. It would be better to stay silent, I thought; but I couldn't stop myself.

"The first Saturday after we'd heard of his death there was a service for him in our church. Ma was the one who insisted, she was convinced he'd never come to rest without it. Gran was dead against the idea; she felt it was tempting fate to have a service without even a coffin. But for once Ma could not be stopped. We meant it for the family only, a small, private affair. Brother Arie got leave from his hotel in Hermanus. Only brother Sonny couldn't come: Oudtshoorn was too far away and perhaps he also felt it wouldn't be quite proper for him to turn up. Gran and Grampa, and her sisters. And that was that, we thought. But when we got to the church there was a crowd such as you'd never seen at a funeral. All Dedda's pals. From the boats. From the trawlers. From all the corners of the Cape, and even further away. Some of them, I couldn't believe it but it was the honest truth, drove right through the night, all the way from Doringbaai and Strandfontein where

Dedda had lived as a child. That church was full to over-flowing, even the aisles were packed. The dominie was ill at ease, anyone could see that; he did it just to please Ma. He kept on paging through the Bible, reading all sorts of passages that had nothing at all to do with Dedda or with death; just rambled, even dragged Jonah into it, and at last it was done.

"After the service everybody came home with us. Bus-loads of them. Ma was quite beside herself, didn't know how to cope with them all; she was no good at multiplying loaves and fishes, she said. But the guests didn't mind about food, and each man had somehow brought his own drink with him. How they'd managed, I don't know, for everything was very prim and proper in church — but we'd hardly set foot outside when the first corks were popping. All the way back to Bonteheuwel on the bus you could hear the bottles gurgling. The crowd swept through the house, spilling into the dusty little backyard and out into the streets.

"I just sat there wishing I could get away from it all, missing Brian. You see, the day we'd got the news he'd taken me out to Steenbras, it was our first time and — anyway, I was still all mixed-up and confused, and a bit sore inside, happy and sad at the same time, and I couldn't stand the crowd.

"You should have seen them drinking. Heavily, seriously, like men who'd come to finish a very important job. No one said a word. Just heaved deep sighs from time to time, then raised the bottles to their mouths again. The sun was already setting when one of the men finally staggered to his feet: one of Dedda's mates who'd been on the last trip with him. 'Ag, jeez, David,' he said, as if Dedda was right there with us, 'how can you do this to us, man? You old bastard!' Then he burst out crying. But the strange thing was that everybody suddenly began to loosen up, as if that was the signal they'd all been waiting for.

"One man started laughing. At first he did it very quietly, all by himself, his body shaking. Then it got so bad he fell off his seat on the back steps. And it was a long time before, still sobbing with laughter, he managed to blurt out: 'You know, boys, if you take a good look at us here — not one of us set foot in a church for years — and you think of David, who also used to wipe his arse on all this holy stuff — and you look at the way he's managed to get the lot of us in church today — I mean, it *is* blerry funny, isn't it?' He had to take another swig from his bottle before he could go on: 'Hey listen,' he said, 'listen: I swear, if David knew about this, no matter where he is, he'd laugh himself to death on the spot. Perhaps he's still swimming about somewhere: but if he knew this, he would start laughing so much he'd drown right there.'"

Mandla also began to laugh. So did I. But I had to concentrate on the road through the tears.

"And that was how the celebration began," I said. "The biggest wake I've ever seen in my life. I don't know where all the drink came from. All through the night there were little boys appearing in the doorway with bottles in brown paper bags, scuttling off like mice if Ma or Gran saw them. At sunrise the next day some were still going strong. Only, by that time the yard was full of bodies who'd passed out, a proper battlefield. Even Ma, who'd never touched spirits in her life, got so jolly that she was singing psalms at the top of her voice; and Gran was staggering on her feet as she moved to and fro between kitchen and living-room serving food. For by that time there was food too. All the neighbours had turned up carrying dishes. Even Grampa began to show unusual signs of life, giggling and feeling up the widows, while the menfolk just went on laughing and talking and singing terrible sailors' songs, fit to make one's eardrums burst. The only times when they calmed down a bit was when someone remembered another story about Dedda and stopped the noise to tell his bit: and then they'd roar with laughter and roll about, breaking bottles and trampling the vegetable beds. Even I, no matter how I was aching inside, longing for Dedda, I tell you, I was laughing so much it was running down my legs. For the sheer joy of it. Because they all loved Dedda so much. Because he was the kind of man who wouldn't mind us drinking ourselves straight into hell to celebrate his death. Gran herself had to admit — two days later, when we'd finally slept it off — that she'd never seen such a funeral in her life. And that was saying something, because she just lived for death.

"That was a great night indeed, when we buried Dedda in our hearts. And ever since then he's been swimming through my memories."

All the stories. He comes home from incredible lands and places — Shanghai, Hanoi, Singapore, anywhere you can imagine — his arms loaded with presents. For his wife, petticoats of the finest silk. Which she is forced to try on immediately. No matter how she protests — "But David, can't you wait till we're alone?" — there's no way out and she knows it: if she refuses, he's quite capable of undressing her himself, right there. And when she comes back to show off, her pale brown cheeks suffused with red, he picks her up in his arms and carries her out to the neighbours for all to see. She screams at him, sobbing with shame, hammering his face with her small fists; but this just seems to incite him further, bellowing with laughter as he dances through the streets to show her off. Until at long last he brings her back, through the front door and straight into the bedroom, kicking the door shut after them, a bang that reverberates through the whole house and sends Gran scurrying about to collect the children and urgently haul them off to the shops.

And then he's off again — impossible to foretell if it will be for a month or a year; once he stays away for fully thirty-six months — and suddenly the house is lifeless and dreary. Gran rules over it with a heavy hand; Ma tries to resist, there are violent shouting matches, and then she gradually subsides into apathy again. Even so, he's never wholly absent from their lives. His picture — taken on board a freighter, in some distant harbour — sleeps under Andrea's pillow. The walls are covered with his bright presents — blue butterflies from Brazil; cocos de mer with their embarrassingly intimate female curves; sea-shells; coral; painted trays; multicoloured tapestries;

297

parrot feathers. And her beloved blanket. Even in his absence his presence looms large, like a fantastic shadow. One knows only too well: no matter what you do, Dedda will come to know about it. Dedda is like God, he knows everything.

Each December, just before Christmas, a car must be borrowed or hired for by hook or by crook — that's Dedda's command — they must travel up to the West Coast to tend the graves of his people. Up there, near Strandfontein, on the coastal farm where he was born, where he used to catch herring and crayfish as a child, his father's ancestors lie buried since long before the time when Gran brought them back to Cape Town. ("Hell, we were poor when I was a child," he likes to tell them, "so poor that when Christmas came along my Ma had to cut open the boys' trouser pockets, just so's they could also have something to play with.") For come Christmas, the dead must be cared for and at ease, every man, woman and child among them. Weeding, shovelling, raking; fresh flowers, new pots to replace the broken ones. Then the long road back again. Dedda will know if his people aren't resting well at Christmas.

One day, one night, without the slightest warning, he's back among them, as if from the dead; it's like a Second Coming. For all of them, but for none quite so exhilaratingly as for Andrea.

If he feels like it, he keeps her out of school ("My Nanna's a clever one, she'll catch up; what I give her they can't teach her at school"), and takes her to town with him. (Probably her earliest memory: Dedda carrying her on his shoulders, walking through the streets, singing at the top of his voice.) Down to the Gardens. To the harbour. To the Museum, when he finds out there are visiting days for Coloureds. There he shows her the Bushmen in the big glass showcases, scaring her out of her wits because at first sight they seem stuffed just like animals; and as naked as her finger, it doesn't seem right. (Just as well they didn't get hold of you too, Grandpa Xhorê, to put you on show in one of their smart display cases.) To Hout Bay. To Kalk Bay, all the places of the Cape. It's he who opens her heart and mind to the Cape, a head-over-heels and lasting love-affair. The Southeaster in summer. The long winters with the rain coming down for three weeks on end. The greenest green.

And once he gets it into his head to take her on a journey through the land in search of long-lost relatives. He's always had this soft spot for family. It's a proper junkheap on wheels, the old jalopy he borrows off a dubious friend, but there's nothing his hands cannot mend or repair. Whatever breaks on the road, he puts right. If a fanbelt snaps, Andrea has to take off her pantyhose to replace it. Otherwise she stands beside him, handing him whatever he needs, until she's almost as good a mechanic as he is.

There's no plan or schedule to their trip. It depends entirely on Dedda's whims; and if a sudden brainwave takes them a hundred or two hundred kilometres out of their way, what's the difference? When he can't find relatives he tracks down old friends, or makes new ones. Trust him always to find a place to sleep. Several nights they spend in the veld: sleeping in the car if the weather is inclement, or in the open if the night is calm. Bushes and shrubs to make their beds. A few odd blankets in the boot, just in case. In the morning he makes coffee. A live coal in the tin mug, and stirring with a specially selected twig for flavour. No sugar. And black. Leaning back against a rear wheel, he talks to her, tells her stories, teaches her about the land, encourages her to taste, to touch, to smell. That's a kiewiet; listen to that hadeda; Jesus Christ, I swear that's a fishing eagle (in the Tsitsikamma, camping on the edge of a sheer red-and-black cliff). Hear that creaking sound? It's a guinea-fowl, sounds just like a wheelbarrow in need of oil. Smell: that's wild olive. Buchu. Cat's tail. Bluegum. Watch that puff-adder. Come closer, look at the ants when I break off a corner of this anthill. Watch out for scorpions if you pick up stones. Got a thorn in your foot, squatting behind a bush to do a wee? Dedda will take it out with his pocket knife. Just clench your teeth, Nanna-girl. Dedda won't ever hurt you.

299

Zigzag through the land, the sound of his mouth organ in her ears.

A man without any learning to speak of. Passed his standard four, then had to lend a hand on the farm and on the fishing boats. Brine in his veins. After his mother has brought them to Cape Town to move into her old family home, the freighters become his life. Not the very big ones: nine thousand, ten thousand tons, travelling from port to port, dropping you when your contract has expired, twelve or twenty-four months later. Sometimes it's a stretch of fifty days on the high seas before you reach a harbour. Then maybe two or three days from port to port. Forty-five men on a boat, half White, half Coloured. You have your own cabin. And the pay's good. Enough to take back to your family and have some left for yourself. Food and shelter is provided; clothes you've got. The rest is profit: eating, drinking, women. You take your freight across the sea — salt, coal, carbon, soya beans, rice, any-thing, depending on where you come from and where you're heading for — and stay on when the going's good. There's always someone to take you in if you play your cards right. Then it's back home and a bit of rest before the itch sends you off again. And home again. When the vineyard sprouts new leaves, the saying goes, the wine is crying in the bottle. And when there's trouble at home it calls you back. A place to weigh anchor. Wife and children, mother and father. Friends. But above all: his Nanna-girl, the one for whom he's prepared to go to hell. (The one for whom he does go to hell one day.)

Just after Malaucène, where the road begins to climb up the Mont Ventoux, a few hundred metres below the camping site, we saw the cyclist again. Unbelievable. But this time the encounter came as quite a shock. Instead of pedalling as usual, he lay beside the road, spreadeagled over his bicycle, his red-and-black cap ten yards away in the grass.

"Can you believe it?" said Mandla. "The poor turd's fallen off. You'd better stop, perhaps he needs help."

I was reluctant — "I'm sure it isn't serious" — but he

300

insisted, and when I pulled off the road he immediately got out and ran back to where the man was now sitting up, rubbing his bleeding knees. In the rearview mirror I watched as Mandla knelt beside him and started feeling his legs to check for broken bones. After a while he looked up and beckoned to me. Of course: there was no way he could communicate with the cyclist.

Not that there was much need to translate. The man was so livid that he could do little more than curse and shout. "Fucking car!" he got out at last. "Blasted its horn right behind me and when I looked round the wheel hit a stone. And all they could do was *laugh* at me. These bloody French drivers—!"

"Aren't you French then?" I asked. Quite unnecessarily, for I should have recognized the accent.

"Of course not. Italian."

"Well, what's he doing so far from his home then?" asked Mandla, after I'd explained to him.

I translated.

"Cycling, of course," the Italian said. "Now they're kilometres ahead. I'll never catch up."

"We've been watching you since July," I said impulsively. "A different road every day."

He gawked at me as if I were soft in the head.

Mandla was still checking his bruises, but didn't seem to find any serious damage. It was strangely moving to watch him.

After a while Mandla got up. "It's all right." Hissing at me: "He's a sissy, that's all." Then he offered the man a hand to help him to his feet. "Can we take you down to the village?"

"No, I can manage." Sulking, the man picked up his cap and dusted it, examined his bike and got on, without a word of thanks.

We went back to the car. "Bloody stupid," said Mandla. "Now he blames the car for it."

"You looked very concerned about him."

"I couldn't leave him lying there like that, could I?"

301

We resumed our drive along the winding road up the slope that seemed to grow steeper with every bend. The whole mountain smelled of pine needles. But there were other trees too, deciduous ones, red and brown and yellow in this late autumn. The effort was almost too much for the little car. After some time we broke through the treeline to find ourselves completely exposed against the barren white sides of the summit; it was growing chilly. Below us the world fell away into the distance, remote like a photograph from space. And suddenly I felt myself in the grip, not just of vertigo but of a terror so primitive and vast that it was all I could manage just to creep on, centimetre by centimetre, nearly stalling the car: but I knew that, surely, if I stopped, I'd lose my balance and fall into that void like a shooting star. The open expanse below was pulling me, an almost physical force that left me panting and wet with perspiration. There was nothing at all nearby to protect us, to offer us the slightest shelter; only the void, the terrifying purity of the air.

Had he noticed my fear? He must have. But he said nothing. Perhaps he, too, felt the menace of that total exposure.

How we reached the top — disfigured by monstrous weather and radar installations — I still don't know. He got out while I remained in the car, my eyes closed, trembling, so nauseous I could throw up with fear. Only after a very long time I felt steady enough to venture out of the car and go to him. He was standing at one of the orientation tables.

Shivering in the cold air we stared into the impossible translucence of the day. The white ridges and folds of Montmirail, the dark grey course of the Rhône, the vague outline of the Cévennes in the far west, the Alps to the northeast, the knuckles of the Alpilles in the south. Beyond the Alpilles, the plains — resembling nothing so much as the Cape Flats — down to the green marshlands of the Camargue. And if one screwed up one's eyes, straining them to the point of drawing tears, one could just make out, with the merest hint of wishful thinking added to it, the sea, a slightly bluer smudge against the pale blue of the sky.

"And beyond the sea," Mandla suddenly said, as if catching his breath, "would that be Africa?"

"Yes, but it's much too far to see."

"Not all that far, if you think of it."

Around us were the quartz-like white rocks of the summit, dandruff on the bald pate of the mountain. And among the rocks, tufts of grass, hardy enough to survive in the cold, with a strong smell of herbs. Small stern flowers. Patches of brittle scrub. Only the toughest vegetation could survive so high, among these barren stones. And below, I sensed the hard essential earth: everything laid bare until only pure stone remained in the steady flow of wind which, I felt, eternally blew up there, stripping away whatever was fortuitous and incidental to leave the barest, merest *I* intact.

"Yes, it's Africa all right." He sounded satisfied.

Stone. Wind. A new anxious awareness of the two of us remote from the rest of the world; he and I; man and woman. With Africa in the distance.

We turned back to the car. For a moment, as the wind suddenly made me lose my balance, he put an arm round me. I could feel the warmth of his body in the wind that had been increasing so steadily that I now had to gasp for breath. Only when we reached the small white car he let go.

But after I'd already opened the door to get in I pushed it shut again. There was not space enough inside. Something in the extreme innocence of the wind lured me back into the open space which, minutes earlier, had almost scared me to death. I walked down the scaly slope, away from the installations at the top, and sat down on a mound of white rocks. He followed me, stopping right behind me, but without saying anything. The wind was very cold now, very pure. I needed that cold, that purity. I wanted to find out how far I could really see. For the first time in God knows how many years I was prepared to look at what I'd tried to forget for so long.

"Andrea," says the big man with the stomach and the crippled

303

leg, "I want you to stay behind after five so you can help me tidy up. It's time I showed you the ropes."

Although his voice has been expressionless, giving away nothing at all, a few of the other girls start giggling nervously, stopping very suddenly as he turns to look at them.

"They're expecting me at home, Mr Wiese," she says. Her mother has the afternoon off.

"It shouldn't take long," he says curtly. "I've been watching you closely. You learn fast, don't you?"

"I don't understand," she says cautiously.

"You will, you will. Now get on with your job, you're wasting time."

That's how he is. No one takes chances with this man. He comes in every morning to do the books; and on Wednesday afternoons he stands in for his wife so that she can go and do her shopping. She's the hairdresser; the salon is in Kenilworth, just off the Main Road. He used to be a builder, they say, but then he hurt his leg in an accident and since then he's never had a regular job again, except for coming in mornings and Wednesday afternoons. They all watch their step with him; he has an ugly temper. Thinks nothing of hitting his wife in front of everybody.

It's just to keep the peace with her mother that Andrea has consented to help out a few afternoons every week. It started during her matric year; this is well into her second year at Western Cape, and it's not easy to cope with both work and lectures, but for Ma's sake —

Her mother has set her mind on it that Andrea must become a hairdresser. Which caused problems when the question of going to university was mooted; and if it hadn't been for Brother Sonny — Ma daren't say a word to him, as he's her living conscience — nothing would have come of it. "You've got hairdresser's hands, Andrea. Those long fingers. Your life is cut out for you. You'll have an easier time than I had, I can tell you."

"But Ma, I thought you also wanted to study years ago. Then you had to give it up because — "

"It was just as well. I got along fine without it and so can you. What's a girl want to do with university? You just pick up bad habits."

You picked yours up before you even got there. But she doesn't say it out loud, it's no use. If you want Ma to clam up, all you have to do is mention university. She seems to take pride in relying on her hands alone; it's become her way of "showing" the world. Just one glance and she knows exactly what is required for every head she has to groom. Face up in the white basin. Measuring out the shampoo in one deft flick of the bottle. Lather. Rinse. Dry lightly with the towel. Then it's cut or style or perm or set. For streaking there's the rubber stocking, strands of hair pulled through the holes, just enough at a time. Curlers. Irons. Under the drier. When it comes to chatting with the customers there's no one to beat her. Not a word too much: just enough to intimate that she's a woman too, she understands, nothing is foreign to her. For the rest it's a matter of listening, slipping in one's "Yes" or "No" or "Goodness Madam" at just the right moments. They also do nails. Nothing anyone can teach her about manicure. Every woman going out through that door must be a living advertisement for Salon Jemima. Word of mouth, that's the only way.

Andrea can't stand messing about with other people's hair. It's all right doing Ma's or Maggie's over the weekend, that's different, they're family. And Dedda's above all, when he's home from the sea: she can wash or comb his hair or scratch his head for hours, anything he asks her to do. But these Kenilworth ladies with their rinses and their streaking and their fancy styles, something new from the overseas journals every week, are the bloody limit. If it hadn't been for Ma — But this is her last year. Next year she'll have to study full-time to finish her degree. She's promised Brother Sunny; she's solemnly promised Dedda. Ma will undoubtedly call down fire and brimstone over their heads again, but that's just too bad. Only this one more year.

She's been hoping to get home early tonight. Johnny is

coming over. Said he'd take her to Mowbray for a movie. Johnny is in his third year, they started going steady a year ago. In the beginning she held back, intimidated by the thought of Dedda; but she couldn't help feeling a soft spot for the man. Very quiet, shy, decent; his father teaches at Hewatt College. In the beginning she just teased him, but Johnny was serious and she could see it hurt him. For her father's sake she still held out: and if he'd been home she would never have dared to let it happen; but then he went off on another of his trips and she was left defenceless. The awakened flesh: touched, opened, surprised. Furtive couplings in the dark. The smell of rubber.

Now this unforeseen setback. What's he mean, "teaching her the ropes"? All she needs to know about hairdressing her mother and his wife have taught her long ago. She feels ill at ease about the others' knowing looks, but when she tries, a few minutes before five, to waylay one of them in the Ladies, the girl brushes it off with a mirthless giggle: "Don't worry, man, it's nothing."

After the front door has been closed — "Good day, Mr Wiese", "'Bye, Mr Wiese", "Cheerio, Mr Wiese" — he still goes on fiddling at the cash register for a while.

"Mr Wiese, you asked me to stay behind."

"Yes. You can check that the combs are all rinsed and that everything is in its place for tomorrow morning. My wife is expecting some early customers."

She feels relieved. This can't take long, a few minutes only, which will leave her enough time to have a bath and prepare herself for Johnny. While she tidies up swiftly and meticulously, Wiese finishes his additions and subtractions at the till, bundles the cash into a bank bag and goes through to the flat at the back, dragging his bad leg. The door is left ajar.

"You can come through," he calls the moment she's finished: he must have been watching her through the slit.

She comes to the threshold. "Mr Wiese — ?"

"Come in."

Hesitant, she enters.

306

"There's another comb over there, by the divan."

She walks right into it. As she reaches the small sapele bedside cabinet he moves over to the door — surprisingly fast with his useless leg — and closes it.

"Jesus, that's not fair," she says in a whisper. "Let me go. Ma's expecting me."

"You've been with us for over a year and I haven't had time to show you the ropes yet."

"I'm not one of the staff. I'm just helping out for my mother."

"Same thing. Every girl that works for us gets the same treatment."

She steps back, holding the dirty comb in both hands, pressed to her chest. "I'm not that sort of girl, Mr Wiese."

"Oh come on. Don't try to tell me you're a virgin." He approaches, dragging his right leg. "You coloured girls start young. And I've been watching you."

(Is it true what Dedda said about one's way of walking?)

Very slowly she draws in her breath. "Please don't make trouble for me, Mr Wiese."

His face grows redder. "Come on, you're wasting my time. Take off your clothes."

Another step back takes her to the edge of the divan.

"Bushman *meid*!" he suddenly shouts at her. "Didn't you hear what I said?"

"If this is what it takes to work here I'd rather go."

"All right, you can go. Tomorrow. Your mother too."

"It's got nothing to do with my mother!" she says, shaken.

"Well, it's up to you." He glares at her in silence for a moment, then loses his temper. "You heard me. Get a move on."

She shakes her head.

He lunges forward to pin her down on the bed, but she manages to roll right over it, out of his way. Where he's grabbed her blouse the whole front is torn open, exposing her bra; she tears herself loose and jumps to her feet, but stumbles, losing one of her shoes, and runs to the door. He cannot catch

307

up with her, not with that leg.

"*Hotnot* bitch!" he shouts after her from the front door.

A whole block away she stops for the first time to pull off her other shoe, staring at it vacantly as it hits her that she's left her handbag behind. Only now does she register the full shock of what has happened. She staggers to a café entrance where she leans against the doorframe, unable to control the sobs.

"Hey, Costas!" she hears a woman's voice shouting inside. "Come and chase this drunken whore away, she's messing up the place!"

She drags herself away before the café owner can reach the door.

Gradually she calms down. It is getting dark. It's a hell of a long way to District Six from here. She'll have to ask for help.

But the people she tries to stop in the street all look at her with a mixture of suspicion and disgust, and make wide detours to get out of her way. She cannot really blame them; she must be looking a sight. And there's the torn blouse and the one shoe in her hand to make it worse. Pulling herself together, she enters a block of flats, takes the lift up to one of the upper floors and begins to knock indiscriminately on the doors. Two of them are barred by safety chains and are opened a mere inch or so before being banged shut again. At the third a middle-aged woman starts shouting at her before she's managed to say a word. The fourth is opened by a young man; behind him she hears the sounds of a party.

"Excuse me, sir — "

He grins, glancing back into the room over his shoulder: "Jeez, Peter," he calls, "come and have a look, man. Come in sweetie."

Their voices are still laughing and shouting behind her as she runs down the fire escape. The feet of her pantyhose are beginning to get frayed.

After another kilometre the street lights go on; the dusk is deepening fast.

She decides to try hiking, cautiously hailing passing cars from the pavement, but not one slows down. After a while she moves off the kerb, into the street where they must see her. They swerve out to miss her, or slam on the brakes to avoid oncoming traffic; heads appear from windows to shout at her. One comes charging straight towards her and she has to hurl herself out of the way, grazing both knees on the pavement; leaving her pantyhose in shreds.

There are no tears left in her. Only a weary emptiness.

In the descending dark she notices the blue lamp of a police station on her way. Without stopping to think, more from desperation than from need, she goes up the red steps, into the angry glare of the charge office, paying no attention to the *Whites Only* sign.

"Hey," says the blond constable behind the counter, eyeing her with suspicion. "What's the matter with you?"

"I want to go home."

"You people!" He shakes his head. "Listen, why don't you go back and sleep it off first? If you feel like it, you can come back tomorrow and tell me all about it. Right?"

"I just want to — "

"Get out!" he shouts. "You think I've got time for every drunken bitch that comes in here?"

She turns round, still holding the shoe in her hand, and goes out blindly into the night.

Half an hour later, after she's given up all attempts to hitch a lift, a car stops beside her, tyres screeching, two wheels on the kerb. A hubbub of male voices inside. The doors on her side are flung open.

"Hi, gorgeous!" someone calls out as an arm grabs her round the waist. "How's it, boys? Just look at this juicy cunt."

She manages to pull free, but the man comes running after her. She hurls the shoe at him but he ducks and it sails harmlessly over his head. A roar of laughter from the car.

"Bloody little cheekypuss!" shouts the man on her heels. "Come on, boys, give us a hand!"

But she darts into a side lane and dives through the hedge into a dark garden where she waits, crouching, for them to go away. It doesn't take long before they give it up.

"Ag, drop it," she hears one of them say. "I bet she's had enough of it for the night anyway. Let's go."

After allowing them another ten or fifteen minutes to make quite sure they're gone, she goes down to the main road again; this time she keeps as far away from the street as possible.

It is very dark now. Only inside her she is aware of a new glare of light, an intensity of insight she will recognize again many years later, in Provence: the discovery, for the first time in her life: *There's no one out there. I'm on my own.*

De Waal Drive. Suppose some of the *bergies*, that elusive clan of vagrants who have made the Mountain their home, come down to get her?

Then it's just too bad. It doesn't matter any more. They may even have more compassion than the others.

Shortly before midnight she reaches home.

"My God, Andrea, where have you been? Look at you! Johnny waited for hours. You're really not playing the game with him, you know."

She doesn't even try to answer. Pushing past her mother she goes to her room and closes the door. After a while Maggie comes in and sits down on her own bed.

"Andrea, you ought to be ashamed of yourself."

"Oh fuck off!" she screams, throwing a pillow at her sister.

"I'll pray for you," Maggie says, stung.

"Pray for yourself!"

Only after the house has grown quiet again does she go to the bathroom where she locks herself in and gets into the bath to scrub herself as if she'll never be clean again.

The next morning, on her way to work, her mother looks in to say good morning (she and Maggie have both spent the night in the living-room; or perhaps with the old people next door), stopping in the doorway when she sees Andrea, in her nightgown, sitting on the window-sill; the bed is still untouched.

"Haven't you slept then?"

"No."

"Why not?"

310

"It's none of your business."

"Why must you make it so hard for me, Andrea?" A sigh. "No one ever thinks of me."

"Just leave me alone, Ma."

"It's easy for you to say. You know I'll be worrying myself sick about you all day. Where were you last night?"

"Nowhere."

"You come home at midnight looking like God knows what and you say you've been nowhere?"

"I left my handbag at the hairdresser's, so I didn't have any money for the bus."

"You could have gone and fetched it. There's always someone. You know they live in the flat behind the salon."

"I'm never going back to that place again."

"How can you say that? Mrs Wiese has always been very kind to us."

"I'm not talking about Mrs Wiese. It was her afternoon off."

Suddenly her mother is very quiet. After a very long time she whispers: "Was it him — ?"

"So what if it was?"

In a rush of anxiety her mother begins to speak: "Andrea, now you mustn't — I mean, the man does it with everybody. Only, I thought because you're not working full-time he wouldn't — But if you stop to think about it, is it really so bad — ?"

She raises her head, her tearless eyes, staring into her mother's tired face. "With everybody?" she asks.

"He didn't hurt you, did he?"

"I didn't let him. You know I'm like a cat, always land on my feet."

"Andrea, I hope you didn't behave badly towards him?" Her voice is suspicious, frightened. "You're not going to let me lose my job, are you? It's all I've ever had. The only thing that's ever been my own. Now you want to take it away from me — "

"I'm not taking anything from anybody. Just leave me alone."

311

Her mother comes a step towards her, yielding for a moment to concern. "You sure you're all right, my girl?"

"Don't worry about me."

She turns her head away. The day is beginning to emerge from the smoke. Far away at the harbour there is the horn of a ship, a hoarse blunt sound, like an animal in pain.

When Ma came home so early that afternoon, bringing my bag with her, I immediately knew it had happened. I didn't try to speak to her; she wouldn't have allowed me either. Just went and locked herself up in Gran's room.

The next morning I took the bus to Kenilworth. There was no clear plan of action in my mind; I just couldn't take Ma's crying any longer. I never thought the man would be so flustered to see me again. Jumped up from the desk where he was balancing the books, sharply turning his head to see whether his wife was watching — she was working on a client under the drier at the farthest mirror — and immediately I could see he was terrified.

"What are you doing here?" he stammered.

"I've just come to pick up my other shoe, Mr Wiese."

"I threw it away."

"Then you'd better find it. The police will need it."

"What's it got to do with the police?"

"I've come to talk about my mother, Mr Wiese. You can't sack her just like that."

"She's not been doing her job properly recently." He was edging back towards the wall.

"You sacked her because you tried to rape me."

Another quick, anxious stare in his wife's direction.

"All these other girls know you, Mr Wiese. If you prefer, we can discuss it with your wife. Otherwise we'll have to go to the police."

He gulped. "Now Miss Malgas, don't act irresponsible. What do you expect me to do? I can't take your mother back like that."

"I'm sure she won't want to come back either. But you can

312

write her a reference. I'm sure she can do with a good testimonial."

I honestly didn't think he'd fall for it. Never seen a man write as fast as that; stopping only to wipe his hands from time to time.

He was halfway through when his wife came to the desk.

"My goodness, Andrea, I thought you'd left us?"

"I just called to pick up a letter for my mother, Madam." Impulsively I decided to push my luck: "And her notice money."

"I thought she got her notice money yesterday?"

"No," I lied, very smoothly. "Mr Wiese said she must send for it today."

He would have killed me if he could, I'm sure. But he was so scared I could smell it.

There was a strange feeling in me as I sat in the bus on the way home. A bitter taste in my mouth. But something else besides. The discovery that I could do anything I wanted with that man. I'd never thought a thing like that was possible. It had never, not for a moment, occurred to me that I might also have a form of power over others; over men. Dedda would have been proud of his Nanna, I desperately tried to convince myself.

Then why was I so scared of his homecoming?

I didn't tell anybody about what had happened. All I did was to cut my hair very short, as I could not bear to see in the mirror the girl I'd been. The Cat had started a new life. And I broke with Johnny. How could I face him after that? He was shattered, but I refused to give him any reason. From Dedda, too, I kept it hidden when he came home a month or so later. But of course he sensed soon enough that there was something wrong: and not just because Ma was working at another place in Wineberg.

At first I tried to brush him off, but Dedda had never been one to take kindly to a cold shoulder. In the end I had no choice but to tell him.

All he said was: "Nanna! Oh my God, my little girl." And

then he stood staring into space as if he neither saw nor believed anything any more.

"Why don't you just forget about it, Dedda? It's all over. I didn't let him do anything."

If I'd know what he was planning I would have done all I could to stop him. Not that it would have been much use, but at least I would have tried. As it happened, I only found out about it afterwards.

He waited for the Wednesday afternoon to make sure the man would be there; then he took the bus to Kenilworth.

Dedda really messed up that man. But Mr Wiese also hurt him badly. Only, that didn't count, for it was Mr Wiese who went to lay a charge, not Dedda. So the police came to pick Dedda up.

At the trial, wanting to protect me, he refused point-blank to say why he'd done it. I was there, I heard with my own ears how he lied to cover up for me. Until that day I hadn't breathed a word about it, not to a soul; after all, it concerned my last bit of self-respect. But I couldn't allow Dedda to suffer because of it. For him I was prepared to throw myself to the hyenas, even if it meant lying.

During a recess I spoke to his lawyer (he hadn't wanted one; Arie and Boetie had seen to it that the man was hired), and then I was called to the witness box. I didn't look in Dedda's direction at all as I rattled off to the magistrate the story I'd made up: about how Mr Wiese had lured me into his room and raped me.

The orderlies had to restrain Dedda in the dock. For myself, it was like dying. I swore to God: never again in my life. This suffering was too much. And what was the use? None at all, for then Mr Wiese countered with his own story about how I'd come to ask for a rise that Wednesday afternoon, and how he'd refused, saying I was just on the temporary staff; if I were to switch to full-time he was prepared to consider it. And how I'd taken my clothes off for him to offer him something for his money; and how he'd then promptly thrown me out, being an honourable citizen and a decent husband for his wife.

314

Twelve months they gave Dedda: assault with intent. Six months suspended for I don't know how many years.

Because of good behaviour he was let out a few months early. But he never was the same again. Before, he'd used to drink because there had always been a reason to celebrate, to be with his pals, to laugh and have a good time. Now his drinking was different, heavier, in a sullen silence, and on his own. He had no stomach for the sea any more. Nor for anything else. It wore us all down. And barely three or four months later there was another blow when we were thrown out of District Six to make way for white development, and we had to move to Bonteheuwel in the everlasting dust and wind. It made Dedda drink even more heavily. I tried to persuade him to do the rounds of the Cape again, like in the past, but he just shook his head, saying I must now spend all my time on my lectures. I didn't dare tell him I'd already given up the university months before, switching to a secretarial course in the city; I didn't want to make things worse for him. This dark, louring bitterness was bad enough. The bouts of self-deprecation and tearful tirades. Or worse, the nights he just *sat* there, his eyes following me wherever I came or went. Those two bloodshot, broken, dazed eyes, staring at me as if my very way of walking burnt him to the quick.

That — the day in court, when I had to strip myself naked before the world for his sake, all in vain; and the way he kept staring at me afterwards — was like a live coal scorching my most vulnerable flesh. It was like blood that never stopped flowing. A suffering so terrible that I never even told Brian about it later (one of only two things I couldn't ever share with him). To no one but Paul did I dare open my heart; the night I returned from Chartres, after Ma's death: and then only because so many years had come in between, and because nothing but her death could finally free me from our terrible complicity. I'm not sure that even Paul could fully understand that pain which had linked me to her so fatally for so long; and the way it had kept us tied to Dedda. Even so, I told him, trying perhaps to shift something of my burden on to him.

315

And now to Mandla, but for altogether different reasons.

I emptied myself completely, feeling quite drained when it was over. Instinctively I took a slightly bruised cigarette from my handbag and fumbled for the lighter. Quickly squatting down beside me, Mandla covered my hand with his. I froze. Then he quietly took the lighter from me and flicked it on. The frail little flame immediately went out. He tried again, sheltering it with both hands cupped around it; and this time we managed to light my cigarette.

He sat beside me in silence while I smoked. Later he took out his *trompie* and began to play, very softly, with a sadness echoing my own. I felt the urge to put my hand on his arm — as if he was the one in need of comforting! — but I didn't, afraid he might not understand.

After a long time he got up again. I threw away my cigarette butt.

"Let's go," he said, and began to walk on ahead of me, back to the distant car.

We drove down the far side of the mountain; at the ski-station we took the road to Sault. Like so often before it was a journey covering not just a certain distance, traversing a particular geography, but a voyage through time as well, back to Brian and me. As we reached the plains below Sault, among the brown fields which only a few months before had been purple with lavender and sprinkled with red poppies, I felt tempted to turn towards the more uneven, rugged landscapes in the direction of Montbrun. Would the first hotel still be there, and the old witch who'd thrown us out? And the other place that had offered us refuge and in which we'd huddled together under a bright umbrella as the rain trickled down from the ceiling on our bed? The sad circus: the motheaten mane of the poor old lion, the monkeys with their thumbs cut off, the cruel children pestering them. And suddenly I knew: no, I wouldn't go back after all. Not just because the memory was unbearable: but because, at last, Brian had also been laid to rest in my

316

mind. For the first time I could acknowledge quite truthfully his relegation to the past.

Perhaps it had already happened inside me long before, but I'd never been able consciously to accept it. Perhaps even my love for Paul had long been an attempt to grope back towards an irrevocable Brian? But I knew now that it wasn't Brian I'd come to look for in Provence: not even signs of him. If I were to meet him again now, in the flesh, he wouldn't evoke any response in me at all. Was it the places as such, then, that had been haunting me? — the geography of so much happiness and torment? Not even that. These towns and landscapes of the South were in themselves but mementoes bearing the traces of other, more remote, less graspable landscapes, spaces, plains and mountains. A world I'd once known with Dedda. A world I'd called my own, knowing I belonged there. That was what had kept me tied to Brian: through Provence — our cramped little rooms witnessing the strenuous spasms of our love, so much fruitless seed and sweat; and the landscapes separating them — I could maintain the illusion of something which had been mine and which I hadn't dared to give up as lost. And that was why it had seemed such an act of betrayal to discover that for him, too, those places had been nothing but stations offering access to earlier, long-lost happiness.

Was I finally free from that now? Of course not. But perhaps I'd found a more direct, more immediate access to the past. At least I was beginning to accept such an alternative as possible.

No, there was no need to proceed to Montbrun.

We drove up the hill to Sault. In a small food shop in the old quarter below the church — winding medieval streets, stone bridges, beautiful doorways, round turrets — I bought the usual provisions for our lunch while Mandla waited in the car. Pâté, ham, cheese, a *pain de mie*, tomatoes, sweet grapes. I was still taking my time to look around when a bizarre procession passing the door made me glance up. I wasn't the only one either: a sudden silence descended on the village as in all the doors and behind the lace curtains of all the windows, faces appeared to stare with a mixture of suspicion and curiosity at the little procession moving towards a microbus on the open square above. They must have been inmates of an institution or a hospital (the sides of the bus bore the name of a place in Aix), people on some kind of excursion, accompanied by male and female nurses in white overcoats. Most of them were old, all seemed disabled in one way or another: some in wheelchairs, others on crutches or sticks; the majority appeared senile or moronic, their mouths open and dribbling, heads lolling on their shoulders, hands floppy and helpless, idiotic grins on their pale faces. In utter silence the townsfolk stood looking on as they shuffled past (one old woman, I noticed, made the sign of the cross); they were helped into the bus, and then it pulled off and disappeared out of sight. Even then nobody spoke. Each seemed to draw back from his neighbour, slinking guiltily into their separate homes, as if ashamed of what they'd seen; as if we all had glimpsed an abyss in ourselves, which we'd rather not acknowledge, something comical, and grotesque, and obscene that had suddenly escaped from the subconscious into the bright light of reason to catch us unawares. I was so upset that I didn't even check my purchases but hurriedly paid for what I'd already chosen and fled back to the car.

"Seen the circus?" Mandla asked as I got in.

I nodded briefly, fumbling for my keys among the parcels.

"Pretty gruesome lot, eh?"

"It's not their fault," I said, irritable.

"I'm not talking about the old ones. I'm talking about the way the townsfolk stared at them."

I found the keys. "Let's go."

"You got all we need?"

"I think so."

He looked through the parcels. "There's nothing to drink, man." He opened his door. "I'll go and get us some wine."

When he returned a few minutes later with a bottle in his hand, he was furious.

"Bloody old shit!" he ranted. "Thought I wouldn't notice!"

318

"What happened?"

"Tried to cheat me with the change. And of course she doesn't understand a word of any fucking civilized language under the sun."

"Mandla, you're being unreasonable. This is France, after all."

"So what? She thought she could cheat me because I'm black. Fucking racist!"

"There may be a hundred different reasons for it. The most likely is that she misunderstood you because you don't speak French. They don't like foreigners."

"Especially not black ones."

I felt piqued. "Of course that's the first thing you'll think of."

"And the last *you* will dare to think of."

"Do be reasonable."

"Why must *I* always be reasonable?" He angrily put the wine bottle among the parcels on the back seat. "You know what she said to me?"

"No, what?"

"All I could make out was *idiot*. That's what really made me the hell in."

I couldn't help grinning. "Well, one thing we know: this place doesn't like idiots."

"It's not just this place." He stayed silent while I drove on along the southern road back to Carpentras, skirting the mountain. After some time he changed his position on the seat so that he could look straight at me, his arm on the back of my own seat. "I don't know what's worse: the ones who either turn their backs on the idiots or insult them — or those who try to 'help' them by fussing over them just to soothe their own conscience."

"Aren't you being very unfair now?"

"You think so? You know how many times I listened to the church people in the townships? There were good people among them. Whites who tried to 'share our suffering'. Some of them had lots of shit with the *Boere*; quite a few were picked

319

up and held in detention. So they knew what it was about. Yet there always was a gulf between them and us. I mean, what were *they* fighting for? — they were doing it either because they felt guilty, or because they were angry, or even because they sympathized with us. But we: we fought because we got no other way to live. See what I mean? For them it was a choice of ideas. Causes. 'Freedom'. 'Oppression'. 'Justice'. For us, it was a matter of flesh and blood. Bone, teeth, hair, nails. We're not people just because we dream about freedom: we're people because freedom lives in a body, because we bleed when we get hurt, because we're cold when it rains and we sweat when it's hot. Because we feel hunger and thirst. And what were they trying to tell us, those good church people? — 'Turn the other cheek. Don't use violence. Blessed are the meek, blessed are the peacemakers. One day, when you're all dead and killed, you'll get your reward in heaven.' And the only outcome is that the bosses get a stronger hold on us. Our problem isn't in heaven, Andrea: it's right here, now. It's in this world where my children are supposed to grow up one day."

"You'd love to have children, wouldn't you?"

"Of course. It's for them that I'm carrying on the fight. You know what my woman told the *Boere* that time they took her in? Spike shouted at her: 'What's that thing you got in your stomach? It's a bloody terrorist. We'll beat him out of you.' So Ntsiki said to him: 'Then we'll just make another to take his place. We'll always make new ones.' That's what she told him."

"What sort of world are you going to give them if your hands are covered in blood?"

"Nobody has ever got anything worth while without blood."

"Please, Mandla! Don't give me those clichés again."

"Suffering is the greatest cliché of all," he snapped back. "That doesn't make it any less real."

The road was getting more and more tortuous as it wound along the Gorges de la Nesque. Precipices so deep one couldn't see the bottom of the chasm; where one seemed to be looking right into the forbidden entrails of the earth.

"Is that what you think of Paul too?" I suddenly asked.

"What?"

"What you said about the Whites who tried to help you."

"I got nothing to say about Paul," he said sharply.

"He did all he could for you."

"Why couldn't he leave me alone? I didn't ask him to do anything. I don't need anybody's fucking help."

And all of a sudden it struck me, as I saw right through all the vehemence with which he'd been reacting every time Paul's name had been mentioned. Deeply moved, staring intently at the winding road, I said: "You have a very soft spot for Paul, don't you?"

"What the hell do you mean?"

"That's why you always react so fiercely whenever we talk about him. It would have been easier for you if he *hadn't* been there, if he *hadn't* helped you: then it would have been a clear-cut struggle, Black against White. Right? But now he's forcing you to make allowance for him. And he means much more to you than you would like to admit, either to me or to yourself."

He didn't answer, but when I turned my head to look at him I noticed the ferocious clenching of his jaws; and in me I felt such warmth, such tenderness for him that I couldn't help putting a hand on his knee.

And that turned out to be the strangest experience of the whole morning: that in the end it was I who felt the need to comfort *him*.

"For God's sake, you must never give up hope, Mandla," I said passionately.

"Why do you say that?"

"Because I can feel it coming. Despair. All that's happened to you — the dead-end you've reached here — perhaps over there too. But you must go on hoping. For my sake as well as for your own."

For a long time we were silent. I had to concentrate on the

321

road; he started playing his *trompie* again, this time without the carefree abandon of before, perhaps doing it deliberately so as to avoid talking. The sound lacked the reassuring monotony of other times: he seemed intent on forcing a response from me. But what? I had no idea. (And if I'd known, would I have dared to do what I did a mere hour later?)

More to silence the tune than anything else, I asked him to take the Michelin from the cubbyhole and read the map, for it was becoming increasingly difficult to stay on course through the network of tiny roads cutting through those mountains. Just before Mazan we turned off and reached the hamlet of Malemort. The name, of course, fascinated me.

"Malemort. Who on earth would live in a place with a name like this?"

He gestured towards an elderly farmer and a youngster pushing a haycart up a small incline. "They look happy enough to me. Does it really matter where one lives?"

"The Plague must have hit them hard at one time, otherwise they wouldn't have chosen such a name."

He shrugged. "You know, it's a perfect name for the fortress in which Paul wants to close up his fancy film people."

"Good idea. I'll mention it to him."

"The *Boere* ought to name their headquarters after it."

"Now you're just being facetious."

The role of blood in combating the Plague. Bloodletting, of course, was one of the most popular remedies. Bowls and baths of blood were drained in the afflicted cities. Ziegler:

> The blood that emerged from the infected would normally be thick and black; it boded even worse for the victim if a thin green scum rose to the surface. If the patient fainted, instructed Ibn Khatimah somewhat heartlessly, pour cold water over him and continue as before. Most surgeons bled for the sake of bleeding, not worrying so much where the incision was made —

And then there were the Flagellants, initially a movement of

322

respectable and devout people, degenerating gradually into collective madness.

> As the fervour mounted the messianic pretensions of the Flagellants became more pronounced. They began to claim that the movement must last for thirty-three years and end only with the redemption of Christendom and the arrival of the Millennium. Possessed by such chiliastic convictions they saw themselves more and more, not as mortals suffering to expiate their own sins and humanity's, but as a holy army of Saints . . . . But as they trekked from plague centre to plague centre, they often bore infection with them to those whom they were supposed to succour.

In some places, says Ziegler, they brought about a spiritual revival, albeit marked by fanatic overtones; at least it was effective enough to persuade adulterers to repent and thieves to return their stolen goods. Elsewhere, alas, the Flagellants inspired the most barbaric persecution of the Jews. Blood, blood, blood. And according to several of Paul's sources, it might be interesting to see the Plague as forerunner of the great social revolution of the same century. Levett:

> The Black Death did not, in any strictly economic sense, cause the Peasants' Revolt or the break-down of villeinage, but it gave birth, in many cases, to a smouldering feeling of discontent, an inarticulate desire for change, which found its outlet in the rising of 1381.

"The first time the SB picked me up," said Mandla, "was in King William's Town. We were having a meeting there with the SAAWU people, just a few days after Vuyizile disappeared. That time they didn't keep me long, about a week, I think. But for three of those days and nights I was forced to keep standing; and then you just got to shit and piss in your pants, for they don't give you a break. Questions, questions, questions. All about Vuyizile. How did I meet him? What's he doing? What books does he read? Who are the people he associates with? On and on, day and night. But suddenly it was over. Back to my cell for a few days, and then they let me go. I found it bloody strange. Only much later I realized that that must have been the time something happened to Vuyizile, otherwise they would have gone on asking questions. Now it was no longer necessary: and he never came back.

"Well, from then on I knew their eyes were watching me. So I got to be careful. Usually it's no more than a game, just to keep you worried. If you're on the road — those days I was travelling to and from between PE and King William's Town quite a lot — then you're stopped all the time. They take the whole fucking car apart, looking for *dagga*, they say. Otherwise they find something wrong with your brakes, or the steering, or the parking lights, or the number plates. If they can't find something, they do it themselves. Kick out a rear light. Rip off a number plate. Waiting for you to protest. Then it's defeating the ends of justice. But one twigs fast. It's the only way to survive. You just keep smiling, taking whatever is coming. Otherwise you've had your chips. And there was more important work to be done than to get picked up for nothing."

"What important work? Was it" — I hesitated — "I mean, was it sabotage and things like that?"

"No. It was MACWUSA. I told you. We had to get the people organized, man. We had something going there which, if it worked out, could give us the first real grip on power we ever had. They couldn't just go on shunting us round. Only, they were picking up the men so fast that we had to be fucking sharp to keep one step ahead, all the time. What with all the arrests, I later found myself on the Branch Executive Committee. And that's when my troubles really started."

"Did they arrest you again?"

"Not just once. Every so often. Seven times in all. Usually it was only for a short while, week or two. Pushing me around a bit, asking questions, their gentle way of warning one. But soon after my parents' settlement was bulldozed and the people taken away to the Ciskei, they came for me again and

324

this time they meant business. What was I doing at the resettlement camp? I told them it was because of my parents. The people had no food, they were dying of cold, I had to help them out."

"That's a bloody lie," says the man with the tanned face. "You went there to stir up trouble. You brought in the Press."

"I went to help my parents."

"You're just using the unions as a front, hiding behind it to do the ANC's dirty work for it. You're a bunch of Communists. You think we don't know? There's nothing we don't know."

"If that's what you think you really don't know anything."

"Who're you talking to, kaffir?"

That's when they get down to business. One night, when your body is still shivery from the electric shock treatment, they throw you in the boot of a car and drive off along a bumpy road. In the middle of nowhere they haul you out again, drag you into the night and shine a torch on a tombstone. There's writing on the stone. Your eyes have trouble focusing, but at last you recognize a name. *Steve Biko*. "Take a good look," they say. "You know what happened to him, hey? You've got it coming to you too. And don't think there will be anybody to hear you."

They take you back to the car. You almost pass out in the boot, but even so it's better than what awaits you at the other end. Especially when they call in Spike. Not a very big man, blond, with a small moustache and red sideburns. Unusually large hands for someone with his build. And it's hands that know their job. You might say the man is an artist in his own way. One of his favourite tricks is to use a small plank studded with nails. You put your cock on the end of the table and he hits you. Guaranteed, he says, to make you piss like a watering can.

A couple of photostat pages Paul had sent along with the others. A quotation from a Hitler speech. And then the author

325

goes on (Norman Stone, Paul had noted in red on the top page):

Behind all this gallivanting was the sinister reality of the police state, the concentration camps, and the exodus of the Jews. Hitler had always promised that once he had power he would never let it go. The consequence was a strong police, and a police to control that police . . . . Hitler despised constitutional forms, and although even he objected on occasion to the "Black Plague" of the SS, he was never a serious obstacle to the growth of Himmler's empire . . . . Nazism had come to power because it promised "order" at last. But the order that it brought destroyed anything it touched —

"This time they kept me for five weeks. Towards the end it was getting very bad. I was beginning to think I'd never see the outside world again." A pause. "I was vomiting blood. I was pissing blood. The one thing that kept me going was the memory of that night they'd taken me away in the boot of the car. The flashlight shining on Biko's name. They thought it would scare me. But instead, that was what gave me the courage to go on. I couldn't help thinking of what he'd said so many times, Pityana's words: *Black man, you're on your own.* I thought of everything that had happened to me, and of how it had turned out. I wanted to study, and they stopped me. I went into the union, and they stopped me again. OK, then I would have to go further. In a different way. That's what they taught me: that with non-violence you get nowhere. They just keep stopping you all the time. They won't believe you. They have no place for you, because they themselves know only violence.

"I don't think they would have given me a chance to do what I got into my head to do: in the end I would have disappeared like Vuyizile. But suddenly there was trouble in the Transvaal — in one weekend two detainees died in the cells; there were

326

questions in Parliament — and without warning they let me go. Sometimes they do get a bit of a fright. And that was what saved me."

"Then you left the country?"

"For a month or so I just lay at home. My head was quite confused. I was as weak as hell, I even had fits. It took time before I began to get well again. I went back to MACWUSA. But one night one of our men came to my aunt's house and woke me up and told me to get out as soon as I could, they were raiding the townships again, rounding up all the leaders of the unregistered unions. He took me away with him. I never committed any crime, same as Ntsiki. Our only crime was that we were black. But for the *Boere* that's the worst crime of all. Millions of us, all criminals. And that was why I had to leave my country.

"We got through to Transkei. It took a whole week, because we had to hide all along the way. From Transkei we went to Lesotho. Some of the ANC people gave me a place to stay; there were many refugees there. I was still hoping just to lie low for some time and then go back. But then the *Boere* raided Maseru. I saw the dead, including the ones who were just sleeping peacefully that night, people like my parents who knew nothing about politics and stuff like that, ordinary poor people. For me that was the last straw. All those years I'd kept on hoping it could be different. I wanted it to be different. But one gets to a point where you know: now I got to do something, else I'll be getting just like my father in the butchery, and I owe something different to my children. Right, so then I left for Mozambique, through Swaziland."

"And there you were safe?"

"I didn't go there to be safe!" he said angrily. "I went because it was the only way I could survive and carry on the struggle." A new tautness in his voice. "And it was far from safe anyway. Soon after I reached Maputo there was a bomb explosion in Pretoria in reply to the *Boere*'s raid on Maseru. Lots of people dead and injured. And then the *Boere* took revenge again by striking against Maputo. You see how simple

327

it becomes once it's started. Black and White. Right and wrong. An eye for an eye. Only, they kept on pretending it was a moral struggle. 'Terrorist nests destroyed', said their papers. It was just like when they raided Angola. Call your enemy 'terrorist' or 'idiot' and you can do to him what you like. Whole camps of refugees wiped out. Women and children. And their own people don't know about it, their newspapers are not allowed to report it. But *we* know. You'll be amazed at what we know in the townships.

"Anyway, those raids were not just retaliation. There was desperation in it too. And it united our people like nothing else. It was another step forward, after Sharpeville and Soweto. Each time a step further. There is a terrible logic in the language of violence.

"On the surface, where the world could see them, they kept on talking about 'negotiations', and 'reform'. But below that surface, where it really mattered, where they could grab us in the dark, there was only violence." He changed position, his large body obviously cramped in the small seat. "So that was when I came over to Europe to get money. George and I."

"And now they've stopped you once again."

He stared fixedly at the map on his knees. Then he said: "Yes. It's really fucked up everything. If I go back now, some people will suspect me of conspiring with George. Otherwise they'll just avoid me, thinking I bring bad luck." A pause. To my surprise he uttered a brief laugh, although there was not much mirth in it. "But you know, in a way it almost came as a relief too. I couldn't go on trekking from one town to the other like a fucking beggar. So what if they treated us like kings? Andrea, that's not my scene. I don't want to be safe and far away from everything. I want to be where it's happening to my people. I want to do something. I want to be running in the night. Blindly, dangerously, but good and fast and open."

We laboured on through the tumbled mountains beyond Venasque. The large oak forests. The gnarled and twisted branches proved how tough it was for the roots to find a grip in that stone-hard soil; how severe the winters must be. The wood itself as hard as stone. But there they were, indestructible even by the Mistral or the worst extremes of heat and cold. The road was narrow, one hairpin bend on the other, so that it took all one's concentration to keep going. Just as well. Both of us needed that concentration.

"What would you say to that?" he asked unexpectedly, when we reached the last ridge and began to descend towards a more gently billowing plateau, in a direction of Murs.

"To what?"

"Running in the night with me."

"Do you really know what you're asking?"

"I know. Do you?"

I didn't answer. But he refused to let me off so easily.

"I'm asking you, Andrea."

"Don't!" I cried savagely, keeping my eyes on the road. "I don't want to be asked."

"But I *am* asking. And sooner or later you're going to answer."

We crossed the last rise before Murs, which had been the final target of my summer journey with Paul, although we'd never reached it after all. Bare branches of fig-trees overhanging stone walls. Cast-iron lamps on the street corners. Houses with grey or red shutters. A village smelling of chicken shit, even though there was no chicken in sight. Where the main road broadened into a small open square with a war monument high above the valley below, I stopped. Opposite us was an old fountain with iron railings. On the surrounding walls the remains of posters advertising the summer's half-forgotten festivals. A small group of old people were sitting in the sun on two benches beside the fountain; all the women in black (all widows?), with knitting on their laps, the men with berets on their heads and pipes or cigarette stubs between their teeth. For them, I thought, there could be no terror in the thought of death. Whatever a human being could experience they'd lived through long ago. Nothing could surprise their sunken, wise

329

old eyes any more. Ten years ago, centuries ago, they would have been sitting there just like that. All the pestilences of the Middle Ages had come and gone; Huguenots and Catholics had laid waste each other's towns and strongholds and fought their bloody vendettas; houses had crumbled and returned to stone and dust: they had remained. They had seen it all, and had survived.

I greeted them. A few mumbled something in reply, not very warmly. Apathetic eyes staring at the intruders.

"We're trying to find the Wall of the Plague," I said, tentatively unfolding my map.

In stony silence the women resumed their knitting.

"Could you perhaps show us the way?" I tried again. Mandla stood to one side, but I noticed how they kept watching him, heads tilted, like chickens ready to squawk.

"Wall of the Plague?" one toothless old woman repeated at last, not looking at me. "No. Never heard of such a thing. What about you?" Nudging her neighbour with an elbow.

"Don't know anything about it," said the second woman.

It didn't sound promising. I was about to give it up when one of the old men reluctantly took his pipe from his mouth. "Which way did you come?"

I gestured. "Over the mountains, from Venasque."

"Hm." He squirted a yellow jet of tobacco juice through his front teeth. "Then you drove right past it. About three or four kilometres back."

I looked at Mandla, but to no avail: he didn't understand a word of what we were saying. "I didn't notice anything," I admitted.

"You wouldn't," grumbled the old man. "Not unless you knew where to look. There isn't much left of the Wall. Not up there anyway. Just ruins."

"Do you know anything about the Wall?" I persisted, knowing I might be pushing my luck. "Do the townspeople still talk about it?"

"No, what would we know about it? It was before our time."

"I told you we've never heard of it before," the first old

woman cut in crossly. "What's it supposed to be anyway?"

"Apparently it was built in 1721 to keep out the Plague."

"So what?"

"Where do you people come from?" asked a woman who'd kept silent up to now. Moustache on the upper lip. A fixed aggresive stare in her beady eyes.

"Far away," I said noncommittally.

"What does that mean? Everything is far away."

"Africa."

"Thought so." She clicked her knitting needles. "Don't tell me you've come all this way to look for an old ruined wall in our mountains."

"We'd like to know more about it."

"Sounds odd to me. Why should anyone want to build a wall to keep out the Plague?"

"They had to stop travellers and vagabonds."

"We have more than enough to worry about as it is," the old woman said sternly. "All these new taxes. Prices going up. And what do we get out of it? They have enough money to pay for truck-loads of wine and fruit from Italy and Spain, but our own farmers are starving. If they really want to build walls they should build them down there on the highways to keep out the foreigners."

Grunts of approval from all the others.

"Well, we'd better be going then," I said. "We'll drive back and see if we can find anything."

"You won't," said the first old woman. "There never was a wall up there. It's just another story the Government is spreading."

We'd already gone halfway back to the car when the old man who'd spoken before called out: "I say, Mademoiselle!"

I looked back over my shoulder.

"If you drive on that way" — he made a gesture to describe a semicircle round the village, to the right and up — "you'll find a few bits of wall that are still pretty intact. But make sure you drive slowly, the road is bad. You can't miss it."

"Thank you very much. We'll go there."

331

"What was all the discussion about?" asked Mandla as we got into the car.

I gave him a brief summary.

"Do you really think they don't know?" he asked. "Or do they just want to keep it to themselves?"

"Your guess is as good as mine." I couldn't help shaking my head. "One would think they'd show more interest. It's something they can show to the world."

"An old broken wall two hundred years old?"

"There was a time when it was of vital importance."

We drove very slowly. And this time we found it, sometimes in the distance, sometimes right next to the road. Long stretches of the thick grey wall, broken in parts, in others surprisingly intact, a good two metres high. A few times we stopped to get out and inspect it from close by. Once he gave me a hand so that I could climb on it.

"Well?" he said sardonically. "Now you've found your Wall: so what?"

"At least I've seen it with my own eyes."

"So now you can believe it?"

"I've never had any doubt."

Bruni:

On 14 February 1721 the Count of Médavy and the vice-legate concluded an agreement by which the trajectory of the second line was defined: from the Durance to the Tour de Sabran, the foothills of the Vaucluse, Bourbourin, Haute Pouraque, Corneirette, Picol Blanc, finally crossing the territory of the communes of Monieux, Sault, Aurel and Montbrun. After the trajectory had been defined, different procedures had to be devised to suit the various sections: barriers, natural obstacles, walls, trenches . . . . The French troops and those of the vice-legate divided the guard zones between them . . . .

As for the builders who went there, they had to take their hammers, ropes, spades and picks with them. Each worked for a period of twelve days and received a maximum of 10 *sols* per day, "so as to have something to eat during the said time, seeing that most of those you have already sent us have been forced to withdraw through lack of food".

In spite of this the problems grew worse, through lack of intelligent and effective leadership: there was flagrant disorganization at the place of work; the amount of money spent soon exceeded all estimates. Several times the labourers gave up working on their section through lack of provisions; as for the soldiers sent to guard the line, they were worn out, as there were no regular replacements. On the verge of total exhaustion some of them gave up. Not only adults were recruited, but children as well . . . . "The wall easily measured six *pans* in height, all the stones being available on the spot, so fortunately our land will be saved . . . ."

The job was completed in August 1721. But by that time, in spite of all precautions, the line had been broken: the Plague was already in the Comtat Venaissin.

We turned left into a forest path running through pines into a thicket of stunted oaks. Soon there was no sign of the Wall any more. Perhaps it had swerved too far away from the road; perhaps this section had been totally destroyed. I wanted to make sure.

But we were hungry too. I pulled the car out of the narrow red path into the shelter of the bushes; we took our food and the bottle of wine and began to walk down the steep incline. There was no sign of any human being or animal or wall. For fifteen or twenty minutes we continued like that; then Mandla stopped in his tracks.

"Look, man, this is enough. I'm not going any further in search of a bloody heap of stones."

"We can have a picnic here."

We cleared a patch of grass in a sunny spot among the trees, and sat down. I broke the bread for us; he opened the wine

333

bottle. Fortunately he'd brought his pocket knife for the pâté and cheese.

We didn't talk much. On us lay the weighty serenity of trees and mountain. No sign of wind in the leaves. There are so many kinds of silence, I thought. There's one kind, oppressive and thick, which makes it impossible to escape what lies beneath the surface: fear, evil, suspicion, dread; even the possibility of love. And another kind, like that early afternoon: an innocent silence, elemental and original, predating sound and world, leaving everything unblemished, unthinkable, and pure.

There is yet another kind of silence, I know now: that which exists in the eye of the storm.

He took off his shirt to feel the spare sun directly on his body. As in the light outside the Palais de Justice in Carpentras I was struck dumb by the beauty of his body. The movement of his arms. His smooth chest and back, a lighter shade of brown than his face and forearms. A lazy rippling of muscles, like a breath of wind touching a liquid surface.

We finished the food; from time to time we passed the bottle of wine from one to the other, until it was empty.

"You still owe me an answer," he said without warning. A few crumbs clung to the corner of his mouth. He flicked them away with the tip of his tongue. A brief glistening of moisture on his lips. "I was hoping you could tell me something by now."

Leaning back on my arms I raised my face to the sun, closing my eyes. But was it to contain myself — or to exclude him?

"I'm scared, Mandla. Whatever one says is so final. Do you understand that?"

His voice grew darker. I was still sitting with my eyes closed.

"I'm not sure I understand. Maybe I should say: I'm not *surprised*. I was hoping — But perhaps I should have known."

"What?"

Every word a small dent on the silence; a smooth flat pebble skimming over it, unwilling to plunge to the depths below.

334

"I know you can never really understand what I'm talking about. To you it can never be more than a 'story'. Something outside yourself. No matter how hard you try, it can never really touch you. Like one can't talk to a fish: it lives in the water, while you're outside."

I opened my eyes. "What are you trying to tell me, Mandla? That you're black and I'm — something else? That I've spent my whole life 'in between', not really belonging anywhere? — neither black nor white, but 'coloured', whatever that may mean?"

"I think you can understand something about being black. We already spoke about that. Whether you really *want* to understand — that's another question. But you can. Anyway, it's not white or black I'm talking about now, Andrea. It's something else."

"What?"

"You see? You still got to ask."

I thought he wasn't going to explain any further; for a moment I even thought he was angry. But he wasn't. In his eyes, when I looked at him, was something almost like compassion; understanding. As if he were looking right through me, from a long way off.

"There's something one can only discover about oneself when they come to take you away from your people, away from life. When the SB comes to pick you up. You can never quite share that experience with others. You can tell them about it, they may listen to you. But to understand it, truly to understand it — that's impossible. It's a kind of loneliness you got to carry in yourself. It's like that man from the Bible, what's his name? — Lazarus — who came back to life: now what would other people understand about it if he tried to tell them about death? There's a wall between the living and the dead, between those who been inside and those who haven't, and nobody and nothing can climb over it."

I whispered: "Just like a man can never truly know what it is to be a woman?" Then I looked him in the eyes again: "You see? Your wall isn't the only one. And in fact, that death you came back from is not so unfamiliar to me either. I also was where you were."

He shook his head.

"I'm not talking about torture." I said. "They didn't hurt me. But I don't think that was the kind of suffering you had in mind either. What you meant was a kind of rape: of the mind, of thoughts, of memories, of hope for the future: the rape of your own possibilities, of your humanity. And that I know. I've been through it, just like you."

In the bare room — a single brown table with a white civil service number painted on its side; two chairs; a grey filing cabinet; soundproof tiles on the walls — under the strong light, the voices taking turns to cajole and threaten, to argue persuasively, to shout at her.

"Surely that's not too much to ask?"

"I cannot do a thing like that."

"What's the man to you? He's a foreigner, an Englishman, all he's interested in is digging up scandals about our country."

"He's a historian. He's doing research, that's all. I'm typing his notes for his thesis."

"Well, if he's so harmless, surely you can tell us more about him?"

"Why don't you ask him yourself? He's got nothing to hide."

"We've already spoken to him. He isn't very forthcoming."

"Then it's your worry and his."

"We're asking *you*."

"I work for Brian Everton. I can't spy on him."

"Are you quite sure it's just work?"

"What else can it be?"

"One never knows. You spend long hours together. Just the two of you."

"Why don't you spy on us then? Do your own dirty work."

"You're just creating problems for yourself. And for your family."

"My family has nothing to do with it. They don't even know him."

336

"We took your brother away tonight. You were there, you saw."

"You'll just have to let him go again. He hasn't done anything."

"What about the books we found in his room?"

"What do I know about his things? Perhaps you put them there."

"He can go to jail for it. For a hell of a long time. We've been watching him. Him and his friends on the campus. Don't think we're asleep."

"Why do you ask me about Brian — Mr Everton — one moment, and then about my brother? They have nothing to do with each other."

"But you're close to both."

"What about it?"

"Do you want us to spell it out for you, Miss Malgas?" A very emphatic *Miss Malgas*.

"Go ahead, I'm listening."

"You're going to report regularly to us about everything Brian Everton says and does and reads. Then we'll let your brother go. Otherwise — "

"You're just trying to bluff me. There's nothing you can do."

"You think so?"

"You can't do a thing like that!"

"Want to bet?"

It feels like hours before she manages to reply, in a voice she barely recognizes as her own: "If there's anything you want to find out about Brian Everton, then do it yourself. I won't have any part in it."

"All right." The man gets up. "We won't force you. But you realize you've just signed your own brother's sentence?"

He comes round the table and stops right in front of her, his eyes a few inches from hers. She cannot control herself. With a sudden jerk of her head she spits in his face.

For a moment she thinks he's going to strike her. But he only brings his hand to his cheek, very slowly, and touches it,

337

an expression of incredulity on his face. There is even the hint of a smile on his lips. "Take her away," he says. "Then bring me her brother."

"Did you ever tell Brian?" Mandla asked after a long silence.

I shook my head. "All I told him was that they asked me about my work. He never suspected anything. In fact, he thought it happened the other way round: he never realized it was because of him that they picked me up. He thought they already had a case against Boetie, and that they were just checking on all *his* connections to make sure. He thought *I* was under suspicion. And if you ask me" — she found it difficult to come out with it — "if you ask me, he felt — I can't be sure, of course, we never spoke about it, but I got the impression that he felt he was being noble to stand by a girl who was in trouble with the SB."

Mandla got up and walked away through the nearest trees. Sun on his shoulders. I heard him urinating. I couldn't see his body, but the sun was sparkling on the jet. I didn't look away. All I wanted was for him to come back and not leave me alone.

For a moment I thought he was going to walk further away into the wood. In a panic I jumped up and called out: "Mandla!"

It was very quiet. Then I heard twigs crackling and saw him coming back through the trees. "What's the matter?"

"Nothing. I just thought — " Embarrassed, I stopped.

Across the distance between us — only a few yards, I should think, but it seemed terribly far, there was so much sun separating us — I stared at him, into the glare, the light falling from diagonally above him.

"We going to look for that Wall again?" he asked.

I shook my head.

"You think we're on the other side already? Or still on this side?"

"Does it make any difference? The Plague is everywhere."

338

"Come to me," he said. He stood waiting for me. In that unbearable light.

I undid the buttons of my shirt, very slowly, one by one, feeling very calm at last, in that surrounding tremendous silence, in that light; and took off my shirt and bra and went to him, unhurried, knowing that what had to happen would happen, and that there were innumerable barriers to be crossed on the way there, but without reserve, in the freedom of everything we were and ever had been.

The hard and heavy earth; its depth.

The illimitable consciousness in the here-and-nowness of that simple act.

I thought: Yes, of course he was right, this is how it is, so self-evident and complex: the truth of the body, which is flesh and bone, which can be hurt, which bleeds, which suffers from hunger and thirst, and from the desire to *know*, which affirms its ineluctable humanity: this was our reality, this the knowledge we had, could have, of world and existence, a knowledge unto death. For never in my life had I been so close to death.

Around us the utter openness of mountain, wood, blue sky; and a single unseasonal cicada shrilling outrageously in what would undoubtedly be the last day of its life. We were like the trees: with branches and leaves that do not simply react to wind but reply to it, rebel against it, co-exist with it, affirming their very treeness in the act — even when the wind strips them bare.

(You would have approved, Grandpa Xhorê: you didn't accept walls either.)

"You no longer have to give me an answer," he said afterwards. "I think I know what it is."

Actually, I thought, in the relationship of any person with another there are only two possible choices: *Will you stay with me? Or will you betray me? What do you ultimately grant me: life, or death?*

Hours later, when the descending cool of late afternoon forced us to get dressed, he put his arm round me and we went

339

back together. From the edge of the grassy clearing where we'd made love I looked back, feeling — strangely — not sadness, but a new assurance.

I was here.

Then we walked on.

We drove back, past Murs; and only then it struck me how odd it was that the village should have been given a name like that centuries before the Plague. A kind of premonition? As if many years and many other, more ordinary, walls had been required to prepare the place for this ultimate Wall. Which now lay in ruins anyway. This I knew for certain, at last: that walls *can* be broken down. Even the walls of Jericho had fallen.

A few kilometres downhill to Joucas. It was unusual for me to reach the village from this direction. On previous occasions — several times in July, with Paul; and the day before, when Mandla and I had passed it on our way to Apt — I had always approached Joucas from Cavaillon, so that the village had always, for me, marked the end of the long open plains: a small brown cluster of houses on an outcrop of rocks signalling the beginning of the Vaucluse range, the great Beyond. But this time, coming from behind, through the savage wooded mountains and oak forests of Murs, the village was the *end* of the wilderness, a final look-out post before one reached the more serene and cultivated plains below. And this not only changed my image of Joucas into a much more complex one than before, but seemed to alter the awareness the place had of itself: now it had to acknowledge, and maintain, itself before the world in the full consciousness of that wild mountainous region, as it stared out across the plains.

On the way to Cavaillon, in the failing light, Mandla said, à propos of nothing at all: "You know, I wasn't being quite fair when I spoke about those Whites who tried to help us in the

340

unions. Some of them were different. I never met Neil Aggett, but when he got killed in detention I realized we could no longer make the same easy distinctions as before. Other forms of solidarity were beginning to take shape. And once there was a woman who came to speak to us, a very tiny, very old little woman, she must have been at least eighty: with thin, wispy, white hair. Arms and legs like sticks. But a surprisingly young face. They brought her from Joburg, when the *Boere* were giving us a particularly hard time. It was shortly after Vuyizile had disappeared. She had no right to be there, she'd been under banning orders for something like fifteen years, but she was prepared to risk it. She spoke in a very soft voice. Nothing could upset her. It wasn't that she said anything special; it was just the way she spoke. As if there was some kind of light burning inside her. I know it sounds stupid but I thought: if ever there was a saint, she must be one. 'I never committed a crime in my life,' she said. 'The worst I ever did was to fight so that people could be treated as human beings.' She wasn't complaining. She never tried to make a show of her sufferings. And at the end she just said: 'If I look back today at all that's happened, I still think it's been worth while. If I had to start again today, knowing beforehand what it would cost, I would still do it. Because it's never in vain. Nothing is ever wasted.'"

"Why are you telling me this?" I asked, not sure that I really wanted an answer.

"Because it's always harder for the women."

"Not harder than for you."

"When they took Ntsiki in," he said, ignoring my remark, "they once worked with her for four days and four nights without stop. When they took her away to her cell afterwards, she pleaded with them not to lock her up on her own, because she was far gone with the baby and so she was scared. They just laughed and put her back in isolation. In the evening she started to scream. On and on, but no one came. She screamed all night. They didn't do anything. When they brought her food the next morning they saw the blood coming from under her door. It was a miscarriage."

I couldn't say anything. My hands were clenching the steering wheel very tightly.

"There was another woman from Mdantsane," he said, without mercy. "An old woman, past sixty. Her son had fled to Botswana after the riots in 'seventy-six. Then one day he came back to visit his family and his mother let him sleep in her house for the night. Afterwards they arrested her. She got five years, for 'harbouring a terrorist'.

"In the prison there was another young woman who heard about what happened to the old mother. So one morning the young one left her a message in the bathroom in the tap, knowing the old one would be brought in just after her. Not even a message: just one word. *Courage*. For that they sentenced the young woman to two years in solitary. No visits, no letters, nothing to read. Two years."

"I want to know *why* you're telling me this, Mandla!" I repeated. It was difficult to speak.

"Because you got to know," he said.

We sat listening to one of my reggae tapes. In Saint-Rémy we went to the same restaurant as the previous day for a meal. We had a lot of wine. I ordered the best dishes I could remember from my visits with Paul. Then we returned to the hotel. There was no need to discuss or arrange anything in advance. As I unlocked my door he followed me inside.

But just as he closed the door behind us there was the sound of a telephone ringing close by, from across the landing. We both tensed as we listened, caught unawares; suddenly the walls seemed to be closing in on us. There was no doubt about it: the sound came from his room.

"It can only be Paul," he said, annoyed; but not without a hint of amusement. "He's the only one who knows I'm here."

"He can ring again tomorrow."

"No, I'll go, then it's over."

"If you must. I'll leave the door open for you."

He came back sooner than I expected. I'd just undressed, and was on my way to the bathroom.

Unlike that afternoon in the wood I felt shy; but I didn't turn away.

"It wasn't Paul after all," he said from the door.

"Wrong number?"

"No. Some stranger. South African accent. All he said was: 'I hope you're enjoying your stay.'"

I opened my mouth to say something, but what could I reply?

He turned back towards the still half-opened door.

"Please don't go," I said. "Stay with me, Mandla. Don't leave me alone tonight."

He hesitated. In his eyes I could see how much he wanted to stay. But at last he shook his head, as if in sorrow. I knew it would be useless to detain him, not with that blackness in him. And I also knew in advance that all night long, as I lay sleepless, I would hear his sound outside in the dark: the sound of his *trompie*, or the heavier, deeper sound of his sighs.

Fifth Day

　　✖　✖　✖　✖　✖

To get up and confront the day, or stay in bed for a little while longer? Not that the bed was so tempting, either for its warmth or for the cherished illusion of security, because after I'd finally fallen asleep — tired, lonely, and frustrated — I'd been irritated by an itch. A flea. It took me over an hour to track it down but at least I derived some satisfaction from killing the little bastard between my nails and flushing it down the toilet. A bite in my groin. In July we'd been tormented by the notorious mosquitoes of Provence, but Paul had soon managed to keep them at bay with a small smoking spiral in the room. The flea was more unexpected, more insidious. Years ago, with Brian, in the dingy little holes we stayed in, they'd been part of our daily, or nightly, lives; but in an hotel of this class it came as an unpleasant surprise.

　　I lingered in bed after all. Not that I felt reluctant to face the new morning: only unbearably lonely, and no longer so sure about the day before. I had no doubt that it had happened (with a brief tension of my thighs or the circular love-muscle deep inside, I could still feel him): but what significance to attach to it I no longer knew. The mere need to "interpret" disturbed me. I didn't want to. Couldn't one, just for once, accept and assimilate the pure physical fact of it? It wouldn't be the only one-night stand in my life (we hadn't even had a night!): but on the other occasions I hadn't been left in any doubt; there had been neither illusions nor unresolved ambiguities: in every case both of us had known what we'd been letting ourselves in for. What had happened yesterday was different. (Wasn't it?) Of course it was. Our involvement had

344

been different; total. That was what had made the unexpected loneliness of the night so unbearable, inexplicable. To lie hunched up in bed, legs pulled up and hugged by my arms, a small bundle of fierce Andreaness under the tattered love-blanket, was neither indulgence nor lust, but simple and necessary affirmation. I was still there! I still bore something of him within me. That had been the one, only, certainty emerging from the past few days (and today was the fifth).

The previous evening I'd taken my pill out of habit, quite mechanically. Only after I'd swallowed it I'd wondered in sudden rebellion: Shouldn't I push a finger down my throat and try to get rid of it? But it didn't seem a good idea. Tomorrow night I would give it up; tonight. The wrong time altogether: it was a mere week before my next period. Oh God, why so much fuss and bother? Why couldn't I just absorb his seed in the knowledge that it would turn into a child? But fruitless or not, I knew I would give up the Pill; as from tonight.

Paul? (— *but I'll always come back to you.*) No, I had been wrong. Whatever might happen from now on — and what else could possibly happen apart from staying with Mandla? — at least this had been resolved. I had put Paul behind me. Even if Mandla were to do the unthinkable and abandon me, I could not go back to Paul again. It wasn't just a matter of being "unfaithful": that is forgivable, acceptable, certainly in the long run, I knew only too well. But something entirely new had begun, something so different from whatever had gone before that it was impossible to compare. Paul himself — and I had loved him, God knows, I'd been addicted to him — Paul himself had become, now that I'd made my choice, part of the past. Mandla was the conclusion and fulfilment of all my earlier possibilities and attempts. *This* was the true meaning of my love. Mandla. Freedom. The Strong Man. Large as a mountain; beautiful as a tree; deep as the interior of an unknown land. Mine. So much my own that in my thoughts I dared to give him my own name, as in my childhood I'd christened everything most dear to me: *Nanna, you're mine, you're part of me, you are I*. And even if he never touched me again in my life that was what he would remain. Even if I went out of this room to find his room deserted, his things gone. (But oh God, not that!) Even if he were to return alone to that distant land he was bearing inside him like a child, the two of us would always be walking together somewhere on the mountainside, in a world without walls, from which even the signs and traces of ruins had disappeared, a world older than gnarled oaks, as old as stone, as new as the youngest blade of grass. If anything in my past had been "coincidence", this was not. Whatever was now, could never have been different. It had been destined since long before the Black Death; long before the first couple had been driven from the Garden into the wilderness, branded by the original white God and his Group Areas Act. Destined: but to what end? — a lifetime of yearning, plagued by hunger and lust, suffering, cursed to bear the sins of a whole country, to be constantly driven back to the barest remains of humanity, the crumbs in the dark corner, burning in an unquenchable fire? — even so we would share it, Mandla and I together, hand in hand; and for us it would be Paradise enough, the only one we might ever be granted.

In sad serenity, empty in Mandla's absence, yet strangely whole in my awareness of myself, drawn up into a small bundle, egg-shaped and complete (yet in that very position so vulnerable, penetrable, accessible!) I drifted back into sleep in the first light of day. A dream. What I can recall of it is distorted by other memories: I was swimming underwater, but without goggles or snorkel, as if it were my natural state, an effortless smooth motion over reefs and ridges, the submarine landscapes opening up below me: but a view so shockingly familiar! — the Hex River Valley, changing into the Karoo beyond Touws River; no, it was the Sand Veld; no, the long plains between the Vaucluse Mountains and the Luberon, below Joucas and Murs — and Mandla was with me, as if he'd always been there (but I knew he hadn't), and we made love under water, his sex like a smooth fish swimming into me;

346

then Dedda's voice was calling in my ears from far away, like water bubbles breaking in my head, a melancholy sound. "Don't worry, Dedda," I replied. "I'll be with you soon." Then I returned to Mandla to resume our lovemaking. But suddenly the voice was there again, not distant and melancholy this time, but shockingly close, a scream of warning or of fear.

The telephone beside my bed.

My heart was thumping with fright — I knew I would be groping back towards that unfinished dream all day — and it took quite some time before I managed to put out my hand and grab the instrument, still quite confused; until at last I recognized the room in the daylight falling through the half-closed shutters. I kept my hand on the telephone, pressing down very hard as if to smother the sound, relaxing only after it had stopped ringing. I knew it was Paul, but I simply couldn't cope with him right then; I felt too naked, and the sound had been like God's voice calling out in the Garden. Behind the trees, I knew, Eve would be hiding, trembling in fear, Adam's warm seed oozing out of her, an entire futile creation dribbling from her womb. Eve, poor Eve. For the first time I understood. Oh God, leave me alone.

After that I couldn't sleep again. Still numb from the effect of the crude awakening, I had to remain in bed for another few minutes before I could get up to run a bath. Once in the warm water I began to relax, as if slipping back into my dreams: except that I felt lonelier than I'd been in sleep, more empty. With my fingers — an old, familiar gesture — I tried to seal up the open wound of my sex until nothing but a scar remained, a neat suture hidden by the hair. But it was wishful thinking. The emptiness inside remained real and undiminished.

I began to rub myself vigorously with a towel. Before I'd finished there was a knock on the bedroom door.

Again that feeling of being trapped. Holding the towel in front of me I went as far as the bathroom door, leaving dark imprints with my wet feet on the carpet.

"Andrea, you awake?"

347

Suddenly I was shivering. I gulped, but my throat was still too dry to speak. Humble and ready, I quietly opened the door for him.

He was clearly unprepared for seeing me like that.

"I just thought I'd — "

"Come in."

He closed the door behind him, and stood with his back against it as if to keep out the world. His shoulders were as straight and square as they'd always been, but his face, I noticed immediately, seemed drawn. Small red veins in the whites of his eyes.

"Mandla, what's happened?"

"Nothing. I came to say good morning, that's all."

"You haven't slept all night."

He shrugged.

"Why not?"

"I'm cornered in this place."

"Because of last night's phone call?"

A gesture which might mean anything.

"Why didn't you come to me if you couldn't sleep?"

"I didn't want to disturb you."

"I was also lying awake, Mandla."

"That's not what I wanted to do to you." He came past me in the direction of the bed, then stopped again to turn back to me.

"Let me look at you," he said quietly.

Unprotesting, almost meekly, I dropped the towel on the floor. He gazed at me from head to foot as if he'd never seen a woman before, not like this. Or was he staring to make sure he would imprint me on his mind for ever? But that wasn't necessary! I was at his disposal. He could take me and have me, I was ready to remain with him for good.

Embarrassed? No, I wasn't. I didn't want to hide or hold back anything from him. But what unsettled me was the expression in his eyes: neither desire nor excitement, nothing as straightforward as approval: on the contrary, it was the most unadulterated pain I'd ever seen in anybody's eyes.

348

"I wish I could be beautiful enough for you," I whispered.

"Don't ever say that again!" He pressed me tightly against him, so hard I could barely breathe; and we stood like that for a long time, in silence, until suddenly I felt his body shaken by convulsions and realized that he was crying.

"Mandla, Mandla, oh God, don't. What's the matter? What's wrong?" I was helpless in the face of the violent feelings that caused him to shake like that.

It went on for several minutes before he let go of me again and went to the window to look outside: no neutral, easy gaze but a stare so ferocious that his whole body was as tense as a bowstring: as if he wished to stare the whole day outside to pieces.

Weak and confused, I sat down on the bed.

"Something must have happened. Please tell me."

"You're asking!" He swung round to face me. "You still asking what happened? *You* happened, damn you!"

"But — "

"I was prepared for anything. Anything, you hear me? No matter what it was. You know it. I told you everything. So what am I doing now?"

It soaked very slowly into me. How could I have been so dumb?

"Mandla, I'm not asking anything of you. I demand nothing, I expect nothing. You're just as free as you were."

"I didn't want to fall in love with you," he said. "What can I do with love? How can I take you back into that hell with me?"

"You were willing to, yesterday."

"Yesterday—!" He came back to me, shaking. "Why didn't you tell me to fuck off? What is it in you that *wants* to go to hell?"

I stared past him. "I'm a witch. You know, so many times in my life I've thought I must be some kind of witch. Nobody ever wanted to believe me. Now I know I've been right all along. Whatever I touch is doomed. I'm bad news."

"It's nothing to do with you!" He grabbed me so violently by the arm that I cried out in pain before I could stop myself; then bit my lower lip. (*Yes: hurt me. Kill me if you wish.*) "It's *me*, Andrea, don't you understand?" Desperate, he fell over me on the bed, pressing me down. "Don't you understand? This is not a time to love."

"Neither of us asked for it, Nanna."

He started, looking at me suspiciously. "Why do you call me that?"

"I didn't mean to." Of course I had! "I was talking to myself."

From many years back a memory obtruded in my mind: those people in London, the exiles whom Brian had so desperately wanted me to meet while I'd set myself so viciously against it. I'd been shocked by them because it had seemed to me they were flaunting their most private hurt: like whores; like terminally ill patients exposing their sores and running wounds and boils and blackened gangrenous flesh to passers-by. It had shocked me profoundly; I'd found it revolting. Because, overwhelmed by my own suffering, I hadn't known how to cope with theirs; even after what had happened to me, I'd still not understood. Why, I'd thought, couldn't they keep their lives to themselves? Why couldn't they love and live and be private like other people? Now at last I understood, as I looked into Mandla's eyes to see my own reflected in them: they'd become like that, not because they'd wanted to, but because nothing private had been left to them. Because they'd been dragged out from among the walls that had always sheltered them, and forced out among the hyenas and vultures of a world pervaded by the smell of death and pestilence. For when you suffer from the Plague you have no privacy left. Any quack, any undertaker, any curious or suspicious passer-by can tear the clothes from your body to watch the progress of the disease — one day, two, three, four, and then the fifth, when the boils burst open — and turn you into a public spectacle. Even if they did it out of compassion: mercy itself becomes cruel when it must expose everything. After all, it's for your own benefit. Offering you, perhaps, your only chance of recovery. So rip off my rags, strip me naked, inspect my

350

breasts and my armpits, drag your nails through what lies hidden under my body hair, tear open my most secret flesh and thrust your fingers into it, make me bleed, let the thick black blood come from my body, hurt me: and heal me, for God's sake, try to heal me, save me, for I can't go on like this any more.

"Perhaps it will be easier to bear if we're together," I whispered. "If I help you. If I go back with you."

"The only result will be that each will bear the hurt of two."

"I want to run in the night with you. Like you asked."

"I didn't know what I was asking. One never knows before it is too late."

"Do you regret it then?"

He hit me with such force that my head was jerked back. I felt a tooth cutting into the inside of my cheek. I tasted the saltiness of my own blood. The pain brought tears to my eyes. I saw him wiping his face with his open hand, unable to believe what he'd done or what he saw. Then he turned away, as if to escape; but after a moment he pressed his head against mine.

"Oh God, Andrea, I didn't mean to." he said.

"Don't ask for forgiveness. I deserved it. I should never have asked a thing like that. I'm not sorry either."

He stared at me, searching my face intently; I kept my eyes unblinking on his. At last he sat up, looking away towards the window and the light.

"There are two ways of dying," he said; I'm not sure he was aware that I heard him. "You can die because you can't face going on, because it's all become too much for you. Or you can die because you choose to. Because you're not afraid. Because you got nothing to lose: because you're free: because there's no way they can touch or tame you."

"Why do you talk about dying?"

"What else is there to talk about?"

"I love you. You love me." I decided to risk it: "We can talk about our children."

"Why you going on about that?" he asked. "Don't, Andrea!"

351

"We'll have to learn to believe in it. It's the only hope we have."

Once again he shook his head, quietly, angrily, without looking at me. "No matter what the *Boere* did to me — standing on bricks, riding 'Boeing' on a broomstick, knee in the balls, electrodes — " for a moment he paused — "even Spike: I could take it all. One can prepare oneself for it. They can't touch you. But this — " Another vicious shake of his head. "I can't."

"I'm not asking anything of you. Except not to deny what is there."

He lay back, next to me, pressing me to him. Still naked, I could feel through his clothes the heavy vital warmth of his body. He held me very tightly, and for a very long time, while neither of us moved.

"Andrea, Andrea," I heard him whisper at last, too softly for me to be sure that it really was my name. Then he relaxed, and rolled away. Staring up at the ceiling, he began to talk more calmly than before, but with such despair in his voice that it gave me gooseflesh as if I were physically cold. "There's only one limit to the power of an oppression, and that's the patience of the oppressed. I am his limit, you understand that? — I'm the line that can stop him. That's why I can't allow anything to hinder me. I can't afford to have a soft spot where he can touch me. If you're with me then you're the soft underbelly, the balls he can grab me by. I told you before. Isn't that so?"

I took his hand and pressed it against my mouth; then held it to my breast. "I'm the same colour as you are. You said so yourself, remember, that day in Avignon; and long before that, in the rue du Four. I never knew it. For years I never wanted to know. Now there's nothing else I want to know. I'm no longer living 'in between', Mandla. I'm no longer in a no man's land."

Almost absently his hand moved over me. I couldn't help moaning in the urgency of my desire. My whole body tensed under his touch. I held his hand against me, feeling myself

352

open to its pressure. "Love me," I pleaded.

He took a deep breath. When he got up, I thought it was to take his clothes off. But he went to the door. There he stopped, his head heavy and bowed. And I heard the sound I knew from the night, that deep lion's groan.

"Put on your clothes, Andrea," he said. "I'll wait for you on the terrace."

Dumbfounded, I pushed myself up on my elbows, but he'd already opened the door and left.

I couldn't think. I was still lightheaded and glowing. Angry? No. Neither did I feel "disappointed"; certainly not confused. On the contrary, I felt stricken by an almost unbearable lucidity: an emptiness, a desolation, an anguish, a terrifying liberation: because now it was up to me alone to solve it — all the more painful, and all the more reassuring too, because I knew that at that moment, outside in the dazzling light of the new day, he would be feeling exactly the same about himself and me.

It was not all agony. In a strange, ridiculous way I was brought back to mundane action by the flea-bite in my groin. Sometimes one is saved by banalities. However irritating it may be.

I got up and went to wash my glowing face in cold water, then chose a light, sober, summer dress for the day.

More than just fleas: the small hotel in the forgotten back street of Saint-Rémy, far from the centre of the town in which only a few gateways of the medieval walls have remained, is ridden with roaches and bed-bugs. The moment the dull light is turned off at night they appear, rustling, from cracks and skirting boards and tattered wallpaper (old-fashioned little men in top hats, dainty little ladies with hoop-skirts and parasols, all in faded, browned pinks). Hours of furious search all over the floor and the bed, shoe or pillow in hand, ready to murder the first insect that shows itself. Sometimes it's hilarious. Not when one is tired. Even less when there's a dark thunderstorm building up inside one, which cannot be shared with anyone else: for it's the week before her period, when she has to keep to herself all the anxiety that will eventually burst out in Aix and lead her to the doctor's surgery.

In the daytime, worn out by loss of sleep, a weariness all the more depressing because there's no way out, Brian insists that she accompany him on all his explorations. He skips nothing: the excavations in the old Roman town of Glanum on the outskirts of the village, where the main road turns into the Alpilles on its way to Les Baux; opposite it, the municipal arch and the cenotaph on the main route from Rome to Spain; museums and churches and chapels of Saint-Rémy; the priory of Saint Paul of Mausole, where Van Gogh was cared for by the nuns for a year, after the people of Arles had signed a petition to rid themselves of the "mad redhead".

For Andrea the priory has a particular attraction, inspired mainly by the beautiful book of Van Gogh prints Brian gave her (a month late) in Arles for her birthday. But their very first visit turns out a failure when the Mother Superior, or whoever she may be, refuses them admission to the long cool building. "It's a hospital, Monsieur, not a museum." "We only need ten minutes, Madame," says Brian. (Perhaps it's his persistence in addressing her as "Madame" that turns her irrevocably against them.) "We came to Saint Rémy specially to look at Van Gogh's room."

She remains unimpressed. "We cannot encourage the worship of mere humans, Monsieur."

"Madame" — Andrea notices how the secular word causes the old grey woman to wince as if she's been struck in the face; then her mouth is drawn into a resolute fold as she seems to resign herself to martyrdom — "Madame, we've crossed half the globe to come here, all the way from South Africa."

A hint of interest in the flickering of her colourless eyes, but she remains firm. "I'm sorry, Monsieur."

Brian plays his trump: "We'd be pleased to make a donation to the Priory, Madame, as a token of appreciation — "

The Mother becomes hesitant. "Well, seeing that you've

354

come such a long way. But only five minutes."

To the left of the entrance she leads them down a few steps to a long dark corridor with doors on either side. Stopping in front of one of them, she glances at her visitors as if ready to change her mind again, before she unlocks it.

A bare white cell with a single rough table, a white jar on the grainy surface. Outside, through the small curtainless window, the summer is raging in a blaze of colours; inside, this muted serenity, as if all tones have drained from the place after the painter's departure.

Even that, Andrea soon discovers, is illusion, as Brian stands looking round, clearly nonplussed, and takes a small notebook from his inside pocket to flick through the pages.

"If you've finished we can go," says the nun.

"How can we have finished?" Brian asks accusingly. "This isn't the right room."

"Monsieur!" protests the dignified, straight-backed lady. "Are you suggesting that I lied to you?"

"Van Gogh's room was upstairs. I made a note of it."

"Do you believe everything you read?"

"My source is beyond reproach, Madame."

Her thin nostrils are quivering, but she keeps an admirable control on herself. "Monsieur — " Followed by a very unexpected about-turn: "And even if he did stay upstairs, what difference does it make? All our rooms are identical."

"Only one was Van Gogh's."

"If you were to go there — what would you see? Walls, a floor, a ceiling, nothing more. You don't seem to realize, Monsieur, that Van Gogh was a poor lunatic just like all the others."

Brian's agitation is to no avail; they leave with empty hands, after a final altercation when he refuses to proffer the promised donation.

Back in the room with the bed-bugs and fleas he takes from his suitcase the condensed translation of Van Gogh's letters he bought in the second-hand shop in Avignon, to show her what he underlined the day before:

355

I have a small room with green-grey wallpaper and two seagreen curtains with a pattern of very pale roses, brightened by a few splashes of red . . . . Through the barred window I can see a wheatfield enclosed by a wall, a perspective like a Van Goyen, above which I can see the morning sun rising in all its glory —

Andrea has opened her own book to look up the reproduction. "Here it is."

"That's it. You see? Just as I told the pious old liar — !"

"We must go back," she says. "Now I want to see it, no matter what happens."

"We won't get past that old witch. No use asking for trouble. And after all, we have the paintings."

"How can they matter more than the man who painted them? Brian, I tell you, I want to get inside that room. I want to stand where he stood. I want to feel what he felt."

"There's no way we can get inside, Andrea."

"Well, if you're too scared I'll go alone."

For two days in succession she makes him go back all the way along the avenue Pasteur, on foot, to the Priory, where they skulk round the buildings like two criminals in search of new ways to get inside. At the back of the hospital some men in blue overalls are doing repair work. And when Brian and Andrea return during the lunch hour on the second day, the workers are off duty, enjoying their food and wine under a large plane-tree round the corner, their ladders abandoned against the brown wall. Not that it makes things much easier for them, for most of the windows on the top floor have closed shutters; others are barred. But after making a quick calculation, Brian shifts the ladder to one of the few accessible windows.

"You can go up," he says. "Try one of the rooms over to that side."

"What about you?"

"I'll keep watch."

"Are you worried about my safety or are you too scared to come up yourself?"

356

"You're wasting time, Andrea."

As a child, among all the kids in the neighbourhood, even when Boetie was present, she always was the first to do whatever was dangerous or forbidden; so in a way it suits her to be sent up by Brian.

The corridor upstairs is deserted, with the builders' paint buckets and other paraphernalia very much in evidence. Following Brian's instructions, she goes to one of the farthest rooms and checks the view through the bars of the window. Then a second, a third, until the landscape begins to match the picture she remembers: the wall, the small vineyard and olive-trees, in the background the rugged shapes of the Alpilles. But there is no miracle. She tries to overcome her disappointment, tries to persuade herself that it *does* mean something to be standing here, looking through the same window at an unchanged world resplendent in the sun. But nothing can convince her. She remains isolated from it: not only from Van Gogh but, in a disconcerting way, from her feelings.

Noticing Brian waving very urgently from outside she hurries back to the window through which she has made her entry. Near the bottom rung of the ladder she lets go and jumps down, wincing as she hurts her ankle so that she has to grab Brian's arm for support. The workers are on their way back, coming round the corner. One of them shouts some hing. Brian replies over his shoulder as he helps her to hobble away; and in a wide circle round the buildings they go up the brief incline towards the weatherbeaten ruins of the old Roman town of Glanum, where they spend an hour among the stones to muster some energy for the long walk back.

"Now you still haven't been inside," she says with a wry chuckle. "And it may have meant more to you than to me after all."

He shrugs.

"You should have come up with me."

"One of us had to keep watch. And I thought it would please you." A pause. "It did mean something special, didn't it?"

357

"I'm not sure that it did. I couldn't picture what he felt at all. I had the feeling that once he'd painted it he was so thoroughly through with it that only second-hand thoughts remained for the others."

"Do you really think anything can be so final?"

"What's the use of something if you have to do it over and over again?"

"Like making love?" (One can rely on him always to return to that; and she cannot help remembering the previous night, and the effect of bed-bugs on passion.)

"Maybe."

"If something is worth while, surely it's important to keep on making it true again, reconfirming it as many times as possible."

"There ought to be something so worth while in itself that it will always *stay* worth while," she says. "So that you needn't go on trying to satisfy yourself with inferior imitations all the time." (One morning in a small backyard under a fig-tree, white washing, blue sky?) "Something you will never ever lose again. But then it can't just be something you're doing to while away the time: I'm thinking of something so important that you're prepared to risk your whole life for it because your whole history, everything you've ever been or can hope to be, is caught up in it. Not something that just happens but something you *will* to happen. Something — how can I explain it to you? I don't know myself — but something which suddenly makes you see very clearly what you're doing here and why you are here."

"That day in the shallow cave at the Steenbras Mouth," he says, "surely we knew it very clearly then?"

She says nothing; her eyes are closed.

"Didn't we?" he insists.

"If it really was like that there would be no need for you to ask me, would there?"

"Andrea!" He gets up, shocked. "Are you trying to deny — ?"

She sits leaning forward, elbows on her knees, cherishing

358

the strange heaviness in her belly. Is there a child inside her? She's five days overdue today. Can it be fear weighing one down like this? Suppose he found out — ? What will happen if she tells him now, in this blinding sun, above this ageless old town dug up from the ground, with the bright blood-red splashes of poppies among the stones? How can one be afraid of something that should be so natural?

She gets up, standing in front of him, searching his eyes.

"What's the matter with you?" he asks. "Ever since we set foot in Provence you're a different person altogether. We were looking forward to it so much. Whatever happened at the Cape is past, don't you understand? We're in Europe now. We're free. Nothing and no one can stand in our way. We can do anything we want to."

"You mean we can fuck from morning till night."

"Must you be so crude?"

"That's all you've been wanting to do lately. As if there's something chasing you."

"You're being very unfair, Andrea. We're spending most of our time going on excursions and doing things, seeing the world. Right in front of you there's a town built by Agrippa which you never even knew existed. Half an hour ago you were standing in the room where Van Gogh lived and painted — "

"I'm sorry, Brian," she says, subdued. "I didn't mean to sound ungrateful."

"But what's wrong with you then?"

"I'm just fed-up with myself. Please don't pay any attention."

"Let's go back," he says, kissing her lightly on the cheek.

"I'm sure the bed-bugs can't wait to see us back."

His face reddens with indignation. "I suppose that's my fault too?"

"That's not what I meant. Oh, Jesus — !" Desperate, she raises her hands and lets them drop back to her sides. "I'm just not able to say what I mean. Let's go back. I promise you I'll be very good."

359

As they pass the entrance of the driveway leading to the Priory she says, wistful: "Perhaps, if there'd just been the slightest mark of his paint on the wall. If he'd cut his name into the plaster or something. That would have made it easier to believe."

"We have his paintings. Aren't they enough? Miserable and poor and rejected as he may have been, he said it all in his paintings. He made it worth while. Not only for himself but for us too, and forever."

"There's nothing *I* can do with what I saw there. I can't relive his life for him. He could paint, I can't. For all the world cares, I need never even have existed."

A snatch of dialogue I remember from Mandla, which he'd taught me that morning:

"*Kunjani?* — How are you?"

"*Ndisaphila, Kuwe?* — I'm well, and you?"

"*Ndingatsho ndithi nam ndiyaphila kuba ndizibona udivuka ndibhinge.* — I guess I'm well too, for I see I'm still getting up and fastening my belt."

No doubt about his belt being fastened as I came down to the terrace. He seemed to have himself under control, but his eyes were still tired and red. I was hoping he would say something — that I looked nice; that he'd seen I wasn't wearing make-up (the only way I could be naked for him in public) — but he was silent, although it was obvious that he'd noticed all right, allowing nothing about me to escape him.

"Have I kept you waiting?"

He shrugged. The *patron*, no doubt watching through the window, immediately brought our breakfast. He was sulky, the way only a man can sulk; as if he'd guessed all about Mandla and me. (If only it *were* like that, Monsieur: if only I *had* spent the night in his arms. Now you've probably taken it out on your poor wife without any reason. Or was it she who took it out on you? Whatever one does, or omits, involves others. *Pardonnez-moi, Monsieur.*)

"Where are we going today?" asked Mandla.

360

I pushed aside the books and maps I'd brought down with me. "Nowhere. Today we can stay right where we are."

"What about your work?"

"We can look around Saint-Rémy. We're both tired."

He gazed fixedly at me; with my naked face I stared back, but neither spoke. It caught me unawares when he put out his hand across the small table and took mine, pressing it hard. A brief smile softened the gloom in his face, as if to say: *Don't worry, we're in it together.*

More at ease now, we finished breakfast; that was when, almost lightheartedly, he taught me my bit of Xhosa. Leaving the books behind at the reception desk, we went through the large stone gate on foot and headed for the town centre. The bark was peeling off the bare plane-trees, leaving the trunks denuded in a patchwork of colours. The summer foliage gone, the boulevard circling the old town now lay totally exposed to the sun and wind.

Through one of the few remaining medieval gateways we entered the winding streets of the centre. Outside, there was at least an attempt at linearity, a determined if sometimes un-inspired attempt to "keep up" with the rest of the world — garages, shopwindows, rectilinear buildings, the large square in front of the Syndicat d'Initiative where the men played *pétanque* in the sand in the afternoons — but inside the old part of town everything was delightfully, humanly unpredict-able, without the oppressive feeling of being cooped up behind walls, which I sometimes experienced in other old towns. Saint-Rémy was relaxed, unselfconscious, Mediterranean, generous. Bead curtains in front of the open doorways, swing-ing like the skirts of a voluptuous woman after someone had entered or left. Red-and-white tablecloths in the restaurants; straight-backed peasant chairs with straw mats, like the ones painted by Van Gogh. Windows and shutters covered with the shreds of summer posters: a chamber concert in some chapel; the festival at Avignon or Carpentras or Aix; a corrida in Nîmes or a local *course aux vachettes*; a cycle marathon (where would our poor rider be today?); a *fête votive* in some near or

361

distant village. The whole summer summarized in bright tatters — sometimes as many as four or five different layers of posters on top of each other, a legible segment of each exposed — just as one could imagine the summer warmth still preserved in the old paving stones buried, undoubtedly, beneath the tarred streets. Music wafted from some of the shops from which women — old and dry, or young and bursting with ripeness — emerged with string bags or with round or long loaves under the arm: the international language of rock and folk, a French *chanson*; once, cool and remote as a memory, Mozart.

The place Jules-Pelissier behind the church lay quiet and unperturbed under its trees, a small group of old men clustered round the fountain, while small children played about under the watchful eyes of knitting mothers, and pigeons fluttered round a window where an old woman in black was feeding them from her breakfast table. These might have been the selfsame people we'd found at the fountain in Murs the day before; or on Sunday in La Motte d'Aigues, or a day earlier in Avignon. Ubiquitous, like the cyclist.

The smell of ratatouille from a side street flooded by the water of a wanton street-cleaner — Algerian or Moroccan? — sweeping everything out of his way with his wide broom while carrying on a loud monologue with himself. Cats dozing on high walls or gliding through small courtyards like memories of lustful dreams: a mere ripple caught by the tail of one's eye and gone before you can turn to look. The cats of Saint-Rémy: they'd been there, several of them with litters, when Paul and I had roamed the streets; and in the dingy hotel where Brian and I had stayed their fighting and lovemaking had interfered with our own at night: long after he'd turned his reproachful back on me, they would go on screeching like lost souls as I lay staring blankly into the dark or trying with my own hand to relieve my frustration or assuage a fear I couldn't, or wouldn't, give a name as yet.

The small ceramic shop on the boulevard Gambetta, past the

statue of Nostradamus at his fountain, and the place Favier, still smelling of last week's fish market. The bent old woman waiting, smiling and patient, while she and Paul are looking round, taking things from the shelves, or squatting to inspect the larger amber jugs and urns on the floor.

He chooses a full dinner service, hand-painted with the emblems of the South, mainly cicadas, decorated in the yellow of wheat and the purple of lavender, an exuberant collection with all the recklessness of summer.

"If you're really so taken with Provence," says the old lady as she begins to add up all the amounts, "don't you think it would be better to come and live here permanently?"

"I've been toying with the idea."

"Are you serious?"

"Yes, indeed."

"Well, if you do think of moving," she says, taking her time to wrap each separate piece in newsprint, "I know of a *mas* not far from here. It's up for rent at the moment, with the possibility of selling in a year or two."

"Friends of yours?"

With a touch of embarrassment she admits: "It's my own. My husband died last winter, you know. I'm getting too old — " Eagerly she adds: "Why don't you just take a look? You may like it."

"You say it's not too far?"

"Ten kilometres. In the direction of Eygalières."

It doesn't take much encouragement for her to draw a spidery map; in a flush of generosity she offers them a water jug as a present.

"Come and tell me if it pleases you," she says as they go out. "I'm here all day."

It's a rambling old farmhouse built of weathered Provençal stone, golden brown in the afternoon sun; a roof of terracotta tiles. Faded green shutters obscured by a luxuriant, unkempt garden: cypresses, hollyhocks, windblown roses. A sprinkling of poppies in the grass. At the back, a stone well, some olive-trees, a vine, another row of cypresses, all of it defined by the

363

sound of cicadas, cutting it into the mind like an etching needle on a copper plate.

"Don't you think we should come to live here?"

"You're joking."

"Maybe I'm not."

(Last night in the Auberge in Eygalières.)

"I was quite startled when I saw that *mas* yesterday," he confides the next day on a café terrace in Saint-Rémy. "It was like something from a dream I'd already forgotten: then suddenly it came true."

"The old South African chauvinist dream of your own piece of land?"

"No." He remains grave, thoughtful. "When I was in the Schloss Judenau, that time we were helping the Hungarian refugees — " He stops, clearly hesitant about whether to go on. "I told you about the girl, remember? Eva Jelačić — "

"Very little."

"In the bit of broken German we shared we used to talk about a house like this one, a *mas* in Provence exactly like the one we saw yesterday. Where we could settle once the war in her country was over, when the world became liveable again. She still remembered a journey with her parents through the South of France, you see, when she'd been a little girl. Somehow it had stuck in her memory. We spoke about the warm, friendly stone, the red geraniums on the window-sills, the vine at the back door, the olive grove. We dreamed about making our own wine, pressing our own oil." Almost apologetic, he returns to reality and to her: "All the dreams of young romantic lovers. And we *needed* a thing like that to talk about, to keep us warm in that frightful cold. To help us forget."

"Did she escape from Hungary all on her own? Were there no other members of her family?"

"No, she was on her own. Never spoke about anyone else either. Only much later" — he hesitates — "right at the end of my stay, after she'd left, we heard from new arrivals that she had had relatives after all. A father, a mother, two or three brothers. They'd all tried to escape together, but the others had

364

been stopped just short of the border. She'd had a younger sister too, but the Russians had killed her."

Now she must know the rest too. "How did she leave the camp? When? Where did she go to?" There is an urgency in her voice, a need to find out everything about this one episode from his past about which he's always been so cagey — even though she is also conscious of an inexplicable resistance against the very wish to know. (How can I deny you your memories if memories are all I myself live by? — Yet, do you know how unbearably jealous I sometimes feel of your unknown Eva?)

Hesitant, without looking at her, Paul answers: "It was soon after Christmas. We had a celebration in the Schloss on Christmas Day. Fir-trees, gift parcels from all over the world, even a brass band from Vienna: little round men with purple cheeks and frozen drops on the ends of their noses. We all tried our desperate best to be outrageously jolly. Bursting with goodwill. But actually it was unbearable, one of the most macabre days of my life."

"And Eva?" she quietly nudges him back to what concerns her most.

"I'd gone to Vienna the previous weekend. Bought her a music box with the last bit of money I'd saved up. A delicate little thing, the kind with an inlaid pattern. When it was opened it played Mozart's 'Là ci darem la mano'." Almost angrily he checks himself: "You must remember, I was head over heels in love. Nothing was too sentimental for me."

"Did she like it?"

"Eva was mad about music. In Budapest she'd been a piano student. It had been her whole life. When the Russians burned down their house — " He falls silent, shaking his head as if to blame himself for remembering. "But why go into that again?"

"I want to know all about her, Paul."

Another helpless movement of his head. "When I gave it to her she started trembling. She sometimes had attacks like that, some kind of epileptic fit, I suppose. I got a terrible scare. But she recovered, pushing the box back into my hands as she kept on saying, over and over: 'No, no. Don't. Don't.'

" 'But I love you,' I insisted. 'It's yours.' "

"She held her two empty hands out to me, pressing them against me, urging me to see that she had nothing for me in return. In my wretched German I tried to convince her it didn't matter. I kissed her hands and gave her back the little box, opening the lid. She just stood there, pressing it against her as the tears ran down her cheeks."

"I still don't know what it has to do with her going away?"

"After ten that evening, when the lights in the refugee wards were turned out, she slipped out to me. She knew I was on duty. In one of the long bare passages she found me as I was doing my rounds. She was terribly excited. In that state she found it even more difficult than usual to express herself in German. In what seemed like sheer desperation she suddenly put out her hand and grabbed me here" — he touches his sex — "in the crudest, clumsiest way you can imagine. With a brave, desperate little smile on her pale face. 'I give you,' she said excitedly, nervously. 'Yes? Yes?' She wouldn't let me go. In the end I forcibly had to push her away from me."

"You refused her?"

"How could I accept a sacrifice like that?"

"Suppose it was all she had? I would have done the same."

He looks at her, almost sadly. "I know you would. And perhaps I would be better equipped to deal with it today. But at the time — Maybe I was being melodramatic and ridiculous, but I just couldn't, Andrea. Because I loved her so much. If we did make love it shouldn't be to thank me for a wretched little music box. I wasn't being puritanical or anything. If it had been Lise or one of the others — But not Eva. I struggled and fumbled to explain it to her in my almost non-existent German. But of course she didn't understand. In the end she turned round and went away, barefoot on the cold stone floor. I could see her shivering. But it wasn't just from the cold."

She nods quietly.

"For a few days she avoided me. I did my best to find her

366

alone so that I could try to explain once again that it hadn't been a way of rejecting her. Christ, on the contrary! But she kept away from me. And about a week later, the first time I went out with the ambulance group to the border again, she left. Just ran away."

"And you never traced her or heard from her again?"

He hesitates, then shakes his head very firmly. "No. Never."

"Why won't you tell me, Paul?"

"It's long past. There's nothing anyone can do about it anymore. It's half a lifetime ago."

She puts her hand on his knee, caressing the faded cotton of his jeans.

"Now you see why I never told you. I didn't want to burden you with it; it isn't fair."

"I'm so glad you did. Do you feel freer now?"

"I can never be entirely free from it. But perhaps I've finally learned to live with my guilt."

"And now you've found your *mas*."

He nods absently.

"But without Eva."

"This time it's with you. This time it's for real. Remember what I asked you."

"I haven't answered yet."

"I know. But I'll wait very patiently. We can't keep that *mas* waiting for us forever."

"Can one ever live in a dream?"

"Eva belongs with the dream. Now it's you and me. And the stone and wood of a real house."

"Perhaps we should consult an oracle. What about your beloved Nostradamus?" She knows with how much delight he constantly returns to the old prophet. "Do you think he'll have a remedy for us?"

"He had a remedy for everything. Even for the Plague. The only problem is that people usually don't understand his prophecies before it's too late."

"Pity."

"Perhaps it's a blessing."

Le Guide Noir:

In 1546 the terrifying Plague broke out which Aix would remember as the "Provençal charcoal" because it made the victims as black as coal. The suffering was horrible . . . . Nostradamus fought against the epidemic by means of a powder with a fragrance of "perfect bounty and excellence", no outlandish smell but one that brought about a happy languor which lasted for a long time. To prepare this powder, Nostradamus mixed the sawdust of cypress wood with irises from Florence, ambergris, cloves, aloes and musk. To these ingredients, shaken carefully together, he added the juice of red petals from roses plucked at sunrise. This powder, "excellent to drive away the smells of pestilence", apparently turned out to be so good as a preventative as well that the inhabitants of Aix, delivered from the Plague, honoured its author with great festivity.

Ziegler:

As well as bleeding, it was useful to open and cauterize the plague boils or buboes. Various curious substances were applied to the boils to draw off the poison. Gentile used a plaster made from gum resin, the roots of white lilies and dried human excrement, while Master Albert was in favour of an old cock cut through the back . . . .

Various soothing potions were prescribed, in particular a blend of apple-syrup, lemon, rose-water and peppermint. This must at least have been pleasant to drink. Even this consolation was removed when powered minerals were added to the mixture.

Defoe:

But there was still another madness beyond all this . . . . and this was in wearing charms, philtres, exorcisms, amulets, and I know not what preparations, to fortify the body with them against the plague; as if the plague was not the hand of God, but a kind of possession of an evil spirit; and that it was to be kept off with crossings, signs of the zodiac, papers tied up with so many knots, and certain words or figures written on them, as particularly the word Abracadabra . . . . Others had the Jesuits' mark in a cross. Others nothing but this mark, thus:

"You see," I told Mandla, "death wasn't altogether inevitable. Some victims were saved, thanks to people like Nostradamus. Even though he, too, was vilified in his old age — can you imagine? — first as a Jew, then as a Protestant." We were standing in front of the prophet's bust, and I held my hand under the clear stream of water running into the fountain, watching it spill over my palm and through my fingers. "Perhaps that's all that really matters? Not the fact of the Plague, but that people try to find remedies, keeping alive at least a hope of being saved from it. Refusing to give up faith."

"There may be different ways of getting saved. For some of the things that people suffer from there can be only one remedy, and that's death."

"There's always an alternative," I said passionately.

"The alternative may not necessarily be better."

"What are you trying to say, Mandla?"

A sudden smile: "Sometimes one doesn't have a stick to test the water before you wade in."

"What's a stick got to do with it?"

"When my grandfather was still alive he used to say: 'Before you cross a stream you must always test the water with your *udondolo* first.' That's your stick."

"And if you don't have a stick?"

"You must always take your *udondolo* with you. If you don't have it ready, you have to wade in as you are."

"Even if it's dangerous?"

"Even if it's dangerous."

369

He took the hand I was holding under the clear stream of water and leaned over to drink from my palm. Still looking at me, he took the fingers into his mouth, one by one. The simplicity of his action turned my whole body into water.

— Hands. Paul taking my hand in the rue Carnot to caress it with a single fingertip, over the knuckles and in between the fingers, from the small webs at their base to the cushions at the tip, across the palm and the hollow of my hand, tracing love- and lifelines so delicately yet so intensely that it leaves me breathless. Brian stopping outside the Hôtel de Sade — the light outside blinding after the cool interior where we've spent an hour among the remains of the most distant past — pressing me against the wall and moving the back of his hand, the hard knuckles, over the surface of my cheeks and jaws and mouth, until I grab the hand and bite into the palm, with a wildness and a passion in me which will dissipate very soon, as he hurriedly leads me back to our bug-infested room where I shall undoubtedly refuse him anew, without either of us knowing why. Now Mandla. Whatever happens is echoed interminably by what has happened, by what is yet to come. I am caressed by the hands of the dead —

I was startled by the thought. Brian was still alive; Paul even more so. Except, for me they were dead, as past as those earlier selves of me they'd known. The only one still alive — and God, how terrifyingly alive! — was Mandla, now, here, with the warmth of his breath and his spittle on my fingers.

We roamed on through the streets to where the traffic of the boulevard Gambetta stopped us like a river in flood and sent us back into the old heart of the town. There was no market that morning, it was Tuesday. Perhaps that was why I kept on wandering, looking for something I felt was missing. The day with Brian, when we'd bought fruit and cheese for a meal, had been my first experience of a Provençal market, which simply takes over a whole village, spilling through streets and sidewalks and squares, impregnating everything, for me, with memories of the Cape and my childhood, the vendors on the Parade, the hawkers of District Six, the blaring of the fish bugle. Upon my return with Paul, we'd bought serviette rings in olive-wood, and a lovely little box for salt; and in the *Souleïado* shop on the busiest market street he'd bought me a summer dress in the most audacious, violent purple we could find, with small flowers in pink and blue. Today the town was much quieter, one could hear the water of the fountain on the place Jules-Pelissier, and sparrows in the high bare trees: as if the town had opened itself more unconditionally to us than before, the crowds withdrawn to wherever they'd come from, allowing us to explore as we wished.

We didn't enter any building. I knew Mandla would be bored by museums and I felt no inclination to return either: but I remembered very well what it had been like before (Roman tablets, and the busts of emperors, and strange pagan Gallic gods, and columns from which the head of the executed had been suspended along the highways; shards of pottery and tools and mosaic and frescoes from Glanum, and the toilet wares of long dead women: tiny containers for mascara and rouge, teaspoons, perfume bottles; even, unmistakably, hair curlers, Ma) — carrying it with me wherever I went, like a subconscious mind adding its dimensions to the simpler world through which we wandered hand in hand.

From the church we crossed over to the place de la République and walked up the boulevard Pasteur. Mandla asked no questions; and if he had, I wouldn't have been able to give a clear explanation. By the time I realized it we were already halfway out of town. Among the cypresses of Saint Paul de Mausole we rested for a while; I showed him the interior of the cloister where the red geraniums were still in flower among the greenery. This time I made no attempt to get hold of the caretakers and seek admission to the hospital; there was nothing I wanted to see inside any more. (Van Gogh himself had in his lifetime spent most of his days looking out.)

We returned to the main road and the *Antiques* on the far side. The tall graceful cenotaph for the grandchildren of Augustus Caesar; and the municipal arch with its friezes still surprisingly intact. No glory to the memory of Rome, how-

371

ever, I thought, like the day before at Carpentras: yet another procession of conquered men and women, slaves in chains. What had been the signs of the empire's greatness were now reminding one of its fall.

Unlike the previous day, Mandla made no comment. Not that he'd become more passive: it was only that we needed fewer words and gestures to communicate.

I wasn't sure whether he would show any interest in the ruins of Glanum fifty yards further on, but he began to walk in that direction on his own. There were no other visitors, unlike the summer when Paul and I had been forced to follow the crowd. In amazing symmetry the heart of the old city lay exposed in stone. The homes of patricians. The streets with their water ducts. The large public baths. Shops, houses, columns, archways. The beautiful "Greek" shrine of Agrippa over the old sacred fountain of the Salyans (now a pool of thick green slime with plastic bottles and cold drink cartons on the surface). The many tablets with their perfectly even inscriptions in unambiguous Roman letters. (*Agrippa was here!*)

It was tempting to yield, like years ago at Les Baux, to the childish urge in me to follow their example. Picking up a shard of stone, I made sure the caretaker at the entrance wasn't looking, and ducked in behind the far wall of the public baths.

Mandla followed me, watching as I made a strenuous effort to chisel the first leg of the A into the stone.

"You'll never finish that way," he said. "You can't cut as deep as those Romans did."

"Give me time."

"There's a much better way." He gave a rare, carefree laugh.

"Show me."

I wasn't expecting the show he put on. Without any hesitation he zipped open his jeans, took out his penis and aimed his jet at the high wall of the baths, writing in crooked, unbroken letters an audacious A.M. and M.M. which he underlined with a final flourish. Then, with crude masculine grace, he shook his eloquent member dry and with a brief jerking motion of his hips tucked it back into his pants.

"There you are! Others may not be able to read it, but we'll know what it says."

A sudden ridiculous, painful image from years ago: a man stumbling about in the moonlight and steadying himself against a water tap to pee: *Let Thy will be done*. And the next day he'd gone away for good.

"When I was small," I told him, "my father always made me stand against the wall in the passage when he came back from his trips, to measure how much I'd grown while he was away. I suppose many fathers do it. Except, my Dedda never used a pencil, he made his marks with spit. In the beginning he did use a pencil, until Ma complained, so he changed to spit. 'It's a secret code,' he always said. 'Don't you worry, Nanna-girl. Even if no one else sees it, *I* can see it.' And every time he measured me he'd keep a poker-face as he showed me exactly where the previous mark had been. And I believed him. I believed him like he was God. And when we were thrown out of that house and had to move out to the little council house on the Flats, that was what I cried about most. It felt as if I'd suddenly lost my whole history."

"Your father was right. Those marks will always be there."

I forced a smile. "As long as those of Mr Agrippa and the others?"

"Longer. They only had stone. What we got — " In a simple, spontaneous gesture he folded both hands over his sex. "All we got to write with is piss and seed and blood and spit and shit. But that's the sort of thing that lasts. People last longer than stone."

"One day we can send our children back here to look it up," I joked. "If they have your eyes they'll find our names all right."

"No need for them to come here," he said in mock sternness. "We'll be writing more than enough for them over there to read." Then, as if he'd suddenly caught on what was happening, he remonstrated angrily: "But I told you not to talk about children again, Andrea!"

373

"How can I not talk about children? I'm a woman."

"The one child that could have been mine is dead," he said, his voice shallow and menacing. "And it was my fault."

"Mandla, how can you say that?"

"It's because of me that they picked up Ntsiki. You think I can ever do that to a woman again? And I'm not just talking about what the *Boere* did to her." He was struggling to say what was on his mind. "You see, there was that wall between her and me, a wall I built myself. Because I used to believe there were things a woman needn't know about. That's something you made me see these last few days: it's no use talking about walls like race and religion. There's other walls too. Anything that can keep one person away from another is a Wall of the Plague. And if you think of breaking things down, that's where you got to start. Right at the beginning, with a man and a woman. A father and his son. Brother and brother." Through layers of suffering he looked at me. "I don't deserve to have children. D'you understand that now?"

"I want to bear your children, Mandla."

He pressed me against him and kissed me with a violence that bruised my lips. Then held my head against his shoulder; I could feel his own shaking vehemently.

"This is the last time, you hear? Never again."

Although I could barely move in his grip, I shook my head against him, protesting in a smothered voice: "I'll go on talking about it. I tell you, I'll go on. I'll never stop. Because I love you. No matter what you say."

I was expecting him to lose control again, like that morning in my room. But all he did was to let me go so that he could stare at me, very intensely; then he raised both his hands and moved his fingers across my face, not a caress but an exploration, the way a blind man would read Braille: my forehead and eyebrows, eyes, nose; my cheekbones and the outline of my jaw, my mouth; then my throat, the hollow between my collarbones, and up to my shoulders, until at last his two hands came to rest on my breasts. He must have felt my nipples contracting under his touch, but he didn't react. All the time we gazed into one another's eyes, each trying as it were to suck the other into himself, herself: perhaps a prisoner released from solitary confinement after many years might react that way, looking at his own face in a mirror for the first time. (On the mountain near the Wall we couldn't find: *Will you stay with me? Or will you betray me? What do you ultimately grant me: life, or death?*)

At last he dropped his arms again, took me by the hand and led me from behind the ruins of the baths, back to the broad flagstones of what had once been a narrow main street. On the kerbs stood tall brittle grasses, their plumes white against the light; among them, tiny mauve and yellow flowers. Small lizards rippled out of our way. There were crows in the sky, a very deep blue sky showing only a few smudges of cloud in the direction of Les Baux. The sharp smell of cypresses in the sun.

Near the remains of the original forum the ground was dug up, the quarries and mounds of earth covered with green plastic. New archaeological excavations, according to the guidebook we'd bought at the gate. For below the Roman town they'd discovered the remains of an even older Salyan settlement. And underneath that, who knows, there might be older ruins still, dating from the Neolithic age or God knows when. Layer upon layer upon layer, one above the other, even though they might be separated by unbridgeable gulfs in time.

Opposite the three tall columns of Agrippa's shrine, where his name was chiselled right across a crack in a horizontal slab of stone, we sat down on the remains of a low wall. From his back pocket Mandla took his *trompie* and started playing again, his eyes closed, his body lightly swaying; he kept it up for a long time. I surrendered myself to the sound, and to the sun, waiting in infinite patience. Until at last, with an irritated gesture — for once the monotonous little tune was not enough to soothe the turbulence in him — he put the *trompie* down beside him. Absently he scooped up a handful of small pebbles and started throwing them at the columns opposite the narrow street, watching them ricochet in all directions, chuckling sometimes like an amused boy. But from his body I could

375

see that he was still tense; the game was only an attempt to control his thoughts again.

"Look at their history," he said, swinging his arm as he aimed another pebble. "All over the place, wherever I went in Europe. Every city, the smallest village. Even out there in the veld are ruins. They live with the signs of their civilization all around them. Everywhere you see it written down, if not on walls then in books. In Azania too. The same books. I read them. I was brought up on their books. Like you. It's the food they feed us: their history." Another pebble, this time hitting the crack running through Agrippa's name. "But what about ours? No sign of it. They swallowed it all, wiped it out. It wasn't moving out of District Six that robbed you of your history: they done that long before. What you thought was yours, was just something they gave you to keep you quiet."

Through the surface calm of his voice I could hear the deeper passion return like a new tide: I'd been expecting it.

"Here from Europe they went out to our Azania. And they weren't satisfied to be boss over us, to get us back to work in their mines and factories, to teach our women to scrub their floors and wash their clothes and eat the remains from their tables: they had to get a grip on our history too. They knew bloody well: take away a man's history and he's no longer human. Then you can force him to bend to your will. Look at what they did to my history: you ever read in their books what they say about the place they call the Eastern Frontier and which used to be, for us, the Western Frontier? You see, we don't even use the same words."

"I know, Mandla. That's what they taught me too. About 'Hottentots' and 'Bushmen'. It was only when I met Brian — "

He went on without listening: "One long story of defeat after defeat, that's all. My people were a bunch of thieves and murderers. If the Xhosas crossed the border it was to steal and plunder their homes. If they crossed it, they said it was to punish the robbers and teach them a lesson. Afterwards they tried to soften us up with the Bible. Even the greatest of our warriors — Hintsa, Makana — were no more than barbarians

376

and vagabonds in their eyes. And the worst is that we ourselves came to believe that we were just a lot of heathens, too lazy and too dumb for anything but whoring and drinking beer and fighting. We also came to believe that Azania's history only began in 1652 when the Whites arrived. We accepted being kicked off their sidewalks or carrying passes or getting thrown out of their butcheries. We allowed them to turn our cocks into watering cans. That's what they did; that's what we permitted them to do. But now it's over. This Agrippa and his lot — " Another pebble in the crack, sending a lizard scuttling off without a tail. "Who turned these old cities upside down? Wasn't it barbarians like us? The same slaves trampled by the horses of the conquerors on that monument over there — "

He got up from the wall and helped me down too. He took his *trompie*, and we began to saunter back.

"What I don't understand," I said, depressed, "is why one must go through the same terrible process so many times? Don't people learn anything then? Must there always be blood and death before there can be change?"

"Look how dry the ground is. This earth will never get enough blood. It's parched. Over there in Azania it's even worse." He turned round to look at me. "That's why I keep on telling you, Andrea! — don't talk about children. A man's blood, all right. Even a woman's, if there's no other way out. But I can't slaughter my own children. And if I get to the point where I must die myself — "

In the bright sunshine I shivered as if a cloud had passed overhead. In the distance I could hear the crows cawing, peaceful specks in the blue sky.

"Don't talk about death, Mandla."

I should have known that he would pay no attention. "It's a very simple choice, actually. Either you live, which you can't do if they've cut out your balls: you live with your pride, with your self-respect — or otherwise you die."

"You can't always choose how you want to die."

"I know. Of course you can't. You can't choose what others will make out of your death either. But there's one thing they

377

can't take away from you: at least, when your times comes, you can choose what you want to die *for*. Maybe it's not much. But it's something. And for me it's enough."

"Why do you keep on like that, Mandla?" I demanded urgently. There was something in him I still couldn't grasp, something which made me unbearably afraid. But he gave no answer.

We began to walk back. Past the wall on which Mandla had written our names. Through the gate, and past the *Antiques*. Between the cenotaph and the arch a group of small children were playing some kind of roundelay — jumping and skipping and falling down, as they screeched and yelled and collapsed with laughter. But like so many times in the past few days I found myself staring at another dimension of reality altogether: not the game those children were playing in front of my eyes, but another dance in a circle round the fig-tree in our small backyard, ducking under the washing on the line — a birthday party? or a spontaneous exhibition of exuberant, violent life? —

Ring a ring o' rosy,
Pocket full of posy,
Hush, hush, we all fall DOWN —

acting out, in that one silly little game, the whole of life and death.

Through the long avenue we walked back towards the town, the sound of today's children forever mingled in my mind with those of years ago. We didn't talk. He was playing his *trompie*, very softly, a ceaseless, unremitting, melancholy tune going on and on, accompanying us like a conscience, staying with us like a shadow, gathering us into its simple rhythm and keeping us going. Impossible to stop: what had begun to move now had to go on all the way.

"Somebody got to know. Anything can happen to me. No matter whether it's now, or in a year, or in ten years. Then somebody got to know about it all."

378

We had something to eat on the way. Back at the hotel the *patron* seemed surprised to see us back so soon. I collected the books and maps I'd left at the counter and we went upstairs. We hadn't arranged anything specific for the afternoon: over lunch, in a small restaurant near the centre, I'd made some casual remark about how tired I was and that it might be a good idea to go back for a nap. All our movements, gestures, even the last few words we spoke, seemed to have been decided in advance for us. I didn't ask him in when I opened my door; didn't even look round — too frightened, not of being turned down, but of seeing once again that anguish in his eyes — as I remained standing with my back to him for a few seconds, waiting: for a footstep, a touch, the sound of his voice. Then I pushed open the door and heard him turn the key in his own lock opposite. *(Look, Dedda, I'm not crying. Your Nanna is being so brave today.)*

"Enjoy your rest."

His casual tone surprised me. I turned round. "You too. Try to sleep. I know you're flaked after last night. After everything. We've been so much on the go all the time — "

"Don't break your head about me."

"Will you come and call me if you — "

"See you." Adding with a small, sudden, lighthearted chuckle: "Sister."

And now I was back in my room again, alone. I undressed and put on my dark red gown. For the first time I dared admit to myself just how exhausted I was. After God knows how long — ten days? a fortnight? — of being on the move, travelling from one place to the other, I suddenly found myself at a standstill. A silence that made my head reel. I had to sit down on the edge of the bed, feeling all resistance in me cave in. It was like standing naked in front of a mirror as I so compulsively used to do (that first evening when I'd set foot in this room . . .) studying my reflection in every detail, inspecting every limb, whatever was part of me, even the most intimate. Only, this time I didn't need a mirror.

— *You must help me look, Grandpa Xhorê. If one has got as*

far as this — where does one go from here? Perhaps you have the answer?

— Tell me about it, Nanna.

I thought of everything that had happened since I had first left Paris. (How gently, how full of love and lust, Paul had awakened me: would he ever do so again if he were to know what had happened in between? And inevitably he would soon know. That was the least I owed him. If he phoned again I would not, like this morning, ignore the telephone or try to smother its sound. He would have to learn to live with that bitter knowledge just as much as I.) The very first turn-off from the road he'd planned for me and which I'd accepted without demur: the impromptu detour to Chartres. Originally with the intention of driving through the Loire valley in homage to the birth of our love; then simply in response to the cathedral itself, luring me to the wholesome darkness behind those smouldering windows. Where I'd discovered what really was at stake in trying to find an answer to Paul's guileless question; and where everything I'd kept at bay for so many years had returned to plague me. The underwater journey through unknown towns, nameless villages, wandering through a lost, enormous land: until at last, recognizing the name of Carcassonne, I'd had to come up for breath in a world more familiar but also more menacing to me. My impetuous efforts to retrieve Brian. (At that stage I'd still thought that Brian held the key to it all!) The slow loosening from my grip of everyhing I'd always thought of as ordered and manageable and mine: the new perspective on what I'd used to regard as too obvious for enquiry.

So many journeys had begun there, on that trip: each new impression, every landscape the point of departure for another. Do you remember the old man of the sea, Grandpa Xhorê, the sordid old creature on the misty beach who tore open his fly for me and with whom I fought so fiercely — what for? to save my "honour"? What honour is left to the two of us, Grandpa Xhorê? And then I drove off with one half of his old flag, leaving him behind in futile rage. Yet, he'd lost but a flag:

what about me? Or are there ways of losing through which something is actually attained? Can what you relinquish open you up to the possibility either of something new or something already forgotten?

Questions, questions, all left unanswered.

The smart hotel in Avignon where I was scared off by the revolting old women who didn't even realize they were teetering on the brink of the grave. Would anything have turned out differently if I'd resigned myself to their presence and acquiesced in whatever had been "destined" for me? If I stayed there instead of driving on to Saint-Remý? At every crossroads on the way: those other options lurking in the shadows around one. In retrospect everything seems so simple and predictable: I drove that way, and then there, and there; here I turned left, there I kept straight on — Yet every single choice excluded innumerable others, changing the entire untravelled course ahead. What would have happened if I'd done this — or that — had gone here — or there? Even this is a simplification. The true question, it seems to me, Grandpa Xhorê, is not what would have happened if I'd made different choices here or there. What matters is: which of those other options was I *conscious* of from one instant to the next? Because like you, Grandpa Xhorê, I carry within me not only those decisions taken but all the unchosen possibilities of myself. They are as much part of me as any choice made by chance at any given moment. To history you, Grandpa Xhorê, is no more than the bit that has been recorded. To those who know me I am only what they apprehend as complete and fulfilled in me. What do they know — even Brian, even Paul, even Mandla — of all that has remained unrealized — the ifs and perhapses and maybes in me — yet which is as much part of me as feet or hands or mouth? In the drawing someone is making of me the world sees but the few lines eventually retained, black and unambiguous: only I know about the countless less visible efforts obliterated and erased, all the failures, hope and despair, frustration, anger, make-believe. (The draughtsman himself is unaware of it: for there is more than one of them.

Whenever one looks away or grows tired or loses interest, another takes over; when they give up I draw myself. Invent myself. Hope myself, think myself. Trying, trying. *Xhorê home go, Cape go, home go.*

And then I had to drive back to Avignon to collect Mandla. That first appearance, when he burst from the small lift, sweeping everything out of his way. The feeling of total alienation with which I woke up in the night, not knowing where I was at all: and the deep moaning sound of his sigh in the dark; and the awareness in myself of the stranger across the landing. (Even now: more of a stranger than ever before.)

Do you remember all the clashes we had, Grandpa Xhorê, that day in Avignon? (More real than anything that happened to us that day: the memory of a sliver of paper pushed through the bars of a cell window and fluttering away on hot currents of air to a distant street without a name. *What are you looking for?*) Until, that evening, turned away from the luxury hotel in the Val d'Enfer, I discovered that it wasn't so much Mandla I'd been fighting against as myself, when I had to restrain him from attacking a stranger because he thought I'd been insulted. Knowing that his presence would not allow me any further escape from what otherwise I might yet have been able to come to terms with. (But that appointment I'd felt approaching all the time: was it behind me now or did it still lie ahead? Could there possibly be anything still awaiting me?)

In Apt there were the black vendors on the market, with their dirty useless wares. And then, in La Motte d'Aigues, we heard that old Monsieur Jaubert had died, so I couldn't keep my appointment with Paul's past. All I discovered in exchange was my own shadow. Had that happened to you too in your foreign land, Grandpa Xhorê? And had it comforted you too, offering you a hint of faith, the knowledge that you still had substance enough to cause a shadow, that you hadn't yet been defeated, that you were still — like any anonymous wretch cutting his initials into the wall of a cell — *there?*

Do you remember the lunatics, the procession of miserable idiots in the streets of Sault, Grandpa Xhorê? The rejected of

382

the earth travelling in little buses to do their sightseeing? While everybody else scuttles out of their way, protecting themselves with furtive signs of the cross against the latest manifestation of the Plague. It's so much easier to pretend that those who threaten you with their deviations from the norm do not exist. The old people of Murs, unaware of the Wall. Or were they just pretending? Or didn't they *want* to know? (What happens to one when you're no longer allowed the safety of your own ignorance?)

And then we set out in search of the Wall ourselves. (Can you imagine, Grandpa Xhorê, that at first we drove right past it without recognizing it?) And found the remains. Only to lose all trace of it in the oak forest. That was where I told him about the night they'd taken me away and given me the choice: the night I'd betrayed Boetie. And then he said: "Come to me."

This morning in the old Roman city he wrote our initials in dark letters on a wall in the sun.

It's a long journey, Grandpa Xhorê, innumerable journeys, I've travelled these five days. And now I'm tired. I don't think I can go on much longer.

I was tired. And I couldn't bear to be alone any more. Impulsively I got up and went to the door, pulling away the bolt, ready to go to him.

But suppose I did? What would I do? Plead with him — to do what? And would he understand? That I wasn't asking him to make love to me, to take possession of my body, but simply to be with me? Of course he would. It wasn't the uncomplicated fear of being misunderstood that restrained me: but perhaps, on the contrary, the much more subtle foreknowledge that he might understand *too well*. And that it would lead to a repetition of what had happened that morning. His wholeness was as precarious as my own; perhaps more so. I couldn't do that to him again. Because I loved him. This certainty, at least, I had, a certainty as deep as a tidal pool in which I could change into a fish.

Allowing the bolt to slide back into its catch, I turned away and went to the cupboard, aimlessly opening and shutting the doors. Then to the window. The imperturbable silence of the autumn day outside. The plane-trees almost totally bare by now. Leaves on the raked gravel. I looked past the garden, far beyond, as far as Mandla had stared the previous day on the Mont Ventoux: all the way to Africa. The land he called Azania, a strangely voluptuous name on his tongue, a beloved more profound and immense than I or any other woman could ever hope to be for him. Jesus, and it was springtime there now.

How limp and sentimental and inadequate to admit that I burst into tears. It wasn't from sadness; and it had nothing to do with myself either. My eyes were simply beginning to leak; I was spilling over the edges of myself. I couldn't help it. Like Gran I began to weep, but for more than just the dead. I was weeping just as much for the living. For Mandla. For his Ntsiki. For Boetie. For Ma. This time I could unconditionally cry for her: a woman for whom nothing had ever gone right and who hadn't the faintest idea of why. I cried for a woman washing and shampooing and tinting and streaking and blow-drying the hair of smart ladies, thinking that could fill an empty life. (*I mean, the man does it with everybody.*) I wept for Brother Arie, the waiter with the pencil-line moustache and the Brylcreem in his hair. For Maggie, who thought she could protect herself from evil by buttoning up to her chin, and by praying or singing in the church choir. I cried for a small coloured girl swimming away from a white beach into the green open sea, preferring to drown rather than be caught; and for a boy watching from a butchery door how his father is thrown out. I wept for those I'd met in London and whom I'd shunned because I hadn't grasped why they'd felt the need to expose their sickness and their bursting boils to the world. Even for those like George, Mandla's companion, who thought nothing of making a living out of treason, because they, too, had no other way of survival. I wept for a generation and a land and a world full of people, all stricken by an invisible Plague.

384

If I were Gran I would never have stopped crying again: for she'd known the exact measure of every person and event, and what I was weeping for had no end. I was simply too tired to stop, I think. At last I dragged myself back to the bed and slumped down on it, too exhausted even to draw the love-blanket over me: simply clutching it in a bundle against my body, like a child. A child with the smell of my whole life. If only I could sleep — Yet I resisted the need. It was important to stay awake, to be conscious of everything, to feel pain; I couldn't afford the effort to exclude or deny any part of it. I had to be prepared — not virginal any more, but at least, oh God, a little bit wiser than before — yet I couldn't explain the object of it: prepared for what, for whom, what bridegroom? What bridegroom would care a fuck about a sobbing, snotty, red-eyed, second-hand *jentoe* like me?

Exhausted, yes. But at the same time, through so much crying, washed very clean inside. I'd never been the weepy type. When it was inevitable it invariably turned out to be wholesome and necessary. I felt drained, but purified. Smooth as a fish. So I didn't lie on the bed for long. There was a strange urge in me to clear up. (A premonition? Apprehension? And yet I swear I couldn't have had any intimation of what was to come: it would have totally numbed me.)

I got up again and rinsed my face in cold running water. Then sat down crosslegged on the bed and began to bring my notes up to date (the previous night I'd skipped the chore). Opening the red covers of Paul's scenario I started paging through it again, stopping from time to time to read a passage or study a marginal comment, although I already knew it practically by heart. On the empty pages facing the typed text I scribbled notes on possible locations from the trips and observations of the past few days: Paul should have no reason to accuse me of carelessness. From time to time I pushed the script aside to look up something in the books and photocopies I'd brought with me. A page from Dostoievsky: I had no idea from which novel it came, his books had always been too thick for me to read; and Paul had simply stapled the page to the other photocopies of Artaud and Kundmann and Chauliac and others: but it stabbed me like a blade in the heart:

He dreamt that the entire world was ravaged by a strange and terrible plague which had passed into Europe from the heart of Asia. All except a few elect were doomed to die. New kinds of germs attacked the bodies of people, but these microscopic creatures were endowed with reason and will. People attacked by them immediately became insane and violent. Yet never had people regarded themselves so wise and unshakeable in their pursuit of truth as these victims, never had they regarded their decisions, their scientific findings, their moral convictions so unassailable. Whole villages, whole towns and nations were infected and went mad. They were in a state of total confusion. Nobody could understand anyone else. Each one of them believed that the truth resided exclusively in himself.

Paul, Paul, I thought: you and your Plague. From that very first day, night (and what would have happened if his blonde filly hadn't interrupted us?): his total involvement in that story. Even I had underestimated it in the beginning, sometimes teasing him about it, or indulging him with, in fact, a kind of maternal amusement. Yet gradually I'd come to understand more about the need it fulfilled in his life, especially as I began to discover more (never very much: it was the one episode from his life about which he'd always remained reticent) about his Hungarian adventure. Those months of isolation in a round stone room in a castle surrounded by snow (skating children singing arias from *Don Giovanni!*), with a never-ending influx of refugees who'd left behind them a horror too vast to express in the broken words at their disposal. His Eve. A single kiss in an attic room amid piles of second-hand clothing. (Could that really be true? Not a single stolen night? Yet I believed him. He had no reason to lie to me. Only, I was jealous even of what had *not* happened!) How could he possibly have come to terms with it in any other way? It was

386

the one thing in his life, I know, that had real meaning for him: all the rest had been evasion, escape, romantic nostalgia or hope. (A single brief cruel conversation between him and Mandla I'd remembered: usually they'd discussed Mandla, not Paul: "It's the one bit of contemporary history I think I can grasp, because I was involved in it." Mandla: "Man, you grew up in the worst tornado of our time: now you trying to tell me you weren't involved in that?!" Paul, with disarming direct-ness: "I was never really 'there', Mandla. In South Africa, if you want to survive, you simply cannot afford to be 'there'." Mandla, like a striking mamba: "You mean if you're white! *I* knew all right. I knew every fucking bleeding instant of my life what was happening to me." What had shaken me most was that, at least up to a point, both had been right.) What better vehicle for that tremendous moment in his life than his story of the Black Death? If only he could find the courage to turn it into a novel, rather than satisy himself with the safer option of a film for which others would eventually take either blame or praise.

"You're just making it more and more difficult for yourself, Paul." (How many times had we had this conversation?) "All this talk about your Great Novel, one day: that's what ado-lescents dream about, it's romantic, it's old-fashioned: you're fifty, dammit. You'd better start *doing* something about it. A novel is not a dream, it's bloody hard work. And you're just too lazy for that."

"Not lazy. I'm frightened, Andrea. If I fail with this — well, then everything will have been in vain. Then it means I haven't been able to make anything worth while out of my life. And what will become of me then?"

"Then you try again."

"It's easy to talk about trying again if you're not yet thirty. After that, everything is measured only in degrees of failure."

"Paul, why can't you believe in yourself any more?"

"I need your help."

"Listen, my love, I can sleep with you, and eat with you, and live with you, but when it comes to believing you're on your own. If you try to shift it on to me you're being unfair to us both."

"Don't you believe in me then?"

I took his face between my hands and kissed him. "Of course I believe in you. Neither of us has ever doubted that. It's your own faith we're worried about."

That, too, we'd thought, would in some way be sorted out by this journey. And now — ? In addition to everything I had to come to terms with, would I also have to learn to live with the knowledge that I'd taken this prop away from him? How endless the circles of water once one has thrown one's stone into it. How marvellous. How awful.

Paul, I think I've lately become acquainted with forms of the Plague that would surprise even you.

Was it my imagination or was there a telephone ringing on the other side of the landing? As soon as it penetrated to me I raised my head to listen more carefully, but by then it had stopped. I could have been mistaken; or it might have been somewhere else in the building. Yet it made me feel nervous. For a while I tried to apply myself to my notes; then, too irritable to continue, I put away the books in a neat pile on the bedside cabinet.

This time the sound was unmistakable: the opening of his bedroom door. My whole body tensed as I waited for it to click shut again. But it didn't. I would have heard it, for one had to use force to pull those doors shut. Were there footsteps in the passage?

I was so tense that I started trembling; I felt dizzy, even a bit nauseous. Perhaps he was standing at my door right now, wondering whether he should knock or not, reluctant to disturb me in case I were asleep.

The thought made me react immediately. I hurried to the door and opened it. But the landing was empty. I went to the balustrade to look down the stairwell, but there was nobody there either.

His door stood ajar.

Perhaps he'd never gone out after all: perhaps he'd changed his mind.

I went across the landing, wondering whether I should knock; then simply went in, my mouth already half opened to say: "I want to be with you."

But Mandla wasn't there. No sign of him in the room. (Nor in the bathroom; the door stood wide open and I could see inside.) His things were still there. The denim shoulder-bag, navy-blue but faded and stained with age and use, the mouth slightly frayed. The contents — the few shirts and underpants, books, a windbreaker — lay spilled on the bed. A pair of sand-shoes on the carpet. That was all. I suddenly thought of that journey with Dedda, long ago, and its sequel with Brian: people we'd passed on the long road between one town and the next, sometimes a family, sometimes just a woman, trekking with a cardboard box or suitcase balanced on the head, God knows where to: and in it, one knew, must have been all their earthly possessions, every single object and bit of clothing. Mandla, undoubtedly, was different; he was a refugee. It wasn't the quantity of his possessions that troubled me, but the ease with which everything could be cleared up. Sitting down on his bed I started picking up his clothes one by one, studying them as if they were of the utmost importance to me. A summary of the man? If so, the result was absolute anonymity. Not even a name tag in the collar of a shirt.

Almost helplessly I tried to convince myself that he would be back in a few minutes. Any moment now. After all, he'd left everything behind. He hadn't even closed the door.

No reason why I shouldn't wait for him here.

My anxiety was subsiding. I lay back on the bed — the spread rumpled where he must have reclined earlier, the dent left by his head still visible on the pillow — trying to fit myself exactly into the outline of his body. I closed my eyes, my head thrown back. Here he'd slept the past few nights. Here he'd lain only minutes ago. It was possible to imagine even a lingering afterwarmth of his limbs. A warmth initially hover-ing on the edge of the perceptible, the merest suggestion, a

389

subtle possibility; but gradually increasing, becoming more certain, undoubtable, overwhelming.

Here he'd lain, here were the signs and traces he'd left. The man with whom I'd fallen in love so entirely without warning, and certainly without wanting to. This utter stranger: even his bed was strange to me; in this room, I'd never set foot before: nothing here belonged to me or acknowledged me: everything was exclusively his.

How much he'd told me about himself; how unbearably little. I tried to recall it all, every imaginable detail. The day in the butchery with his father. Moving to PE, driven by the passion for learning. His aunt's shebeen. The noisy nights. The dirty streets, the open drains, the shithouses, the smoke of early mornings. New Brighton. Soweto. The schoolchildren going on strike; the buildings and buses burning, the smell of tear-gas; the police van. Fort Hare. Vuyizile clearing out. Mandla following him back to PE. Reading, reading right through the nights in the light of the oil lamp. The meetings. The unions. His parents' settlement razed to the ground. The *Boere*. Ntsiki: blood coming from under her cell door. Never another child, not before the sun reddens the new dawn. Spike. In the light of a torch, one night, a name on a tombstone: *Steve Biko*. Lesotho. Mozambique. The mission with George. Paul's flat. (*Mandla is different from anybody else you've met — Hi, sister!*) A meal in the rue du Four: "Sister, you're black. You got my colour. So what you fucking about here?"

Black man, you're on your own.

(One night, that interminable walk home from Kenilworth. *There's no one out there. I'm on my own.* Was that what each of us had recognized in the other?)

Will you run with me in the night?

Jesus, Grandpa Xhorê, what has happened, what's still going to happen?

For God's sake, Grandpa Xhorê: *What is happening?*

The thoughts, predictable to start with, began to merge in unexpected new configurations as if I were staring at them

390

through an uneven pane of glass, seeing their separate shapes running together as in water, changing all the time.

This man whom I loved, who'd pissed our initials on a wall. Who'd pressed me to the ground with the weight of his body and loved me right into the earth.

This stranger whom I didn't know at all: I knew his way of laughing, or of making love; and how he sighed in the night when he was alone; and how he played his *trompie*. What else? My God, there was nothing else. The Stranger. And here I was lying in the space that was his, this anonymous hotel room pervaded by him, his taste, his smell, his presence, his absence, his strangeness. This bed that was his. In which he might have spilled seed that should have been kept for me.

Mandla, Mandla, Mandla.

I didn't know what happened, nor how it came about: only that it was something which had never happened to me in my life before. I was lying there, my eyes closed, surrendered to him in his absence. Did I actually fall asleep? — but how can one sleep with a body so taut that one's muscles are aching? Whatever happened was something I would never have thought possible, not even in the purest physical sense. And if in fact I were asleep, and if it were a dream, then surely the most vivid, the most shatteringly real dream of my life. I lay surrendered to him in his absence: and in that absence he must have taken me: without laying a hand on myself, not even the most tentative touch of a finger, I felt my body becoming more and more tense, until I was trembling all over, abandoned to a man not anywhere near me — but knowing with great conviction that he would be coming back soon, oh very soon, coming, any moment now, finding me here, taking me, coming — and then I felt the sudden rush of blood to my face and the warmth spreading in my belly, and the first shock shuddering through me, like a stone thrown into a bottomless pool, and I came with a violence I'd never experienced or imagined in my life, either with a man or on my own.

For a long time I lay quite motionless, spent, feeling the moisture from my deepest insides oozing slowly out of me.

391

Stunned, ashamed, for what would he do if he were to come back now and find me in that state? (Maggie had surprised me like that a few times in our childhood. *God will wither your hand if you don't watch out. He'll strike you with a bolt from heaven.*

Then it began to subside. The warmth ebbed away, leaving me exhausted, limp, sated. Still incredulous, dazed perhaps by sleep, I shook my head, then pushed myself up on my elbows, wondering whether I should stay there or return to my own room. (Suppose the *patron* came past and found me there — ?)

On the small table in front of the window I noticed a few more of Mandla's possessions. A leather belt with a large brass buckle. Two or three paperbacks. His passport (no doubt false, made in Mozambique). His *trompie*.

For a moment I looked at it, almost lovingly: its sound had become such a part of our relationship. Then a sudden twinge of anxiety caused me to draw my breath in sharply: if Mandla had meant to stay away for some time, to go for a walk, if he hadn't just gone out for a minute or two, surely he would have taken the *trompie* with him? He was never without it.

Now I was frightened. Too frightened to move. For the first time I knew fully and without doubt that Mandla hadn't just gone out somewhere: *this room was empty.* I could feel my heart pounding in the emptiness: in that one room I sensed all the empty rooms of my whole life. A kind of emptiness, I think, only a woman can recognize.

It took an effort to get up, to go back to my own room and take off the red gown, put on my clothes. I didn't allow myself the time to brush my hair. In fact, I even forgot to put on my shoes.

Barefoot I went downstairs.

There were more people than normally at the reception desk. The *patron* with his sad moustache, his suspicious wife, two *femmes de chambre*, and four or five strangers, all men, two of them *gendarmes*.

As I arrived in the lobby their agitated conversation stopped very abruptly and they all turned to look at me. I was conscious of my own footsteps whispering on the cool terra-cotta tiles.

"Here she is," said the *patron*'s wife, a triumphant sound in her voice, as if she'd been waiting for just this moment: woman against woman.

Her husband appeared ill at ease. He half emerged from behind the counter, apologized to the *gendarmes* as he pushed past them, and grinned foolishly in my direction.

"Ah, Mademoiselle. Perhaps you can help us."

Kundmann:

In Ludwigsdorf, where the Plague was raging with the utmost violence, a young peasant girl was infected. As soon as her lover heard of it he went to her in the night and indulged so long in lovemaking that he brought home a plague boil as reward. But this had not happened in sufficient secrecy for the parents of both to remain unaware of it; but although all the parents harshly reprimanded their children for their crime, they could not prevent them from meeting every night, now here, then there. Dr Eggerdes happened to arrive at the home town of the lovers' parents, and they begged his permission for the love of God to summon a priest from Oels to marry their children before they died of their sin, as both were infected by the Plague, yet could not be restrained from meeting every night and indulging in what they had no right to do. A few days earlier the boils had actually burst. The doctor said to the mother: "As your children's boils have already burst, yet leaving them strong enough to go on meeting and making love, they will certainly not die of the disease."

There's no one out there. I'm on my own.

Back in my room. The dusk is deepening inside. Outside, the sun has just gone down.

393

I am alone. Nothing stirs, not even the curtains, not even a fly.

It's been a long afternoon. Hours ago already I thought I was tired! If I was tired then, there is no name for what I'm feeling now. And yet, although my body is exhausted, I feel a strange clarity in my thoughts.

To be present wherever one finds oneself: with the full weight of one's whole history, one's whole self, all one's possibilities. (Did I really know what I was saying, one distant weekend in a beautiful hotel room on the Loire? — *In every moment one lives one's whole life.*)

So this is the appointment I've been expecting all the time: an hour ago in that cool interior; now here, back in what for days has been "my" room. (Never as truly "mine" as the small flat in the rue Bonaparte. And much less mine than the room once shared by Maggie and me in another world, the only one that has ever been fully my own: where we were disturbed at night by the coughing and shuffling of the old people next door; where one could be awakened very suddenly by the noise of Dedda's boisterous homecomings; where, from under the fig-tree in a cramped little backyard one could be startled by the sound of a fish bugle.)

How many different people have others tried to make out of me over the years. There was Gran who believed she could teach me all she knew about knitting or cooking; Ma who tried to train me as a hairdresser. Had Boetie been allowed to have his way he'd have turned me into a revolutionary; Brian wanted to make of me a rebellious exile fighting for the "cause". For Frank I was a protégé, sometimes a model. One of his successors used me as a photographer's assistant; my boss in the office used me as a secretary by day, a mistress at night. For Serge I was a script-girl. For Paul — ? Research assistant, companion, support, beloved whore; eventually to be his wife. Drawn in, every time, into someone else's existence. A chameleon, sophisticated by years of unbridled reading, guided by Brian and his successors, by Paul; devouring their worlds (or devoured by them?); a smooth and eloquent talker — films, fashions, philosophy — who never puts her partners to shame: but still the chameleon, adapting to survive. The nearest I ever came to being someone in my own right, was with Dedda. His virgin daughter, oh undoubtedly. But he knew who I was, who I could become, should like to be. *Nanna*.

I, Andrea Malgas. For that is what remains at last, when one is left as utterly alone as I am now. Not virginal, not by a long shot, thank God. Not whole or complete or neatly rounded off. Just I.

(Thanks to Mandla? The irony does not escape me. The difference is that he never tried to claim me as his own. On the contrary. He knew how to deliver me to myself. *Running in the night*.)

It was so easy to take the decision when he was beside me: I'll go with you wherever you want to take me, even if it means roaming about in a wilderness, or walking back into the fire of hell. There was something exquisitely simple about it, a logic, a complete assurance of this-and-nothing-else. Now it is much more complicated. Not obscure or confused — in fact, a painful luminosity — but inexpressibly more complicated.

All the other, innumerable journeys leading to this single point.

Through the land with Dedda, in the borrowed old jalopy. His mouth-organ moaning in the dark. The sound of his voice when he erupted into the house of a night, Sindbad the Sailor with his blanket loaded with presents. His smell. His thin arms around me, the stubbly feeling of his skin against my cheek.

The smell of hair conditioner, of shampoo, the burnt pungency of the irons. A Wednesday afternoon with Mr Wiese. *I'll have to show you the ropes.* The endless road home. Ma's face. Maggie reading from the Bible. *Fuck you and your Bible, you're just being jealous!* Johnny who cannot understand why. His only bitter reaction, undoubtedly: *Women!*

The day Maggie telephoned with the news of the wave that had washed Dedda from the deck. The hollow cliff at the Steenbras Mouth. The bright brown water, just like Coke. *The man is white.*

395

Boetie is taken away. *You're going to report regularly to us about everything Brian Everton says and does and reads. Then we'll let your brother go. Otherwise* — His face through the pane of wired glass. Now he's off to the Island.

The night they came for us. The sheets, everything. The stupid girl vomiting all over the carpet.

At a time like that one's feet are insecure: it's like having birdlime on one's soles, one gets stuck to the tarmac of the runway, terrified of the narrow steps leading up to the plane. When we land at the other end, there's the stunning transition to the rhythm of a train speeding through a landscape both alien and disturbingly familiar; he's sitting next to me, exhausted, sleeping with his head on my shoulder, his mouth half open, a thin line of spittle down to his chin. When the train stops, it's Avignon, where we are turned away from the hotel. (Because we're not married. Not, as I first thought, because of my colour. In the Val d'Enfer all the tables are taken, *je m'excuse, Monsieur-dame.*)

A miserable little circus company at Montbrun. Drenched animals in stinking cages. The sound of the old sick lion in the night.

London, a grey stain on the earth, dull smudges of colour blurring in the rain. People, quarrels, bouts of desperate passion. Days of helpless sobbing in Hyde Park. Frank's face as he opens the door in the grey building on the rue Mouffetard. *I hope you can help me. Only, I want to make one thing very clear before I come in: I'm not going to sleep with you.*

Paul. To whom I'd been unfaithful years before anything as definite as an affair had started between us. Could either he or I, no matter how we loved one another, ever have foreseen a different end? We needed each other; we made ourselves available to each other. And that was good. There was a deep compassion in it. We cared for each other. But looking back as I do now — ? The delicate traces of birds in the snow of the Luxembourg Gardens. To be remembered; but impossible to retain.

Mandla.

It isn't easy to think his name. Everything is still too exposed, too raw, too immediate. Only much later will I be able to face or digest it. Not that I shall ever be able to feel detached; there will always be something infinitely precarious in the thought. Beautiful and dangerous: that's what he was. Those deep groaning sighs as he walked about in the night like a dark predator. The whispering voice of the earth itself in his music.

He often spoke about hate. He must have known as well as I that it was no more than a boy's clumsy attempts to cover up. He'd never been destined for hate: love was his natural state. From the beginning. Even when he thought he was hating it was but the bitter flipside of his love. Hate gets buried with one, and that's the end of it. But love is indestructible, all the more so if it is a man's love of the earth, his Azania, his Africa, more immense and eternal than he or I or we. He was hurt too deeply, he'd suffered too much, he'd seen others suffer too much, ever to risk having a child. In a few days his own last seed will be washed from me by my futile blood. But the love can never be destroyed.

The Gideonite Bible beside my bed (how many years since I last paged through a Bible? — it's like my heathen sinning Dedda rounding up all his pagan friends in church!). I knew exactly what I was looking for. Ecclesiastes:

> To every thing there is a season, and a time to every purpose under the heaven:
>   A time to be born, and a time to die; a time to plant, and a time to pluck up that which is planted;
>   A time to kill, and a time to heal; a time to break down, and a time to build up;
>   A time to weep, and a time to laugh; a time to mourn, and a time to dance;
>   A time to cast away stones, and a time to gather stones together; a time to embrace, and a time to refrain from embracing;

A time to get, and a time to lose; a time to keep, and a time to cast away;

A time to rend, and a time to sew; a time to keep silence, and a time to speak;

A time to love, and a time to hate, a time of war, and a time of peace.

Over and over, for the words to burn into me; to burn away the last bits of redundancy. For this was my time. My hour had come.

Only a few pages further in the same book — perhaps this was the last certainty I still required? — : *To him that is joined to all the living there is hope.*

Behind me: a life in flames, like a wheatfield into which two careless happy children have set free a burning cicada. The only difference is this: that I have to turn back into the flames myself.

I know what I have to do now. It needn't take long either. To clear up what I still have left, and then to pack. For Paul's sake I must bring my notes up to date, so that I can leave them behind for him. That is the least he deserves, however inadequate an explanation it may be. This will not be easy; I know my hand will be trembling on the paper.

The notebook I'll leave with the *patron*; and a letter.

Then I must settle the account: hopefully Paul will grant me these last expenses on the credit card of the film company. I'll make sure he gets refunded later; somehow. And then I must be off. Stupid of me, probably, as it's already dark. But I needn't go far tonight. Perhaps to Eygalières — I think I can at last assume responsibility to face that memory — and very early in the morning I can go on from there. My time here is past. And the evening and the morning were the fifth day.

And now the letter. I hope he'll understand. (*Someone must!*) We all seem to send off our helpless hopeful letters like this,

398

thrust through the bars of our cell windows, out into a faraway street. Who knows — ?

— into a faraway street. I'm not sure that others will ever understand my doing what I'm doing now. I *must*, and I'm *going* to. I hope you won't see it as some kind of romantic self-sacrifice: I'm not young enough for that any more. Rather think of it, if it doesn't sound too precious, as a way of taking up a responsibility I've long tried to deny. Perhaps in this way one can reach out to a precarious peace. Though I don't think it's just for the sake of peace that I'm choosing it.

Is there anything more difficult, more unnatural, that can be asked of any human being: to choose freely, in full consciousness, in the scorching knowledge of exactly what is at stake, to give up what you've got, including your own safety, to turn your back on comfort, and to choose hell because it's yours? Will you understand this choice? And will that free you, at last, finally to write what you've been wanting to write for so long, shaking off the fear that has paralysed you?

You've left the end of your story open. I know you hoped I would offer you a solution. But each person can only live his own story, Paul. Each has to find his own conclusion. Your people caught in the Plague: will they live on in their Schloss Judenau — whether in orgies and merriment or in a wild madness that rages on until not one of them is left — or will they go back to the world, no matter how empty and dangerous it has become, how uncertain and unpredictable, simply because they cannot survive without it? Only you can decide, Paul.

What a beautiful, marvellous world it is one sees underwater if you dive in with goggles and snorkel, a dream more fantastic than anything you can imagine. The only sound is that of one's own breathing (*I'm alive!*); apart from that it is silent, everything is smooth, liquid, gliding, incredibly lovely. But sooner or later one has to go back to firm earth, that earth where one belongs. We don't have gills, but a nose. Not a smooth oval whole of head and body, streamlined like a penis: but five limbs. We must go back. And sooner or later, if one dares to face the agony of seeing clearly, one knows — painfully, but very surely — that one *wants* to go back.

This is what I've come to understand: crookedly, tentatively, crudely, but without a doubt. But what about you, Paul? I wish I could have sat down with you somewhere — on a café terrace, or on the heights of Les Baux far above the Val d'Enfer, or in the churchyard of the little village of your clan, La Motte d'Aigues; perhaps in Murs, or even in Avignon, wherever it might suit you — and talk it over at length. But I know that in the end this would only complicate things for us, make it more painful. I'm not avoiding you to hurt you, that much I know you'll understand. Don't think for a single moment that I underestimate what we had together. I know how much I'll miss it in the darkness ahead; how often I'll blame myself for having done a stupid, senseless thing. But I must. For both our sakes it must be a very clean cut. I'm not just "disappearing" from your world. I want you to think of it as a positive and decisive, lucid act of going away, no matter if it hurts. Even my memories I shall jealously withdraw from you. This is what I so urgently want you to understand.

That's why I'm asking these questions, Paul: not for my sake, but for yours.

Do you understand, do you really understand, *why* I can see so clearly today? *Why* I've recognized this emptiness and this light the moment it occurred?

Do you know where I get this knowledge from — less than knowledge? or more? this passionate faith, this deep awareness in the guts — of having arrived somewhere: not at a destination, but at a moment of choice, of decision, call it anything you wish, perhaps truth; perhaps the threshold of myself?

The very first night we met you asked me what I was running away from: do you know the answer now, the way I know it? and do you realize why I no longer *want* to run away? Can you see that what I've tried to escape from is the very thing I've always been heading for?

Do you know this now, Paul, as fatally as I do?

And do you know, at last, why I'm writing at the end of this letter: not *Andrea,* but,

With love,
Nanna?

PART TWO

And now
we must from the beginning justify the fact that we are
still living

Yannis Ritsos

No, Andrea, I don't understand. I still don't; or not yet. But I'll try. That much, at least, I owe you.

I'd imagined my journey to the South in such a completely different way. Whenever I had a chance, in Paris at first, then at the conference in Strasbourg, and back again in the boulevard Malesherbes (as well as a few times, thanks to the spare key you'd given me, in your own little flat in the rue Bonaparte, high above the courtyard, resounding with pigeons and sparrows nesting in the ivy on the high walls), I tried to picture our meeting. Perhaps in the Auberge in Eygalières. It would satisfy my writer's instinct for a conclusion, the security of the circle. For that is where I'd first asked you. Or would it be in Avignon, the City of the Plague, perhaps on the square in front of the Palais des Papes? Less dramatically, on our sun-drenched terrace — even though the sun would be more spare and transparent now — of the Mas des Herbes Blanches at Joucas? Or at the monument for the dead of La Motte d'Aigues where my Huguenot ancesters had come from? Or quite simply in your hotel room in Saint-Rémy? — but that was difficult to imagine, as I didn't know the hotel; and it was quite disturbing, an obstacle whenever I thought about you, not to be able to visualize your surroundings. Had that always been a lacuna in my experience of you? However intimately I'd come to know you in Paris — that first night in Frank's flat, behind the green velvet seat from a train of the Bel Époque, as if right from the beginning we'd been preparing for a journey; the terrace of the Mahieu or one of the cafés on a boulevard near the Opéra; a wide flight of stairs in the

404

Luxembourg Gardens, surrounded by statues and pigeons and playing children; the throng in the Louvre of a Sunday; or in a stuffy film studio at an editing table, the air dark with smoke — or elsewhere in Europe on any of our many expeditions (that unforgettable weekend on the Loire; Provence in summer), I'd always, inescapably, known that your "own" environment was different, and distant. Even when I recalled the Cape, a memory sometimes so acute that I had to catch my breath, I couldn't place you in it. So there'd always been a secret territory in you I'd never reached — and there were moments when you seemed to derive a curious pleasure from seeing me grope for it in vain. Which would explain that ferocious independence (all the more deceptive because you can offer yourself so unreservedly to the man you love; an impression of complete devotion) which no man before me had been able to tame; and now I must also admit failure. Was that the reason for my interminable interrogations about myself, my urge to know more and more about you, trying perhaps to gain a more comprehensive grasp on you? Never suspecting of course that this collection of "facts" (how much of it true, how much invention?) would be all I'd be left with in the end.

If I pronounce your name, even soundlessly, "Andrea" (whatever other names you may choose to call yourself, that is what you are for me), what does it conjure up? Your bitter-almond girl's body (your deepest taste still on the tip of my tongue). Your fierce lean beauty: the lithe, smooth hardness of your limbs, a tough shoot, wild-olive, supple enough to bend without breaking or splintering. Your narrow face with the unexpected fullness of your mouth, the dark enormous eyes, slightly slanting; your long-legged stride, defiant, free. Animal vigour. That air of cool detachment, yet with an intimation of something smouldering inside: an aggressive self-reliance inspired by your own assurance, both of the strength of your mind and the resilience of your body.

All of this I'd expected to find on my return to you: you would await me with all the violent simplicity of your *Yes*. Not

405

for a moment had I doubted it, not even after our last stilted telephone conversation (although, in retrospect, surely those terrible opening words should have warned me: *Who am I speaking to?*); not even when you didn't reply that last morning.

The telegram was cryptic to the point of being noncommittal.

Mandla dead. Am leaving. Ask for message at hotel. Love—Andrea.

I telephoned immediately, of course, but you'd already left. The evening before, the hotel manager said. When I mentioned my name he recognized it. "Monsieur Jaubert?"

"Joubert."

"That's what I mean. Well, she left a parcel for you. Said you'd come to collect it yourself."

"I will. Please keep it for me until I arrive."

"Where are you phoning from ?"

"Paris."

"Good God. But — "

"I'll be there this afternoon."

Just over eight hours by autoroute, stopping only when it couldn't be avoided.

I had no idea of what to expect. Perhaps I should have pressed the *patron* for more particulars: he sounded eager to talk. But, unreasonably perhaps, I felt it should wait until I arrived in Saint-Rémy. Only after I'd left Paris did I discover how agonizing it was to know nothing at all, apart from those laconic words: *Mandla dead. Am leaving.*

Leaving for what destination?

Might we, I wondered in alarm, be travelling past each other on the way, in opposite directions?

And: dead? One doesn't just die like that. Mandla was young enough to be my son.

There was nothing I could do about it. I had to suppress the thoughts as much as I could, concentrating only on the road before me, unaware even of the landscape. Nothing but that black autoroute, interrupted from time to time by a *péage* or a complex of garages, restaurants, shops, smelling of old cigarettes and stale beer, littered with cigarette stubs and cans and papers; sticky stains on tables and window-sills; dirty toilets.

Perhaps, I thought in a surge of vicious helplessness, people only love one another so they can have someone close enough to wound.

At Cavaillon I turned off the autoroute. Twenty minutes later I was in Saint-Rémy, my head throbbing, my neck stiff, dazed from driving. Another fifteen minutes to find the hotel, as I'd forgotten to ask for instructions on the telephone. The sound of the tyres on the gravel grated my ears as I turned into the front garden to the parking bays. The sun was down already. At the swimming-pool — dark blue, a spread of fallen leaves on the surface — a lamp was burning on a tall post. Another above the entrance in the corner of the L-shaped stone building.

"Monsieur Joubert!" The man with the moustache seemed both elated and relieved to hear my name. "Have you really come down all the way from Paris?" He raised both arms above his head. "What a mess. Who would have expected something like this to happen? But of course I told my wife the very first time I saw them — " (he gave a loud shout over his shoulder in the direction of a glass door with lace curtains, through which one could see the flickering of a TV screen) "— Lisette, come here, the gentleman from Paris has arrived, the one who's come about the dead man — I told her one couldn't trust these people, you know. I mean, I live in peace with everybody, Monsieur, I bear nobody any grudges, I'm against apartheid and that sort of thing, but I told her — Lisette, where are you? — one can't be too careful these days. I must say, the young lady looked very decent — "

"It was clear at first sight that she couldn't be trusted," said his wife, coming through the glass door, as if she'd been eavesdropping, waiting for the most propitious moment to make her entrance. "I know her type. Very smart and all that, but no man is safe near her."

"Now come on, Lisette, the young lady obviously was —

407

how shall I put it? — well-bred and proper. Actually, she was extremely attractive."

"If that's your idea of beauty! Just as well tastes differ." The woman, pale, with dark rings under her eyes, sniffed derisively. "But of course you couldn't keep your eyes off her. And what with those tight jeans — "

"The man was something else," her husband interrupted hastily. "We don't discriminate against clients, Monsieur. And it was quite late in the evening when Mademoiselle brought him in, so one couldn't possibly — But I always say — now isn't that true, Lisette? — if a black man wears his hair like this — " (he gestured) " — then you can expect problems. The whole trouble started when De Gaulle moved out of Algeria. If he'd listened to Salan the world would have been a better place today. I grant every person his place in the sun. But his sun is over there, in Africa. Mine is here. I just knew there was going to be trouble, but so as not to affront the lady — "

"Just as well the man stayed here," said his wife bitingly. "At least he kept her occupied. Otherwise there would have been no end to room service, day and night."

"Monsieur," I said when at last I could get a word in. "The man was a very close friend of mine. I'd be most grateful — "

"A friend of yours?" He made a deft adjustment in his attitude. "Mark my words: I didn't say anything against him. It's just that I didn't know what to expect. One can never be too careful. But I can certainly say this for him: he never gave us any trouble. They were very well-behaved in all their comings and goings. They were always together. Were" — he hesitated — "were they, you know, engaged or something?"

"Mademoiselle Malgas is my fiancée."

"*Oh là!*" said the woman before she could check herself. "Gaston, now just shut up before something is said that should better be left unsaid."

"I didn't say a word, did I?" he snapped. Leaning over the counter he put his hand on my arm in a comradely gesture. "You know what women are like, Monsieur, one can't open one's mouth — " He stood up again. "No, I was just asking, no offence. You see, when I asked her something about her friend the first morning she came down for breakfast, she gave me a pretty sharp answer. Didn't want to know anything about him. But afterwards" — he winked — "oh well, they say it's a matter of chemistry. In my time it had more to do with biology."

"Gaston, for God's sake, keep out of it. Once you get drawn into a sordid business like this — Just think of it, the police and everything — " She turned to me, but it was hard to say whether it was in supplication or reproach: "It's a decent hotel we have here, Monsieur. Twenty years we saved up for it. We've only been in the business for two years now. As it is, we're just beginning to find our feet. And it isn't easy, I can tell you, given the economic situation in the country. So we really can't afford to have any trouble."

"It's not your fault at all, Madame," I said.

"That's what I keep telling my husband."

"All I want to know from you is what happened. I received a telegram from Mademoiselle Malgas and that's all I know about it. She didn't give any particulars."

"Yes, I really became suspicious when she left in such a hurry," said the *patronne*. "I mean, why couldn't she have stayed till this morning? But she'd barely come back from the morgue and the *gendarmerie* when she asked for her account. Said she had to leave. Not a word about why or where. She obviously had something to hide."

"Now what could she have to hide, Lisette?" her husband protested, suddenly indignant. "She was in a state of shock, poor girl."

"You'll always side with another woman against me. Why don't you just give Monsieur the parcel she left with us? I still think we ought to have given it to the police straight away."

"Thanks for keeping it here," I said eagerly. "May I please have it?"

It was a clumsy parcel of rather indefinite shape, wrapped in a newspaper and tied with a dark red cord.

(You in your loose gown, Andrea. Moving through your flat in the old grey building with its smell of cats and the food of many years: the cord untied, the flaps swinging open as you turn: the smoothness of a thigh, the tender, paler shadow of a breast. Were you conscious of how nonchalantly, how utterly and easily you ruled over that small space?)

"If it's possible I'd like to stay over for the night. Do you have a room for me?"

I was hurried now, breathless, anxious to escape from their possessive conversation; feeling the weight of the long journey pressing me down.

She nudged her husband with an elbow, but I wasn't sure whether it was meant to warn or encourage him.

"Of course," said the *patron*. "We have lots of space. This time of the year, you know — "

"Here's a *fiche*," the woman said quickly, slipping the small form on the desk in front of me. "I trust you brought your passport?"

"I have an identity card."

"I see. Well, in that case — " She looked up to her husband for advice, then took her own decision: "Fill it in, all the same. One never knows. After what's happened — "

"I still don't know what happened," I said bluntly, mechanically filling in the required details.

"Neither do we. At least not everything." A Gallic shrug. "Will one ever know — ?"

"How did he die?" I asked, almost desperate.

"Why don't you go round to the *gendarmerie* in the morning?" said the *patron*, evidently pleased with the idea. "They can fill you in with everything. I mean: we're just laymen — "

"We're all laymen when it comes to death, Monsieur," I said, more sharply than I meant to.

"That's so true. A very profound thought." He nodded several times, his lower lip thrust forward expressively. Then he raised both palms again. "But sometimes one feels more at a loss than at others."

410

"You spoke about the morgue," I insisted. "Is it somewhere in Saint-Rémy?"

"No, no, in Tarascon. To think of it, such a healthy man. You should have seen him" — he bent his arms in the posture of a body-builder, then dropped them again — "but of course, you knew him well. Oh dear. Poor chap."

"An accident?"

"Now, what some call an accident — " He moved his head to and fro.

"How can we be sure?" asked the woman, as if it was my fault that they were so much in the dark. "It was all so unexpected. When the *gendarmes* came in here — I got such a shock, I thought it was bad news."

"Wasn't it?"

"I mean in connection with my family. One always expects the worst, doesn't one?"

"My wife's father died last April, Monsieur," the *patron* offered by way of explanation. "It was a terrible blow to her."

"What did the police tell you about my friend?"

"Your friend — ? Oh, of course. Monsieur — oh dear, you must forgive me. I won't even try to pronounce his name. These Africans — "

"Mqayisa. It's not such a difficult name."

"Yes, but it's — Oh well, each to his own taste, eh?"

"A car accident?"

"I'd rather not say anything about that, Monsieur. It seems there was a car. From behind, I gathered. But that's just about all we know. According to the police — "

"Watch out, Gaston. Before you know where you are you can be in trouble. Leave it to Monsieur to go to the *gendarmerie* himself. Then our hands stay clean."

"All right, all right," he sighed. "But you know how careless these people can be — you'd say the whole road belongs to them. Don't care a damn about others. And when something happens the poor driver gets all the blame — "

More than that, I realized, I wouldn't easily prise from them. As quickly as possible I completed the formalities, refused his help in carrying my overnight bag, and went upstairs alone — following their instructions — to unlock room 6. On the threshold I stopped, suddenly apprehensive: I'd forgotten to ask whether this had been Mandla's room, or even yours. But reluctant to face another barrage of useless comments I decided against going downstairs again and went inside, closing the door behind me. On the bed I eagerly untied the small bundle. If I'd expected something special — a revelation, an explanation, something intimate — I was disappointed. There was little besides the pile of books and papers I'd sent with you, wrapped in a tattered piece of tricolour (what black humour could have prompted it?)

Looking more carefully through the books I found the green *cahier*, the type you always used; the notes of your journey. Some of the pages were written out neatly, as if you'd taken your time to formulate your thoughts. Most of the jottings however, were simply scribbled down, almost illegibly at times, telegram style, not very revealing at first sight. But there was a letter too, written on pages torn from the back of the notebook and bearing my name; five sheets in your hurried handwriting. I read through it several times, for at first it didn't seem very illuminating — except that it finally cleared up some of my most immediate questions about Mandla.

— and the more I think about it the more certain I am that he must have known about it. Not just a vague premonition but a very definite expectation. He may not have known how or when, only that it was coming. A kind of heaviness in him, a gloom. He never discussed it with me although we did get very close these last few days. I ascribed it to his shock because of what had happened with George in Paris, the story you told me on the phone and which made me so mad.

Yesterday we drove through the mountains between Carpentras and Joucas. The one place you've always wanted to go to and which for some stupid reason we never actually visited together. The Wall of the Plague. A kind of conse-

412

cration of your film. (We worked damn hard too, you see!) But I don't want to hide anything from you. You've got to know: we made love. I found a final answer to your question, and please forgive me, Paul, but it can't be Yes. With Mandla I discovered for the first time that I'd been trying to live a lie for too long. Even if it will be painful for you, you must grant me this frankness. Because I love you I cannot leave you with any illusions. What I had with him was new and necessary. His furious dark body. A lifetime in a couple of days.

Just as we were ready to go to bed in the evening the phone in his room rang. Some stranger wanting to know whether he was still "enjoying his stay", something like that. So you see, they must have been on his tracks all along. I suspect they phoned him other times too, only he didn't tell me about it. It upset him so much that he didn't spend the night with me (if that will console you, my dear, possessive, jealous Paul!)

Today we felt exhausted. We came back for a nap after lunch, he in his room, I in mine. I heard his telephone ring again. Just after that he went out. I presume they arranged to meet him somewhere, but how can I be sure? He left his door open; he even left his *trompie* behind, so it was obvious he meant to be back in a few minutes.

Then he was knocked down by a car. Killed instantly, the *gendarmes* told me at the morgue when I got there. I had to identify the body. They found his room key with him, which is why they came to the hotel so quickly. It was on the road to Cavaillon, about a kilometre out of town. The car hit him from right in front, which proves my suspicion. It was near a stall beside the road, perhaps you'll still remember, where they sell copperware and stuff. A hundred yards or so before the Avia garage. Apparently there were no eye-witnesses. When people heard the crash and went to have a look, it was all over. The car had raced away. One of the people from the garage said he thought it was a dark blue Peugeot.

413

I cannot cry about it, Paul. I have no tears left in me. It's like a terrible freedom that's suddenly opened in front of me. Like that endless space surrounding one on top of the Mont Ventoux.

It's no use postponing or hesitating any more. My mind is made up: perhaps it happened long before I properly realized it; maybe even that very first night you introduced him to me in your flat. How were we to know? — it was just as impossible as it had been for us to predict our future that first night at Frank's party. One lives, it seems to me, like Gran's knitting, from one stitch to the next, and only after a long time you realize it's a jersey. Now it's time for me to clear up. When one has postponed for so long to accept what is really self-evident, there is no point in waiting any longer. What I have to do now —

You've always been so thorough in cleaning up. Even when we came in late, long after midnight, tired or tipsy, eager to get to bed, you wouldn't be satisfied unless everything was tidied first, whether in your flat or mine. "Gran's influence," you would say, remember? " 'What if the Lord comes in the night and finds your house in a state?' " However playfully you said it I knew you meant it seriously too. Even in my flat, where you knew my Spanish char would come in early the next day (doughty old Pilar, strong as a mule, whose hands could tackle anything), you couldn't be talked out of it. "I clear up my own mess. No one else will do it after me."

Which was why it was so disconcerting to me to find myself alone in your flat sometimes, when you came in late or when I prepared a meal for us: nowhere the smallest sign of my predecessors in your life. (Why not admit it now? — I *did* hunt for their traces; I'm a pryer, I'm a writer, I leave nothing untouched.) With other women there's always something: a box or a drawer filled with letters; old theatre programmes, birthday cards, gift wrapping, a book with a special inscription, a man's jersey, a button from a jacket or a shirt, an empty

414

cigarette packet, a tube of shaving cream, photographs. In your place, nothing. As if you'd had no previous existence. That's why I could never give up nagging: tell me, tell me, tell me. (Thank God I did!) I could never quite fathom or explain it. Had you simply shut off your early life? Or were you embarrassed, or frightened, or angry to be reminded of it? I know Frank gave you a few of his paintings while you were with him, you were particularly pleased with one portrait; and there was a nude I was terribly jealous of. But what's become of them? In your Serge period your walls were covered with film posters or stills. During the year or so when you were a secretary your room overflowed with match boxes from luxury hotels, restaurants, cafés. Gone, all of it. A virginal beginning every time. Have you at last, my darling, come to terms with the fact that it isn't possible?

I remained sitting on the bed with your letter in my hands, overcome by grief and fatigue. I was hungry too. Perhaps I would be able to think more clearly, methodically, once I'd satisfied the more mundane needs of the body.

It was pure release to stand under the shower and wash the day from me; to put on fresh clothes and go out in search of a restaurant. I took my room key with me, hoping that would leave my few possessions — yours — more secure. As I went through the front porch the glass door to the living-room was opened and I saw the *patron* appearing on the threshold, a checkered dressing-gown over his shirt and trousers. But before he could drag me into conversation again I hurried out.

Somewhat to my own surprise I spent more than two hours over dinner in the Castelet des Alpilles: I'd meant to return to my room as soon as possible; but as on many previous occasions, with you, the ambiance was so relaxing, aided by just more than a bottle of Trévallon, that I tried to draw it out, reluctant to go back to that lugubrious hotel. I was frightened too. So much had been stirred up by the first skimmings of your letter. In silence I toasted Mandla with one glass after the other. (Remember what you told me about your father's funeral? My toasts to Mandla were much more sober and

415

restrained, and of course there was no one else to share them with; but a strange feeling of peace began to ease the shock and the hurt in me, like relaxing in a warm bath.) Above all, it kept me from thinking.

Outside, when at last I reached my car again, there was an aggressive white moon in the pitch-black sky. The stars pierced the outlines of their constellations in clear, shameless dots, as on a winter's night. (A sudden inexplicable longing for the Southern Cross! And I remembered something about Mandla, late one night when the two of us had driven back from a meal with friends outside Paris: he'd been whiling away the time by playfully asking me riddles. Most of them I'd forgotten. But there'd been this one: "Guess what? — my lost cattle, I cannot find them because they're grazing in a far country." "What is it?" "What d'you think? — it's the stars, man.")

I was back in the dull light of my hotel room, with the books and papers, the senseless piece of flag, the dark red belt like an umbilical cord over the edge of the bed. I was tired, but I knew it would be useless even to try to sleep. Deep into the night I lay reading your patchy, sketchy journal. A single reading didn't take long — no more than fifty or sixty written pages, with lots of open spaces in between. But I reread it all, many times, trying to grasp, through your staccato phrases, something of what had happened to you while you'd been away. Surely there should be clues. Oh and there were. But how to interpret them! Those words scribbled down day by day, tentative, searching, sometimes confident about a day gone by, but always hesitant about the morrow. Words not yet quite sure which way they were heading: innocent words, nibbling away very slowly at the fruit of knowledge.

Andrea, you: with your celebration of passion, any passion, provided it was unreasonable, violent, overwhelming: as long as it could keep you in touch with whatever you conceive of as "life". Or am I patronizing you now? Perhaps I'm simply trying to exorcize the hopelessness of all my efforts to understand you sufficiently, to do justice to you. Does one inevitably create to one's own image the person one loves? But then

416

love is not more than another form of imperialism. And that would be unworthy of you. In your final notes I sensed something different which both frightened me (because it excluded me so resolutely) and left me with a feeling of awe. Yet I had no certainty, not really, not yet.

Also, one cannot grasp everything at a first reading — not even at the second, or third. And your handwriting, to say the least, leaves much to be desired, especially when you are sleepy, or frustrated, or in a hurry. So it was very deep in the night before I noticed the reference to Eygalières. And immediately I recalled the *mas* we'd gone to see, which the little old lady at the pottery shop had wanted to rent to us, thinking we were newly-weds (and not wanting to disillusion her, remember, we didn't let on); and I thought of the night we'd spent in the Auberge, when in an impetuous moment I'd asked you to marry me. Why not? It had seemed such a logical thing to do. And yet I'd felt startled as soon as I'd asked you. I didn't want you to know about my apprehension, you were in the grip of a passion building and building to the moment of explosion, and the joy kindled by my question was part of it. But I stayed awake for hours afterwards, wondering whether that really was what I wanted. Could I possibly go through with a thing like that? Looking down on your sleeping face — through green foliage the light from outside fell into our room, I could see you very clearly — I felt not only uncertainty, but anguish, mortal terror. What would I do if you really said yes?!

Of course something deep in me profoundly desired it. A need, perhaps, to be forced for once to accept a foregone conclusion; to be tied irrevocably to a decision taken: to wake up one morning knowing it was a fact, no longer illusion: this was how it was, and there was no way of avoiding it — Would that also be a way of forcing myself to get down to work? I'd never, until you'd stated it so bluntly, realized to what extent I'd been shying away from the novel, however urgently I also wanted to write it too. There was simply too much at stake for me, a middle-aged writer with a reputation greater than my achievement. I'd become scared at the mere thought of failure;

so it was much safer to content myself by dreaming about possibilities. The appearance of faith. A parody of hope. Counterfeits of love. *Verba, non res.* In my case even the *verba* had become dubious. All these years writing had lain dormant in me like a plague ready to break out in black stains on white paper. Fear of death. Fear of loneliness. Films and women: all of them substitutes. Then you, changing for the first time my fear of dying into a rage to live. You urged me on. You refused to leave me alone. It made me all the more afraid. To fail in your eyes would be infinitely worse than any ordinary mess I could make. Because you were beginning to become dependent on me too: I know how much you yourself were frightened of, and what you needed from me. Does everything really, ironically, turn out for the better after all — ?

All right, then: Eygalières. Only after I'd deciphered the name did it strike me that you might have gone there from Saint-Rémy. It made sense. It wasn't far, and it had been dark by the time you'd left. I was already on my feet, ready to get dressed and drive off immediately, when I discovered it was only three in the morning.

At least I'd now begun to find some direction again, instead of the darkness and confusion I'd first felt. Impatiently I waited for the day to break; falling asleep from exhaustion and only waking up, much to my annoyance, past eight. Irritable, I submitted to the *patron*'s ministrations at breakfast; thank God, he was less talkative than the previous evening. At last I was ready to leave. But I drove too fast and missed the first turn-off — such a small road branching off to the right, the signpost half obscured by grass — and because of traffic both from behind and ahead I couldn't just brake and reverse. Driving on slowly, I saw the second turn-off well in time. On the farms beside the road the people had already begun working in their plastic tunnels for winter vegetables.

My instinct had been correct; but I was too late. You had indeed slept there the night before, said the friendly *patronne*, but you'd left very early in the morning.

418

"Did she say where to?"

She pulled an eloquent face as if to say: *Maybe, maybe not: it's a secret between us ladies*. Then changed her mind, when I was already turning away to leave, and said: "She mentioned something about 'going home'. I didn't ask her where it was. But I had the impression she was going on a very long journey."

Exactly as I'd expected. And yet it was a shock to hear it confirmed.

On the way back to Saint-Rémy I drove very slowly, abandoning myself to my thoughts. *In the end they all go back. Only I stay behind. Why — ?*

I'd already reached the outskirts of the town before I realized the flaw in my argument. It wasn't I who was reacting unnaturally by staying behind. It was you. Just like Eva, so many years before. I think you knew I would never be able to understand what had driven her to what she'd done; which was why I'd never told you the whole story. Now I wish I had.

Eva in that throng of refugees. Subdued, her large dark eyes — appearing so much larger than they were because of her blonde hair — always obscured by an expressionless shadow. Often wholly detached, absent, as if walking in her sleep. With those large dark eyes, wide open, she stared into the void, not appearing to notice us, seeing only what lay beyond. For she'd survived a burned-out world of which we could not form any conception. She had nothing *left*. Her movements as mechanical as those of a little ballerina in a music box. Something submissive about her, like a cringing dog, ever since the day I'd plucked Brückner away from her. Always keeping near me, scared it seemed that something like that might happen again if she ventured out alone. And yet *not* submissive either! A hint of pride, if that's the right word. No, rather something detached, as if she had in advance cut herself off from anything, including the worst, that might ever happen to her. Perhaps because nothing could conceivably happen that would be worse than what she'd already experienced. The house set alight over their heads. The Russians

419

beating them back into the flames with their guns, because a few young resistance workers had been discovered in their cellar. In the end the family had broken right through the cordon of soldiers to escape from the fire. Then they'd caught Eva and her younger sister and raped them, passing them from one to the other. In her nose the smell of her own scorched hair. The next day she'd torn herself from her father's anxious arms to steal back to the ruins of their home. To see if her music could still be saved. Through the black holes of the windows she looked at the rubble inside, the caved-in, burnt ceilings. The remains of her father's library. Grey ash, twisted bindings, here and there pages with the middle sections still partially legible, the edges blackened. In the midst of it all, her grand piano, a black monster, a skeleton with discoloured grimacing teeth. Then the flight to the Austrian border, where she got through while the others were caught.

Eva standing at a window in the round tower: the children outside on the frozen river, skating, singing. She begins to cry, her body contorted as if to force all life from it. I try to comfort her. Not even realizing who I am, she attacks me with her small fists. When at last she calms down, still sobbing, she holds on to me. For a few minutes only. Then we hear the other workers coming back (they've gone down to collect more boxes of clothing for us to sort); the work must go on.

Outside in the dazzling snow, just before Christmas, after a heavy new fall: the sun has come out, everything is glistening, impossibly white. Crows swooping overhead.

"Why can't they stop cawing?" I ask.

In her halting German: "They are too black on the snow, yes?"

In the large dining hall, the clattering of hundreds of spoons in the soup plates. Eva suddenly pushing hers back, her face dreadfully pale, her hands on her throat, ready to throw up. Shaking her head fiercely when she's approached. Until one of her compatriots — a gentle, mildly surprised old man with a mane of white hair and heavy spectacles, a professor in linguistics — begins to talk to her softly, translating for our

420

benefit: "She says she cannot eat. While she is sitting here at table her people are starving at home. She says it does not matter that we are safe here: *they* are still there. They are living and dying all the time."

And just after New Year's Day she was gone.

All these years I've been going about with the romantic feeling of guilt that it had been because of my reaction to her pathetic offer of sacrifice on Christmas night. In a sense, I suppose, it was easier to bear this guilt than face the whole truth: that her reasons for escaping were less relevant than the simple *fact* of her escape. Namely, that she'd chosen to return across the border, back into Hungary, into hell, back to a burned-out piano with skeletal teeth in a burned-out house in a burned-out city. Of her own free will: that above all. Against all reason and logic: because there was no reason or logic left.

Late in January, shortly before I left, one Hungarian family who'd recently crossed the border, brought me news of her. She'd been arrested and thrown into jail. Just before it had happened she'd told these friends about the Schloss Judenau and given them my name. If ever they managed to get through, she'd told them, they should try to give me her message: I was not to worry about her, she was back with her people.

That is what, these many years, I've never been able fully to grasp. This is what I've been unable to share with you, Andrea. What a pity, I realize now, too late; for I know you would have understood it so much better than I ever can.

My last telephone conversation with Mandla. According to my calculations that must have been barely an hour before his death, that Tuesday afternoon, when I called him from Paris. He was just as surprised to hear my voice as I was relieved to get a reply.

"I don't want to be a nuisance," I told him. "Actually I meant to talk to Andrea. But when I tried to phone this morning there was no reply."

"I can go and call her, but I think she's having a nap."

421

"Is anything wrong?"

"Why you asking?"

"You sound strange. Different. Blunt. Did I wake you up?"

Instead of answering, he asked: "Was it you who phoned last night too?"

"I? No. Why?"

"There was a call for me, here in my room. But when I picked up the phone it was silent. Then I heard somebody putting it down at the other end."

"Must have been a wrong number."

"Ja, suppose so."

"Mandla?"

"What?"

"Is everything all right? With you? With Andrea?"

"Why shouldn't it be?"

"I'm just a bit worried — "

He suddenly became aggressive: "Paul, I bloody well told you not to send me to this fucking place!" Then, after a brief pause: "And not her either."

"What on earth do you mean?" A sudden suspicion lodging like a lump of porridge in my stomach. "Has something happened — ? The two of you — ?"

"What's she got to do with a film on the fucking Plague? Why do you use her to do your dirty work?"

"It's not dirty work. All these years she's been nagging me to write the thing. Andrea's the one who — "

"Why you hiding behind her? You're just fucking her around."

"I don't understand what you're trying to say. Is she unhappy?"

"I didn't say she was unhappy. I said you're fucking her around. For me too. I'm not going to stay in this place. You should have known better."

"I'm already making arrangements for you. I'd rather not discuss it on the telephone. But give me another week or so, then I'll have something organized."

"Can't you come down straight away? Come and finish the

film work on your own if you got to. But leave Andrea alone, you're poisoning her."

"Why are you suddenly so worried about Andrea? Here in Paris the two of you were always in each other's hair."

"I'm not worried about her. I'm worried about nobody. Why didn't you just leave me alone right from the start?"

"If only you would tell me what you're trying to accuse me of — !"

That seemed to calm him down a bit; perhaps he was just very tired. "I'm not accusing you of anything, Paul. It's just that it shouldn't have happened. It's each man for himself. A man can't afford to get infected by others."

"Look here, Mandla — "

"If I were you I'd come and fetch Andrea straight away. I'm not good for her."

"One moment you tell me I'm fucking her around. Now it's you."

"Neither of us is good for her."

He put the telephone down.

That "heaviness", that "gloom" you spoke about in your letter.

I wanted to phone him again immediately. I felt a need to speak to you. But he'd said you were having a nap. I know how moody you can be if your sleep is disturbed; and after our tatty conversation the previous morning I didn't want to upset you again. Perhaps I should follow Mandla's advice and drive down? But I couldn't make up my mind. If it really were that urgent, I felt, you would have let me know yourself.

Still, I was very confused. I know it occurred to me once that I was sitting there like old Oedipus in his town stricken by the Plague, with everybody expecting me to find a solution:

. . . a tide of death from which no escape is possible —
Death in the fertile blossoming of the earth;
Death in the fields; death in the wombs of women;
And the Plague a fiery demon holding the city in its grip —

423

How on earth could I be held responsible? Hadn't I done all I could to allow you the breathing space you wanted and Mandla the time we needed to solve his problems? Where do I find an oracle?

Even after eighteen years of exposure to French bureaucracy I could still not accept with equanimity the red tape it required to dispense with a simple enquiry at the *gendarmerie*. The three-storeyed building on the boulevard Gambetta: only on the two lower floors the grey shutters were open. (What happens on the top floor?) The small tarred yard in front, behind tall railings. The hospital-like interior: pale grey; dull green lino tiles; neon lighting; a large map of the area on the wall.

The officious prelude: who was I? What were my relations with the deceased? Could I prove it? How did I learn of his death? Where did I live? How and when did I come to Saint-Rémy? Did I have any concrete evidence to shed light on the matter? (If not, what was I wasting their time for?) If it was true that Mademoiselle Malgas had informed me, why hadn't she come with me? Where had she gone to? — Followed by infinite variations of the same inquisition as I was passed on from one official to the next (with unnerving lacunae in between, when such-and-such was not available), as each had to be brought up to date from the beginning. If I was no relative, what concern was it of mine? Was I an eye-witness, and if not, what was I doing there? Some curt, others downright rude, still others more congenial but long-winded, others quite simply obstreperous.

At long last — by which time it was afternoon already — I landed in the small clinical office of a rotund middle-aged officer: once again the shiny lino tiles, the tube lights, the grey filing cabinets. One of them stood half open, offering a view of rows of orange files inside. On the wall the framed picture of a shot wild duck hung upside down. (In a butchery?) At least he was prepared to offer some information on Mandla (gleaned from a written sheet in the open orange file in front of him), in exchange for a recapitulation of all the details I'd already supplied about myself. Not that it was worth much. According to one witness Mandla had suddenly jumped right in front of the approaching car. According to another the car had been travelling at a reckless speed, swerving out for a stray cat or dog in the road, and driving off without even slowing down after he'd hit Mandla. The classic hit-and-run.

"Can't the driver be traced?"

"Stolen vehicle. Picked up in Aix. Found in Nîmes this morning. That doesn't bring us any further."

"Could it have been deliberate?"

"It could have been anything. Perhaps an ordinary car thief who got a fright and raced away because he couldn't risk getting caught." A narrowing of his dark eyes under the heavy grey brows. "Why do you think it might have been deliberate? Did he have any enemies?"

"Not in France as far as I know. But he fled from South Africa. Have you contacted the embassy?"

A gesture which might mean anything. "What do you think of the possibility that it might have been suicide, Monsieur Joubert?"

I replied with a mime of his own gesture.

(Because after George's betrayal he couldn't face a new start? But he'd survived worse blows than that. Because he'd felt guilty towards me? That was no reason to kill oneself. Because love had taken away his power to act, paralysing his will? Mandla was no romanticist.)

"What's going to happen to the body?" I tried again.

"It depends. If his family wants it back — "

(What will they do with him? Bury him somewhere in the Eastern Cape on a bare hillside among rows of others, graves marked with twigs or boards carrying names written with ballpoint pens; some of the smaller ones marked only with a doll or an empty feeding-bottle propped up among the stones?)

"I can pay for a funeral if he's buried here."

"You're not a relative."

"Does it matter?"

"What will we write in his dossier? We can't start distributing corpses to all and sundry." A flickering of interest. "Did he leave a testament?"

"Not as far as I know."

"Then it doesn't seem as if you can help us much, does it?"

"I was hoping you could help *me*."

"If you want to, you may try the morgue in Tarascon. Not that it would be of any use." He made an attempt to sound more sympathetic. "The dead are dead, Monsieur. The living should look after themselves." He rose and offered me his hand. He closed the orange file. Perhaps it was really closed now, as far as he was concerned.

On a café terrace I ordered pastis. In the boulevard the afternoon traffic was coming past in fits and starts, but I didn't pay much attention. It was difficult to order my thoughts; there was too much to contend with, and all of it in too great a confusion to know where to start.

Was that the end of it then? What else had I expected?

It was no use remaining where I was. I had one final appointment to keep; that I knew only too agonizingly well. There was no logical reason for it: I only knew it was unavoidable. I made up my mind very abruptly. Gulping down my pastis, I called the waiter and paid him; then went to my car a short distance up the boulevard.

Of the fifteen or sixteen kilometres to Tarascon I remember nothing; I drove mechanically, not even thinking. Just off the playground opposite the castle I found a parking place from where I walked to the Syndicat d'Initiative to ask for directions. Narrow streets smelling of old cheese; down-at-heel seedy buildings. The lady eyed me very suspiciously when she heard my request: I don't suppose they handle such queries very often. She made it very clear that it was much against her liking to telephone first the hospital and then the morgue; when someone replied at the second number she unceremoniously thrust the telephone into my hand and sat watching me beadily while I spoke. A female voice with a very broad

426

southern accent gave me confusing and rather loud directions: some five hundred metres out of town, on the road to Mezoargues.

"Where is Mezoargues? I've never heard of such a place."

A long, convoluted explanation followed, rounded off with an emphatic correction: "It's not a morgue like in most other places, Monsieur. What we have here is an *athanée*. We don't keep our bodies in drawers, you know. They have their own small chambers in which they can receive visitors. Now who did you want to see?"

It was such a straight question that for a moment I was completely at a loss, thinking: My God, so he's still alive!

"Mandla Mqayisa." I had to repeat the name several times.

"Oh." Did I detect a note of hesitation? Then, in a very matter-of-fact voice, she asked: "At what time can we expect you?"

"Immediately." I had to check a macabre impulse to say: "You needn't warn him, he's expecting me. We've had this appointment for a long time."

Whether the lady at the Syndicat had deliberately given me the wrong instructions, I don't know; but I got lost several times before I found the road to Mezoargues. And at last there was the small villa the woman on the telephone had described. I didn't taken in any particulars. That morning at the *gendarmerie* in Saint-Rémy nothing had escaped my attention: I'd wanted to etch every detail on my mind, attaching great moment to the most insignificant observation. Not any more. I won't even recognize the receptionist if I were to see her again.

An office, a corridor, a small cool *salon à l'américaine*. Then Mandla's body.

This wholly unnecessary death. Or was it, on the contrary, the most ineluctable of all that had happened to us?

I stood looking down at his dark motionless face. What was I doing there? What could I possibly have expected?

All I was aware of was *distance*. I could touch him, but it wouldn't bridge the space between us. He, I. Black, White.

427

Man, man. This ultimate Wall separating the living from the dead.

But also: the incredible dignity of his death, as he lay there. Invincible. Nothing could touch him any more: police, vans, batons, nail-studded planks, lies, hate, suspicion. Nothing.

One of his hands lay empty beside him, palm up, fingers open, as if expecting something to be placed in it, something on which he could gain a final satisfying, fulfilling grasp. What was the myth I'd once read about a dead man holding out his hand just like that? — rich men came and filled it with gold, but it refused to clasp it; the aldermen offered him the keys of the city, but he wouldn't budge; women came and shed their tears in his palm until it was brimming with their sorrow, but the hand refused to close; virgins offered his palm and fingers their kisses, but without response; until at last one man approached with a handful of earth and placed it in the dead man's hand, and this he grasped, and held. But I had no clod or lump of the red earth of his Azania to offer him, and I knew that nothing else would ever put his hand to rest. Empty-handed I stood beside him, head bowed, staring, moved.

Mandla, my friend. Whom now I would never come to know.

Even right there beside him, close enough to touch him — but I didn't — I could not reconcile myself to his death; couldn't even believe it.

(This body had loved yours!)

It wasn't this thing, this corpse, that concerned me. What I tried to do, what I should have wished to do, was, I think now, to stare right through him, to whatever lay beyond him: like an archaeologist digging up the remains of one city above the other, one below the other, layer after layer. Or like peeling an onion to the nothing in its core.

That big, strong man, who even when he sat down gave the impression of energy bundled up inside and waiting for a pretext to burst out. The deceptive lethargy in his movements: if necessary, one knew, he would react faster than a cheetah bringing down his quarry. The violence of his laughter, when

428

one least expected it. The youthfulness of his gladiator's body; the gravity more suited to a much older man. Mandla Mqayisa who'd burst into my life four months ago, without warning or notice, and who'd now left it just as suddenly, for good. (For good? No. I don't think I'll ever be without him again.) Who'd taken you from me with so much ease, a Pied Piper casting his spell over you to follow his music and leave me behind with nothing.

Our endless conversations, often right through the night, especially when you'd angrily left us alone and gone back, in a huff, to your own flat. Invariably the same point of departure:

"You scared of today then that you keep on running back to history? This stupid film of yours — "

"The Plague is the best image I can think of to express the one moment in history that shocked me to my very guts."

"You mean that Hungarian shit?"

"Yes. Because I was part of it. I watched from close by while a whole nation was being besieged and conquered, until there was no freedom left at all."

"Did you have to wait for Russia to invade Hungary to understand that? In your own country people are living in a permanent state of siege. Or did you side with the Russians over there?"

"You should have your head read!"

Was it a change of subject? — "You know, there's one book you wrote years ago: I read it in London the other day, somebody recommended it to me. *Survivors.*"

"The only one that's still being reprinted. Thanks to the film."

"The blokes who survived after their country was destroyed. There was one of them, a white man, who fled because he couldn't take it any more. It all began with a very small thing for him, one day when his car was stopped on the road by a herd of cattle. Remember? — of course you remember, it's your book. The black herdsman can't control the animals. His boss arrives in a bakkie and starts laying into him with a sjambok. The traveller jumps out to stop the man, thinking

429

he's doing a good deed. Later he hears that after he left the farmer killed the herdsman, most likely to avenge himself for being humiliated by the traveller. From there you take it further, step by step, as the traveller gets drawn into other people's lives. The murdered man's family. The farmer's people. The whole goddamn country. His own life is threatened and in the end he's got to leave — just because one day he dared to ask a question about the system he'd always lived by. A bit simplistic, I thought. A bit 'white' if you'll forgive me for saying so. Even so, you had something there which was the naked fucking truth. Not mucking about with Europe and Hungary and Plagues and stuff. Why haven't you ever written a thing like that again?"

"It was something I saw when I was a child. Only, unlike the traveller in the book, my father just drove on. He didn't try to interfere. He was a *dominee*, you see. And he was in a hurry to get back in time for the evening service after we'd spent the afternoon on a farm. The whole boot was loaded with pumpkins, mealies, carrots, beetroot, half a sheep, a basin full of *wors* — " I drew myself back from the memory. "I think what I did in the book was to write the whole country out of my system. I had to, for the sake of my own survival."

"You thought you could get rid of it so easily?"

"I'm living in Europe now, Mandla. I'm involved in a new kind of life."

Where did the shift in our conversation take place? Impossible to pinpoint now; by the time I became aware of it, the inquisition was already in progress — but very calmly, almost casually, as if he was attracted to the dialectic for its own sake (and I'd already discovered that he could be a formidable sparring partner).

"Right, so you're not a political animal. But you must have certain convictions."

"Naturally."

"I assume you're against straitjackets — politically speaking? That you don't approve of government power, corporate power, institutional power?"

430

"Right. But what are you trying to prove?"

"Give me time, man. Tell me: would you agree that institutional power inevitably leads to institutional violence?"

"I'm afraid so, yes."

"Which is why you support the freedom of the individual?"

"Yes, indeed. Provided one individual's freedom doesn't threaten another's."

"Right. So you're against exploitation in any form?"

"Absolutely."

"You're painfully aware of the fact that the great majority of the world's population is exploited, no matter if it's on the basis of race, or religion, or sex, or whatever?"

(What else could I believe, after Eva?)

"I've always fought against it in my work, yes."

"So you support the underdog?"

"Of course. It's a question of human dignity."

"And you believe that, certainly in South Africa, racial exploitation is a form of class exploitation? That the capitalist system, the mines, the industries, make it easier for the Government to keep the labourer 'in his place'?"

"That's how it works out, yes."

He looked satisfied. "So you accept that it is part of the whole South African strategy — ever since they got more sophisticated and started clothing naked domination in pin-stripes — to create a black bourgeoisie? And to lure Coloureds and Indians to their side?"

"Undoubtedly. In that way the ruler safeguards himself doubly: he uses the labourer to do his work for him and at the same time manages to persuade him that property is the highest virtue."

"Right. So all the shit can really be traced back to property? In other words: blow up the mines, shoot the capitalists, burn down the factories, and it's the beginning of the Millennium?"

"I never said that. I've never condoned terrorism."

"But you already admitted that the state rules through institutional violence, enforcing its power through the exploitation of the majority? That property is the final obstacle? If you

431

really believe that, how come you can't agree that it must be eradicated boots and all?"

"Because I can't approve of countering violence with violence. Then your own hands are as dirty as those of your opponent."

"Who talked about clean hands, Paul? I thought we were talking about the *world*?"

"Without violence."

"I see. You want to get a dialogue going with the bosses. You want to tell them: 'Hey man, it isn't nice to exploit people.' You want to persuade them to give up all their power just like that and divide their possessions among the poor so that the world can suddenly become a better place for all."

"Mandla, now you're trying to make a fool out of me."

"I'm trying to show you what a fucking fool you already are! You stand for everything that's good and right, but you don't have enough faith in it to do something which will make it possible. Nice words you can stuff up your arse, man. It's what you *do* that counts. The rest is bullshit."

"Mandla — "

"Come on, tell me: what are you going to *do*?"

I stared at him, cornered, furious, helpless, glowering.

To my amazement he burst out laughing. I'd been expecting anything — a new round of invective, a fierce retort, even that he might spit at me or hit me — but not his laughter. As if he'd never seen anything quite as funny as I.

"I wasn't expecting an answer, Paul. What's it matter what you say to me? It's the answer you give yourself that counts. Nothing else."

I should have known better. But seeing him move off the attack, as it appeared to me, I tried to compensate for my embarrassment. "When I write a book or make a film," I said, "it helps other people to see what's happening. At least it's a beginning."

"You think you can tell a black man in South Africa what it means to be black?" He quickly came right up to me. "You want to tell *me*?" Again that sudden change to laughter: no bitter, dark laugh, but a liberating howl, as if he really found it wildly funny.

"There are white readers too, you know," I said after a moment. "People who in all sincerity are not aware of what they're doing."

"And you want to open their eyes so that in future they can start refining their crudest mistakes?"

"No. Once a person has become aware of evil he can start doing something about it. And it's not only a question of South Africa. It's the whole world; wherever one class exploits another."

"Don't fool yourself with class." He pressed his clenched fist under my nose. I gave a step back, he refused to let me get away. "Look at this fist, Paul. It's black. It's not a worker's fist, it's a black man's. It's with this skin that it all started. Because I look like this and not something else. So when I react it's got to start with the colour of this fist. For years your people tried to make mine believe that it was a shame to look like this. Not because we're poor, but because we're black. But those days are over. We discovered that a man can be proud of being black too. You'll be amazed to see what difference it makes."

"Why do you talk about 'your people' when you speak to me?" I asked.

He stared at me in silence for a minute, then thrust his hands in his jeans pockets and walked away from me. But, no doubt conscious of the histrionic effect — I could see why he'd been so successful in the unions — he turned back at the door and said with a smile: "Sorry. Of course you no longer live there. You're — how did you put it? — 'involved in a new kind of life'."

The most remarkable thing was the way in which these violent arguments became the very basis of our relationship. He could rage against me in the foulest language so that not even the sea could wash me clean again. And whenever he resorted to his own brand of rhetoric — the slogans I'd heard reverberating for so many years through Europe: Sartre and Marcuse and their followers for the "thinkers", Fanon and

433

Guevara and others for the "doers" — it was my turn to give him hell. Perhaps it helped to keep both of us on our toes. Or was that what, certainly for me, was wrong with it? — that it always remained something of a game, an exercise at a safe distance? Did I fully appreciate, even when we heard about the treachery of his "comrade", how radically different it was for him? That, in the most literal sense, his life depended on it?

The enthusiasm with which I'd accepted him as a protégé in Paris: making arrangements for him, introducing him to people, offering him shelter, giving him money. A way of "getting involved", or at least of creating for myself the illusion of commitment? — but so safe, so vicarious, so second-hand.

Here he was now. Through his death he had, whether I liked it or not, changed it for me too. (How it would have amused him to know!) I could no longer keep it at bay. The answer I'd been unable to give him I now owed myself: it could no longer be postponed. Through his death I had become involved.

"If there's nothing else one can do," he'd once said, "then at least you can withhold your consent. Whether it's in a specific situation — when a Boer tries to pull the wet canvas bag over your head or to throttle you; when a factory tries to force you to accept inhuman wages — or in a more general sense. A man must never become guilty of giving his consent, collaborating, condoning. Whatever happens, *they* must take responsibility: don't make it fucking easier for them."

I'd drawn my comfort, however meagre, from knowing that I'd left the country, that I was no longer there. Surely that, too, was a way of withholding my consent?

Or had that been the final evasion?

I went out of the ugly little villa, back into the thin sunlight.

Mandla was dead. I was still alive.

The crows are cawing because they are too black on the snow, yes?

What had the day yielded to me? A feverish pursuit of

memories; blind alleys; disturbing possibilities; no answers. And too much pastis. For on my return from Tarascon I once again went to the café in Saint-Rémy. I suppose I was simply feeling reluctant to return to the hotel, unable to face that depressing room. But what else was there to do? It was too late to think of driving back to Paris; and anyway, I was feeling too depressed and dazed to risk it so late in the day. Impulsively I thought of La Motte d'Aigues. Would there be any comfort among the remains of my ancestors? You'd already told me that old Monsieur Jaubert had also died. But perhaps my restless thoughts — an arid mental lust — would find some peace there?

I returned to the hotel, packed my few belongings, and went downstairs to check out. Outside the sun had already set.

The *patron* was disapproving and indignant. "I don't understand you people. This is no time to leave. You should have checked out before noon, it's written very clearly on the notice behind your door."

"I'll pay for the extra night."

He appeared more mollified, although he kept on muttering for a while. "Well, all right, then. But think of all the extra trouble. If we'd known earlier we could have changed the sheets this morning. But all right. Nasty business, isn't it? Heard anything from Mademoiselle?" As if he had a personal interest in finding out.

"No."

"Really, these girls."

Whatever that might mean.

Then I was on my way. But shortly after Cavaillon it was dark and I had no desire to drive through the mountains at night, so I turned off to Gordes where I found a room for the night. Had too much to drink (again), and swallowed a sleeping pill to make it worse. Inevitably I woke up in a foul mood the next morning, almost *wanting* the day to turn out a disaster, miserable and sorry for myself: Mandla dead, you gone, and no one thinking of me — !

All I could still hold on to was the film; and even that

thought couldn't comfort me. The screenplay was still without a proper end. Your departure had been a tide receding; and what was exposed on my bare stretch of beach and among the rocks was not an appetizing sight. Meagre, unsightly, tatty. Seaweed and broken shells, bamboos with a sickly rotten smell, red-bait, perhaps a dead sea-gull or gannet; driftwood and tangles of nylon line, plastic bags, broken bottles and rusty cans, torn condoms, unmatched shoes —

On my left, perched on its hill, the hamlet of Joucas. I could drive on to Apt and La Motte d'Aigues as I'd planned, or turn off here first. Why not? For a variety of trite, wholly unconvincing reasons I'd never gone to the Wall myself, coming to within a few kilometres of it in July, the few days we'd spent at the delightful Mas des Herbes Blanches; but no closer than that. Not, I think, because there had been any significant obstacles in the way, but because the mere idea of the Wall had always seemed more important to me than a reality which might turn out deceptive or disappointing. A literary Wall; like my literary Plague. True to the pattern of my life? — excepting, always, that one tremendous episode which might have been the final demonstration of my help-lessness against the world: the ultimate impotence of the writer.

(From where, what forgotten piece of reading, this sudden echo: *The worst crime is to do nothing, for fear that we cannot do enough?*)

All right, Andrea, I decided: I'll go there to see for myself, at last. In your footsteps.

Up into the mountains behind the hamlet, to Murs. Remembering from your random notes your comments on the inhabitants, I decided to try my luck without them, turning into the narrow short-cut towards Sault just before the village. To my surprise I found it without any trouble. Stopped, and walked towards it.

Well! Hello, Wall. So this was what all the fuss had been about, this line of tumbled stones dotted across the ridges and through the valleys and canyons of the long mountains: a serene landscape — hazy, misty, melancholy in the rapidly changing weather — and as I stood looking, a single spearhead of birds came streaking past overhead, heading very resolutely south. Swallows? They seemed larger. Wild geese? Storks? Too high to make out. On their way, undoubtedly, to a distant summer. With my head thrown back, I stared at them until they'd disappeared into the clouds over the Luberon. Then, in the beginnings of a light drizzle, I walked up to the Wall and ran my hand across the surface of the stones, picked one up to feel its weight, then looked round, at a loss.

Something was nagging my thoughts, a passage from Johnson which I couldn't quite retrieve; only afterwards, back in Paris, I looked it up. Here it is, in the stern old man's unintentionally comic turn of phrase, dating from 1778, when Boswell intimated that his fervent desire one day to visit the Great Wall of China was inhibited by the demands of his children:

Sir [said he] by doing so, you would do what would be of importance in raising your children to eminence. There would be a lustre reflected upon them from your spirit and curiosity. They would be at all times regarded as the children of a man who had gone to view the Wall of China. I am serious, Sir.

At least the Wall of China had kept out its enemies. This Wall had had no hope of keeping out the Plague. No wonder the people of Murs didn't like to be reminded of it. Will all our own efforts to ward off our plagues, to pretend they don't exist, one day be of no more than touristic value?

I felt out of place and ill at ease. Let down, like when one is stood up by a very special woman after many assiduous efforts to make a date. You keep on hoping that she only, inadvertently, made a mistake with time or place, but deep inside you know it reflects on an inadequacy in yourself.

I tried to imagine the feverish activity of two hundred and

437

fifty years ago: old men and youngsters, soldiers, peasants, all possessed by the need to finish in time. The famished, the runaways, the criminals, the notables: in the face of the approaching Plague there was no distinction among men. And then it all turned out to be in vain, too late. It's easy to be amused by it afterwards; to say they should have known better: how could the Black Death be stopped by a man-made wall? What hurts, is not the comment it offers on the dead but on the living.

The wetness was beginning to penetrate right through my jacket. I had to go. (Thank God for the pretext.)

Yet I was reluctant simply to go away. I started the car and drove on very slowly. After a while the Wall began to recede from the road, until it disappeared completely among the wild oaks. Somewhere here you must have turned off. Somewhere near — You gave very few details in your notes. But it couldn't have been far away: a clearing in this wood, a no man's land where you could no longer see the Wall.

For the discarded lover the worst (I first meant to write "the most inhuman", but then realized: the worst of it was the very humanness of it, the totally exposed humanity) is to imagine the beloved in the arms of another man: a younger man. *His furious dark body.* (There was a time, do you remember, when it was *my* body you called "furious"!) Nothing else confirms, in advance, so deeply, the inevitability of my own death. (Even though it is he who is dead, and I who go on living!) What had been most intimately mine — every texture of your skin, every variation in your breathing, every murmured word or moan — had now become part of another "us", making me irrelevant, replacing me, excluding me. Or had I always been an outsider to your life? This thought didn't make it any easier. Please don't think of it as anything so uncomplicated as "jealousy", Andrea. It is I myself, my whole life, suddenly at stake again. And yours no less than mine. Because the most terrifying knowledge of all, I think, is this: that I cannot achieve any grasp on what is "mine" unless I've first come to terms with *you*. You once said that the lover knows his beloved least of all, because he's blinded by his own image of her. It is this blindness I shall have to confront if I have any hope of ever working my way through it.

When it became clear that there was little hope of finding any more traces of the Wall, I turned round and drove back until I could see it again, glistening in the drizzle. There I stopped and, the wipers moving monotonously with their mechanical whirring sound, sat staring for I don't know how long; reluctant to go on; sensing it would be like cutting a final umbilical cord. For how many years had I been nourished and inspired and sustained by the thought of this unprepossessing, unimpressive boundary wall (between what and what)?

The panic-stricken people of that remote century, blindly stacking their stones, stones, stones against Death — their own futile imitation of the original Tower of Babel! — without ever grasping what it had really been about (ignorant even of what the Plague itself was!). However terribly mortal we all are, it remains impossible for the individual to perceive beyond his own end the end of space and time: the end of his history, of whatever particular group or society or nation he forms part of. The individual may die, but the group must remain: this is the illusion that keeps us from going mad. That was what the people of Venasque had tried to assure with their Wall which, like all the other walls in our unillustrious history, now lay crumbling among the trees in the wet mountains.

When I'd gone to the Schloss Judenau to help the refugees, those Hungarians — and we, too, the helpers (each a refugee from his own everyday world?) — had seen it as an effort to build a wall against the flood of history. Trying to "salvage" something, to offer some redemption, to achieve something durable. It had shaken me so deeply that for a quarter of a century I'd struggled in vain to come to terms with it. And, since then, how many more times, in how many variations, had the world witnessed the same spectacle? — the Congo, Biafra, Bangladesh, Vietnam, Czechoslovakia, Somalia, Uganda, Iran, Lebanon, Afghanistan? And South Africa, a

439

volcano smouldering through it all to remind one of the persistence of the Black Death.

Angry, rebellious, helpless — yet again! — I thought: how can I possibly fight against so much violence and inhumanity? What is the weight of a book against the turmoil of history?

I started the car again. Impossible to remain there all day, in the rain beside a pile of stones. There were many more stones than those to be cleared up inside me.

Deaux:

> It is one of the tragedies of the Black Death, as it is one of the tragedies of the world after Hiroshima, that men did not, could not, suddenly and *en masse*, change radically their conception of things. It is one of the triumphs of the period that, in spite of being unable to do so, civilization endured and men moved on to a new order . . . . For all the horror it held for those who endured it, in the perspective of time the Black Death is a triumph of life.

A short distance below Joucas, at the junction with the main road, I stopped to spread the map across my knees, pondering the various possibilities. Should I continue to La Motte d'Aigues as I'd meant to? But the excursion behind me had made me restless; what could I hope to find, especially in this bad weather, in that remote village with which I no longer had any ties?

Or should I drive back to Cavaillon and take the autoroute to Nice? My little villa at Villefranche was available; at this time of the year the summer visitors had long left. And I would undoubtedly be revived by the sea. For a moment there even was the exhilarating thought that you might be there to catch your plane; suppose we met by "accident"? But I knew it was an idle hope. Even if the encounter were possible I owed you the freedom you so urgently demanded; the only conceivable freedom left to you. In a way it was even harder than facing Eva's return to Hungary: there had been absolutely no chance

440

of following or finding her; however agonizing to accept, I'd had no choice but to resign myself to it. But you could still be followed. I might go back with you. But what would be solved by it? Perhaps, somewhere along the way, I had acquired a bit of respect for another's freedom.

Once, only once, remember?, I'd thought of going back. When there had been the possibility of joining Dirk and Johan in Amsterdam. I'd never told you the whole truth: they hadn't gone on to Johannesburg without me because I'd missed my plane. There had been other planes I could have caught. But I'd quite simply grown too scared. I knew I was a coward and couldn't go through with it. And when they ended up in court and broke down and began to sob and plead for mercy, I couldn't find it in me to despise them. I knew the same might very easily have happened to me. It's like dying: only by entering into it can you discover how you will react to it. Still, it seems to me today that if it were to happen now I would find the courage to go. This time it's for your sake that I am staying behind; this time staying is harder than going.

But if I stayed: where should I go to, what could I do?

All my vacillation was no more than the postponement of what was really very obvious. And after a few minutes I turned back towards Cavaillon and the autoroute, back to Paris.

The night in your flat. You must forgive me my last romantic detour: but after the long journey I couldn't face the emptiness of my own flat. The shock when I saw the little Renault parked at the very entrance to your building (a whole array of parking tickets fluttering on the windscreen). I was dizzy at the sudden wild thought that you might have changed your mind after all. I should have known better, of course! There was no answer to my knock. And when I unlocked the front door with my duplicate key I immediately knew it was empty inside.

Another jump of my heart when I saw the large envelope bearing my name, on the telephone table. But all you'd put in it were the documents of the car; and the credit card of the film company, wrapped in a sheet of notepaper that said no more

441

than *Thanks!*; and the worn-out holder — a few gilt letters still bravely trying to spell *Amboise* on the leather tag — with the keys of your flat and car. Part of your thorough clean-up. You had already taken your leave of me in the letter of Saint-Rémy: and that neat end, you no doubt thought, should not be frayed again by postscripts. (*For both our sakes it must be a very clean cut.*)

From the first moment I set foot in the terrible physical emptiness of what had been your flat, I knew it would be useless to hunt for further signs or clues. You had *meant* to go away. You'd known I would go there, but at the same time you'd wanted me to realize fully and finally that for me you do not exist "in a state" of being away: your existence *equals* being away. We must all believe in death, the empty flat said, for death is true: pure, innocent, painful, lucid. In spite of it I couldn't restrain myself. Until long after midnight, like a private detective, a burglar, a security policeman, I sifted through your possessions: all of it so intimately known to me and yet, in your absence, totally strange, because you weren't there to give meaning to it. Perhaps the most unnerving discovery of all: the fact that you'd obliterated whatever traces your flat had borne of my own share in your life. Now I was as much relegated to oblivion as Brian or Frank or Serge or any of the others. You'd warned me, hadn't you! — that you would withdraw even memory from me. All that remained were the signs of your own independent existence. You, Andrea Malgas.

The search was like a journey in itself — a night journey through an avenue like the one running from Saint-Rémy towards Eygalières — where individual, unrelated objects suddenly appeared in the headlights (a trunk, a rock, a figure on a bicycle) and disappeared again; darkness all round.

Exhausted I fell asleep in your bed at last.

A brief unsettling dream. I was back at the *gendarmerie* in Saint-Rémy. This time, after an endless interrogation, they took me through a long corridor and down a flight of stairs to a cellar where I saw Mandla's body on a table. There were many people milling around it. Most of them I couldn't recognize, and when they spoke it sounded like foreign languages. You were there too. What shocked me was that you had no clothes on. You beckoned to me to come and have a closer look. I went to the table, and suddenly we were alone, he and I; even you had gone. I grew unspeakably afraid. For all over the body black spots appeared. Gangrene or something. The boils of the Plague in his armpits and groin. I moved my eyes slowly along the full length of his body, from the feet up, growing more and more terrified as my gaze went higher. Only when I reached the head did I realize why I'd been so frightened. For it wasn't Mandla at all. It was myself.

And now I'm back in my own flat. Came in early this morning. Stood for a long time in front of one of the large windows, staring at the traffic far below in the boulevard Malesherbes. The wheels hissing on the wet street. Inside I was isolated and comfortable; the heating had already been turned on.

Now I could no longer postpone it.

For hours I sat rereading the notes of your journey to the South, analysing every phrase, looking for hidden meanings, unintentional undertones. Your last letter. All the questions you concluded with, and which will never leave me in peace until I've at least attempted to reply to them.

All around me, all my life, there has been turmoil, while I've tried to remain immobile in the eye of the storm. Even my love for you was, I think, a part of it.

Now you have gone. You've made your choice, for better or for worse. What will become of you I do not know. You may choose to plunge into romantic action; or it may be sufficient simply *to be there*, to do what at any given moment you believe you must. That in itself demands a special kind of courage.

(My only worry, if I dare voice it: you went to make a new start. Your letter intimated as much; the thorough clean-up of

443

your flat confirmed it. The "clean break". But you yourself must know, much better than anyone I've ever met, that no one can ever make a completely new start. We drag with us, sadly and gloriously, all our loves, failures, happiness, suffering. Memory can never be destroyed, not even denied. Remember the night you so often told me about, when you and your father had been sitting together, unable to talk? — because to him it had still been the night before, while to you it had already been morning: that's how the two of us also find ourselves today. I'll have to learn that tomorrow has already begun; you will have to live with the knowledge that last night can never be past. You're on your way already: your decision has been taken.)

Like Oedipus in his stricken city I have to take my own decisions here and now: wherever they may lead me.

No, indeed, a book does not weigh much against the violence of the world, Andrea. It can never become a substitute for reality. Yet what would have become of the world without the word? Brute beasts killing and maiming one another? An eye for an eye, a tooth for a tooth, blood, blood, blood.

According to one hypo'.esis humanity has two distinct places of origin in the world, two beginnings, two essential connections. One of its birthplaces, it is alleged, was the Ural Mountains: the earth, the dungheap, to which all that is physical and concrete in a human being responds. Its type is the peasant. But another line goes back to the Middle East, where the Word had its beginning. The *Verbum*. Mind. Spirit. The urge to invent. Hence, in order to evoke a response from the very core of a person's humanity, one should appeal to either of these two instincts that have shaped him. One can appeal to the hunting instinct, to the violence latent inside, the urge to change and destroy what comes in its way, to conquer; or to the imagination, to the human being's ability to create.

If this is true I have only one possible choice. My answer to Eva. In the final instance my answer, Andrea, to you.

444

For how many years have you been pestering me to shake off the fear, to look my world in the face, to risk everything, to write what I have within me?

I will. At last.

Over ancient Europe winter is settling in. But I shall write.

The only way I can possibly do justice to you is to try and imagine what it is like to be you. But does this also predestine failure? — how can I, how dare I presume to form you from my rib?

("How can you ever understand? That terrible instant when you come into me — sometimes I wish you could be a woman for a few seconds to experience it — when you break into me, rejoice into me: my stomach muscles jerk, a sudden shock, as when one receives an unexpected message. How *can* I convey it to you?")

To do justice to you an essential injustice is required. That is the heart of my dilemma. I can never be you: yet in order to be myself I must imagine what it is to be you.

Is that why you asked in your letter: *Do you understand, Paul, do you really understand, why I can see so clearly today? Why I've recognized this emptiness so unfailingly the moment it occurred? Do you know where I get this knowledge from —?*

I've surrounded myself with all the piles of notes from these many years, trying to find a starting point in the innumerable quotations I once thought I could use as mottoes for my book. Remains and relics from my unwritten book on the Black Death, now a mere supplement to what I have to write (or is it the other way round?). Boccaccio. Petrarca. Guy de Chauliac. Defoe. Camus. Artaud. But how could I deprive myself in advance of the freedom the book demands to become itself? I must not prescribe expectations to myself: at most indicate a broad, general, dangerous world yet to be discovered, a provisional dialectic brimful with possibilities: something not preceding the text but flowing from it.

Or should I dispense with mottoes altogether? Except, perhaps, for the moving, terrifying slogan from the fourteenth century: *In peste Venus pestem provocat?*

445

I tore up the first few tentative pages. This could wait for later, after I'd seen what had come to light.

A dedication. *For Andrea?* For a book that is sufficient. But more than a book is involved: it concerns a life. Even then: *For Andrea?* Or something more intimate? But that, too, can wait for later. Once I know where everything has taken me. A dedication, mottoes, belong to the openness of an end, can never be a gate at the beginning.

Try. Make a beginning. Anything. Just try.

I turned a new sheet of paper into my typewriter, trying to type whatever came into my head: not about the Plague, but about you.

Back to the same landscapes, over and over —

A new sheet, another start:

"I was here." Scratched into the gritty plaster, right through the paint, through tendons and nerves, into the mind —

If only I can find the right beginning. In a beginning all the rest is contained. The perfect egg. In every word the history of an entire life.

Once again I read your questions. The aching clarity with which you challenged my confusion: *Do you know — ? Do you really know — ? Do you know — ?*

No, I do not know yet, Andrea. But I'm going to try. So help me God.

Because I was there; had been there. (So many journeys travelled on a single trip.) Because I'd been exposed before to the quality of that light which once again struck me

Grahamstown — Eygalières, 1983

446

Acknowledgements

Thanks are due to the publishers concerned for permission to quote passages from the following copyright works:

René Allau (ed.), *Guide de la Provence mystérieuse*, Paris, Tchou, n.d.

Antonin Artaud, *Le Théâtre et son double*, in *Oeuvres Complètes*, IV, Paris, Gallimard, 1979

René Bruni, *Le Pays d'Apt malade de la Peste*, Aix-en-Provence, Édisud, 1980

George Deaux, *The Black Death 1347*, London, Hamish Hamilton, 1969

Johannes Nohl, *The Black Death*, trs. C.H. Clarke, London, Unwin Books, 1961

Norman Stone, *Hitler*, London, Hodder & Stoughton, 1980

Barbara W. Tuchman, *A Distant Mirror*, New York, Alfred A. Knopf, 1978

Philip Ziegler, *The Black Death*, London, Collins, 1969

Other sources from which passages have been cited include:
James Boswell, *The Life of Samuel Johnson*
Guy de Chauliac, *La Grande Chirurgie*
Daniel Defoe, *A Journal of the Plague Year*
Fyodor Dostoievsky, *Crime and Punishment*
J.J. Jusserand, *English Wayfaring in the Middle Ages*
Johann Christian Kundmann, *Seltenheiten der Natur und Kunst*
A.E. Levett, *The Black Death on the Estates of the See of Winchester*
Sophocles, *King Oedipus*

447